MW00512283

Books by Alexander Blackburn

Author

Novels

The Door of the Sad People

Suddenly a Mortal Splendor

Kitty Pentecost

Literary Criticism

The Myth of the Picaro

A Sunrise Brighter Still: The Visionary Novels of Frank Waters

Autobiography/Biography

Meeting the Professor: Growing up in the William Blackburn Family

Essays

Creative Spirit: Toward a Better World

Editor

Anthologies & a Collection

The Interior Country: Stories of the Modern West (with Craig Lesley)

Higher Elevations: Stories from the West

Gifts from the Heart: Stories, Memories, & Chronicles of Lucille Gonzales Oller

Literary Magazine

Writers' Forum, 21 vols. (with Craig Lesley, Bret Lott, and Victoria McCabe)

THE DOOR
OF THE
SAD PEOPLE

Alexander Blackburn

RHYOLITE PRESS LLC

Published in the United States of America by Rhyolite Press, LLC
P.O. Box 2406
Colorado Springs, Colorado 80901

www.rhyolitepress.com

Blackburn, Alexander
The Door of the Sad People / Alexander Blackburn
1st ed. July 2014

Library of Congress Control Number: 2014942762
ISBN 978-0-9896763-4-2

PRINTED AND BOUND IN THE UNITED STATES OF AMERICA

Book design/layout by Donald R. Kallaus
Cover design by chileary.com.

Reproduction of portrait of Howard Lathrop from "Bow Street, Portsmouth with Howard Lathrop," oil on canvas, 1937, by American master Russell Cheney, courtesy Portsmouth Public Library, Portsmouth, New Hampshire. Photo from the Ludlow strike entitled "Rows of miners' cabins and ore pit carts on tracks" (Call X-61220) is reproduced courtesy of the Denver Public Library, Western History Division. Not only are carts empty, but also families have been evicted from the company-owned cabins.

The author expresses thanks to Chi Leary, cover artist, to Angela Calloura, typist, and especially to John Dwaine McKenna, Publisher, for his timely and gracious leadership.

Inés, always

THE BROTHERHOOD OF MAN! It will always be a dreary phrase, a futile hope, until each man, all men, realize that they themselves are but different reflections and insubstantial images of a greater invisible whole.

There are those who have eyes and cannot see, who have ears and cannot hear. They are blind, they are deaf, they have no tongues save for the barter of the day. For which of us now knows that awakened spirit of sleeping man by which he can see beyond the horizon, hear even the heart beating within the stone, and speak in silence those truths which are of us all?

A means, a tongue, a bridge to span the wordless chasm that separates us all; it is the cry of every human heart.

Frank Waters

PART I

Chapter One

That October of 1903, just a couple of months shy of my thirteenth birthday, I fell in love, faced a military firing squad, was locked in a bull pen, kidnapped, pistol-whipped and thrown from a moving freight train into Colorado's Comanche Grasslands, but I hadn't kissed a girl or killed anybody yet. Also, though I knew lots of Webster's, Shakespeare, English poetry and my *Book of Knowledge* practically by heart, there were times when I didn't have enough sense, as they say, to pour piss out of a pot. My greatest achievement had been to change my name to Tree. My old name, Rountree Penhallow, Junior, stuck out like a horse turd in a pan of milk.

Actually, I'd been right proud to have been named after Daddy, Dr. Rountree Penhallow of Colorado Springs, Colorado, until he honeyhumped Mrs. Pia Dare of Los Tristes, Colorado, whose husband was an officer in the Philippines fighting a stupid war. Suddenly my world was full of bull feathers. I not only created for myself a name but also escaped to faraway places.

Mum, Daddy, and I, and Ruby, our aging cook, cleaner, nurse, photographer and factotum, had lived until August of that same year of 1903 in a two-story white clapboard house on fashionable Wood Avenue, altitude about 6,000 feet with a fourteener, Pikes Peak, in our back yard. Daddy was Director of the Sun Palace, a sanitorium for rich lungers from Back East, and a pillar of society. He knew no more about curing people with tuberculosis than he did about branding mosquitoes. Still, he impressed flatlanders and rustics alike with his authoritative manner and English accent.

Colorado Springs was popularly known as "Little London." Anyone of English birth with a demeanor however frosty and an accent however fruity was there regarded as naturally superior. So, Daddy's London goose was in Little London a swan. Nor did it hurt his reputation that his boss was one of the richest tycoons in America, Mr. Alpheus Woodbridge of New York, Chairman of an imperial enterprise called, simply, Corporation. He, Woodbridge, was the wrong pie to stick your nose in and virtually owned Colorado from sheriffs to governors because Corporation owned or controlled most of the mines and mills. Even the Sun Palace was his property. For reasons unknown to the family, Woodbridge had taken a shine to Daddy.

He had a lab and a clinic on the ground floor of our home. My bedroom was directly above those facilities. Not an eavesdropper by preference, my curiosity mostly confined to language and literature, history and geography, when Daddy was seeing patients downstairs I usually paid no attention. However, when Mrs. Pia Dare arrived for her TB cure, instead of a prick from a hypo needle she got a romp. I heard stuff in spite of putting hands over ears. She showed up only when Mum and Ruby were out shopping. Why didn't Daddy cure Pia while I, also, was out of the house, like at school? I think he had it twigged that I was rowing a boat near the South Pole or riding stallions in Mongolia or conversing with Kubla Khan in Xanadu.

Four events preceded my violent departure from home and callow youth.

First, Captain Kyle Deville Dare, U.S. Army, retired, returned from the Philippines and resumed married life with Pia at his ranch in Los Tristes. Unaware he was a cuckold and grateful to learn from Daddy that Pia had been cured of her TB, he brought her to our house in order to thank Daddy and pay him. I met Dare the first time then. We hit it off right away. I be dog, he didn't look like a cuckold he was so handsome.

Second, when he was visiting us, still wearing campaign hat, tunic, belt, puttees, boots and all, Ruby got her Kodak out and snapped a picture of him. Although this event had no immediate effect on my life, in the long run it would have enormous influence.

Third, Daddy, insisting that Mum was dying of TB, had her entombed at the Sun Palace in the aforementioned August, 1903. Confined to a private room in which a music box played *Nearer My God to Thee*, she was denied visitors except once a week; she was also denied access to postal service, telephone, and telegraph. The sanitorium was surrounded by high walls and patrolled by off-duty militia of the Colorado National Guard. Now, in truth—and Mum, Ruby, and I knew the truth—Mum wasn't and never had been a lunger. If she had been home, I might have gone back after I didn't die in the Comanche Grasslands.

Mum being locked up, I depended upon Daddy for existence, and he was tighter than a matador's trousers, never having given me a cent for allowance. But, as long as Mum was home, if I needed cash-money, maybe a nickel to buy chocolate, she would give it to me, no strings or guilt attached, saying, "We'll deduct the advance from your inheritance, pet lamb." At the age of thirty-five in 1905 she stood to inherit a fortune. One day I, in turn, would inherit some of it from her. I'd be lucky to inherit from Daddy a morsel of undigested food toothpicked out from between his molars.

Mum's being locked up, Ruby, too, got cut in heart. "I'll no longer have that old woman with a touch of the tar brush sleeping under my roof," Daddy had announced to me in August. Ruby stayed on to cook and clean but moved nights to a bungalow she owned on Shooks Run. She had paid-up mortgage and savings and could have moved out for good. She loved me, though, I her.

Fourth, the Woodbridge family arrived in Colorado Springs on October 23, 1903. The young Mrs. Woodbridge, Elizabeth, she really *was* dying of TB. Woodbridge had built the Sun Palace in Colorado Springs so that he could dump her in it and begin a new life in his mansion in New York. Once he dumped her, he was going hunting in the Rockies, leaving the two children—Alpheus Woodbridge, Jr.,

"Alphie," seventeen, and Felixine Woodbridge, "Scampy," thirteen—alone in a suite of rooms at the luxurious Antlers Hotel close to my home.

"You'll be in charge of the young chaps," Daddy disclosed to me to my surprise before the Woodbridges' arrival. Ruby was serving us breakfast, and we usually ate in silence, but Daddy had been talking about his boss, the dumping and the hunting, and I had been riding on the steppes with my friends, the Mongolians.

"Sir?"

Daddy looked at me as if seeing me for the first time. Actually, he *always* looked at me as if seeing me for the first time. "Entertain them. Escort them to the Braemoor and Cripple Creek. Pay their expenses."

I considered myself a friendly person, but I didn't cotton up well to rich kids. Besides, my services had been offered up without my knowledge or say-so. On the other hand, for the first time in history Daddy was giving me permission to go to the Braemoor Hotel, the most glamorous resort in the West, and to Cripple Creek, the rootinest-tootinest town in the West and source above 9,000 feet on the far side of Pikes Peak of the world's richest gold mines. Perhaps, after all, I could show Alphie and Scampy around. But how?

For the first time in history Daddy divined my thought. He reached for his wallet, extracted cash-money from it, and slowly counted out ten ten-dollar bills, licking the corner of each bill like a hounddog. "I'll want a full account of all your expenses. Judas Priest! If anything's amiss when I get back, you're in for a what-fer!"

A "what-fer" in our country lingo meant a whipping. "What do you mean, sir, when you get back?"

It turned out that Daddy had been invited to join Woodbridge on the hunting expedition. If there was anything more ridiculous than an image of Daddy's giving me, at five-foot, 100 pounds, a what-fer, it was an image of him out in the wilderness with scouts, cooks, hunters, and other grownups smelling like porkers in a mud hollow, talking stories around a campfire, rubbing ringworm between the toes and passing around jugs of lightning!

I transferred the bills to my wallet, next to the picture of a belly dancer I'd stowed there after a hard-on. It didn't feel good, having so much cash-money on my person. A miner earned scarcely $600 a year, and I was carrying one-sixth of that sum to waste on rich kids! No, it didn't feel good, but maybe I had to stop feeling sorry for poor people if I was ever going to be a correct grownup.

Daddy was studying me from behind his pince-nez. "Jolly good," he muttered. "The brats can visit Mr. Woodbridge's gold mine in Cripple Creek. Simply hours of entertainment. I insist! Soaping the stairs to hell will give them a sense of accomplishment! The law against gambling at the Braemoor isn't being enforced. If the brats want dope, I'll leave you the key to my medicine cabinet. By all means sell them tinctures of opium—of course at their own expense." Daddy pounded his fist on the breakfast table.

A few days later, while Ruby was serving us fried chicken for dinner, I was feeling so sad about Mum that I blurted out, "What will happen to me if Mum dies?"

I thought Daddy was going to ask me what my name was. He chewed his chicken slowly. It was his dictum that one mustn't speak with a full mouth. I aged a bit before he finally dabbed lips and mustache with his napkin, cleared throat, and assumed a crack and pontifical pose.

"Pity Me was a good man, but Shut Up was a better man than he."

"Welcome home to Xanadu, Tree," said Kubla Khan. "There's a damsel with a dulcimer waiting for you in the pleasure dome."

Apparently the Woodbridges arrived, because, one morning, Daddy dressed himself up to look like Teddy Roosevelt on safari and joined the hunters at the DRG&W, the Denver, Rio Grande & Western Railroad depot. Daddy then having been whisked away to the mysterious Land of Misogamy, I made ready to meet Alphie and Scampy at the Antlers next morning at nine.

I slept little that night, wondering what was going to happen to us with Mum so exposed to bacilli that she might in fact die, leaving

Mrs. Pia Dare, who had been waiting in the wings for the romps, a Mona Lisa with pus drooling out the sides of her enigmatic smile. Eventually, though, I slept and dreamed a dream.

In the dream the sky is intensely black except when lightning daggers clouds which are snagging and bursting on snow-trapezoids of the Continental Divide where Daddy is shooting a wolf. Heavy rains are falling, arroyos are flooded, cliffs toppling over, forests uprooted, white snakes with debris poking through skins are slithering down fourteeners, twisting steel bridges into pretzels, smashing houses into kindling, drowning people with sad expressions in their eyes. In the floodwaters a girl is struggling. She looks like the picture of Napoleon in my *Book of Knowledge*. I extend my hand to her. I pull her body into my puberty-tormented one.

I was remembering the dream next morning when I sauntered into the Antlers for the first time, rode an elevator for the first time, and for the first time in my life knocked on a door behind which, like dragons in a myth, coiled the brood of a tycoon.

The door was opened creakingly. Standing before me was the girl in my dream. She looked like Napoleon, dark bangs over brow, eyes mysteriously downcast.

Chapter Two

No way I intended to escort the kids to Cripple Creek. Having just fallen in love for the first time, I had to protect Scampy from the violence in Cripple Creek.

Normally just riotous, Cripple Creek had become a war zone. The hard-rock miners there, thousands, had come out on strike against the mine owners, the complaints the same there as they long had been in mining camps everywhere in the United States: dangerous working conditions, virtual enslavement, no recognition of Union. Opposing the miners' peaceful requests were established powers: the mine owners, the executive, legislative, and judicial branches of government, the National Guard under command of a Denver dentist named General Case, the Pinkerton Detective Agency and an assortment of "sucks" or spies. Without explicit permission from the Governor of Colorado, Case had put in place martial law. Thereby, after a beating called a "kangaroo," a striker could be arrested and taken "prisoner," locked away in a "bull pen," and, without due process, "sent down the mountain," in other words, deported out of state. According to what I'd been reading in newspapers, Cripple Creek miners by the thousands had lost their jobs, some their lives. Their families had been evicted from their homes in the "company-town," and replacement workers called "scabs," recruited not only from other states but also from Mexico and the poorest countries in Europe, had enabled gold-mining operations to continue unabated. Pinkertons, known as "dicks," were doing most of the dirty work, including the demolition of printing presses favorable to Union, and the militia armed with Krags and Gatling machine guns did the rest.

Most papers condemned the strike. One of them described miners as "depraved beasts, harpies, decayed physically and spiritually, mentally and morally, thievish and licentious, descended from Sythians, eaters of raw animal food, and fond of drinking the blood of their enemies." The few papers sympathetic to unionization were expressing, without demonstrable effect amidst a cowed, compliant, or simply complacent public, outrage at Case's disregard for the law and liberty.

In a recent development, as I had read in *The Gazette* and *Denver Post*, a judge not on Corporation payroll had ordered General Case to turn certain of his "prisoners" over to proper authority, this showdown scheduled to take place at the Cripple Creek courthouse on the morning of October 27, 1903.

The girl who looked like Napoleon with downcast eyes lifted them to meet my stunned gaze.

Being a phlegmatic American of half-English descent, I couldn't heave my heart into my head without first making sure I wasn't just infatuated and she wasn't already spoken for. Besides, she was unobtainable, and I was a bum. It did seem to me she was the one I'd been looking for ever since my sexual organ peered from the bush.

I gawked.

"Rountree?"

I corrected her.

"Super." She pronounced the word in a whispery way, making it sound like *Sue Puh* and letting it push her lips forward as if she were sipping sarsaparilla through a straw or sucking nourishment like a blowfish. "*Comment allez-vous, Arbre? Je m'appelle Scampy.*"

Mum spoke French. Ganny, my grandmother who lived in New York, had been born in French-speaking New Orleans before the Civil War. I knew a little, too. "*Enchanté, mademoiselle,*" I said swiftly and bowed. Believing ice broken, I essayed polite conversation.

"Have you read Darwin's *Origin of Species*, Scampy?"

Her face clouded over. "Is it a book?"

Flummoxed, I said nothing more. I followed her into a living room with real electric lights. I imagined hidden somewhere a guillotine just for me. I had come prepared to die in style: instead of dungarees and shitkickers, I wore knickerbockers, white shirt and collar, bow tie, tweed cap and black shoes with a shine on. I had taken a bath and washed and combed my hair. Daddy was fond of describing it as "an unmade bed in a flop-house."

Out of a corner of my eye I spotted Alphie, a lanky 200-pounder with greasy black hair parted down the middle, standing, waiting for me. From the way he was dressed he seemed to have arrived without any intention of roughing it in our West. He was wearing a high-winged, starched white collar, silk necktie with diamond pin, black chesterfield coat and wellingtons. Sporting a mustache that looked like the beginning of pubic hair, he was smoking a cigarette and taking sips from a leather-diapered brandy flask. Scampy, at least, would not embarrass me with her jodhpurs, airtight blouse, velvet jacket, lace-up black boots. Her pink cheeks could have adorned a box of raisins.

"Would you like to see my photograph album?" she asked, indicating that I should sit beside her on a plush sofa.

"Love to," I lied.

"Sue Puh."

Normally, I hated to have to praise images of strangers grinning like Cheshire cats with Niagara Falls or the Eiffel Tower in the background. With Scampy beside me smelling of lavender water from Provence, Mum's favorite, the album spread out upon our knees, the pictures could have been from the realms of gold. The Woodbridge family's camping trip on Mount Desert Island, Maine, could have been in the Garden of Eden. There was a Maxwell happily wrecked against a telephone pole, beside it a coachman who looked oddly familiar. I was taken by a portrait of Woodbridge, the Bismarckian mustaches, the steely eyes, the thin lips. If he resembled an emperor in Scampy's eyes and therefore in mine, he was a kindly bloke who had never burned heretics at the stake without good reason. I did feel genuinely sorry for Elizabeth Woodbridge in wedding dress. She who was about to die reminded me that Edgar Allan Poe believed that the greatest story was that of the death of a beautiful young woman. Still, in my opinion, however prejudiced I was in favor of sudden breasts, the best picture was the one of Scampy identified in white ink on black paper as "Felixine as the Snow Fairy in school performance of *Nutcracker Suite*, December 1902."

"Felixine?" I queried.

"Pa-pa calls me Scampy." Scampy half giggled. "He says I'm 'a tempestuous petticoat'!" Alphie, stifling a yawn, came and hovered over us. "Give Brother the album, Ugly Duckling darling." His croaky voice had inflection of boredom. Scampy, casting a worried look in my direction, passed the album over to Alphie. During the next few minutes all I could do was stare at him as if he were out of his mind.

He *was* out of his mind.

Calmly, he tore from the album two pages. Glued to the first page was that portrait of Woodbridge looking like an emperor. Glued to the second page was the picture of Scampy as Snow Fairy. Without hesitation Alphie slipped from his coat a Colt's pistolet, aimed it at the portrait of Woodbridge, fired, and removed his father's face. After stowing the pistolet back in his coat, he proceeded to slip from it a pair of cuticle scissors and to snip Scampy's face out, handing the locket-size headshot to me. "Yours for a keepsake, old bean," he said, quite pleasantly. "Is love real? Yes. Will it last? No. Do feel breathless with admiration, old bean. If you try to climb into Sister's pants, I'll shoot your balls off."

"May I have the picture of you?" I asked Scampy, making an effort to blot out Alphie.

"Sue Puh."

I tucked the picture into my wallet next to the booty and the belly dancer. "Tell your brother," I heard myself saying, "that my dad is a crack shot who charged up San Juan Hill with the Rough

Riders." Immediately I felt so ashamed of myself that I wanted to go home and crawl under my bed like a bad dog. I glanced sideways at Scampy, expecting looks to kill me. By a stroke of luck she was too busy glaring at Alphie to be paying attention to me. However, I was so keen on pretending to be clever that, combining the image of Fairy with Spenser's *Faerie Queene*, I outdid myself with sappiness and said, "Shall we go pricking on the plain?"

"Pricking on the play-ane?" Alphie's sarcastic emphasis demolished my dream of knighthood on horseback with maiden. "Smutty, old bean."

"I'll not be mocked," I said, and then I did the worst thing I could possibly have done: I tried to defend my boorish propensity for smartaleckiness. "From the time I was kicking in my crib I have loved words," I said. "Mum would sing lullabies and read stories to me, and words created pictures in my mind. I wanted to live inside them forever. Later, they swooped down on me like hawks to tell me the sad story of the difficulty and nobility of being human.'

"As much as I enjoy playing baseball and football after school," I continued, unable to stop myself, "I have from that early age felt content to stay home and read. The habit of looking up meanings of words in Webster's led Mum to invent Shootout. It's a game in which we try, as in a duel, to 'shoot' each other with big words instead of bullets. She gunned me down with *superannuated, ubiquitous,* and *obsequious.* I annihilated her with *euphemism, nebulous, exoteric, discombobulated* and *disestablishmentarianism.* By the time I entered grade school I was a verbal gunslinger and had to keep my mouth shut in order to make friends with teachers and classmates.'

"Mum, you see, has never been to college. She's as keen as I to become a thinker and free person. She permits me freedom to roam about and experience the rough and tumble. By the way, Alphie, old bean, when a bully as big as you put a garter snake in Sally Krapinski's bloomers, I tackled him and bloodied his nose and made him cry so bad I gave him my jackknife to make all square.'

"Mum has me at a disadvantage where culture is concerned. Having grown up in New York and traveled abroad before her marriage, she had symphonic music and Broadway theater going for her. My musical education has been limited to Sousa's marches performed by a high-school band. The only live theatrical performance I have attended is a Christmas pageant with eight-year-old actors playing shepherds to bleating, defecating sheep. Mum decided to wean me away from children's books. We read Shakespeare's plays aloud, identified spot quotations according to title, act, scene, who was speaking and why. No matter how hard I've tried, words such as *fardels* in *Hamlet* have me hogtied, I admit. From Shakespeare Shootout we graduated to English poetry and a Bible read as literature. On my own I explored each year's edition of *Book of Knowledge*, and anything banned from libraries, for example, Darwin's *Origin of Species*—a book—and the *Rubáiyát* of Omar Khayyám."

Realizing finally that the kids weren't paying me much attention, I stopped myself. Alphie said, "If you think you're so goddamn intellectual, little fart, shoot me."

"O.K.," I said. "Misogamy. I'll count to three."

I counted. Alphie's expression went blank. "Misogamy," I said. "Hatred of marriage . . . Now, today we rent mounts and go riding in the Garden of the Gods. There you'll observe a rock formation called 'kissing camels', and in cutbanks there are shark's teeth proving the Rockies were once upon a time a seabed . . . Paleontology, Alphie. I'll count to three."

"Paleontology," Alphie repeated without pause. "Study of fossils."

"Splendid," I said. "Fifty dollars to make all square."

I handed over to him half of Daddy's cash-money. If he frittered it away, it would no longer be my responsibility to keep him entertained. Hadn't Daddy mentioned opium?

"Do you want to buy some opium, Alphie?"

"O.K.," he said, face brightening. "Where?"

"Mexicali," I said. "Chinese smugglers, I'm told."

"O.K.," he said. "Thanks." He frowned. "Where's Mexicali?"

When I told him it was across the border from southern California, he looked sunk. I could have kicked myself for leading him on and accidentally stripping off his mask. Beneath appearances he was a big baby. He needed my protection just as Scampy did. I had run the course from innocence to irritation, but I was now resolved, if I could, to befriend and enlist him in my courtship of Scampy.

"Garden of the Gods O.K. with you, Alphie? Scampy?"

"Sue Puh," she said, bestowing upon me a smile.

Looking back, I've often wondered why Alphie's behavior, especially his packing a pistolet and using it to strike his father dead, as it were, hadn't disturbed me more than it did. Partly, I was so in love I assumed the world had gone mad. This was good. Partly, I assumed that seventeen-year-old boys from New York were already entitled to be armed and dangerous. Actually, though, I believed that rich people lived by rules differing from those conventional ones with which the rest of us had been indoctrinated. In a way I envied Alphie and gained a kind of osmosis confidence lacking in myself up to that time, being a lonely westerner beneath the salt.

The first few days with Scampy and Alphie were among the happiest I had ever known. Wherever we went, Scampy went out of her way to walk by my side, to hold my hand, to tolerate my awkwardness and "intellectual" rot, to giggle at my jokes. Best of all, she loved the outdoors as much as I did and was not in the least restrained when it came to expressing wonder, whether it was the sight of golden aspens or the sound of mountain streams or the scent of pinesmoke in autumnal air. On one occasion the three of us hiked to the top of Mt. Manitou not far from the summit of Pikes Peak. When we reached an elevation of 10,000 feet, Alphie passed out from altitude sickness combined with a hangover and cigarette smoke. Scampy let me put my arm around her shoulder. We gazed in rapture at immeasurable America, tawny plains spreading out to the east. Suddenly Scampy tilted her head and said, "Would you like to kiss me?"

"Actually," I said.

She closed her eyes. At that moment Alphie stumbled into

view, saying, "Tip a raree bird . . . off Pikes Peak . . . and ish a long way to Tipperary."

We did go to the Braemoor. While Scampy and I watched a polo match and ate cotton candy, Alphie lost his remaining dollars playing blackjack in the casino. On the way back to the Antlers in a hackney I had hired, he announced that he intended, next day, to visit his mother in the Sun Palace. Evidently, the visit came as a surprise to Scampy, but she was excited at the prospect and, upon arrival at the hotel, at her own expense ordered for delivery to the sanitorium an exquisite bouquet of irises and roses.

"I want you to meet Mom," she said to me.

I must have blushed.

"What's wrong, Tree? I love my mother to pieces. I know she would love to meet you. Say you'll come. It will be super."

I had to explain that Daddy had prohibited me from visiting my Mum more than once a week, and that I'd just seen her—having walked a ten-mile roundtrip to do so—only a few days earlier.

"Oh, poop." Scampy stamped her foot, giving me first glimpse of the "tempestuous petticoat." "Pa-pa owns that stupid hospital and can fire everybody in it, including your precious Daddy. Promise you're coming?"

"I want my Mum to meet *you*," I said. To overrule Daddy with Woodbridge pull was indeed a triumph to relish.

Next morning we took a hackney to the Sun Palace.

It was, as I've previously intimated, like a closely guarded fortress. To enter it one had to pass through a gate after a security check by armed militia who were earning extra money during off-duty hours in Cripple Creek. Daddy took great pride, I happened to know, in having a contingent of young American soldiers at his beck and call. He was particularly pleased to have as Head of Security one Lieutenant Fredson Shiflit, appointed to the position by Woodbridge, himself. According to Daddy, Shiflit's record as a mercenary in Cuba and recently as an Army officer in the Philippines was extraordinary, his rank there and in the Guard, in light of his heroism, a disgrace. "Why," Daddy gushed, "Roosevelt should put him in charge of the Department of Good and Evil!" Daddy was so ignorant of our government that I refrained from enlightening him, nor, having encountered Shiflit briefly at the sanitorium, was I sure which side, good or evil, he was on. Of medium height with a thick neck, a large black mustache, a badly stitched cheek wound and a perverse look in his eyes, Shiflit, in my opinion, gave nightmares a bad name.

Shiflit, himself, stopped us at the gate and greeted Alphie and Scampy like old friends, inviting them—not me—to share a coffee with him in his police shed. He eventually waved them on to hospital grounds with a hearty laugh and the bonhomie of a King Claudius. Me, he held back.

"Can't he come with us?" Scampy pleaded.

"Sorry, dear Miss Woodbridge," Shiflit said with tight smile, "regulations . . . Master Woodbridge," he went on in another voice, addressing Alphie, "if you would be so kind, see me on your way out, and I'll have the safe conduct ready for you."

I cooled my heels outside the gate for an hour. When the kids reappeared, Scampy rushed into my arms and sobbed her heart out. I did my best to assure her that Daddy would be doing everything in his power to get her mother cured, using the most modern techniques, and that, upon her return to New York, I would write her daily about her mother's progress. I could hear the chattering of Scampy's teeth as well as feel her heaving against my chest.

While consoling her, I was casting furtive glances at Shiflit, wondering what his relationship to the Woodbridges might have been. Then it hit me: he had been their coachman as shown in a yellowed photograph in Scampy's album. In light of this revelation I'd made a hasty judgment about him. Perhaps Daddy was right about Shiflit's rank representing a disgraceful lack of good judgment on the part of military authorities.

Back at the hotel Alphie showed me a letter signed by Shiflit on official government stationery granting "safe conduct for members of the Woodbridge family and friends, for the purpose of attending courthouse proceedings in Cripple Creek at 11:00 a.m., October

27, 1903." When I asked Alphie if he was aware of what was going on in Cripple Creek and of the dangers of violence there, he shrugged and said he and Scampy wished to visit the Woodbridge gold mine there and could do so safely now that they were under the protection of the Guard.

"You go," I told him. "I'm taking Scampy to a Ute Indian pow-wow in the Garden of the Gods."

"You're a fraidycat, old bean," Alphie said. "Sister's coming with me, isn't that right, Ugly Duckling darling?"

"You stop calling her names!" I burst out, face hot all over. "I've had enough of your guff!"

Just then Scampy, hands on hips, came, glared at me, and said, "I'll thank you to apologize to Brother! All you think of is yourself! Our Mom is dying in your stupid hospital, and we have a right to visit Pa-pa's gold mine!"

Blood rushed to my temples. I'd turned her against me for the rest of my life. "Sorry," I managed to say above a whimper. "We'll all go."

"I suppose," Alphie said, "we have to take the stagecoach?"

"We take the Midland Railroad after breakfast," I said. "Let me lard the details for you."

"Praise the lard," Alphie said.

From that moment on I pitched Cripple Creek as a showcase for the Wild West from desperadoes and floozies to Scythian harpies lapping puddles of blood up from the streets. To my infinite relief Scampy was smiling a small, nervous smile.

I rose early the morning of the 27th, tossed my wet-dream-enriched pajamas into the laundry hamper, drew a hot bath, washed myself with Mum's scented soap, and shaved imaginary whiskers with Daddy's straight razor, taking care to cut my chin a little. According to *The Gazette*, snow could be expected in the higher elevations as Halloween approached, but, for the high plains, Chinook winds were in the trend, keeping us warm during coming days. I put long johns on top of cotton underwear, cable-stitch sweater on top of flannel shirt, but otherwise dressed myself up, like a tweedy golfer, in a New Yorkerish outfit Ganny had bought me. Later, when Ruby came to serve me breakfast in the dining room, she, standing in the doorway to the kitchen, studied me with a quizzical expression which seemed to say, You, Little Lord Fauntleroy?

An hour later I picked up the kids and took them by trolley to Manitou Springs in order to board the Midland for Cripple Creek. Alphie was dressed up in a tuxedo and wearing a black homburg in the style of tycoons. Scampy was wearing jodhpur breeches and a fur coat. There was no way I was going to tell them they should have been wearing dungarees, frock coats, woolen hats and shitkickers. Even though my own clothes stuck out as badly as theirs, Scampy's floppy hat with a peacock feather in it like a quill pen did seem a bit *too* provocative for residents of Sodom and Gomorrah.

A train with parlor car and three coaches was preparing to depart. Two of the coaches had shades drawn and were patrolled from outside on the platform by soldiers with bayonets fixed on rifles. I approached a conductor and inquired what was going on. He checked his watch before replying, "A sad sight. Scabs they be noo, bohunks and wops, pore lads orphaned in the land they have yet to see with possessin' eyes. Their brothers' bread 'tis they be taking unbeknownst."

When I asked the conductor why shades were drawn, he lowered his voice to a raspy whisper. "If Union fellows or they wives and children were but to know this day them scabs are coming, there is divil to pay, I say. Who 'tis throws first rock at them windows—or stick o' dynamite, to be sure?"

We boarded a third coach filled with sleepy miners and cigar-smoking merchant-types. They snickered at sight of us.

"Crip-ple CREEK, CRIP-ple Creek."

The conductor's announcement is followed by a clang of bells, a screech of wheels, a hiss of steam. Reaching my ears in a rippling effect are sounds of trombones, tubas, flutes and cymbals. A small military band is playing *America*. A crowd waves hats and handkerchiefs in the direction of the parlor car. They cheer as from it descends a white-haired, potbellied general dressed in campaign hat, sky-blue tunic with yellow epaulets, frilly leather gloves, boots with spurs, scabbarded saber at side. Extending from his upper lip to mid-cheeks are white mustaches which look as if glued on to his fiery countenance. He salutes, mounts a white horse, and canters off with other horsemen. Cartoons have not done justice to General Case's cold, blue, feral eyes.

Bandblare is receding. I sing words in my head: *land of the pilgrim's pride . . . let freedom ring*. We are engulfed by masses of people surging down Bennett Street. I am swept along as part of a crowd of a thousand people, angry people, some wearing red bandannas of unionists, some hammering blue sky with fists and waving muckers. Far from feeling threatened by the crowd, I am on equal terms with it, sharing its goal and adding my steps to the footsteps of others in a display of invincible unity. I tighten my grip on Scampy's hand. We are swept along. Furious faces aim wild eyes and obscenities toward the roof of a redbrick bank building. I see soldiers up there crouched behind a Gatling gun. I scan the roofs of other buildings and see sharpshooters aiming rifles at us. We are swept along. I hear the crash and tinkle of broken glass and see boys tossing bricks at store windows. I hear rifle shots reverberating distantly among hills and canyons polka-dotted with mine shafts. Hearing screams of terror, I see suddenly swerving from a side street and bearing down upon us a squadron of cavalry, sabers drawn, brandished, catching splinters of bright sun, hoofbeats thundering. Our crowd is parted down the middle, scattering willy-nilly, stumbling into heaps on boardwalks and seeking shelter behind wagons and barrels. At the braying of a panic-stricken horse I turn, see it rearing up and pawing air, see a boy about my own age dashing at the horse and swinging a crowbar at fetlocks, see the horseman slashing at the boy's arm, cutting it deeply, I see the horseman galloping toward a thinly-dressed girl, slashing at her, missing her, then see him galloping toward me and

Scampy. I pull her back into my arms. He leans out of the saddle and with a swish of saber at her bonnet cuts its peacock feather off. I see it seesawing in the windy wake of horsesnuffings.

"I love you, Scampy," I murmur into her hair before letting her go.

"Where's Brother?" Her voice is too calm. I spot a homburg bouncing like a black tea cozy above the melee and roiling tide of crowdflesh: Alphie. Bobbing to the surface with a cigarette dangling from lips, he takes his way at the vanguard of the crowd until he and it, tidal wave against a wall, are halted by a long row of cavalry, the surge now a sprawling and a withdrawing, a subsidence and disintegration. Alphie is chatting with a mounted officer, Shiflit, beckoning us to hurry and join him, waving the safe-conduct letter in the air.

"Jolly good," I say to Scampy, using my father's English expression in a tone of sarcastic understatement. "He owns Cripple Creek." Against the flow of the crowd we go until, abreast of cavalry, we stop near Shiflit who salutes, two fingers to hatbrim in a vulgarly familiar fashion, Scampy. He doesn't dismount. We pass through the wall of cavalry. We are going, Alphie explains, to the courthouse. Later, Lieutenant Shiflit will personally show us the gold mine.

I can visualize connections as they were anticipated in the newspapers. Because General Case has been ordered to surrender his "prisoners" to the jurisdiction of the court, miners and their families have turned out to protest proceedings. Lieutenant Shiflit's horsemen have formed a barrier to prevent the crowd from storming the courthouse while allowing antiunion persons admission to it.

A pall of cigar smoke coils over heads of a hundred spectators in the courtroom. We take seats in the rear of the room. Up ahead at the bar and bench where flags hang limply there is as yet no judge. Seated next to me, I notice, is a reporter scribbling in a notebook with a Denver newspaper's logo. He wears the obligatory starched collar over striped shirt, galluses, and fedora.

Hi, I say.

He squints at me. Hi.

21

I'm with the Woodbridge kids, I say. They own the gold mine.

You don't say, says the reporter, squinting at Scampy and Alphie. If you ask me, I wouldn't advertise the presence of Woodbridges. Folks here might . . . The reporter makes a choking gesture at his neck.

What's going on, sir? I ask. Wait and you'll see, says the reporter. General Case is going to come in here and tell the United States to piss off.

I overhear Scampy. *I want to go shopping*, she is saying to Alphie. His reply is lost to me in the hush and footscrape following a functionary's order for everyone to rise. I can see by the crimsoning of cheeks and puckering of lips that Scampy is riled up. I am tempted to tell her that local shops will prove about as interesting as wallpaper unless she buys postcards of Pikes Peak and Geronimo.

We are ordered to sit down after a small, gray-bearded man in a black gown seats himself at the podium, *thwocks* a gavel, mumbles inaudible words and peers over the rim of spectacles to impress us with the majesty of his calling: judge. From the closed doors behind me comes a heavy *stomp stomp* of boots on marble. The sound is stopped by a command. Then I hear *clack thwack* of what must be rifles shifted in unison. Doors are flung open, militia, platoon-size, march, bayonets fixed, down center aisle. Soldiers stand to attention in columns alongside the aisle. A whistle is blown. Six miners, handcuffed, chained together, disheveled, unshaven, bare-chested, pit-clothes smeared with dirt and streaks of blood, are, each one, prodded like Jesus down the aisle until yanked to a halt in front of the judge. He bangs gavel, calls for order. Along comes General Case, eyes front, spurs jingling as he strolls at a leisurely, menacing pace down the aisle. *AH-bout HACE!* General Case's command is followed by silence. The judge drops gavel, adjusts spectacles, slumps in swivel chair. I hear a scratchy noise, try to read what the reporter is scribbling in his notebook with a pencil. He is making a sketch of a naked woman. The model, if nothing else, is in his head. *HARCH!* General Case's command soon empties the room of his men as, one by one and out the doors, the six miners are prodded, followed by stomping columns of militia, followed by the general. Doors are slammed shut. The judge's gavel is *thwocked*. He is saying something about the destruction of liberty. I am leaning forward to fill my soul with his words, glancing aside to share the moment with Scampy and Alphie.

Their seats are empty.

I dash into the street. Mounted on his white horse General Case is leading militia and prisoners through subdued crowds. I see no sign of Scampy and Alphie.

BINDLE STIFF! The screech of a man who has clamped me from behind in powerful arms is so startling I can hear my heart thumping in my ears. Unable to free myself from his grip but able to spin around, I stare into the marble eyeballs of a blind man whose hands are traveling up my neck and across my face like sucking spiders. He has no front teeth. His grizzled beard is flecked with vomit. Again he screams, *Bindle Stiff, me highgradin' sweet-eart, where av ye stook me specimens? An dinna give none of yer lyin' tongue to Old Neddy . . . Under yer bulgin' pants ye be walkin' lumpily, be ye not? Or 'tis it in yer high walkin' boots ye av stook me ore? Sweet'eart, canna fool Old Neddy! Th' cage will git yer! Inter the'cage w'yer, may she grind ya inter pulp! Put out yer shoe, luv, put out yer shoe! . . . Easy . . . Shove yer dinner pail back from the edge! Oh! Yer foot be caught tween risin' cage and shaft? Drawn and grinded through th'openin', yer pore leg, luv, pulled from socket 'tis, pieces of yer skull and brains a-smeared on rock, a thousand feet down shaft 'tis cold, Bindle Stiff, 'tis cold water at bottom, yer body grinded inter pulp! . . . Ye be dead but fer Old Neddy at highgradin' shop!*

I break the blind man's grip and run, run to a side street as far from Old Neddy as I can get and am out of the sun. There are piles of unmelted snow. I am trying to catch my breath, my back braced against brick wall. I close eyes.

And open them after my heart is no longer wildly beating.

The scarface of Lieutenant Shiflit is not two feet away from my face, behind him six militia, bayonets fixed on rifles.

Rountree Penhallow, says Shiflit, you are under arrest for vagrancy and incitement to violence.

A thick-necked sergeant comes and cuffs my wrists behind my back. Bull pen or dig, sir? he says.

Dig, says Shiflit.

Sir, I say, there's a mistake. Alphie has your safe conduct.

He doesn't say anything.

I am marched for several blocks to a vacant lot littered with broken bottles and wind-flipped newspapers. The sergeant unlocks my cuffs, hands me a trenching tool, points to the hard ground at my feet and says, Dig. Two foot by four foot by four foot. Shiflit comes and points a revolver at my head. Dig your goddam grave, Rountree Penhallow, Junior.

The militia chortle, sit, light cigarillos. Dig my own grave? This is all a Halloween prank. You're joshing me, I say to Shiflit. Here's the shovel.

Shiflit half smiles. You don't care to dig, Rountree? Perhaps you'd prefer to be thrown down that mineshaft over yonder? . . . Sergeant! Bring Penhallow, Esquire, pencil and paper.

The sergeant brings pencil and paper. Shiflit barks at me, You have five minutes to say goodbye to your loved ones. Do you see my trick or treat firing squad over there?

I begin to believe he is not joshing me. I lift my eyes to the immeasurable mountains. I lower my eyes to the paper. Mum, I love you. Scampy, I love you. I don't want to die. The sadness is too much for me. Tell Daddy I only took the kids to Cripple Creek because he and Alphie and Shiflit made me do it. Alphie told a joke. It's a long way to Tipperary. I met this crazy old blind man named Neddy. He thought I was a bum and a thief. Forgive me.

Time's up, says Shiflit. I am handing him the blank sheet of paper when it is whipped out of my hand by sudden whirlwind. Like a kite, the paper rises, sinks, rises before finally plunging into the black maw of the abandoned mineshaft.

Gentlemen, says Shiflit, bow your heads.

My executioners toss cigarillos away, stand, bow heads.

The end-time prophet Ezekiel, says Shiflit.

For some reason I, too, bow my head. I keep eyes open. There is an anthill at my feet where I will fall. I slide my feet sideways.

And when the living creatures went, Shiflit says in prayerful tone, *the wheels went by them: and when the living creatures were lifted up from the earth, the wheels were lifted up . . .* The words of the Lord. Amen.

The executioners murmur, Amen. They form themselves into a line in front of me, rifles unslung.

Shame is with me. I cannot move legs. I move hands up to cover my face.

By virtue of the authority vested in me, I hear Shiflit saying. Bolt-actions go *click snick click snick.*

The sadness is too much for me. I sink to my knees. I smell my own sweat under the long johns. I durst not cry.

Ready!

Shiflit's voice.

Aim!

Shiflit's voice.

FIRE!

I hear shots reverberating near and far. I open eyes, peep through spread fingers. My executioners are lowering rifles, slapping sides with merriment. The sergeant comes and handcuffs my wrists in front of me, pulls me to my feet, pushes me toward town.

Close to the depot I am pushed inside a high-walled compound. Prisoners have blank expressions on their faces. A man with a glass eye studies me. A soldier prods him with bayonet, draws blood. The glass-eyed man laughs, A good day is today, then, indade. I don't fancy having any truck with blind men.

I approach a beardless young man. Is this a bull pen? I ask. He holds palms upwards. Me Nor-vay, he says. I approach a black man and ask the same question. She, he replies, it.

Under armed guard we are herded into one of the Midland coaches with shades still drawn, though the scabs are gone, and we go down the mountain to Manitou. We are transferred to a Pikes Peak Avenue trolleycar. Nosy parkers, old ladies, whisper loudly behind kid gloves, *Doc Penhallow's boy . . . shame . . . be the death of his mother . . .*

I and others, including the bleeding glass-eyed man, have our handcuffs removed by Pinkerton dicks who have deputy sheriff badges and shotguns. They march us to the DRG&W depot, push us into a boxcar. By slanting of sunlight through bars I can tell that the train is moving in a southerly direction. Motion rocks me to sleep. I wake. The train has stopped. A dick drags me to my feet, makes me jump out of the boxcar into darkness. Hulking figures of other prisoners are herded, as I am, through a network of railroad tracks until we are pushed into another boxcar, still guarded by the dicks. I can tell by the slanting of moonlight through the bars that this train is moving in an easterly direction. Motion rocks me to sleep. Suddenly I am pulled to my feet by a dick. He pats me down. He opens the boxcar door. By dim lantern light I see the other dick coming at me with a pistol raised. I begin to wrestle with the dick who is trying to push me out of the fast-moving train. The other dick's pistol is a moon-splinter crashing down on my skull . . .

Chapter Three

Diamond dust woke me. The icy crystals tiptoed on melting fairy feet across my cheeks. The feeling of being intimately in touch with splendors of the universe was not previously unknown to me. Permitted by Mum to follow the wind of my will, I had been alone in wilderness before. I had broken trails into mountains at treeline beneath Pikes Peak, had discovered pristine soda springs bubbling up, hot and ineluctable, from bowels of the Earth, had saluted mothering bears as they feasted on chokecherries in meadowlands. Indeed, on one occasion many miles from home, I had leaned into the icy blast of a blizzard as it pierced through layers of clothing almost to the marrow-bone and set my soul on fire with the awe of an other-worldly force and dimension.

Blacksmithy poundings against the base of my skull were causing me to slip in and out of consciousness and back and forth between time-present and time-past, giving me Rip Van Winkle puzzlements. It was, I felt for sure, an hour or two since my adventure with Pinkerton dicks. The moon lighting up the prairie was a Galilean celestial body, not a hallucination, not a dream, not dyspepsia. If landscape was a Dalmatian dog, here were dark clumps of scrub-oak, juniper, piñon and sagebrush on sheet-linen-white plains and hillocks. If I had moments of feeling as dizzy as a blue-bottle fly in a manure factory, and had, as well as a concussion and vertigo, the worst thigh bruise since Jacob wrestled the angel, I had indeed been thrown from a train: I was lying at the bottom of a sharply sloping railroad embankment. Silvery tracks vanished to a distant point. Once, lightbeams, moanings, and hootwhistlings of a real train were manifesting themselves out of that very point. After a while this train, chugging and wheezing like an asthmatic giant punching himself in the gut, loomed above me, then rumbled past where I lay, leaving a diminishing *clickitty rackitty clickitty rackitty*. Silhouettes of passengers were celebrating with bottles. A Sabbath stillness enveloped me.

There had been words scrawled on the walls of the yellow boxcar, most of them with the erotic etymologies of *fruit* and *cup*. A swaying coal-oil lantern cast flickering light. Two shotguns held by Pinkerton dicks left me indisposed to make conversation. There were three bearded miners, including the glass-eyed one I'd seen in the Cripple Creek bull pen, and the two dicks, bearded with handlebar mustaches, cheeks marked by what seemed to be healed knife wounds. Whenever they looked my way, I flashed them a smile of bonhomie, wanting them to know that their derbies, serge suits, gray spats and black hobnailed boots showed *real* class.

I passed out again.

When I opened my eyes, sunshine lay on the land like a golden *rebozo*. Far off to the west of me tiny pink breasts, which I identified as the Spanish Peaks, swam into my ken, behind them the wide expanse of the Sangre de Cristo Mountains a jagged line of blue sawteeth. Close to me by half a mile a silver river ran: the Purgatoire. Specks of geese were swooping and looping in mistpatches.

I felt as separated from God as Sunday School in baseball weather.

I was lying on my back, I now realized from my study of maps, in the Comanche Grasslands of the Great American Desert. I'd been pistol-whipped with enough force to crack my skull open and hurled from that moving freight train. Prior to being whapped like a cockroach, I'd been led to believe I was being executed in Cripple Creek by Shiflit's firing squad. Facing it I had felt at the anticipated moment of death so overwhelmed by shame that I couldn't move my limbs—a feeling, as I would later in my life learn from Scampy, akin to that of a victim of rape.

I was remembering what I'd read in my *Book of Knowledge* about the Spanish conquistador, Francisco Vásquez de Coronado, how in 1542 he had hacked, looted, raped and murdered his way through Indian pueblos until his search for gold ended in what was now southeastern Colorado, the very ocean of grass I was lying in. I was lying just fifty yards or so from a weather-beaten sign, PENIEL, probably a whistlestop on a bend in the Santa Fe line. Peniel may have been a real station with ticket agents and spittoons and caved-in adobe *casitas*, shanties, stores, saloons, churches, and whorehouses, but obviously when I hit, literally, town, I was its entire population.

January, 1903 . . .

Woodbridge has asked Daddy to do a locum at Los Tristes. Miners employed in Woodbridge's St. Mabyn's—in fact, miners and their families everywhere in the Los Tristes district—are reported to be suffering in unusually large numbers from a variety of diseases, including TB, typhoid fever, black lung, and rickets. Although, according to Daddy, Woodbridge believes the reports are exaggerated in order to enlist sympathy for "anarchists," it would be, he says in his telegram, "useful to receive first-hand information from a physician of such eminence as . . ."

Ruby will take care of Mum. School is closed. We will be staying, Daddy says, "in a luxurious hotel" on Main Street. "Rountree," Daddy says, "I believe it's time, now that you are growing up in the world, to see for yourself the importance of scientific morality. It is the cornerstone of my profession. Whatever sentiments one may wish to indulge in the presence of misery, we must cling to objectivity at all costs. If one allows oneself to become involved with the pathetic and often specious lamentations of the unwholesome masses, one will go stark, raving mad! Facts are facts. We have the secret nostrum to relieve mortals of suffering, to wit, faith,

faith, faith—faith in the possibility of a cure where all is hopeless, faith, above all, in the doctor, himself. This, you might believe, is my overweening conceit, but, mark my words, unless the doctor is a god to the patient in every particular, impressing upon him a doctor's authority and the necessity of submission to that absolute authority, no remedy is bloody likely. All the shilly-shallies of apothecaries prove of no avail. I set forth with the solid basis of a definite intention in a perfect soberness of spirit to possess souls in the curvature of my hands until death wearies of attacking me through the agency of some wretch's sullied flesh!"

This, perhaps, is the most passionate speech Daddy has ever made, at least to me. I'm not sure I can separate the wheat from bull feathers.

A parlor car of the DRG&W will carry us the 175 miles from Colorado Springs to Pueblo, Walsenburg, Aguilar, Quivira and Los Tristes.

Once on our way I look to the east and see plains with snow sprinkled on them like powered sugar, here and there cattle like cinnamon-colored almonds, cottonwood log cabins with flat roofs of mud, horses tied in the shade of corral shelters, corn *milpas* and alfalfa fields. According to my *Book of Knowledge* the plains stretch eastward about 150 miles to the Comanche Grasslands, La Junta, and the Kansas border. The foothills of the Rockies rise to the west of our train. Southwest of Walsenburg the Spanish Peaks, thirteeners, inspire Daddy to make a joke. "The Indian name for them translates as 'Breasts of the Earth.' The Grand Canyon must be the reeking slit, by Jove! That sort of thing."

I am riding in Mongolia.

Los Tristes is cramped into spaces where hills slope to the Purgatoire in a valley floor. This little city must have taken in a smutty-nosed cat: it wants to be prosperous. It has brick and sandstone buildings aligning a main thoroughfare. It has a five-story First National Bank, a six-story brewing company, and a three-story hotel, the Imperial, complete with ballroom, a restaurant with chandeliers, brass spittoons, and a special staircase to enable

Texas cattlemen to take their horses upstairs to bed.

Out West, Los Tristes is old. Conquistadors came through it when it was just grass. When a couple of them were murdered and left unburied and unshriven, they were immortalized in water: *el río de las ánimas perdidas en el Purgatorio*, or The River of Souls Lost in Purgatory, was named after them, becoming Purgatoire when French trappers explored the by-then Mexican territory. Finally there sprouted by the river the little town, mostly populated by Mexicans from down Taos and Mora way. After the United States grabbed the land, the DRG&W was pushed into the vicinity, followed by AT&SF, Atchison, Topeka & Santa Fe Railroad. Coal was discovered. Pretty soon it was fueling Woodbridge's iron and steel mills in Pueblo, the "Pittsburgh of the West."

Thrilled as I am to be where generations have trod, over the next few days as Daddy and I in a rented buggy make rounds of mines and company-towns in the hills surrounding Los Tristes, my heart is cut. *Stark twisting canyons. Bleak, unpainted shafthouses, breaker buildings, fan houses, spindly-legged tipples. Corrugated iron sheds for mules which have spent their lives underground, coming up blind. Infernally smoking piles of slack. Coke ovens flaring luridly at night. Treeless rows of weather-beaten, two-room shacks for families and boarders of ten or more men, women, children. Yards strewn with refuse. Powder-box shanties climbing above dust-bearded slopes. Black coal cars, coffin-shaped, trundling and rumbling and clanking and screeching through soot mists at all hours. Surfacing into bitter cold, miners, bodies heated from twelve-to-sixteen hours of labor underground, are momentarily enveloped by mist as if they are Homeric gods. Children stealing lumps of coal, filling burlap bags with it. Children with heads misshapen, skinny legs, chests narrowed and breastbones forced unnaturally forward and outward.*

The first most interesting thing about the Imperial Hotel, apart from the fact that Daddy's idea of "luxurious" is a windowless dungeon of a room, is the number of raccoon-coated gentlemen who enter the revolving front door by walking through it backwards, hawkeyes upon Main Street. When I remark upon this custom to Daddy, he lowers his voice and says, "Pinkertons. If they turn their backs to the street, it's a sticky wicket: they can be bumped off by union agitators . . . They can't afford to let down their guard, but they have artillery under their coats, enough to make short work of the bloody buggers." The verb "bumped off" is new to me. I get the idea and soon practice backing in through revolving doors and firing imaginary Winchesters from the hip.

The second most interesting thing about the Imperial is that Daddy doesn't come to sleep in his bed there in our cheap accommodations until three or four in the morning. He explains that he is exhausted from treating one of his patients. One moment he moans, "My prostate is buggered." The next moment he chants almost deliriously, "Poontang is my delight, poontang is all my joy . . ." Whatever the meaning of his babbling, I plan to escape, without cash-money, across the Mexican border on the AT&SF to Lamy and Albuquerque and from there to El Paso by stagecoach.

On the morning of our departure we take a buggy ride to a spread called Homesteader's Ranch. While I wait outside in the cold, Daddy goes in to the low adobe ranchhouse to see a patient. He neglects to take with him his black leather medicine bag. When he returns to the buggy hours later, he waves to the window. The figure of a pale young woman who looks like Mona Lisa in a dressing gown parts the curtains there and blows him a kiss. I be dog if she isn't the same Mrs. Pia Dare who comes to our house in Colorado Springs for the honeyhumping! I try to blot out the pictures in my head of morose sex organs by focusing thoughts on baseball. As we head toward the depot, I bring up the subject of medicine to show Daddy I am keen on having a successful career like his, playing god.

"How did it go at St. Mabyn's? Did you find it difficult to help sick coalminers there?"

He flicks reins. "Kippers' knickers," he says.

"What did you do?"

"I had them sacked."

"Sacked?"

"Fired."

"They have leprosy?"

Daddy doesn't crack a smile. "St. Mabyn's is now the healthiest colliery in the nation. Woodbridge will break out champers for me." There is a pause. Daddy, looking sad, sighs lugubriously and mutters, "I'll always be only halfway between the dustman and the king."

The sun had just begun its westering. Even though my head was still spinning, I hoped eventually to crawl to the tracks and get a passing freight to stop. If it went west, I now knew, it would need only about sixty miles to fetch up at Los Tristes. If it went east, on account of my having leftover Daddy-dollars in my wallet, I might's well pay my way to Topeka, Chicago, and New York and hole up with Ganny on Park Avenue. Any which way, I needed to saddle up. I might could be easy meat—frozen meat. Another night of diamond dust and I was hors d'oeuvres for any wolf, coyote, mountain lion or bear.

My tweed cap must have fallen off when I rolled down the embankment. Whatever its monetary value in New York, without the cap I would be in Scampy's eyes a tramp. My wallet, too, was missing from the rear pocket of my knickerbockers. The Pinkerton dicks had probably robbed me. Daddy would not accept excuses when his cash-money was missing. I might really be in for a "what fer," and I later was headed for poor-house and potter's field. Most devastating, Scampy's photograph, like the Holy Grail, had disappeared.

Hoofthuds, horsesnuffings, wheelsqueakings, jingling and clinking of tracechains. I, squinting through mirage of heatblur, saw a buckboard drawn by a pair of sleek sorrels and filled with four men, three of them hatless and bearded, a fourth, the driver, sporting a widebrim Stetson and a clean-shaven face. I shut my eyes.

Someone shouted.

Whoa-there. Whistles. Yo. "There is good," someone said.

Gravelscuffings.

Heavy breathing next to me.

"Well," said a deep, gentle voice next to me, "stump my toe."

Another voice said something I couldn't hear. "Yup," said the man who was next to me, "I know this young gentleman. Lives in the Springs. Doc Penhallow's boy. Goes by Tree . . . Tree? Can you open your eyes, son? We've had a little search party out for you. If you want to just lay there, we'll come back for Thanksgiving with turkey, yams, sweet corn, pumpkin pie and turnip greens."

"I don't like turnip greens." I popped my eyes open.

He was a big man with a sad countenance, but his blue eyes twinkled. This appearance of peaceableness clashed with the .45 caliber revolver holstered at his waist. He had bully straw-colored hair, like a sailor's in *Treasure Island*, falling from Stetson almost to his shoulders. I recognized the cuckold all right, as he me, and by my proper name, too, but I kept cards tight to my chest in case he was playing the jack. He asked me how I was feeling.

"Fine," I said. "Who would fardels bear?"

"You who have 'a native hue of resolution'," he fired back with *Hamlet* precision. He was good, fast on the draw. Cradling my neck with one hand, with the other he poured water from a canteen down my throat and over my head. "You have a nasty wound, *monsieur* . . . I'll put coal-oil on it. Scalping party?"

"Pesky varmints," I said. "I sharpened their heads and drove them into the ground."

"So that's why you're covered in blood and smell like crap." He was pressing a hand against my brow, feeling for fever, lifting arms and legs gingerly. "Tell me if it hurts," he said. To my amazement, though my thigh had been so sore I believed I was paralyzed, I could now not only move limbs but also sit up. My main problem apart from the concussion was, to my shame, the soiling in my underwear. "I stink," I said. "I'm sorry."

"Not to worry," he said.

As he was pulling on my shoulders, I felt a flash of heat lightning in them and groaned.

'Hurts?"

"Bit."

"You're not cut out for a gravedigger," he said.

A few seconds must have passed before my brain stopped whirling like a ball in a revolving roulette wheel. He knew! Cripple Creek, Shiflit, trying to dig my own grave, the lot: he knew. His name was coming back to me: Captain Dare. "How come, sir," I asked, "you remembered I don't go by my dad's name, Rountree?"

Dare shrugged. "I could tell you had an Indian sign on you there . . . The truth is, I couldn't make heads or tails out of Dr. Rountree Penhallow, if you don't mind my telling you flat . . . We came to your house to thank him for curing Pia, and he bows and scrapes and quotes Dante's poetry . . . It was cheeky. I grew up in France. When a drunk excuses himself to take a piss, he'll say, *Il faut changer l'eau du poisson*—'I'm going to change the water in the fishbowl.' It's a droll euphemism which gives no offense. But if an English gentleman fondles your wife's hand and tells her in Italian that she has 'gentle qualities,' I dunno . . ." Dare finished stretching my limbs, sat back on heels, and rubbed a fist across his nose. He resembled a fighter satisfied he had delivered a knockout punch. "Nothing broken, Tree."

I decided to ask him, and did, about the gravedigging. He nodded his head in the direction of the three men who were building a fire. "Glass-Eye Gwilym yonder, he saw you in Cripple Creek yesterday. He saw you attacked by a crazy blind man. He saw what Lieutenant Shiflit was up to in a vacant lot. He saw you in the bull pen. He saw you in the boxcar. He saw the Pinkertons throw you out last night here in Peniel."

The man called Glass-Eye Gwilym was the one-eyed man I had seen in the bull pen and boxcar.

"A man who lays on the ground—," Dare began.

"—lies," I cut in. The lie/lay problem in English grammar always brought out the wise guy in me before I could shut my mouth.

"A man who *lies* on the ground on an October night in Colorado where the 'lone and level sands stretch far away'—"

"I like that," I said.

"*Ozymandias*, by Percy Bysshe Shelley. Do you always teach your grandmother to suck eggs?"

Even though Mum and I had read aloud to one another the English poets, including Shelley, *Ozymandias* had escaped attention. I giggled, the word felt so savory on my tongue. I would like to buffalo bullies at school with it in future. *Take that back or I'll ozymandias your candy ass*. Dare was saying, "A man who lies on the ground, and so forth, needs hot black coffee and vittals."

"Victuals."

"However," he sighed, "I can't do anything about your face."

He was so fast on the draw, before I realized that he was joshing me I was passing fingers over my face. I might could be another Tomato-Face Paic, the Croatian boy at school who spilled coal-oil on a woodstove and set himself on fire and was saved by a passerby who rushed into his house and put olive oil and baking soda on Tomato-Face's face and made it human again, sort of.

"Your face looks like the south end of a mule going north," Dare said. I fired back, "That was a chestnut when Methuselah bamboozle yuh." I really liked Dare now.

He rose and went toward the fire. That time when he returned from the Philippines and came to our house with Pia he was still in uniform with campaign hat and putties and ribbons, handsome as he was, I'd been prejudiced against him for being a cuckold. Now, though, he was wearing Mexican boots, dungarees, the Stetson and a bully Indian shirt—soft white-tanned skins sewed with sinew, natural edges fringed, deer tails dangling from neck flap. I wanted to grow up and be like him.

Memory was wrapping itself around that time when Daddy and I and Captain and Pia were saying goodbyes at the front door of the house on Wood Avenue, Mum, as usual, having been ordered by Daddy to remain in bed upstairs in her room. Daddy had made introductions, Dare as *one of our fighting boys back from the Philippines*, me as Rountree. Pia, as usual, was slender and full-bosomed, smile like Gioconda's depicted in my *Book of Knowledge*. Eyes were her most remarkable feature, a light-green turquoise pair of opaque swimming pools peeking through dark long hair. Wearing a voluminous gray satin dress, skirts of which brushed the floor as she walked, she might drive Daddy potty, but I, at least, knew her for what she was: a floozy. That Daddy was "bowing and scraping," as Dare had said, was true, as was quoting from Dante, a bit of persiflage all the more astonishing as Daddy didn't know enough Italian to order a plate of spaghetti. Kissing the gloved hand Pia held out to him, he said, *"Donna pietosa e di novelle etate, Adorna assai di gentilezze umane,"* whereupon I dashed to our family library and found already open there on a table our bilingual edition of *The Divine Comedy*, the "Pia" canto marked. After memorizing the lines as Daddy had done, I rushed upstairs and repeated them to Mum, to whom they rightfully belonged. When she asked me to translate them, I was ready and said, *"A lady compassionate and young, richly adorned with gentle qualities."* She opened her arms and hugged me into her French perfume and said, *Dante fell in love when he was only nine years old*. Some time afterwards I found Daddy humming to himself, *Qual maraviglia! Qual maraviglia!* Seeing me, he gushed, *That chap believed I cured her miraculously! She clasped her hands as if in prayer and thanked me with 'Qual maraviglia'!* Dare fell for it! *Her father was a wop from Los Tristes*. The musical Italian language reminded me of the *dong ding ling dong-a-ling-a-ding* of convent bells in Woodmen Valley which I had listened to during my wanderings in the hills. As for Pia, though she was a floozy, I didn't like Daddy's calling her father a "wop" when he had been slobbering over her like a hounddog.

Dare had put a speckled blue kettle on a trivet over the campfire. Surrounding it were the miners with their masses of matted hair and bushy beards. Pants of a canvas material were stuffed into their steeltoed boots and suspended by galluses over frayed, sweat-stained long johns. As often as I'd seen working men similarly dressed and unwashed, I had not realized until now how much hardship had been etched in otherwise youthful features. Glass-Eye Gwilym was tilting a bottle to his lips, the neck under his beard looking like that of a skinned fish, the kind of sickly white you'd expect to see in a dead man before undertakers rouged him up.

I've seen a foal seemingly dying of colic suddenly spring up on shanks and go frolicking in sunny pastures. I now, like that foal, without vertigo or much pain in thigh jumped up, went and sat on a log by the fire. Dare wrapped a Navajo blanket around me, fetched from the wagon a rag soaked in coal-oil, and rubbed it into my scalp. The medication stung as if a Roman candle had been lit and left sputtering at the base of my brain. Dare had done, I realized, the necessary before howling could be formed behind my teeth. He tied another rag around my head. "There," he said. "Glass-Eye Gwilym has your grog."

Glass-Eye Gwilym stood nearby, a half-empty, amber-colored bottle in one hand, tin cup in the other. From the kettle he had poured black coffee into the cup until it was half full; from the bottle he had poured into the cup, filling it, what I assumed to be whiskey. He came and presented me with the cup. "There is good you are, boy," he said. Holding the cup in two hands and sniffing the aroma of its contents—coffee and, for sure, whiskey—I had the wonderful sensation of acceptance into the world of real men who worked and stank. Glass-Eye Gwilym, indeed, smelled like skunk cabbage visited by alley cats. His drinking made the good eye red as an autumn leaf. The glass eye, sloppily imprinted with a blue iris, resembled ivory-colored porcelain used for toilets. He belonged in my *Book of Knowledge* under Homo Neanderthalensis.

I took a first sip and gasped. I took a second sip. Wildfires raced through my belly. I took a big swallow. The Tipperary song sneaked into consciousness. I closed eyes, hummed it to myself. Glass-Eye Gwilym and Dare were talking about me.

"There is terrible. Cracked his noggin on a stone, may hap, after dicks they wrassled and robbed, thewing him oot like a sack of spuds."

38

"You told me he was pistol-whipped."

"Aye, that, too."

"Luckily, he landed softly, rolled down here," came Dare's voice. "If you didn't actually see him kangarooed, our case for attempted homicide might be shot."

"There is silly." Glass-Eye Gwilym's retort had an edge to it. "I wonder did you know, Mr. Captain Dare, we was sleeping, me and Huw and Sean . . . I wake up to commotion. Pinkerton opens door. There is the lad squealing like stuck pig and he is pistol-whipped hard enough to kill him and, heave-ho, I see oot boxcar door the sign, Peniel, it says. This I have told you plain to be heard."

"Don't take on," said Dare. "Without your navigation we would not have found him . . . His father's a stingy so-and-so. Strangely, he never charged me for treating an illness which, thank goodness, my wife never had. He must pay you a reward for saving Tree."

My shoulder had a hand on it. It felt good, but Dare didn't know that Pia was a floozy. I opened eyes. "Sir?"

"Listen, Tree."

He and Pia still lived together near Los Tristes, I was sorry to hear. Upon his return from the Philippines, he had been, he said, "performing services" for Union leaders in Denver, intercepting trains with boxcars used for deporting strikers. Because he had a home telephone, Union had informed him that a number of Cripple Creek miners guarded by Pinkertons had been sent down the mountain and were probably headed for La Junta and the Kansas border on the Santa Fe line. He had called the sheriff in La Junta, knowing him as one of the few public officials in southern Colorado not on the payroll of mine owners. Together, once Dare had driven his team a day and night to La Junta, they had been boarding freights, searching boxcars. Finally in one of these they found Glass-Eye Gwilym, Huw, and Sean guarded by dicks named Gott and Mush. Aware that these Pinkertons just brought in from New York had not been properly sworn in, the La Junta sheriff arrested them on a charge of carrying concealed weapons, this booking made in order to hold them until more serious charges such as attempted homicide should come to light.

Nodding with a wry smile, Dare concluded the story. "Concealed weapons? In addition to shotguns and revolvers, those gentlemen from Sing Sing had enough dynamite caps to turn an anarchist green with envy. But not until our friends here were about to hop a freight back to Denver was it revealed that a certain young gentleman who was not a striker but who had been tortured and deported with them may have been murdered by the Pinkertons, body hurled from the boxcar at this whistlestop called Peniel . . . You have Glass-Eye Gwilym to thank. If it had not been for his insistence that we come look for you—the Pinkertons denied everything and claimed that this Welshman, as is true, is a thirsty sot—we might have let him return to Denver."

"Shanghaied, kangarooed, and sent down the mountain," Glass-Eye Gwilym piped up. "A miner the boy is already indade." I studied him, remembering detail from the bull pen, how a militiaman prodded him with a bayonet and drew blood, the one-eyed man laughing, *A good day is today, then, indade.*

Dare's expression was deadpan. "The boys and I," he said, "are having a fry-up. I don't suppose you'd care to join us for bacon, eggs, and baked beans?"

"There is good the boy is!" The bronchitic screech in Glass-Eye Gwilym's voice sounded like someone's rubbing a hand on a tight balloon. Shielding good eye from sun and scanning horizon, he stumbled off in the Grasslands.

While I had been recovering consciousness, I'd been concerned about those whose hearts might be cut if my disappearance were to come to their attention. Mum worried about me all the time, my grades at school, my access to Daddy's medicine and liquor cabinets, my dropped testicles. Although I had no intention to become a moron, a dope fiend, an alcoholic and a jerk-off, and she had always trusted me to find my own way, now that she was locked up her worries could be unbearable. I knew that patients at a sanitorium had to be spared emotional disturbances of any kind. Hence they were prohibited from using telephone, telegraph, or postal services. So it was unlikely for the time being Mum would learn what had happened to me. As for Ruby, she was accustomed to weird behavior in our family and would be unlikely to raise an alarm. Finally, the principal of my school, Mr. Lily, had already been alerted by Daddy that I would be absent until further notice due to obligations to the Woodbridge family.

Daddy, Alphie, Shiflit and the Pinkertons had all, one way or another, been involved in my disappearance. Had they conspired together to make certain I showed up in Cripple Creek? Alphie could be mean and impulsive. Shiflit knew Alphie and worked for Daddy. Perhaps Daddy's hunting trip had been designed to provide him with an alibi, leaving my disappeaerance in the hands of a Guardsman beyond the reach of the law—Shiflit.

Scampy, I loved. I could not bring myself to place her under a loathsome suspicion. Although she must have realized that something had happened to me in Cripple Creek, she was almost certainly too terrified of her brother to seek help for me from the authorities. And was she in some way connected to Shiflit?

When I was looking at her photographs, I had read, written below the picture of Woodbridge's wrecked Maxwell, "Mr. Shiflit, the coachman, wrecks our car because Alphie put opium in the radiator."

I was splattered with blood, black and glossy as a raven's wing. Someone had wanted me to die.

I survived.

Not too damn bad.

Years later, in Paris in 1908, Scampy revealed to me why neither she nor Alphie had been concerned about my disappearance. Shiflit had told them that he had been hired by Daddy to put me through a course of military training in Cripple Creek. Scampy and Alphie had left me in the courtroom because, they believed, I was scheduled to remain under tutelage of the Guard. I had resisted taking them to Cripple Creek because I was trying to dodge discipline.

~~~

An hour later I revealed to Dare my suspicions about Daddy though nothing about his adultery. When I came to Daddy's possible setting up of events with Alphie and Shiflit, I admitted, "I don't really hate my father, and I don't fancy squealing on anybody, and I hope I'm wrong—but I'm scared for Mum. Things are only now coming into view like stars in daylight . . ."

I had stopped myself just as I was blurting out my hypothesis, one, that Daddy wanted to lay hands on Mum's inheritance, two, that he was so infatuated with Pia that he wanted me and Mum to die, I by "accident," she by disease. Informing the man who had helped to save my life about his wife's infidelity might lead to his using the revolver for ventilation. The truth might prompt Dare to revenge.

"On the other hand," I tossed out as if inspired, "I wouldn't put it past Alphie to play a pre-Halloween prank and Lieutenant Shiflit to carry it to an extreme. What do you think, sir?"

Dare looked me in the eye. "What do I think? I've known Fredson Shiflit for years. Some day I'll tell you about him . . . For the time being, I'd say I agree with you: I wouldn't put anything past him. He's like a wanton boy with a butterfly, stripping off one wing at a time, only very patiently and deviously. When you think you've got him figured out, he's actually aiming at something else . . . Suppose, for example, my wife were having an affair with your father. I know it's absurd. Suppose it were true, though, and Shiflit knew about it. What would he do? . . . Well, if he were an ordinary *maître-chanteur*, he would blackmail your father for hush money. Shiflit, however, doesn't operate that way. He wants, above all, the satisfaction of believing he is God's scourge, an avenging angel, an instrument for extermination . . . He would torture you and plan to have you kidnapped and murdered in order to pin the blame on me. He has a score to settle with me . . . By the way, Tree, give me your money."

Dare's uncanny speculations required on my part nervous giggles and sharp intakes of breath. So absorbed did I become in this pretense, albeit I felt some relief in having suspicion shifted from Daddy to Shiflit, I reacted to Dare's demand for my cash-money as if I didn't already realize my wallet was missing. I reached for it in the back pocket of my knickerbockers, again thinking, *Daddy will whip me for My Adventure with Depraved Beasts.*

"Glass-Eye searched Gott's pockets," Dare was saying. "He found a wallet and a cap."

A few minutes later I was wearing my tweed cap and searching through my wallet. Dollars, Scampy's photograph, belly dancer were accounted for. To show my appreciation I joshed the Welsh miner.

"Say, Glass-Eye," I said, "you stink."

He blinked the red eye, hung head, croaked, "I know it."

I waited to see if he had another hand to show. After a while I believed I had hurt his feelings. "Sorry," I said.

He jerked head up. "You stink, too," he said. "There is sorry."

I clutched my stomach as if I'd been shot. I muttered famous words: "You got me!" He grinned. His teeth were yellow. "Say, Glass-Eye," I piped up, "what did the raree bird say when General Case tried to tip it off the top of Pikes Peak?"

After twisting head about and stroking beard, he said he gave up.

"Well," I said, "when General Case tried to tip the raree bird off the top of Pikes Peak, the raree bird said, 'It's a long way to Tipperary'!"

"There is terrible," Glass-Eye Gwilym said.

The sun was really westering now, gathering its Joseph's coat of colors for the big disappearance behind the Sangre de Cristo Mountains. While the "boys" were breaking camp, Dare explained arrangements to me. Glass-Eye Gwilym and the others would catch an eastbound Santa Fe to La Junta and from there head back to Denver. Dare would take me in his wagon to the Purgatoire to have a bath and then to his Homesteader's Ranch where I could recover from my wound. He would telephone the news of my rescue to Daddy, Mum, and Ruby, and to Union lawyers in Denver that they might take legal action against the Guard and the Pinkerton agency.

He and I headed west. The sorrels pricked up their ears, anticipating the great life awaiting them around every bend in the trail. Sunblaze snagged on rims of the Sangres. If I had been a tree like one of the golden cottonwoods leafed out along the Purgatoire, I would have been ravished by the beautiful illusion of a permanence in my gold.

I broke a long silence. "Do you reckon, sir, it would be all right to consider Glass-Eye Gwilym in a Jesus-y category, a savior of situations?"

Peering down the trail, Dare replied matter-of-factly, "He saved your life."

"Some people I know," I said, "consider poor folks evolutionary throwbacks. What do you think, sir?"

"Well," said Dare, "when I was in the Philippines, I learned a proverb: *En casa del ciego, el tuerto es rey.* 'In the country of the blind, the one-eyed man is king'."

I squinted against the burnt reddish-orange of the setting sun. It wasn't Sunday School, the ocean of grass I was leaving, but it had taught me a lesson: it could not be divided into peoples and territories, it had only one language. Even though it seemed to be composed only of lone and level sands, there was some greening in the sloughs. The sun made me think of Glass-Eye Gwilym's good and merciful eye, the one with a savior's soul in it.

Chapter Four

Where wheels fitted into parallel ruts, no grass had grown for a long time. Dare told me we were following the Old Santa Fe Trail. To my delight the barren landscape had a history, one I had read about, and now I was participating in it as if I were hearing thunder of buffaloes, hoofbeats and wagonrattles of conquistadors, of French trappers, of merchants and, indeed, of an army. In 1846 Colonel Stephen Kearny and his Army of the West had followed this very trail on their way to the conquest of Mexico. As I recalled, there had been 1,500 wagons, 15,000 oxen, and 4,000 mules in that cavalcade. I could almost hear the clinking of traces, the shouts of skinners, the clop and thud of shod hooves on gravel.

A blast of cold air pelted our faces with sand and brought from faraway the howling of coyotes. The horses, stepping uneasily, had heard it too. I glanced at Dare. He looked imperturbable. He had a box of rifle shells on the seat beside him and a Winchester .30-.30 leaning within easy reach of his hand. "I reckon the coyotes won't bother us," I remarked. I sounded like what I was, an urban brainfart.

"Oh," he said, "they're snooping around all right. Soon's we left Peniel they picked up the scent of bacon in the grub box . . . Not to worry. They won't attack us unless they're frothing at the mouth with rabies."

"Frothing at the mouth?"

"Depends. A rabid coyote will come at you with head low and swinging from side to side. He'll be coughing and whining . . . Sometimes he's so quick, before you can line him up in your sights, he'll be sinking snapping wet jaws into your horse's legs."

"Honest? What do you do?"

"You have to shoot the horse."

It was almost enough to make sweat trickle out all over me, Dare's coyote tale. He liked to josh me, though, tongue-in-cheek like. I wished I was back home in civilization. There, at least, coyotes would only be looking for kittens. Lamps, there, would be lit. Indians might be holding a pow-wow in the Garden of the Gods, but they weren't on the warpath. Bears might come prowling before hibernation, but they preferred garbage dumps to church picnics.

A big moon began to rise into an inkiness that was pricked with early stars. Dare turned the team off the trail and brought it to a halt in a meadow of windrippled grass. Thickets of willow bushes grew between the meadow and the Purgatoire. I had known we were approaching it because, smelling wet air, the horses had whinnied. Having learned I was no longer immortal, I wasn't sure I could stick my apprehensions about wilderness.

"Looks snaky," I said.

"Why don't you help feed and water," he said. It wasn't a question. "We'll bed down a spell until the moon is high enough. Then we'll plow a straight furrow home . . . Meantime, unless you're fixing to take your bath in a cup of water, I suggest Lost Souls Laundry yonder will remove crap from you and your store-boughts, dude. What about snakes?"

I wished I hadn't brought up the subject.

"Don't worry about rattlesnakes," said Dare in tease-tone. "Say there's a prairie rattler down there in the willows where you'll be walking barefooted. Say he hears you coming from a hundred yards away. Say he sticks out his forky tongue and coils up, rattles going like castanets in *Carmen*. Well, he's flush to your full house. He can strike only twelve feet or so, giving you time to scoot before he coils again. Besides, he's probably had dinner already—a fieldmouse or a yummy wild duck. He's sleepy and doesn't want to kill unwashed boys. When you come right down to it, snakes are like flies: they won't hurt you if they're well cooked."

"I'm real tired," I said. I stretched myself. "I'll just lay down in the wagon."

"*Lie* down." He was paying me back for priggishness. "Can't recommend my wagon. It has more fire-ants and cockroaches and ticks than Napoleon's army had lice . . . You didn't know about Napoleon's army? Could've fooled me. Thought you knew everything . . . Well, what was left of Napoleon's army after the Russians and the winter had finished with it was destroyed by lice . . . Yessiree, I'd think twice before bedding down in my wagon. Other day, I found me a cockroach in the oats there as big as a Pacifican king-crab. He had a carapace of hard scales like an armadillo's. I had to hit him with a shovel. It just bounced off. And he started singing . . . *de colores se visten los campos en la primavera* . . . and telling me he's hungry, pass the biscuits. I got so mad I finally crushed him with the butt of my rifle. He made a cracking-up sound like popcorn in a blast furnace . . . Did I say ticks? Sleep in my wagon, and the ticks will come crawling and sucking blood through your scalp until they are bloated like Humpty Dumpty. You die of Rocky Mountain Spotted Fever. All that's left of you is the red grass which grows on the soil where there has been a murder . . . Now, I'm not saying you can sleep on the ground without molestation. If there's a thunderstorm tonight, the crockydile will crawl out of the river. If there's one thing your crockydile likes better than hogturd tied to a swollen gland, it's a boy who tries to cure freckles by refusing to take a bath . . ."

I wouldn't have named a dog after me after he finished. "I reckon I'll go down to the river directly," I said with an effort at bravado, alighting from the buckboard and springing into the wagon's load. I removed a piece of sacking over a water barrel, filled pails of water from it, jumped down and gave these to the horses to slurp up. Then I slopped them with grain and hay, rubbed them down, blanketed them. Dare gazed at me, perhaps impressed, not realizing I had seen these chores performed in barns and livery stables. He was laying sheep pelts on the ground, bedrolls on top of them, and fetching canned peaches and soda crackers from his grub box. After a while we squatted side by side and ate the peaches and crackers. I was like his pal.

Not too damn bad.

Dare tossed me that Navajo blanket. "You'll need this while your clothes are drying," he said. "In any case you'll not get blood stains out until we leave them at a Chinese in Los Tristes. You can buy what you need at the Pluck Me."

I left shoes, socks, wallet, cap and the rag, the one which he had tied around my head, on my bedroll, then ran through willows as fast as I could, barefoot, and cannonballed into water so snowmelt cold it would have put steel to shame. I wriggled, frog-kicked, dog-paddled and breast-stroked, meanwhile stripping off sweater, shirt, leggings, knickerbockers, long johns and underwear, fixing to rub them the way Ruby would have rubbed them, only without benefit of her washboard and lye soap. But, when I was nigh frozen, I lost my grip on the stupid clothes. They sank in swift current and must have mingled with rusted sixteenth-century Spanish breastplates on the bottom.

Not long afterwards I stood over Dare. He was snoring while I, teeth chattering, was wrapped in the blanket. "What's the Pluck Me?"

"Go to sleep, kid."

"I haven't anything to wear."

"That's what my wife always says."

"The river snatched my clothes."

"They say," he said, "if you stick a rusty nail in the ground, you can hear Mrs. Devil crying. That doesn't mean she forced you to do it . . . Do you wake up your father when he's sound asleep?"

"No, sir."

"Well," he said, "that's good. I thought he might have an honest motive to kill you . . . What's the Pluck Me? After I answer your question, will you promise to sleep until reveille?"

The Pluck Me, it turned out, was the name given to company-owned supply stores in company-towns and company-controlled towns. By paying workers in scrip instead of in dollars, the company monopolized business, forcing them to buy in the stores at inflated prices. If workers exchanged scrip for dollars and avoided company stores, taking business elsewhere, they were apt to be sent down the mountain. Since regular paid-up work varied according to seasonal demand or strikes, and since the company deducted doctor and other fees from wages, the workers were apt to run up ruinous debt at the stores and end up jobless and homeless, evicted from company-owned houses—in sum, plucked clean as a chicken on Sunday.

Since I had some dollars I could buy new clothes at the Pluck Me and worry about exploited workers later. I crawled into my bedroll and seemed to make renewed contact with civilization. The Lost Tribes of Israel must have camped in the meadow, because the small of my back was lying on the Ten Commandments, as well as on arrowheads, bullet casings left by Billy the Kid and Wyatt Earp, and porcelain dolls smashed by pioneer girls and boys. Coyotes were sneaking up to get bacon, snakes were waiting to poison barefoot boys, cockroaches were singing Mexican folksongs. I listened to the annihilating night so hard my ears hurt. The river and a million crickets kept up steady ripplings and murmurations. Once, a train mournfully wailed . . .

Next thing I knew, Dare was shaking me awake. The moon was high and bright. Against the ink-blot of the Sangre de Cristo, extremely distant city lights twinkled like thousands of giant lightning bugs.

Dressed in shoes, socks, cap and blanket but with nothing to cover my buttocks, I sat on the bucking buckboard and accumulated splinters. Still half asleep, I broke trails to home, conjuring up images. No, I really didn't hate my father. When he clipped pince-nez to the bridge of his red nose, he studied you as if you were an insect. His lips twitched beneath his mustache. If Mum tried to make conversation at the dinner table, his legs jiggled about in nervous agitation. Regarding American fashions as low-class, he had three-piece suits sent from Saville Row; at home or at the Sun Palace he wore his Guy's Hospital high-buttoned cutaway coat over striped trousers. When he stepped out of the bathtub, he neglected to towel off droplets of water clinging to the hairy upper part of his back, a Van Dieman's Land beneath his dignity to bother himself with. Consequently, as soon as he put on the starched white shirts and collars Ruby had carefully washed and ironed for him, they became soaking wet. Thoughtless about Ruby as well as me, he loved only himself, for sure. Yes, his faults were thick as fiddlers in hell, but, no, I couldn't really hate him. For one reason, I needed to hate all my own faults.

There was so much to love about Mum, born Anna Maria Dautremond in New Orleans, that it was easy to put her on a pedestal and to eulogize her properly with words such as *kindness* and *generosity* and *steadfastness*. She had flaws: flighty moods, fits of anger and melancholia, above all, abject, soporific submissiveness to Daddy. He was devouring her bit by bit. She, it seemed, had increasingly little will to resist him. However—and this was the most astonishing of her attributes—she was rebellious. Daddy might be ignoring her, threatening her with abandonment, humiliation, even death, but she was defying him. Daddy sent a coachman in a brougham to fetch her to the Sun Palace. The coachman restrained her in a strait jacket even though she was not struggling. I was allowed to accompany her on the journey from home, which she would probably never see again, to hospital, from which, it seemed, few emerged alive. At the corner of Cascade and Cache la Poudre, we passed some healthy-looking, respectable-looking ladies. Mum asked me to lower her window. I did so. She stuck her head out of the window and her tongue out at the ladies, this gesture joined to a sputtering fart of a raspberry and by her favorite cussword, "Bull feathers!" Then, too, a dangerous secret had been revealed to me by Ruby. Daddy, had he discovered it, would have been mad enough to make red peppers grow. When he was at the Palace and I at school, Mum would glue on a mustache, wear a wig covered by a Russian astrakhan, dress in a man's suit and tennis shoes, sneak out the back door and go hiking for miles, after which exercise she'd have a hot bath, school herself in college-level letters and sciences, and only by mid-afternoon return to bed and try to look sick enough to drink the blood of a black cat. Although Mum was really fit to climb fourteeners, Daddy was getting credit throughout our city as a caregiver devoted to a doomed, neurasthenic invalid.

He had diagnosed her with TB from the time he first met her in Italy. When she was pregnant with me, he believed that I was weakening her resistance to the tubercle bacillus; my birth, he once told me, had almost cost her her life. "She threw a hemorrhage the moment you were delivered," he said. The dead albatross of guilt around my neck began to weigh about a ton. One afternoon after school, as I was giving Mum a cup of tea in her bedroom, I burst into tears.

"What's the matter, pet lamb?"

Placing the teacup on a table and opening arms to me, she hugged the be-jesus out of me. I stopped bawling and sniffling and blurted out the reason: I had caused her to throw a hemorrhage.

"Where on earth did you get such a silly idea, pet lamb? I've never thrown a hemorrhage. I gave birth to you on December 18, 1890, in a lunger's cottage in the Adirondack Mountains. I warned Daddy, who was in attendance, that if he gave me chloroform he'd come in for grumbles he'd never forget!"

I was just learning at that time from Ruby that Daddy had a red nose and twitching legs because he was a liar. Therefore, because he didn't deserve respect, I snitched on him, pointing out his malpractices, not his adultery.

"Well," Mum said, "he's the doctor, a genius. Who am I to question him? He's right: he says I am uneducated. And he has helped so many people. It's a small thing I do, resting in bed and out on the sunporch and working up a cough evenings when he takes my temperature . . . Selfish me! When he isn't looking, I stick the thermometer in the steam of the vaporizer to get my normal reading heated to over 100 degrees! And then, if only then, he speaks to me so kindly, so tenderly . . . Of course, he believes he is perfect! I have to do everything I can to spare him the pain of self-reproach. Where would he be without his authoritative manner? . . . Maybe if I hadn't gone along with his nonsense about having TB, he wouldn't have proposed? He needs to see me in all that spiritual purity which is supposed to result from the wasting away of our mortal flesh . . . Imagine. I married him in Rome when I'd barely turned eighteen . . ."

Dare halted the team at dawn. "Scarecrow," he pointed.

We were surrounded by fields of pumpkins. Squawking crows, who were feasting on them, were ignoring a scarecrow which resembled Ichabod Crane, exceedingly lank with narrow shoulders, long arms and legs, a broom in straw hands.

"Want a puff?" Dare was lighting a sulphur match, sucking flame into tobacco in a briar pipe, then taking a few puffs and blowing smoke into cold air. Right there, by once again treating me on equal terms, he soared to the top of my list of Never Befores. I'd never been in love before, never faced a firing squad before, never been kidnapped before but, hully gee, I'd never smoked anything before except a little rabbit tobacco wrapped in tissue paper.

"Pre-chate it," I said, "but no thanks."

"See here," he said. "You can't shop in the Pluck Me wearing nothing but a blanket. If you dress like a scarecrow you'll pass for one of the regulars. Anyway, Halloween's coming . . . Here's the human dilemma. You can't smoke all the time. You can't drink all the time. You can't sleep all the time. You can't make love all the time, and you sure can't run around naked all the time unless you're so bugs you're aiming for the lunatic asylum . . . So . . . The farmer failed to harvest his pumpkins on time or to put a twenty-two in his scarecrow's 'hands' instead of a broom. Why don't you get some of his clothes? In exchange, you can give those crows a hard time."

" '*Let*'," I quoted after some thought, " '*the shades of the prison-house begin to close upon the growing boy*'."

" '*Trailing clouds of glory*'," Dare quoted quickly and correctly from Wordsworth. " '*Trailing clouds of glory*'."

He really was fast on the draw. He had gotten me with *Ozymandias* and blazed away with *Hamlet* and now he was shooting me with *Intimations of Immortality*. I wished he and Mum could play some Shootout together. It would be bully to see them together, I was thinking.

I ran into the pumpkin field and returned a few minutes later dressed in rags for a Halloween party on Robinson Crusoe's island. I had on faded cotton trousers, a linsey-woolsey shirt, and a dark frock coat, items so shot-up by cowboys that warp threads rubbed my skin like sandpaper. But I was free of splinters. I did try to pay for theft by leaving my New York cap on a pole, but my efforts to frighten crows by flapping arms and cussing proved hopeless. I expected to see a thousand squawkers furiously rising and blackening an already gray sky. Instead, the crows, hearing me yell at them, stopped pecking pumpkins just long enough to stare at me as if to say, Mercy, What's the Young Generation Coming To.

We hit the trail. That other trail composed of mixed memories continued to open out. I wasn't altogether certain of their source, whether Mum or Grandma Ganny, scrapbooks, letters or my own deductions, but the reverence I had for history forced me to acknowledge as real the skeletons we had in our closets . . .

Colonel Rufus Obadiah Dautremond, my maternal grandpa, had made his money in the New Orleans slave trade before the Civil War. Lucy Dautremond, my Grandma Ganny, predestined to be a belle in New Orleans, grew up penniless, orphaned when her mother died of typhoid fever and her father, while serving under Rufus Obadiah's cavalry command, received a minié ball in the chest. At sixteen, in 1869, she met and married old Rufe. "I was so ignorant," she told me with her querulous laugh, "I thought money and babies came from sugar barrels. A nun at my convent corrected this impression, explaining that babies came out of a doctor's saddlebags, and a mole on the neck brings money in by the peck."

After the wedding the Dautremonds moved to New York and lived in a house on Washington Square. Grandpa said he was in the "export import" business. It required his long and frequent absences from home, leaving Ganny to raise Anna Maria, born in 1870, with the help of servants and governesses. On the rare occasions when Grandpa showed up in New York, she, who by now understood how babies originated, locked him out of her room and sent him to sleep in a deck chair in the hallway. When Anna Maria reached the age of seventeen and Ganny the age of thirty-four, the question about the origin of money was clarified where the family was concerned: it had come and continued to come from human trafficking.

Colonel Rufus Obadiah Dautremond up and died in Salvador of Brazil in his office next to the market where he had been importing, not exporting, slaves. Fugitive slaves had murdered him and abducted his mistress.

"His business was *his* business, not mine," Ganny told me with a toss of gray hair. She specialized in sophistry. "I am quite sure he has gone to hell, bless his heart . . . Imagine: if Athens had not had slavery, we would not have had Socrates and Aristotle and other smelly old fools. Imagine: if Bristol had not been built on the proceeds of slavery, we would not have had the divine *Rime of the Ancient Mariner* by Samuel Taylor Coleridge. He was, you see, writing within sight of slave ships rotting in the Bristol Channel. He pictured a skeleton ship with ribs as bars on the face of the setting sun."

When I repeated this bit of literary criticism mixed with callous rationalization later to Mum, she made a face and said, "Ganny's a moral imbecile."

Grandpa Rufus Obadiah, it turned out, was careless. The Will he had drawn up with the help of a Jesuit priest, had, first, to be translated from the Portuguese into English. Ganny had inherited a fortune tied up in a trust fund with peculiar stipulations and legal blind spots. The most important stipulation had to do with Mum: when she attained to the age of thirty-five in 1905, half of Ganny's trust fund was to be paid out in cash to his "dearly beloved Anna Maria." But the trust was not irrevocable. There was nothing to prevent Ganny from looting it long before her daughter became an heiress. Grandpa, apparently exacting revenge for deck-chair nights, bequeathed Ganny a fortune only to have half of it eventually snatched away, but he hoisted himself with his own petard. Given her ignorance about money—she had once tried to exchange Confederate bills for greenbacks—he may have expected to exercise control over her from beyond the grave. He underestimated the power of Ganny's moral imbecility.

Phase Two of the money trail began when Anna Maria, aged seventeen, learned of her "good" fortune: she repudiated it when, hiring a lawyer from Wall Street, she drew up a Will of her own. According to its terms, when she attained to the age of thirty-five, the cash she received from the trust fund would be given to charities designed to help former slaves get education. To her way of thinking, justice had power to be a living thing. She wanted great expectations to be anonymously locked-in to a worthy cause. She made it clear, furthermore, that Ganny was not to leave the remaining estate, should occasion arise, to her—perhaps to children in some future but not to her. Ganny thought her daughter *une folle*. With a shrug she made plans for a tour of Europe, bought a poodle named Muggins, and noted in her silver hand-mirror that she could still pass for a young bride inconvenienced by a daughter.

They went abroad.

Just before Mum's eighteenth birthday, Ganny fell in love. It was hot. They were taking English tea on the *loggia* of a *quattrocento* palace, a *pensione* in Florence just across the Arno next to the

Carmine. All day as she and Mum had been wandering through shops and museums, buying shoes and jewelry and sundry what-nots, she had almost decided that the life of a rich widow in New York should not be sacrificed to the slavery of marriage. As soon as a man had her hand, he'd find a way to get her money, and as soon as he had control of her money, he would lie and cheat. Still, if she could find a man as sweet and moral as *some* Americans and as charming and attentive as *some* Europeans, she might, provided he was also handsome, invite him to bed. Such a creature, in her opinion, was more likely to be discovered in Florence than in any of the other cities, including Paris, she had seen. In Florence, it seemed, beauty was a way of life, beauty and the expression of natural feelings, passionate and meridional. How could any man in Florence, native or stranger, not acquire gentleness and artistic sensibility simply by breathing?

Finishing tea, she strolled to a five-foot balustrade from which she could get a rare whiff of fresh air and a view of Brunelleschi's Duomo and Giotto's Campanile. So what if the Borgias and Medicis had been murderous tyrants? The arts they supported had outlasted them. She heard shrieks of children in cobbled streets a hundred and more feet below. Near the Carmine, girls and boys, unabashedly naked, were playing in a fountain. She lifted Muggins up so that he, too, could enjoy the Renaissance.

Then it happened.

A tall, darkly handsome young man with pencil mustache and wearing a rumpled white suit, silk cravat, white shoes and Panama hat was entering the *loggia*. Ganny was about to put this dandy down for a gold-digger when Muggins wriggled free of her arms, dashed across the tile floor, and sank his teeth in the stranger's ankle, whereupon he calmly exclaimed, "Crikey! What a go!" With sangfroid like that as he tumbled to the floor, he was obviously English. While Anna Maria was busy capturing and strapping Muggins, who had never before been known to growl and bare fangs, let alone bite anyone, Ganny held this palefaced fop in her arms, wiping sweat from his brow with her very own monogrammed handkerchief and apologizing for everything except the War of Independence.

He came to. Immediately appearing awestricken at Anna Maria, he said, "Hello-a-low-a-low-a-low." Unaccustomed to being stared at, she gave Muggins to a servant so that she could feign indifference. The stranger, after rummaging in a black bag he had dropped, produced a syringe and a small vial of liquid, filled the syringe with it, and proceeded to immunize himself against tetanus by sticking the syringe in his forearm. "Right as rain," he said (pronouncing the words as *royt as reign*). Whether, as Ganny believed, he traveled with vaccines sealed against the heat, or whether, as Mum believed, he had simply shot himself with saline solution, he achieved an effect: an invitation from Ganny to join the ladies for tea.

He said, presenting Ganny with his card, "I'm *Mister* instead of *Doctor*, as you can see there . . . We surgeons from Guy's preserve the old tradition of the barbershop, as it were. The original 'doctors' were practicing alchemy or talking rot from the pulpit for centuries before we medical chaps stopped cutting hair and began calling ourselves 'doctors' . . . There you are. It is my very great honor to present myself to you, *madame*, or, if I may say so, young lady. Mister Rountree Penhallow at your service."

"I can read," Ganny said with heavy sigh. "My late, well-to-do husband—he passed away in Bahia, losing his head to a machete—was also a traditionalist, bless his heart . . . Are you a scoundrel, Mr. Hollow?"

"Penhallow. I should bloody well hope so, dear lady. Of course, I'm only halfway between the dustman and the king . . . I do so love you Mericans! With you lot, one needn't pretend to be worth more than a thr'uppenny bit. By Jove, bugger what others think! . . . And is this lovely girl with the sweet dog your sister?"

Ganny fiddled with a pearl necklace in perspiration at her throat. "Anna Maria is my little girl. One day she'll be an heiress, too. In the meantime, as we say in N'Orleans, I'm the red-hot mama." She paused as if to conceal a blush. "I hope you're not one of those romantic gentlemen who believes Romeo climbed up the wall to the balcony? Of course he wouldn't do such a silly little *thang* like that, would he? Juliet left the doors just an iddy-biddy teensy-weensy ajar, don't you think? He spent the night with little old Juliet, don't you think?"

Mr. Penhallow deployed a modest smile. "Tykes the mickey, don't hit? Way I see it, what you lose in the round-abouts you gain in the swings."

Rountree, as he came to be called, spent the next few days escorting the "Mericans" to the Uffizi and Pitti galleries, to Santa Croce, the Medici Chapel and the Campanile, Muggins being locked in Ganny's room. Following each excursion Rountree had flowers delivered separately to each of the ladies in their rooms and tucked billets-doux under their doors. When the contents were shared between them, the notes were found to contain exactly the same terms of endearment, a fact which Ganny regarded as an implied preference that she was equal to any eighteen-year-old girl. Thus she was the real prize. As time went on she brought conversation around to the subject of American law as it pertained to inheritances and trusts. Finally one afternoon on the *loggia*, while Rountree was stuffing himself at Ganny's expense with buttered scones and marmalade, she explained the Dautremond legacy. One, she had the money. Two, when Anna Maria, after an interminable waiting period of eighteen years, inherited her share, she was throwing it away.

"To black folks, can you imagine?" Ganny made an up-to-here measurement, hand to brow. "And she doesn't even have –"

"—a touch of the tarbrush?" Rountree suggested, helpfully.

"Exactly," said Ganny. "And her Daddy slaved to get that money." Realizing a moment later that she had spoken the truth, she changed the subject. "Don't you believe, dear Rountree, that it's a man's duty to provide for his family?"

The English doctor nodded in agreement. "Mrs. Dautremond, the head of the family, . . . Lucy, if I may be so bold . . . ought he not, in addition to his duty as provider, to manage his wife's affairs? For instance, and I trust you will pardon the indiscretion of one humbly dedicated to the advancement of science and saving of lives, if our Anna Maria, God forbid, were to die after the age of thirty-five, would it not be more fitting to see her fortune bequeathed to scientific studies of disease than to nebulous educational benefits for people stranded behind her in progressive evolution? Far be it from me to criticize her intention, which is noble, but, woe is me, there is in Anna Maria's eyes a softness, a languor. I fear she may be wasting away to nearly ethereal delicacy. She may die of phthisis before she has had a chance to reconsider the nature of her contribution to, er, humanity. Frankly, I propose that she change her Will so that the fortune may be managed for the advancement of science . . . I fear I have said too much, Lucy."

"I'm not stupid," Ganny countered with a wink. "I myself, with more money than I know what to do with, would never dream of trusting its management to myself. Women have so little savoir-faire in these matters. On the other hand, a sensible gentleman, once he marries into a family, ought, as you say, to manage his wife's affairs . . . Perhaps between the two of us we can persuade my little girl to change her Will?"

Next morning Muggins was found dead in the street. He had somehow managed to get over the balustrade of the *loggia*. "The gall, the absolute gall," Ganny said, tittering, to Mum. "Rountree has done it, throwing poor Muggins over the wall so that he can have me all to himself!" Anna Maria pointed out that Muggins had been locked in her mother's bedroom all night. This argument continued for some time, but in the end Ganny let slip that her door had been left ajar. No Romeo had appeared. Muggins had, *faute de mieux*, just run away, caught scent of a bitch in Renaissance streets, and leapt to his horrible death. *Pauvre petit.*

Ganny decided to have Muggins buried in the Protestant cemetery in Rome alongside Keats and Shelley. While she was making preparations for a casket, Rountree and Anna Maria had enough time alone together—a few hours at most—to plan for an elopement. As soon as they were in Rome, they would go to the American Embassy. She, first, would have her Will changed so that Rountree became her beneficiary on her thirty-fifth birthday. The idea—Phase Three on the money trail— had Ganny's approval in advance. Second, while Ganny was at the cemetery the lovers would get married in a civil ceremony at the embassy. Having made inquiries on the Ponte Vecchio, the bride-to-be soon found a counterfeiter who altered the date of birth on her passport to prove that she was of legal age to take Mr. Penhallow away from her mother.

The three phases could be summed up in a few words: Phase One, Grandpa Rufus Obadiah gave everything to Ganny in a trust fund that she could invade and out of which she was to make half over to Mum on her thirty-fifth; Phase Two, Mum's Will repudiated the money and gave it to charities associated with Grandpa's victims; Phase Three, Mum's new Will made Daddy her beneficiary that he might use the money for unspecified scientific research. If Ganny, herself, had not come to visit us in Colorado Springs for Christmas just after my birthday in 1901 and cleared the decks for the future where everyone's prospects were concerned—but only I was let in on the secret—the existence of a Phase Four would not have come to light until Mum's attainment of the famous middle of life's journey.

Ganny had no sooner stepped down from her train from Denver than she took one look at snow-covered Pikes Peak and shrieked, "That *hideous* mountain!" Although it had inspired Katherine Lee Bates to write *America the Beautiful*, the peak shrank after Ganny's pronouncement. It was no longer sacred, as Indians believed, but a pile of rock, no longer a beacon for progress, as pioneers believed. According to Ganny, the Penhallow family, once it had in-migrated from the northeastern United States to the Rocky Mountain West, had fallen into a cultural backwater.

I knew from Mum how Ganny had reacted to the elopement in Rome. "First of all," Mum told me, "the functionaries in charge of the Protestant cemetery refused to have Muggins buried there. With great tact they agreed with my mother's opinion that the bones of a poodle were intrinsically worth as much as those of Keats and

Shelley, but without evidence that Muggins had been baptized, had read the Apostles' Creed and believed, for instance, in the Virgin Birth, they had no choice but to give directions to the nearest incinerator. By the time Mommy had finalized arrangements for a cremation, I had changed my Will and married Daddy. Your grandmother swore she would never speak to us again. She went to Capri in the company of a gigolo who claimed to belong to the Black Aristocracy. In spite of vows of chastity, some popes have children. These descendants, known as the Black Aristocracy, are venerated and sometimes given titles such as *principe*."

I felt sad for Ganny. Unrequited love I well understood from a life of expecting love and not receiving it from Daddy. In my innocence, for in spite of some precocity I was naïve, I brought the subject up one afternoon as she and I were playing backgammon in front of the fireplace near the Christmas tree. Dressed all in black as usual, her lips painted red, complexion sallow and wrinkled, her gray hair tied into a bun, she had rolled dice so successfully that I remarked, "Gee, Ganny, you're lucky in everything!"

She drew herself up. "Everything except love." She made this pronouncement with a forlorn expression.

I went a step further. "Didn't you love Daddy before Mum did?"

There was *definitely* a silence. She threw her head back and studied me from a distance of a thousand miles. "That wasn't love, *mon cher garçon*," she said at last. " That was despair. He stole my being from me." She leaned forward and added in a dark whisper, "I got it back."

People have a way of telling me stories. They confide in me, usually without prompting or warning, secrets about which I haven't the slightest curiosity or in which, conversely, I am implicated, thus burdened.

"You're a very bad boy,' she declared, wet eyes darting about behind menacing bifocals, "but I love you."

"I'm sorry," I said. "I've been impertinent."

Smiling intensely, she held my cheeks in the palms of her hands. "Do you think I'm an old, fussy, stupid woman? Have they told you I'm rich?"

I nodded my head. The cold hands which she pressed into my cheeks gave me the creepy cruds.

"Have they told you that half of my estate goes to Anna Maria in a few more years and is then transferred to your father?"

I thought I should pretend to ignorance but nodded.

"Well," she said, "I suppose they've turned your head with visions of a bountiful inheritance?"

I said nothing. Mum's references to a future inheritance had always conjured up the image of a magical grandmother rather than a prospect of Easy Street.

Ganny gave my head a shake and wasn't smiling. "Your father won't get more than a few pennies on your mother's thirty-fifth birthday. Why? I've wasted all the estate I could except what I need for the rest of my life . . . Do you think it's easy to lose a fortune? Think again . . . At first I divided my estate in half. Then I invested your mother's inheritance in the most worthless stocks on the market. My brokers, mistaking my intention, instead of liquidating her half so that there would be nothing left for an English gold-digger, sometimes converted worthless stocks into a bonanza . . . I had to be very firm with them: lose the goddam money, *mes chers amies*, or I'll have your *petits testicules!* They became so adept at losing money in securities and dry wells and hideous mountains that I not only lost your mother's half of my estate, but two-thirds of my own remaining half! . . . You will of course inherit from me whatever's left of paltry riches . . . on one condition . . . Can you keep a secret?"

"Yes," I smiled brightly. "Lie follows."

She pinched my cheeks, lowered hands. "You little rascal," she said. "I've already told you my secret . . . If your father were to hear of it, he would murder your mother as he murdered my Muggins!"

Almost two years after Ganny's visit the secrets I had been faithfully keeping threatened, like tuberculosis or cancer, to spread. If, in fact, Daddy were dominating Mum in order to hasten her death, spiritual as well as physical—"stealing her being from her," as Ganny might have put it—he would be doing it because he wanted her money and his freedom. Why else would he want Mum out of the way? The answer was clear: Pia, my other secret. If in fact Pia was making plans to desert Dare in 1903 and marry a free and presumably rich Daddy in or after 1905, would Dare ever forgive me for keeping him in the dark? Finally, if in fact Daddy wanted me out of the way, was his motive not obvious, to isolate Mum in the Sun Palace completely and to leave him free to live with Pia in my house? And yet . . . and yet . . . for all his eccentricity, muddleheadness, incompetence, lies, conspiracies and possible violence, he still might be little worse than a Mr. Hollow in Penhallow.

Mr. and Mrs. Penhallow sailed from Genoa to New York and went to live in the Adirondacks where Daddy had a job at a TB sanitorium. "Bugger it," Daddy said to his bride with post-marital delicacy. "We'll have to cope with a lunger's cottage, but rest outdoors, drink hot toddies, and breathe fresh air according to *vis medicatrix naturae*, dearest." Early on a December morning in 1890 when the temperature in the New York mountains hovered below zero, I was born.

"It was really a big order to pull you into the world," Mum told me. "The winter was so cold that the bag of waters might have frozen upon bursting. Your father delivered you without forceps. You looked like a purple salamander. I had so much milk I had to give the overflow to a baby goat."

"Go-goat?" I stammered. I was shocked about sharing her breast milk.

"I was ignorant! Daddy didn't know any better, and neither did the great doctors at the sanitorium. Only a nurse there advised me: the more milk you give, the more you produce . . . If I'd kept on I would have been wet-nurse to all the babies and animals west of the Hudson River."

We moved to Colorado in 1893 so that Mum could benefit from mountain air and Daddy could pick up his M.D. degree in Denver. To the attractions of Little London as a resort had been added the gold-mining boom of Cripple Creek and, now, the Satanic mills of the TB sanitorium industry. While Daddy spent most of his time removing goiters, ovarian tumors, and inflamed appendixes—and, in Mum's words, "any opinions differing from his own"—he was also publishing papers in medical journals about treatment of TB patients. Lungers, he argued, had to be isolated in institutions at high altitudes because the diminished amount of oxygen in the air would force an increase in respiratory activity, thus expanding the lungs. High-velocity winds, moreover, would blow away putrid matter and keep the air fresh and pure. Lungers should rest in bed in the open air even during the most frigid weather, making breathing as shallow as possible. In short, the cure for TB was to go west and hibernate like a bear. By the time I was ten I was reading off-prints of Daddy's papers. Any footnotes in German had me stumped, but the manner in which my very own father wrote about his theories gave me the impression that he was indeed a genius, his icy control of Mum justified.

On one occasion in the year 1900 Daddy was honored at a formal dinner at the El Paso Club downtown. To my amazement, since, like Mum, I was proud of him, he invited me to come along; he rented a small tux for me and reserved a table for us with the city's dignitaries. I had my first raw oysters, filet mignon, truffles and champagne. There were about a hundred people present, ladies in gowns, furs, and ostrich feathers, gentlemen in tuxedos, Prince Alberts, and top hats. I entertained myself by separating the gentlemen into categories according to mustache (pencil, handlebar, walrus), beard (Vandyke, Burnside, Ulysses Grant, Jesus Christ), and countenance (bricklayer, apoplectic, whiskey puce, Dracula anemic). Finally the Mayor introduced Daddy, proposed a toast to him, and had everybody singing *For He's a Jolly Good Fellow*. Daddy mounted a podium. The dining room quieted down to sibilance. Daddy began his speech with an anecdote about student days at Guy's Hospital.

"We were so obsessed with the advancement of science," he said, poker-faced, "we considered diagnosing syphilis in the Holy Family."

You couldn't, as they say, hear a pin drop.

"By Jove," Daddy resumed, "we couldn't hold the Holy Ghost down long enough to treat Him with mercury and iodide of potassium."

A man with walrus mustache guffawed. Suddenly the whole room erupted into raucous laughter and wild applause. There, beaming, was spellbinding Daddy, *my* Daddy!

Our house served as a home, and, as I've said, a clinic and a laboratory. Outside was a long-pillared, sagging porch above which on an open balcony Mum sunbathed and fed seeds to small birds. We had gas lights and bells, hot-air vents in every room, bathrooms off of bedrooms, fireplaces fitted with ash disposal chutes, living room, dining room, library, kitchen and pantry. About half of the ground floor was given over to the clinic and lab. There Daddy read English and German journals, measured opsonin levels by centrifuging blood samples, adding emulsion, and counting bacilli enclosed in leukocytes, and experimented with medicated vapors —creosote, chloroform, iodine gas, hemlock extract and turpentine. When, uncharacteristically, Mum complained that the "stink" was "intolerable" and experiments could be conducted in the coach house in the backyard, he retorted with an English schoolboy's Latin boner: " 'Achilles's mother dipped him in the River Stynx until he was intolerable'."

My bedroom, as I have said, was on the second floor directly over that clinic. Here I had my *Book of Knowledge*, dictionaries, Shakespeare, KJV Bible, Robert Louis Stevenson, *King Solomon's Mines, Youth's Companion*, Darwin and other banned authors, maps, globes, baseball gloves, coloring sets, stamp collections, a log-cabin construction kit which would have baffled Lincoln and a sepia portrait of the author of *Treasure Island* in Bohemian costume.

When Mum was incarcerated in the Sun Palace, I was not allowed, as I've mentioned, to visit her more than once a week. Having no allowance to pay for cab or trolley fare, I made the roundtrip on foot and was passed through the gates by Shiflit and guards. I didn't mind walking at all, having Pikes Peak for companionship, and an hour's visit with her did us both good. A little bit, I'd figured out what made her so submissive to Daddy. She saw herself through his eyes as a burden who threatened him, as a useless wife, and as an object of scorn and ridicule who'd be better off dead.

She talked with me as if she hadn't enjoyed human companionship for a long time. I reckoned that was true, too.

"He," she said, meaning Daddy the Director, "insists upon absolute silence. The buzzing of flies and rattling of radiators begin to sound like the *Anvil Chorus*. Once in a while the part-time security guards shoot off their rifles on the campus just below my window, and dozens of patients faint and almost die of heart failure due to the big excitement. At 8:00 p.m. nurses come and wind up our music boxes, the ones that play *Nearer My God to Thee*... It's amazing how eagerly my fellow patients sing along with the boxes. It's like a Moody and Sankey revival meeting in Madison Square Garden: this world's not for love, buy eternity now, hark the herald angels.'

"We are allowed to speak with one another only when we're eating or copulating, which is called 'cousining.' On a typical day patients ghost out of their rooms and gather in the dining room. We have swell meals, the theory being that we must counter the effects of wasting away by eating stale bread, eggs, mutton chops, sweetbreads, sardines, boiled mush, raw oysters and jelly sandwiches. After lunch we walk or are wheeled to the Cure Porch on the roof. We are supposed to be soaking up sunlight, inhaling fresh air, and cousining. We who are about to die salute sexual intercourse. If we show no increase in temperature after orgasms, the theory goes, we must be almost cured. If we show an increase in temperature after orgasms, the theory goes, we have no reason to be coy and should screw anything handy. Gather ye rosebuds while ye may... Personally, cousining isn't my cup of tea. The cadaverous old goats with penises the size of okra might be millionaires, the homosexuals might yearn for a last chance to liberate themselves from their dominating mothers, and the wraith-like women in white robes might be looking for real love, but I say it's necrophilia, and I say to hell with it.'

"Following Cure Porch, we are sent to our rooms for a sponge bath—in 40-degree water. Numbed with cold, we are stuck with pneumothorax needles whether we have fluid in the lungs or not.'

"The purpose of your father's administration is not to drain a patient's lungs but her or his capital. He either prolongs your 'cure' indefinitely or he permits the patient with hacking cough to be released to society after he or she makes the Sun Palace primary beneficiary of a Last Will and Testament. I'm sorry to tell you, Tree, but your father is like the city dog in the country: stand still and he'll hump you, run and he'll bite your ass."

On my last visit to the Sun Palace I was alarmed to see Mum beginning to resemble one of the wraith-like women. All those years when she sought Daddy's affection by pretending to have tuberculosis, he was claiming that her spotless handkerchiefs were "stained with her blood-flecked sputum." He burned them. Upon taking her temperature, he would shake his head dolefully and study her sputum cups, the ones she filled with watery drops of tomato ketchup. At the dinner table he covered his face with hands and lamented, "O the horror and the beauty of consumption! It conquers the flesh, it spiritualizes its victim! Yes, yes, it is true as Henry Wadsworth Longfellow observed of creative genius, 'No truly sensitive person can be perfectly well,' and my own dear Anna Maria isn't even a genius! What can I do? O God!" Now that Mum had lost her home and the loving care of Ruby and me, she was slipping away. As for Ganny, the Christmas when she had revealed to me her plan to leave Mum and Daddy without any substantial inheritance had been her last visit. Perhaps she was not as financially impoverished as she had given me to believe. She still had an apartment on Park Avenue, and she had indulged in a round-the-world cruise for herself. Was she unable or unwilling to rescue Mum should I tell her what was going on?

In one postcard Ganny had written me, "America is divided into two parts, New York City and the unfortunate rest of it." Another postcard, one which she had mailed after a visit to India, consisted of one sentence about the symbol of Love: "The Taj Mahal was interesting." With a style as pithy and cool as this, she could save a fortune in postage stamps.

One thing I had been forgetting about my last visit with Mum at the Sun Palace:

She was lying propped up in bed. I was looking out her window at Pikes Peak. I saw on the campus below me the militiamen. There were six or seven of them, all still in uniform after their hours in Cripple Creek, all armed with rifles, all idling about, chatting, laughing while a certain doctor in a high-buttoned Guy's cutaway coat was, some fifty paces away from them, fastening a dressmaker's dummy to a cottonwood tree. When Daddy had finished setting up this target, he retreated to a safe distance, picked up a stick, and began to twirl it as if he were leading a marching band. The militiamen lined themselves up in a row, apparently having received a command, and fired shots in the direction of the target. The enamel breasts and belly of the dressmaker's dummy exploded. Daddy raised his arms in a gesture at once triumphant, obscene, and mad.

Chapter Five

Having come close to dying on October 27-28, I was by
dawn of October 30 grateful just to be alive. More than
ever I found beauty in ordinary things. They were, as
I, ephemeral, but, I believed, all was implicated in a numinous
order. Where, before, I had associated Los Tristes mainly with the
ugliness of industry and with the misery of hardscrabble lives, now
when redbrick and sandstone buildings loomed up ahead I felt
an urge to preserve them in pictures. It would be presumptuous
to assign such a feeling to conscious awareness in myself of an
artist's compulsion to escape through the door of Time. It's fair to
say, however, I was looking at the world, for all its good and evil,
with charmed eyes and regarding my fellow mortals with a, for me,
more than usual compassion.

"Sir," I said, "I've been thinking. Maybe Daddy's just a bit of old
ham."

After reminding Dare of our previous conversations concerning
the Penhallows, the Woodbridges, and Shiflit, I mused aloud,
"Maybe there are fewer maggots in Daddy's brain than I've led
myself to believe. I can understand his wanting to lick Woodbridge's
boots. Pecking order. I can understand his wanting me to take
Scampy and Alphie to visit their father's gold mine in Cripple
Creek. Polishing the apple. If Daddy wasn't planning to have me
killed, using Alphie and Shiflit as accomplices, someone other
than Daddy must be suspect. I've had suspicions about Alphie.

Westerners, to him, spit in pianos. He's a gambler. He would love to buy some opium in Mexicali. He's crazy. But would he have me roughed up for the Halloween fun of it? Gratuitously?"

"Gratuitously?" Dare had been steering his team along the trail. He glanced at me, grinned. "You've got a bump on your head the size of half a tennis ball. Did the Pinkerton dick do that to you for the fun of it?"

"Perhaps no one was intentionally plotting to bump me off," I said.

"From 'gratuitously' to 'bump me off'?" Dare whistled. "What sort of Moby-diction is that? Tell me, do you really believe your father is innocent? . . . He has been persecuting your mother, according to her and to you, for a disease she doesn't have. What if Pia, too, didn't have TB? What was he up to during my tour in the Philippines?"

"Do parents kill their children?" I fired off the question before he could pursue his "up to" line of thought.

"Abortion?"

"I didn't mean."

"Infanticide? Victimizing any child up to the age when he is big enough to fight back or run away? I see that struggle every day. Bosses beat and kill workers until workers get unions. Dictators kill millions until they revolt . . . Let's have a little pedantry. The killing of children by parents is such a prominent motif in ancient literature that even God the Father sacrifices Christ the Son. With a few exceptions it is the most horrible taboo on the menu . . . For starters on this *table d'hôte*, we have Abraham and Isaac: your interpretation, *mon élève?*"

It was an easy question for one with my flippant answers. "Abraham and Isaac . . . Abe was so potty he thought God would like to see how far His servant would go to prove his devotion. Since Abe loved Ike, the sacrifice of his first-born son would be excellent proof. Just as dear Abe prepared to plunge the knife into lucky Ike, along comes a hallucination, 'God' in the form of a ram. Abe spared Ike. No runs, no hits, no Ur."

"Smart aleck," said Dare. "A previously sanctioned primitive sacrifice is now biblically discerned as forbidden . . . Aeschylus has a similar attitude. He has Agamemnon sacrifice his daughter, Iphigeneia, as a sign of commitment to war with the Trojans. For this and other foolish acts Aeschylus has the Greek king murdered in the bathtub by a vengeful wife, mother of Iphigeneia . . . What is your analysis?"

"Unpronounceable king sacrifices unpronounceable daughter for a selfish or blind reason and gets his comeuppance. Arrogance is punished, wife buys new bathtub . . . Daddy kills me. Mum bumps him off. The law convicts her of murder and hangs her. Whatever happens to me, I wouldn't want my mother to take revenge."

"Aeschylus would have agreed with you," said Dare. "One forbidden crime is chained to the next forbidden crime . . . Generally, jurisprudence divides justice into divine and secular branches. Thus, for example, the biblical injunction, 'Vengeance is mine, saith the Lord,' becomes Hamlet's dilemma: take personal revenge by killing his father's murderer and he burns in hell, or wait until there's enough evidence of providential intention to act not for himself but as an instrument of God's justice. The problem for post-Enlightenment humanists is that God's purposes are beyond humanity's finding out. That problem, by the way, doesn't prevent Shiflit from claiming to know them. There are plenty of god-men in the modern world and plenty of god-people who believe love is on their side, justifying war against sub-humans . . . For the *plat du jour*, we have three more Greek *spécialités*. The father of Oedipus, fearing that his son would grow up to kill him and marry his mother, trusted a servant to take the baby to Mount Cithaeron, with heartless cruelty stake his foot to the ground, and leave him to the wild elements . . .'

"Next *entrée*," Dare continued after flicking reins. "Atreus, feeling annoyed with Thyestes, hacked the sons of Thyestes limb from limb, boiled morsels of their flesh in a cauldron, and fed the remains to their father. A monstrous crime, murders of children, corpses served up to an unsuspecting cannibal! The most monstrous of

71

tyrants was Saturn. Fearing that one of his sons would dethrone him, he set about eating all of his children—in effect, exterminating the human race. The myth doesn't make clear whether Saturn needed dental work and bicarbonate of soda. Luckily, one of his sons, Zeus, did escape and dethroned his father. People today still dream, like Saturn, of the total extermination of human beings. There's a new story in *Maga* by a writer named Conrad. It's called *Heart of Darkness*, and it's about a so-called 'civilized' European who wants to exterminate the Africans . . . For wine we have some excellent Medea today. She secured the Golden Fleece for Jason, married him, bore him children. The cretinous husband brought his young mistress home to live in a *ménage à trois*. Medea murdered her children because they were his, an almighty male's. According to Euripides, she escaped punishment. That was his shocking message 2,500 years ahead of his time, that a mother who had no legal rights to sue for divorce and take her infants into custody would kill them . . . *Bon appétit!*"

After driving his team along for another mile, Dare resumed his "pedantry." "You began by asking whether parents kill their children. I fed you horror stories in which they do exactly that. Of all murders, the murder of a child is the foreclosure of the future. It is hideous, primitive, unjust. Prohibitions against it are everywhere in most societies even though religions envision the End of Days with salvation of the few (and these not necessarily children) as a situation devoutly to be wished. I take your point, Tree. In sum: you generously doubt your father would try to kill you. He understands prohibitions, restraints, probabilities. Would he be so stupid as to trust Alphie Woodbridge, who is mentally disturbed but too rich to be bribed, with a murdersome scheme, or to ignore witnesses, Miss Woodbridge, Shiflit, the militia, citizens observing deportations, Gott, Mush, Glass-Eye Gwilym, Uncle Tom Cobley and all? I think not . . . All the same, if he is a monster, why? What's his motive?"

Dare's question sent a shock wave through me. The story of *Medea* had connected unspeakable violence against babies to the peccadillo of a motive, adultery. Probing for Daddy's motives, Dare was invading territory over which I already had some serious sway: Ganny's money, Dare's wife. For these, would Daddy kill? I must have looked pale. Dare asked me how I was feeling.

"Fine."

"Let's forget the preachiness of the old myths," he said. "Your father may merely act the part of a god. Maybe, as you suggest, he is just a ham actor. If he really believes in his omnipotence, that would explain why, as if he were God, he introduced you to me as his 'only begotten son'. Personally, I have no sympathy for your father, but I don't think he's a killer. He's not like Shiflit."

It was a good time to change the subject. "Sir," I said, "Mum is losing her will to resist. Before, when she was obedient and submissive, she was fooling Daddy in ways known only to me and Ruby, particularly by exercising when he wasn't looking. Daddy has her imprisoned, isolated. She is forced to concentrate thoughts on dying. She'll go potty . . . Suppose I go home, evade the nurses, the security guards. We could live in New York with Ganny. Will Mum have the sand to start a new life, work at a job, get a divorce?" I paused. "She must save her soul . . ."

"Suppose," Dare said, sparing me ridicule for hifalutin soul-language, "you had a friend, someone able to penetrate defenses at the sanitorium. Do you think he could persuade your mother to flee with him? Or does she depend on your father too much to leave him?" He placed a hand on my shoulder. "Anybody, not just a married woman," he said gently, "can feel dragged down to the point where she or he thinks nobody cares what happens to her or him . . . You feel abandoned. You feel it's a pity you're alive . . . Think of a victim and her assailant as related to one another. The assailant needn't be a father or a husband. The assailant can be an 'It'—a culture, an environment. In Europe that is often the case. You live in an ancient village. Nothing changes. You go to church. You go to school. You get a job in a sweet shop. You make babies. You see yourself in your own ruin. You give up. You're already spiritually dead. The *patrón*, for a fee, sends you off to America where you save up to return to the old country. Whether you return or not, and, chances are, you can't or won't, the 'It' still has you trapped. You accept your inferior position. You actually desire what made you despisedly used in the first place. . . Tell me more about your mother. Are you absolutely sure your father misdiagnoses her with TB?"

I summarized the situation for him, how, when Daddy met Mum in Florence, he was already pretending or convinced she was wasting away, how he took her for a honeymoon in a lunger's cottage in the Adirondack Mountains and forced her to breathe frigid air for years, how for ten years in Colorado Springs he had virtually tied her down to the house, few visitors, no vacations, no parties, no trips to Denver for theater or opera, and now how he had her locked up in the Sun Palace where there was nothing for patients to do except sleep, eat, fornicate and wait to die. To please Daddy, Mum had for years faked coughing, faked fevers, faked spitting of blood. In hospital she could no longer deceive Daddy.

In the outskirts of Los Tristes my eyes feasted upon the warmly Mexican looks of things, adobe homes with window frames and doors painted blue to ward off evil spirits, chile peppers tied into *ristras*, piñon smoke rising in straight plumes from the chimneys, outdoor ovens for baking bread, high woodpiles signifying prosperity, wooden-wheeled wagons, horses munching hay, statuettes of the Virgin, flower-strewn *camposanto*. Although I had but limited acquaintance with Hispanic culture and language, I wondered if Dare had been exaggerating the "It," the negative aspects of traditional life. The people of Los Tristes seemed to live happily on their *tierra* with *la familia*. One could do worse, I reflected, one could really do worse. As, for example, grow up an Anglo without firm roots or a happy family. Daddy, for another example, didn't even know the identity of his father.

"Excuse me for interrupting your reverie," Dare said, "but, since we're about to meet Pia in the afternoon, I should clarify that I respect her—and your father—and haven't meant to imply that they've been having an affair. I apologize if —"

"—Oh?" I affected indifference.

"You see," Dare went on, "there was a letter written in ink on your father's Sun Palace stationery and addressed to me instead of to Pia, his former patient."

"Oh," I said. "A cock-up."

"Doc Penhallow wrote me that letter just a couple of days after my return from the Philippines. He wanted me to know that Pia had been 'cured' of TB and would require his services no more, 'no clinical visits, no hospitalization.' She was, he wrote, 'discharged.' I was elated to receive the news, even though, during my time overseas, I had had no clue that Pia had been ill at all. Of course she never wrote to me."

"Cock-up," I said.

"Cock-up?"

"A mistake. One of Daddy's words."

"Well," said Dare, "he does seem to have a pattern of cock-ups. What really grabbed my attention was his failure to charge me a fee . . . He had come hundreds of miles to treat Pia dozens of times at our ranch in Los Tristes. By my reckoning, his expenditures in addition to services rendered should have been in the hundreds of dollars. He must have known I had the ability to pay—ranch, savings, property in France . . . His letter made no mention of a fee. When Pia and I caught the train to Colorado Springs and came to your home for the purpose of showing gratitude in person, I brought up the subject of a reckoning. I took out my wallet. It was, as he could see, bulging with dollars. Do you know what happened?"

I replied that, if Daddy opened his hand, he did not do so out of a generous disposition. His refusal to accept a fee was, therefore, very odd.

"He got red in the face and excused himself from the room," Dare said. "When he returned, composed, he said that it was 'unprofessional' for a doctor of medicine to accept money from the son of another doctor of medicine. Rubbish. Secondly, he said that your mother upstairs in her bedroom had not been cured of TB. Therefore, because he had successfully cured Pia of it, he had gained confidence in his methods. Dubious. If now he cured his wife, he really owed us some remuneration! Preposterous. Thirdly, the least he could do for us 'fighting boys' was to offer us free services. Sappy. We shook hands. His hand was limp . . . There is something else."

"Oh?"

"Dawn Antelope. He's been managing the ranch for donkey's years. Before I left for San Francisco and the war, I asked him to keep an eye on Pia in case she were sick or needed help. I didn't consider this request to be spying. To ask him to spy would have offended him. But just because he lives alone in the old smokehouse behind the barn doesn't mean he lacks the nose of a bear and the ears of a wolf. He can smell or hear things like a Paleolithic hunter. Unasked, he told me that Pia never coughed, day or night, over there in the ranchhouse, and she never burned anything with an odor of blood . . . I better shut up. That suit you, Tree?"

"Suits me," I said. I hoped, indeed, to hear no more about Pia and Dawn Antelope. She for sure and he possibly had seen me at the ranch in January. What if Dawn Antelope revealed Daddy's nocturnal visits to the ranch while I was alone at the Imperial Hotel?

"I'm off to the Pluck Me!" I said to myself. Oddly, I no longer seemed to need imaginary journeys to faraway places.

I had never bought my own clothes before. Mum had mended my socks. Ruby had taken my worn-out shoes to a cobbler on Shooks Run. Other than Ganny's gifts of New York clothing, my clothes were bought by Mum at hick haberdasheries on Tejon Street. As fullback for after-school pick-up football games, I liked to have my shirts and trousers smeared with blood and lime and ripped up. In my heart of hearts I probably did have an inchoate dream of becoming an artist. I yearned to be dressed not as a "gentleman" but as Robert Louis Stevenson in my sepia portrait of him. If the Pluck Me catered to Bohemians, I would soon be appearing in baggy velveteen trousers, a wide-collared sailor's shirt, painter's smock and beret.

We crossed the railroad yards near where the Colorado & Southern approached the AT&SF. Here, probably, and not at the DRG&W several miles to the north, the Pinkerton dicks must have transferred me and Glass-Eye Gwilym from boxcar to boxcar.

Dare drove us across Commerce Street bridge and up a muddy incline where wooden arcades topped with balconies fronted stores. We stopped before a brick building on which had been painted in black letters, WESTERN SUPPLY CO.

"The Pluck Me," Dare said. "We'll cross trails and meet again in an hour at U.S. Livery on Main up yonder where you see electrified cars of the Los Tristes Street Railway Company. My father used to tell me about the not-so-long-ago days when Texans would drive cattle smack through the middle of town where Main Street is. It might take all day to get the herd through. Afterwards the street resembled a hog wallow of mud and dung. The cowhands would get roaring drunk and go stampeding to the whorehouses up there on the west end. Now we have, instead of bellowing and thundering and whistling and yippeeing, this horrid screeching and clanging and little electric discharges. Pretty soon they'll be paving the street with bricks!"

I was beginning to discern in Dare a hankering for the old days when a man had a harsh wind in his face instead of the noise and stench of modern times.

A crack of whip was followed by his "Hee-YAH!" I watched the team until it disappeared at the crest of the hill.

The door to the Pluck Me was blocked by a hulking, bull-necked giant with a handlebar mustache as big as a horseshoe and a Texas hat as big as a bull's muzzle. As he shifted tobacco from cheek to cheek, his mouth became cockled. His teeth were brownish-black as scat. His coat bulged over a gun in a hip pocket. If, as I approached the door, I had been this fairytale giant, I would have seen in me a choirboy's countenance and a Halloween scarecrow's bullet-riddled wardrobe.

"Good morning, sir," he said in a cultured tone of voice. He gave me a pleasant nod. Boy, was I dumb.

The store had the dimensions of buildings I had only imagined from sketches in books of the Coliseum in Rome, Paddington Station in London, Madison Square Garden in New York. From a domed ceiling frantic with pigeons to a floor heaped with merchandise must have been a drop of four stories. Electric lightbulbs, still, I had heard, a novelty in some towns, festooned aisles between departments. Noises of loadings and unloadings, mingled Babel voices of a hundred or more customers, and screams of scads of children drifted, as did the smoke of cigars and coal-fired hotdog grills, into the atmosphere.

I wandered about the store studying sad people. Some of them I thought I recognized from profiles in my *Book of Knowledge*. There were tall blonds from the north of Europe, long-bearded Jews and Slavs from the Balkans, olive-skinned Greeks, dark-eyed Italians, hollow-cheeked Croats from the Mediterranean, Japanese with small black hats, Chinese with pigtails, American-Africans whose upper arms were thicker than my thighs, Mexicans like Aztec pictographs, rosy-cheeked Irish and gaggles of gaunt, homely-looking Welsh, Scottish, and Cornish immigrants as well as their New England counterparts with rigid faces and catarrhal twang. I could only guess at occupations. If a man had stooped shoulders, he was probably a miner. If he had reddish-brown complexion and stubby fingernails, he was probably a farmer. Men with groomed beards might be clerks, engineers, waiters, salesmen. Those with fierce eyes might be Old-Testament-style prophets, or ex-cons from the penitentiary at Cañon City, or, simply, crapulent drunks. Most of the women were, if young, laundresses or grade-schoolers, if sixteen or older, wives, mothers, housemaids, nuns or schoolmarms. Some women wore calico dresses, others wore tucked blouses with leg-o-mutton sleeves; a few wore makeshift fabrics and covered feet with burlap sacks. Typically, the women had disheveled hair knotted at the nape of the neck, missing fingers, racking coughs. I snatched at fragments of speech: " . . . top drift, mun . . . heet heem in the *cojones, compadre* . . . whupped to a frazzle . . . washin and arnin', washin and arnin' . . . *volontà di Dio?* You crazy in the head . . .

Non c'é piacere nella vita . . . No, *Signore*! I'll never go back to that accursed place. Italy is a beautiful country for kings and tourists but a bad hole for a man who must earn his living. . . ."

The Bohemian fashion had not flourished in Los Tristes. Here and there an immigrant might be sporting a beret he had brought with him from Crete or Genoa or Catalonia, but berets were not to be found for sale among coalminers' pit caps, farmers' straws, cowboys' low-crowned Stetsons. Trousers were made not from wool or twill but from denim or canvas. Hobnailed pit boots and Mexican boots were not meant for artists in Scotland, Monterey, or Samoa. I decided to abandon the Robert Louis Stevenson style and dress as Dare did. I bought a black Stetson, a pair of dungarees with silver buckle, a pair of boots. I indulged myself in long johns for 65¢, a red bandanna for 25¢, a blue wool shirt, galluses, underwear and a toothbrush. For Pia, my hostess, I bought a box of chocolates, for Dare a tin of Prince Albert pipe tobacco, for Mum and Scampy turquoise and silver brooches. All in all, I "borrowed" $12.35 from Daddy's remaining $31.00 and still had enough cash-money left over for a one-way rail ticket home.

Dressed as a cowboy at last and with small purchases plus old shoes wrapped in brown paper and tucked under my arm, I, like the immigrants, felt seduced by the Pluck Me, trying to identify carbide lamps, breast augurs, cans of double-f black explosive powder, Singer sewing machines, a gramophone with morning-glory horn, notions, trimmings, laces, pins, cuffs, collars, crazy quilts, checkered tablecloths, mangles, handwringers, candles, sink tubs and crosses, *kachina* dolls, ribbons, *metate* for grinding corn. There were plenty of gadgets for which I had no name or conceivable use.

Paying in cash-money for purchases, I was treated deferentially with a "Thank you, sir" and a "Good day, sir," but customers using little booklets of scrip had embarrassed looks as if they should apologize for being diddled. Those buying necessities in spite of obvious penury—"Could yer put it in the store book, please, Charlie?"– looked sunk. One emaciated miner in rags pleaded with one of the managers for an extension of credit. He was told in cold tongue, "It's your Christian duty to be rich!"

As I was strolling along Main a few minutes after leaving the Pluck Me, I couldn't help but stop now and then to admire my new clothes as reflected in store windows. Some time later, when I was outside GRANDE GROSSERIA ITALIANA smelling the aroma of garlic and cheese and *caffe dolci* and salivating over displays of sausages and sliced salami, tinned eels and pickled olives and macaroni, Dare snuck up from behind, spun me around, and nodded his head. He approved of me—something Daddy had never done. A few moments later I had another Never Before: a girl about my own age strolled by and said to me, not to Dare, "Good morning, sir." Fetched by her coy smile and flash of slanted eyes, I returned the greeting and tipped my Stetson. Her half-unbuttoned blouse revealed breasts deserving of a psalm from King Solomon. Her cheeks were smashed cherries. Her perfume was wafted out of the pages of *Arabian Nights*. Hers was the sweetest assembly of body-parts ever to sashay down a street in the vicinity of virginity.

Dare also stared at her. She joined a group of girls smoking cigarettes and leaning against the wall of the First National Bank. Each girl supported herself on one black-stockinged leg while raising the other leg.

"That's what I like about Los Tristes!" I exclaimed. "The folks here are so polite."

After some hesitation during which he was, I could see, trying to suppress a smile, Dare sighed, *"Faire le pied de grue.* They stand on one leg like a crane to show they honor the penny and are worth the dollar. While I'm glad our folks are making you feel welcome, I'm afraid I have disturbing news."

He withheld it until we had picked up the team at U.S. Livery and were headed southeast into the foothills rising from the river. He had been on a telephone line from Union headquarters in Los Tristes to officials in Denver, his intention having been to report his success in picking up Gwilym and the other deported miners and leaving them to hop a freight back to Union Station.

"They hopped a freight all right. However, upon arriving in Denver, Gwilym made a beeline for a tavern on Larimer Street, got drunk, and assaulted a Guard. He was arrested. To expedite his return to Cripple Creek, he was escorted by the Guard to Colorado Springs. There he has been turned over to the tender mercies of an old friend of ours, someone who now almost certainly knows my whereabouts and yours, someone who, unlike your father, likes to kill people."

"Shiflit?"

"Shiflit."

Lizards slither-twitched on boulders beside the road. Chipmunks in grama grasses stopped to stare at us, probably expecting a shower of bread crumbs. Black clouds, piling up, launched blue caravans of shadow over *chamisa* fields buttered with the last of swaying sunflowers. A wide valley spread out before my eyes. Rain from a thunderhead on the faraway horizon walked on black legs across it. Dare halted and hitched the team to a log-rail at the top of a mesa beneath evergreen ponderosas. Strange-looking potholes appeared in a cutbank.

"Prairie dog town?"

"Rat holes," he said. "Some folks say they go for miles underground to the mines . . . I want you to sweep your eyes over the valley and tell me if you see anything unusual."

Having been once before, unknown to Dare, to Homesteader's, I had to survey it with a pretense of amazement. A switchback road led downward to an irrigation ditch; the road ended about a hundred feet from the ranch buildings. Out in pastures, cattle and half a dozen head of buffalo were grazing.

"Hully gee! Buffalo!"

"Keep looking," he said.

A log fence surrounding the buildings was hung with Apache plume like purple wigs. The buildings were typical of *ranchitos*:

corrals, a water tank on stilts, a large red barn, stables, haystacks, woodpiles, the old adobe smokehouse and the sprawling, faun-colored adobe ranchhouse entered via an adobe wall which sheltered lilacs, hollyhocks, and tiger lilies. From the chimney of the ranchhouse wisps of smoke inscribed S-shapes in dry air. In shadows of a long portal supported by *vigas* and corbels, witchproof blue window frames and a blue door were certainly not unusual in southwestern Colorado, nor were the two shepherd dogs stretched out sleeping in patches of sunlight. Although a black object resembling a pillow lay next to a rocking chair on the portal, I could not identify it as unusual. Squinting hard, I finally brought my attention to rest upon an area to the rear of the house. Near a fishpond shaded by cottonwoods four saddled ponies had been hitched, and a horse-drawn hackney carriage, its driver apparently asleep, had been parked among apple trees.

I pointed. Dare nodded. I had passed his test. He lowered voice. "One's a mare. Crease at the withers. Western saddle. Rented out from U.S. Livery is my guess. I recognize the hackney. It can be hired down at the depot . . . Now . . . See those other ponies sort of strung-out looking? No distinctive stirrups and cinches. They're Army. Takes a pitchfork to get a trot out of them . . . Now . . . The strike in Cripple Creek and northern Colorado hasn't reached Los Tristes yet. There shouldn't be any milish here as strikebreakers . . . Those ponies arrived by train . . . Who are our visitors?"

"Shiflit?" I, too, spoke in low voice. It felt good to be sharing in his alarm. "You said."

"That's my guess, son. Shiflit and some milish—and maybe Gwilym, prisoner under the undeclared martial law. Two bits it's them . . . Shiflit knows about me and you and the Pinkertons . . . Here's what I want you to do. Listen."

Dare slipped his revolver from holster, spun its chamber, slipped it back to holster. He bit his lip before speaking. "I want you to take the Winchester and some ammo to Dawn Antelope. I want you to tell him three things. One, call the dogs. Two, saddle up Natural Selection. Got that? Three, if you hear any gunshots, you are to mount

Natural Selection and get the hell out of here. Go to the Union off
of Main Street . . . If there are no shots fired, he's to keep the horse
saddled . . . Now, listen. Sneak down the *arroyo*. Follow the irrigation ditch, keeping head low. Run for the barn. If Dawn Antelope's
not there, he'll be in the smokehouse. If you can't find him, I want
you to high-tail it back to Union on foot and tell the folks there,
friends of mine, to stash you out of sight. Got it?"

"Those girls were prostitutes." I meant to prove to Dare I was
no fool. He looked at me in a queer way. "Just because she was a
whore, it doesn't mean she wasn't polite."

"O.K., pal," Dare said, handing me the Winchester and shells.
"As soon as you reach the barn, I'll know Dawn Antelope is there
because the dogs will run to him. Then I can reach the blue door
without my dogs raising a ruckus welcoming me . . . I don't know
what to expect from the person who hired the hackney. Pia's all
alone by herself in there . . ."

I stopped listening and ran a hand over the Winchester. I was a
rifle boy. Nobody could cut me down. Rascals must scurry to cover.

I ran, crouching, until I reached the barn. "Mr. Antelope?" My
voice resounded among small startled birds in the ricks and a
couple of hoof-nervous horses in stalls.

"Mr. An—"

He appeared suddenly. Having seen Utes and Arapahos
harmlessly smoking, dancing, and singing at pow-wows in the
Garden of the Gods, I gave the rifle and shells without hesitation
to the old Pueblo Indian. He was short and bandylegged, his skin
light brown and raisin-wrinkly, his tightly braided, pigtailed hair
dangling out of a Texas hat. His obsidian-dark eyes, while I was
relaying Dare's commands, seemed, though, to be focused on my
own hat as if he wanted to steal it. Without uttering a word, he
did in fact lift my Stetson off and begin to run gnarled hands over
the half-tennis-ball lump on my head. Then he went to a corner
of the barn and returned with a gob of axle grease in one hand.
Again without uttering a word he spread the grease over my wound
and gave me back my hat. "Maybe him liked it skillet grease," he

said gently with a half-smile. It took me a while to understand his meaning: he was apologizing for giving me what he considered to be inferior medical care. While I was standing there awaiting Dare's moves, Dawn Antelope glided to the barn door and whistled softly. Seconds later, we had those sleepy shepherd dogs sniffing our crotches and rubbing wet noses into palms of our hands. Before long, too, he fetched from a stall a powerful roan and saddled it —Natural Selection incarnate. I peeped beyond the corner of the barn. Dare had cleared the adobe wall. Revolver in hand, he was sneaking up to the blue door under the portal. I again saw that black object I had previously thought was a pillow.

It was a leather bag.

A doctor's bag.

Daddy's bag.

My mind back-flashed to January. When Daddy had gone into the house to have floozy-time with Pia, he had left his black leather bag with me in the buggy. He was trusting me with his tinctures of opium because I was in a rowboat at the South Pole and all that. So now, because the driver of his hired hackney, though asleep, was not to be trusted, Daddy had put himself to the trouble of lugging the drug-filled bag to the porch. Believing it possible he had come to save me, I decided to disobey Dare.

As he was opening the blue door, I was springing from the barn, entering the house at his heels, hoping to fling my arms around my father, perhaps a man in the last analysis *there* when I needed him.

I am agape.

Shiflit really is in the house with two milish and Glass-Eye Gwilym. The bedroom door is opening. Daddy and Pia really are emerging from it. Dare is leveling his revolver at them. Me, I hang head, take inventory of feet. Gwilym wears pit boots. Shiflit and the milish are wearing military boots. Dare and I have on cowboy boots. Pia and Daddy are barefooted.

Raising head, I have to *think*. Daddy, I conjecture, has returned from the hunt and been informed by Shiflit, who has been informed by Gwilym, that Dare and I are expected to arrive at the ranch in late afternoon. Daddy has come for me all right but not to comfort and collect me. Shiflit collects Guards and ponies. This posse comitatus catches a train from Colorado Springs, arriving about mid-afternoon. Dare must be suffering horribly, but he is disguising how deeply cut is his heart.

Parallelograms of smoky yellow sunlight printed on wide floorplanks. Piñon logs crackling and hissing in a large stone fireplace. Fire shadows dancing on varnished *vigas* and *latillas* of the ceiling. Plastered walls decorated with Navajo rugs, oil paintings of Indian braves, an elk's head, an officer's saber. We have seen these things when we burst through the blue door, seen also Mexican chairs, a Morris chair, a hand-carved refectory table, a bookcase filled with leatherbound volumes, Dare's telephone, a statuette of the Virgin. Is it Pia's? We have also seen Gwilym tied with rope to a Mexican chair. Shiflit, smoking a cigarillo, has to himself Dare's Morris chair. Bottles of wine and tequila, glassware and chinaware and half a ham are scattered about the table. The milish have stacked rifles by the fireplace. They really are, unlike the Pluck Me giant, Corporation goons. When the bedroom door opens, we, Dare and I, see an unmade bed, articles of clothing strewn about the floor. Pia, blowzy, is wrapping herself in a gown, smile ready for Leonardo's brush. We, Dare and I, see a half-naked Daddy who is not opening his arms to give me an *abrazo*. This is just a feeble fornicator, shirtless, hairy-chested, trying to pull up Guy's Hospital trousers, and he acts as if he has correctly interpreted the function of Dare's revolver: ventilation. He drops trousers, standing in pink drawers, retreating backwards slowly into the bedroom.

Shiflit rising, flipping cigarillo into fireplace, intones, *"He that is without sin among you, let him first cast a stone at her.* John, 8:7. Cap'n Dare, you got the drop on us."

"I'm sure, Fredson," says Dare, "had you been present when the Man spared the adulteress, you would have cast the first stone—at Him."

"They tell me you hold up trains now."

"I don't hold them up. I get a search warrant and have your friends arrested."

"It's illegal to carry a concealed weapon."

"Would you like to see my game warden's permit?"

And Shiflit: "It's illegal, aiding and abetting deported felons and other fugitives."

And Dare: "Gwilym has never been convicted of any crime. The boy has never committed one. The last I heard, though, kidnapping and conspiracy to commit homicide are still punishable in a court of law."

Rushing forward, Pia explodes at Dare, "What are yer grinning about? What's so funny? Have yer no decency?"

Dare turns to Shiflit, sings, " 'Oh, I come home the other night' . . . Remember that one, old buddy?"

Shiflit grins, sings in a pretend-yokel's accent:

> " 'Oh, I come home the other night
> So drunk I could not see,
> Found a head on the piller
> Where my head ought to be.'"

I look up, agape. Shiflit goes to the refectory table, pours a shotglass full of tequila. Dare levels gaze at Pia, says in whimsical tone, "It has been aptly said, love, that when the English landed in this country 'they fell on their knees and then on the aborigines'— to which we now add, And English doctors collected their fees."

"There is sorry." The voice has everyone glancing Gwilym's way. His face is red and puffy, good eye bruised, lower lip split and bloody. Gwilym drunk in a tavern on Larimer Street? Nothing wrong with that. Snitching on Dare and me? Yes—but after a kangaroo.

Shiflit crosses the room and pours tequila down Gwilym's throat. "Drink hearty, *mun*. Bard of the eisteddfod, tell us about the affidavit, the one you signed before notary public. Nothing to feel sorry about now, is there?"

Gwilym, gaze to floor, speaks in a low, slow monotone. "Cap'n, he says he is going to give the boy a bath . . . There is bugger all indade."

"Go on, *mun*."

"There is sorry." Gwilym lifts his good, red eye to Dare. I am as immobilized as I had been in Cripple Creek before Shiflit's firing squad.

"Don't worry about it, Gwilym," says Dare. Pia slaps him across the face, voice at a boil: "Pervert! Sadist! Yer make me sick! Go on, hit me! Coward! I'll put yer in the penitentiary for the rest of yer life . . . if yer try to take my house away from me."

And Dare: "If all you want is real estate, you don't need bearers of false witness present and soldiers who pretend to be police . . . Once you invite the police into your house, love, it's hard to get them out."

And Shiflit: "The Penhallow boy is accused of rape, resisting arrest, and planning to murder his mother."

And Dare: "Humor here is getting so dry, trees will be bribing dogs."

And Shiflit: "Crimes of Rountree Penhallow, Junior. Vagrancy in Cripple Creek. Arrested by detectives of the Pinkerton Agency on suspicion of rape. Escaped . . . The good doctor had to move his mother to the Sun Palace to protect her from Junior . . . Something else . . . Doctor? Now that you've dropped your cock and picked up your sock, perhaps you would be so kind as to enlighten Mrs. Dare's guests about your security arrangements?"

Daddy has emerged from the bedroom in Guy's uniform and silk cravat, pince-nez, top hat. His mustache and balding head with patches of gray hair lend themselves to a lordly demeanor. "Where on earth," he asks, locating me even though I'm actually in an ox-drawn cart on my way to Azerbaijan, "did you find such a ridiculous hat?" He stands over me, looks me up and down. "I see your tailor has a sense of humor." He snaps fingers.

"Sir?"

"Quids."

I hand my wallet over to him. From it he removes the dollar bills, counting them, returning five, pocketing the remainder. He removes, too, the photograph of Scampy and the sketch of the bellydancer. Holding these items up to the light, he shakes his head slowly. "To think all I've done for you, boy . . . Begin poor and rise. Stay poor, despise . . . Filth!" He tears the sketch of the bellydancer into bits and tosses these over his shoulder. Pia glances at me. Her features melt. "My husband is a sorry remlet of a man," she purrs, "touching yer in a private place, lyin' naked with yer. I know yer can't talk to me now. When yer poor dear mama's gone, bless her, yer'll find good comfort here! What carryin' on! Yer had a good bringin' up, and yer daddy loves yer with all his heart."

"He's for the high jump," says Daddy.

" *Ginger red hair*," singsongs Dare.

> " *Ginger red hair*
> *Went to the fair*
> *And bought an old stallion*
> *Instead of a mare*. . .

With such shows of praise and love for my young friend, perhaps you'll tell me what in the name of claim-jumping is going on?"

"Partic'lars, Lef'tenant," says Daddy, making a bruffing noise in his throat.

I lift eyes up from shoes. Shiflit unfolds a document and bows to the statuette of the Virgin.

" 'Whereas'," he reads from the paper, "meaning no offense to lady present, 'Mr. Alpheus Woodbridge, Junior, did observe Rountree Penhallow, Junior, Esquire, to insert a finger under dress of Miss Felixine Woodbridge in the Midland Railroad coach near Cripple Creek, Teller County, Colorado, at zero-nine-three-zero hours, and whereas aforesaid Mr. Alpheus Woodbridge, Junior, did seek out and report to Lieutenant Fredson Shiflit, Colorado National Guard, Cripple Creek, with information pertaining to this assault, and whereas said Lieutenant Shiflit under authority vested in him did arrest aforesaid Rountree Penhallow, Junior,

Esquire and expeditiously did deport and send him down the mountain, and whereas Mr. Alpheus Woodbridge, Junior, escorted Miss Felixine Woodbridge to the Antlers Hotel, Colorado Springs, El Paso County, Colorado, to have her examined to determine the presence'—meaning no offense to lady present—'of sperm'."

Dare interrupts. "May it please the Where Ass, the defendant would like to masturbate his finger, meaning no offense to lady present. If sperm is ejaculated from his finger, babies mustn't suck thumbs."

Shiflit reads, " 'Miss Felixine Woodbridge wept piteously and copiously, crying out the name of her rapist, whereupon Mr. Alpheus Woodbridge, Junior, pulled a Colt's pistolet out and told her to shut up until the arrival of her father, Mr. Alpheus Woodbridge, Senior, and Dr. Rountree Penhallow, Senior. Whereas these gentlemen arrived at the Antlers Hotel, Colorado Springs, and whereas Dr. Penhallow used his stethoscope to examine said victim.' . . . Tell us what you found, sir."

And Daddy: "The patient had a 50-75% stenosis within the profunda extremity and hemodynamic trauma to the triphasic flow as well as blunt trauma to the labia majora."

And Dare: "Excuse my presumption, but my father, you know, was a doctor . . . It would seem you used your stethoscope to listen to the legs."

And Daddy: "Lef'tenant?"

Shiflit's militiaman hands him another document. He reads, " 'Charge 1, conspiracy in violation of the Code. Specification 1. In this, that the said Rountree Penhallow, Junior, Esquire did feloniously and unlawfully combine and conspire together with Mr. Kyle Deville Dare, Captain, U.S. Army, retired, and Mr. Gwilym (no middle initial) Thomas, no fixed address, for the purpose of inflicting bodily injury upon one, Miss Felixine Woodbridge, and that the said Rountree Penhallow, Junior, Esquire in pursuance of such combination and conspiracy did inflict bodily injury upon Miss Felixine Woodbridge, by then and there feloniously and unlawfully assaulting the said Miss Felixine Woodbridge, with intent to maim, disfigure, disable and rape . . . Charge 2, Accessories after the fact. Specification 1. In this, that the said Mr. Kyle Deville Dare and the said Gwilym (no middle initial) Thomas, then and there knowing that a felony had been committed, that the said Rountree Penhallow, Junior, Esquire feloniously, willfully, maliciously, deliberately and unlawfully . . .'"

Dare sings, softly:

> " '*The dirty little coward*
> *Who shot Mr. Howard*
> *And laid Jesse James*
> *In his grave . . .*'

Jesse was going by 'Howard' when Ford shot him in the back, I think . . . Ford used to hole up near these parts, Pagosa Springs way, I think . . . You must believe, Fredson, that you're impressing Tree with this nonsense."

And Daddy: "We're not impressing charges as long as Rountree stays away from Colorado Springs . . . If I tell his mother that her son is a rapist, it will kill her. Come to that, he's no son of mine. Up in the Adirondacks while we were on our honeymoon, she refused me her bed, complaining about the fatigue which comes with the accursed disease. I refrained from conjugal duty. She went cousining with every scruffy tubercular chore boy she could lure to the cabin. Here is fruit of her lust . . . The bastard is not to see his mother ever again . . . Security arrangements? I believe, Rountree, you and Lef'tenant Shiflit are acquainted? Try to break in to my Sun Palace, you'll find him there, Head of Security, as usual. You'll regret the encounter . . . If you or any of your accomplices dare to visit dear Anna Maria or send her messages by one means or another, it'll be no skin off my nose, what happens, as, I believe, you say in the colonies . . . Nonsense? Not bloody likely."

I hear from faraway in the direction of the barn the whinnying of a horse. I lift up my eyes unto Daddy and to the photograph of Scampy in his hand. I snatch the photograph, slip it into my dungarees, and glare at Daddy.

"She wasn't wearing a dress! She was wearing jodhpur breeches and a fur coat! Abraham!" I scream at him. "Agamemnon! Saturn!"

I run out of the blue door. Like a bird in grief, I cry and my cries are left trailing behind me.

The mesa near the buckboard was being overrun by hundreds of rats. I had read that rats sometimes emerge from hellish habitats and overrun entire villages, devouring food supplies and babies. I had witnessed during my first trip to Los Tristes in one of the company-towns a child without nose or ears. Rats had eaten them, I was told. I had read, too, that father rats eat their young.

I, then, had run out blue door, vaulted over adobe wall, and continued to run along the sandy road braiding among sagebrush and up via the switchback to the mesa where Dare had hitched wagon and sorrels. I had no clear idea what I might do. I figured to collect from the wagon that package containing among other items my old leather shoes, now magic shoes enabling me to go back to the Forbidden City of Colorado Springs and set Mum free. If memory was serving me correctly, the passenger-and-mail train out of the depot down by the Purgatoire was scheduled to depart at seven o'clock. I had an hour to catch it. I would hide in the mail car. Upon arrival past midnight I would run to the Sun Palace before Daddy could kill Mum.

When the sorrels came in sight, they were screaming and stomping and kicking, trying to free themselves from traces and hitching post. There had to be, I surmised, a prairie rattler nearby, possibly digesting one of the small birds whose dusk-songs were mellowing out the day. All I need do was pick up a stick and charm the snake into side-winding away. Upon my close inspection, though, I saw a horde of black rats streaming out of those holes purportedly leading for miles to mines. Squeaky-squealy-squirming vermin were crawling and leaping into the wagon, becoming a heaving heap. As soon as one batch would finish whatever it had been doing in the wagon, it was replaced by another batch. A black wave would spill over the sides of the wagon, tumble and weave about on the ground, and hurl itself against the fetlocks of the sorrels who, panic-stricken, trampled and crushed rats until there were already piled up enough dead ones to fill several sizeable bathtubs. I realized I must unhitch the team and send it galloping to the barn, but I thought the biggest rats would attack me. Their leader, perhaps the missing link between rats and wild boars, had but like Roosevelt at San Juan Hill to give the order to charge and I would be one et-up boy, chewed, swallowed, and excreted. But just as he rallied his troops with a cry of *squeeeeek*, he flipped over on his back, pawed the air, jerked like a believer possessed by the Holy Spirit, and took a siesta. His troops resumed their attack on the sorrels and died, their incisors sticking out like buck-teeth. Upon peering into the wagon, I could see that rats had gnawed through the grub box and devoured its contents, then gobbled up the hay, the oats, and the contents of my package from the Pluck Me. Having unhitched the sorrels, slapped them on their rumps, and ordered them home with a "Hee-YAH!," I watched them shed rats onto the road by the dozen, squashing some who emitted sounds like bicycle pumps being compressed.

As I started walking toward town, I noticed a rat which was dragging one of my missing shoes down an *arroyo*. I followed the rat into the *arroyo*. From there I heard the thundering of approaching hoofbeats and was just in time to see Dare galloping toward town on Natural Selection. "Mr. Dare! Over here! Help! Mr. Dare!"

He didn't seem to see or hear me.

PART II

Chapter Six

Why had Dare bolted past me? Had he rejected me, believing Daddy's lies? Surely Dare would come galloping back for me! He had been a swell guy from Peniel to Los Tristes. He had deployed sarcastic remarks and songs in the ranchhouse to show defiance to our enemies. No, he couldn't have been deceived about the clumsily staged "legal brief" presented by Shiflit. Dare's heart, surely, had been cut by a woman whom, he had suddenly realized, he didn't know, his wife, but he had not lost his wits. Had it not have been for his protection—Shiflit and Daddy had actually scared me—I might have felt like the dog whipped so often he must either cringe and wet the floor or run away. I had run away. In Dare I had a new, kind master. After I had unhitched the sorrels, they had raced pell-mell back to the ranch. Dare would have seen them and deduced where to find me. By jinks and by jiminy, he would retrace his tracks, pull me on to the saddle, and think up some slick adventures for us out yonder in the Territories!

I scanned the road for about twenty minutes. Buzzard hawks canted in the sky. Dare, I finally realized, wasn't coming back. I kicked dirt. I hated my new boots. "Tell me," I muttered to myself, "did they poop into your brain and forget to put lime in it?"

I dragged myself out of the *arroyo* and up to the mesa where I found hawks already tearing and gobbling up ratflesh. My Pluck Me long johns, ripped to shreds, were strewn about the road, an acid tang to the air, harbinger of snow, underscoring the fact that long johns would soon be coming in handy. My toothbrush and red bandanna, as well as the chocolates, tobacco, and brooches had either been swallowed by rats or taken in the wagon. And yet I couldn't go back to the ranch to look for them.

By a sudden reversal, instead of bewailing my new condition as an outcast, I rather fancied it. I had Scampy's photograph and five dollars. Who could ask for more? I was going to catch the stupid mail-train home.

I didn't know that the train was down on me. I didn't know that the schedule had been changed since January. I didn't know that that train was actually leaving the Los Tristes station while I was still down in the *arroyo*. I didn't know that Dare, after leaving Natural Selection at U.S. Livery, had caught *my* train . . . I didn't know, didn't know . . .

What I didn't know but would come to know through the power of remembering Time was this . . .

In Paris in 1908, months before my eighteenth birthday, who should show up in my life again but Scampy and Pia, the former disowned by, the latter evicted by Woodbridge, aetat. 68. What I didn't know about Shiflit and didn't want to know, some of his story being perverse and bogus, I learned from Scampy. And, of course, I dreaded what would happen if the girl I thought I really loved back in Los Tristes were to discover that Scampy was living in my digs on the Rue des Beaux-Arts. Would my true love understand that Scampy, during her residence *chez* Monsieur Pen'allow, had come genuinely to believe that I was her nephew, even though I knew perfectly well that I wasn't? Already, I thought, inclined toward suicide when she arrived, she couldn't be told the truth, namely, that she had married, unwittingly, her biological father, lest she go over the edge. I was compelled to join her in pretending that we were "nephew" and "aunt." I couldn't bring myself to put Scampy out on the street. More about that later.

What I didn't know in 1903 but would learn in 1908 was that Scampy and Shiflit had recently—and very briefly—been married. Moreover, Woodbridge, still pretending that he was her father, had insisted upon the union and had given the bride away at the high-society wedding. He steadfastly regarded Shiflit as the person to succeed him as Chairman of Corporation. What, to his way of thinking, could possibly be wrong with a marriage between a daughter and her father as long as the family, if that was the word, retained control of the Woodbridge empire?

As soon as the wedding was over, the couple went to the Waldorf-Astoria for the honeymoon, and as soon as they were alone together in the bridal suite, Shiflit tied Scampy hands and feet to the bed and raped her. Whereupon she managed to escape from the hotel, go home, and cry in Pia's arms for a week. Whereupon Woodbridge, who knew nothing of the rape and thought Scampy must be suffering a mere attack of virginal jitters, ordered Pia to talk the runaway bride into doing her duty and returning to her loving husband's arms. Whereupon Scampy recovered herself and had the marriage annulled. Whereupon Woodbridge dispatched Scampy and Pia on a cruise around the world. Scampy, he believed, would come to her senses. If she didn't, and in Paris, though penniless, she still repudiated the proposal that she marry Shiflit a second time, she could, ungrateful wretch, go to the devil as far as Woodbridge was concerned, Pia, too, now that she was fat and full of years, twenty-seven to be exact.

Scampy had been aware for some time that I had carried her photograph in my wallet from the day I met her in 1903 to the time, several years later, when I gave the photograph to Woodbridge. Both she and Woodbridge believed that I had been carrying the torch for a rich girl beyond my reach. When Scampy arrived in Paris, she assumed that I was in love with her. Actually, I considered myself almost betrothed to my girlfriend in Los Tristes and believed I should have no feelings for Scampy except fear—fear she would commit suicide. Fortunately, after Scampy and I met my grandmother, Mrs. Irene Penhallow, in London and learned that

Woodbridge was my grandfather, the taboo against incest came to my rescue. I was protected by the "nephew-and-aunt" confusion. More about that later, too.

One morning in Paris Scampy had nothing better to do than part the curtain separating us, she in my bed, I on the floor, and proceed to tell me the story of Shiflit. When she finished, I asked her to write it down for me. I still have her notes . . .

He was born in 1872, he told Scampy, in a log cabin in Utah in a polygamous community. Exactly where in Utah he was born he had forgotten, he said. He believed the cabin was located in a valley in the Wasatch Range about a week's ride north of Salt Lake City. The practice of polygamy had to be hidden from political and religious authorities in Salt Lake City.

Solomon Shiflit, self-proclaimed prophet, was his father and his great-grandfather, he told Scampy. Solomon's first wife, Molly Fredson of Hangman's Creek, West Virginia or Kentucky, was not his mother. Having hitched their destiny to pioneers, Solomon and Molly moved from Vermont to Illinois, to a half-deserted city, Nauvoo, where they discovered a principle, Plural Marriage. If a man married more than one wife and a wife more than one husband, he and she could have good reserved seats in Eternity. Soon Solomon, ready to hang out his shingle in Nauvoo as a Plural Marriage prophet, married a fifteen-year-old girl whose sixty-year-old first prophet had died of a heart attack. There was another prophet who wanted the girl for his forty-third wife. He didn't take kindly to Solomon's triumph in the Celestial Sweepstakes. The two prophets had a verbal duel, each excommunicating the other, the unsuccessful one with the threat of a gun. Solomon immediately received a revelation from pieces of parchment hanging in the night sky. Written in ancient Egyptian hieroglyphic, these pieces of parchment were deciphered by Solomon, their message put in effect. Placing Molly and fifteen-year-old Number Two in a prairie schooner and leaving the armed prophet to search elsewhere for Number Forty-three, he decamped. After many moons, he found the nameless valley where he gave local Indians firewater and settled down. Eventually there were dozens of Shiflits living in fetid cabins scattered through the valley, as well as some non-Shiflit pioneers who needed the opiate of Solomon's prophesies to sweeten the cup of oblivion. For them Solomon erected a church in the middle of the settlement between the whorehouse and the saloon.

The methods of farming in the valley were little changed from those used in the days of Nebuchadnezzar. Oxen drew wooden ploughs. The bare hoofs of cattle threshed grain. The feet of corpulent damsels trampled kernels into flour, and the wasted kernels were gobbled up by locusts and seagulls. There was no common school, no library, no post office, no printing press. Although, after a while, a general merchandise store and a shop for gingerbread, boiled eggs, and root beer were built, the people of the valley were too busy getting plurally married to bother with civilization. Most girls were mothers by the age of sixteen. Most men were content to fish, fight, sit, spit, drink, gamble, sleep seriatim with wives and beat their children.

Meanwhile, Solomon introduced his doctrine of Tithing for God in Social Contact. For contact with himself he collected 50% of his flock's earnings and locked the proceeds in his Mexican box. No one complained. His prophetic secret was to paint in the sermons he delivered in church such an intolerable picture of life that his flock wanted glory to come lickety-split. Solomon had incontestable biblical proof that flesh and spirit were opposed, that souls were overwhelmed by evil, that forgiveness of sins was inconceivable, that the End of Days was fast approaching and that obedience to God's minister, himself, had to be absolute.

Some of his hair-raisers, one day to be memorized by Fredson, were: *"For that which I do I allow not: for what I would, that do I not; but what I hate, that I do. Romans 7:15," "Whosoever therefore resisteth the power, resisteth the ordinance of God: and they that resist shall receive to themselves damnation. Romans,"* and the call to rid God of enemies through a bloodbath, *"Do not I hate them, O Lord, that hate thee? I hate them with perfect hatred. Psalm 139:21-22"* and *"The nation or kingdom which refuses to serve you shall perish, and wide regions shall be laid utterly waste. Isaiah 60:12."*

Lo, it came to pass that some of the non-Shiflit pioneers who could actually read their Bibles began to discover passages missing from Solomon's sermons. The epistles of St. Paul, for example, had not been quoted by Solomon in full. A passage such as *"Though I speak with the tongues of men and of angels, and have not charity, I am become as sounding brass, or a tinkling cymbal"* was, for Solomon, a mistranslation. When non-Shiflit pioneers threatened to leave the valley over this theological trifle, Solomon promised to speak to the Lord about their marriageable daughters. Lo, non-Shiflit pioneers with daughters now hastened to leave the valley as swiftly as possible. As a result the availability increased of Shiflit daughters and granddaughters for plural matrimony with fathers, grandfathers, uncles, great-uncles and cousins once or twice removed.

A head-count in 1870 revealed that Solomon had seventeen wives, seven of whom were his blood relations, twenty-five children, eighty-seven sons or daughters "in law," and 433 grandchildren, 203 of whom had survived to the marriageable age of puberty. Only twenty-seven of his descendants were prone to suffer from grand mal seizures.

Lo, it came to pass that Solomon took as his eighteenth wife his thirteen-year-old granddaughter, P.C. Shiflit. He had baptized her himself, the "P.C." standing for "Pizzum Civ," his pronunciation of Psalm 104. He liked to choose for his offspring names from Books, for instance, Genesis, Deuteronomy, and Lamentations for girls, Chronicles and Revelations for boys. Mrs. P.C. Shiflit, in giving birth to Solomon's Number 26, a boy, died. Since he had used up the Books for given-name purposes, Molly gave the boy her maiden name, Fredson. She had no extra spouses, herself, and had a name to spare.

Fredson was raised in a granite mansion big enough to

accommodate many of the wives and little children, the remainder of the continually increasing and multiplying ones relegated to fetid cabins. Molly taught him to read. Solomon bloodied little Fredson's back and bottom with a hippopotamus whip that was "good for the soul." Fredson wondered, if the human soul wasn't worth two bits, why did his Great-Grandpa-Daddy make the effort to improve it? The answer was, Solomon, just before lashing him with the hippopotamus whip, could be heard tapping his remaining front teeth with his fingernails.

When Fredson turned thirteen and theoretically became Great-Grandpa-Daddy's rival for plural mates from the polygamy pool, he was sore afraid. Other young men had been known to disappear in similar circumstances; subsequently, their fathers "sealed" pretty chicks, often blood kin, to celestial contracts. Fredson decided to pretend he was an "abomination" with no interest in girls. By breaking his wrist at a 90-degree angle, by lisping, and by staining his lips with the pulp of pomegranates, he qualified himself for the priesthood. He conducted "sealing" ceremonies for Solomon and assorted brides.

"After," Shiflit told Scampy, "I found a likely girl in one of the cabins, even if she was dressed only in a bearskin, I persuaded her to come to church with me. There, after pinning her arms behind her back, I waited for my old man to come tottering into the church to join us at the altar. While he was tapping his teeth with fingernails, I would say to his new beloved, 'Honey, you are to be Brother Shiflit's wife. God has commanded the marriage through an angel with a drawn sword. If you will accept of him he will take you straight to the celestial kingdom, and if you will have him in this world, he will have you in that which is to come. You can be married today and can go home this evening, and your parents will not know anything about it until you are embarrassed—that is, with child. If you reject this command, the gates of heaven will be closed to you. Go ahead and be blethed.' As soon as the girl gave her consent, which she invariably did as soon as she was drugged, I escorted her into a back room where plaster of Paris angels were stored in a circle around a fourposter feather bed. Once I had the bride stripped naked and tied down to the bed, my old man would slouch into the room, wearing nightgown and nightcap and tapping teeth with fingernails. I would give the couple my 'blethings' and leave the room."

Lo, it came to pass when Fredson turned sixteen, a dark, serious-faced girl with hazel eyes rode bareback on a burro into the valley. Even though she was not a Shiflit, she was, oddly, already pregnant. Fredson hid her in the whorehouse before she could be noticed and married. According to her story, her parents had been scalped by Indians and she was put to work as a scullery maid in an orphanage in Kansas. One day she escaped with a traveling salesman. He abandoned her in Denver. Lately, she'd been trying to get to Salt Lake because, she believed, the men there never abandoned a woman in this world or the next. But she had to get an abortion first.

"Honest," said Shiflit to Scampy, "she was my chance to tithe for God in social contact. Sunk in sin, I begged the young lady to accept my hand. Together, we would care for her love-child. She accepted. We needed a grubstake. I thought of the Mexican box. The prophet owed me back wages. He'd whipped me for free. He'd made me procure wives for him. I opened the Mexican box and paid myself some silver dollars. I bought me a horse and buggy, took me and my betrothed to Salt Lake . . . Sumbitch! She robbed me and had an abortion! Damn her lights after all I done did for her!"

He rode the rods from Salt Lake to Denver, Chicago, and New York . . .

I couldn't, I thought, admit to myself I still loved Scampy. "I understand your sadness," I said. "Shiflit must have had a pretty rotten childhood. One of his characteristics is to be whimsical about brutal matters. Since his story shows some of those characteristics, perhaps he was telling some of the truth."

"You always understand me," Scampy said. "When my mother was brought to die in the sanitorium, I behaved toward you like a spoiled brat. You saw through my rich-kid bitchiness. You kept my photograph in your wallet for years, as I have learned from Pa-Pa. You proved you cared for me . . . Perhaps you think I swallowed Fredson's story hook, line, and sinker?"

"Me?"

She gave me a hard look. "I haven't filled my mind with wind. Like William James, the philosopher, says, I'm 'tough-minded'."

"Yes."

"I knew," Scampy said, "Fredson liked to embellish his stories and cast his motives in a favorable light. My father was the same way. I kind of married my father, I think . . . Does some of Fredson's story have, as you suggest, a ring of truth?"

Scampy and I discussed Shiflit's story in historical contexts. Polygamous communities had indeed sprung up on the frontier and formed part of the westward movement. Countless families throughout history for thousands of years had been incestuous. Ubiquitous was the violence against children, often sanctioned by religions. Granted, one had to doubt that Shiflit's child-mother was named "Pizzum Civ," but untold millions of people believed in the holiness of the names of Books in the Bible. The bit about the nameless girl with hazel eyes who used his money to get an abortion had probably been sugared over to conceal, one, that Shiflit was responsible for the pregnancy, two, that he had forced the girl into having an abortion, and three, that he abandoned her. As for "paying" himself, he had clearly stolen the money.

Scampy hadn't finished telling Shiflit's story. When she was five years old in 1895 a, to her, "handsome young man" had been hired as a coachman and bodyguard by Woodbridge, the man she considered her father. His name, he said, was Fredson Shiflit . . .

Young Shiflit in New York sought to pattern himself after men who had achieved Success. He had clothes tailor-made. He taught himself the art of living beyond his means. He lounged about in clubs, hotels, and charitable organizations. He frequented taverns and restaurants in the financial district by day and in the theatrical demimonde by night. He made a list of the members of the board of directors of companies. He sailed to and from Europe on an ocean liner, albeit as a waiter. By the age of seventeen in 1889 he had compiled an index to the wealthiest and most influential families in the city and whittled the list down to tycoons who were philanthropists and taught Sunday School. In this way he focused his attention on Mr. Alpheus Woodbridge.

"Books were a rarity in my native valley," Shiflit told Scampy. "Once or twice a year peddlers showed up and sold, in addition to snake oil and almanacs, inspirational literature of the rags-to-riches variety and biographies of great men like Ulysses Grant, Andrew Carnegie, and Jesse James. When in New York I heard about your father, what a great man he was, what a humanitarian, I knew I had to meet him and offer him my services. At that time I was earning purses as a prizefighter known as the K.O. Kid. I had a hell of an uppercut. I broke a few jaws with it, killed a fella fair and square.'

"But, you see, your daddy was Jesus to me. If I were to attend his Sunday School, a sinner like me, I'd like to of ruint his reputation. I prayed, prayed real hard to stop myself from polluting him. One dark night I took a long walk in the Bowery and ended up in an Irish saloon with sawdust on the floor. As dear St. Paul warns us, we do that which we hate. I had too many O-be-joyfuls of John Barleycorn, got into an altercation with some gentlemen who were using totally inappropriate language. They crowded me into a corner, made some unkind remarks about my having sexual intercourse with my sainted mother, and demanded my money. By the time the police arrived, I had cold-cocked so many of those leprechauns that the sawdust turned red with blood. I was arrested for drunk and disorderly, assault and battery, and informing an officer of his canine ancestry. But when I told the magistrate I was the K.O. Kid, working for Mr. Alpheus Woodbridge at cleaning up the city for decent folks, he asked for my autograph and let me go. I now had to introduce myself to your Pa-pa."

Mr. Alpheus Woodbridge taught Sunday School in the vestry of a Gothic monstrosity on the Upper East Side. One Sunday morning while he was lecturing to a group of well-dressed ladies on the topic of scoundrels who entice maids to whom they are not betrothed, a tall youth came and seated himself on a bench in the front row. He was wearing a morning coat and clutching a Bible and looking as if he had enticed a maid. All of a sudden this stranger hurled himself to the floor, made apish grimaces, and commanded Satan to get behind him. The well-dressed ladies rushed and gushed forward and revived him with hot tea and salami sandwiches. Before leaving church, the stranger distributed a card engraved with his name, "F. Shiflit, Esq."

He attended Sunday School the next week. The well-dressed ladies buzzed with excitement, but Mr. Woodbridge paid him no attention. The lecture was about the evils of trade unionism. Evidently, when union "agitators" were "pretending" to make improvements in workers' wages and conditions, they were actually committing "treason." Every mine worker had the right to make an independent contract with a mine owner, for example, and any union which "interfered" with this "noble" relationship was just as much "in restraint of trade" as any other monopoly. Shiflit, noting that some of the ladies were nodding off to sleep, decided that the time had come for him to get biblical. Leaping to his feet, he recited with vehemence, *"The wolf also shall dwell with the lamb, and the leopard shall lie down with the kid ... They shall not hurt nor destroy in all my holy mountain. Isaiah 11:6-9!* Hosanna! Hallelujah! Sir! Mr. Woodbridge! You have spoken with the tongues of angels!"

What followed this outburst surprised everyone, Shiflit most of all.

Mr. Woodbridge stood as if transfixed, staring into a middle distance, countenance seemingly lit from within by an extraordinary light. After a prolonged silence he smiled in a tight-lipped manner and finally lowered his gaze to the ladies. "Sisters," he said quietly, "do you know who has been in your midst today?"

Shiflit studied the ladies. They sat in motionless silence. Almost inaudibly a small lady said, "Jesus?"

Mr. Woodbridge's eyes watered. He said with a sigh, "The Savior has been in your midst, concealed from your view, though not from mine . . . Thank you, Lord."

At the conclusion of Sunday School Mr. Woodbridge requested that F. Shiflit, Esq., stick around. When they were alone, Mr. Woodbridge growled with clenched teeth. "I know who you are, K.O. Kid. Drunk and disorderly, assault and battery in the Bowery, lying to a magistrate. You are an impostor. . . What the devil do you want?"

"I want to be like you," Shiflit replied unhesitatingly, "sir."

As early rays of dawn part a clouded sky, so a sly smile slowly spread across the tycoon's radiant face . . .

"When Shiflit was telling you his story before you married him, did he happen to mention the Philippines War?"

My question elicited Scampy's quizzical expression. "Yes," she finally said. "Yes, he did . . . He was so brave . . . I think I thought I was in love with him on that account."

"Oh," I said as indifferently as I could. I told her what Dare had told me in 1904 about Lieutenant Shiflit's "heroism" in Cuba and in the Philippines, how he led the charge against an enemy redoubt, how he got shot in the face, how he killed an aboriginal in hand-to-hand combat. "Captain Dare, as you call him, told me about Shiflit one day when we were buddied up in a coal mine in Los Tristes. He said he was a real hero."

"Fredson showed me and Pa-pa photographs of some Filipino village. Bag-something."

"Bagapundan," I said.

"Well," she said, "Fredson told us about Baga . . . whatever . . . and the people, the Goo-goos? He was soooo great. God, he was great!

The Goo-goos had massacred our American boys, a thousand of them. We had to capture the village. Fredson led the charge with his automatic gun. There were bodies all around, buildings full of bullet holes. There was a picture of an insurrectionist who looked like Abe Lincoln in a stovepipe hat. Fredson had the dreadful duty of hanging him from a belfry. The prisoners he took were murderers. His superior officer—Pia's ex, Captain Dare—ordered him to have them blindfolded and executed by firing squad . . . Fredson didn't want to show us these pictures, but I'm real tough-minded, and Pa-pa wanted us to see them. You know what he said that evening after Fredson, to whom I was engaged at Pa-pa's urging, left us alone together? He said about Fredson, 'You've won the lottery there, Felixine,' he said. 'He's a rough diamond with a heart of gold and a corking good patriot, lots of snap and ginger!'

"Pa-pa was grooming Fredson to take over Corporation because Alphie was too mentally disturbed to take it over."

"Changing the subject, auntie," I said, "Pa-pa hired Fredson as a coachman? If he was being groomed to succeed Pa-pa, why would he have to start off at low-level jobs? Why was he allowed to seek military adventures?"

"Well," said Scampy defensively as if I'd touched a nerve. "He wasn't just an old coachman. He drove our Maxwell into a tree, but that was because Alphie stashed opium in the whatchamacallit—the radiator. You know what Mr. Shiflit did then? We called him 'Mr. Shiflit' in those days. He drug Alphie into the garage and beat him with a hippopotamus whip . . . Know what? After that, Alphie was like Fredson's, I mean Mr. Shiflit's, dog. Anything Mr. Shiflit told him to do, Alphie did it, including selling drugs to kids . . . Mr. Shiflit used to take my mom out for long rides in the country. He was the first person in the family to suspect my mom had TB. He got Pa-pa to call the doctor. The doctor verified the diagnosis and said, 'Witchcraft!' He didn't believe a bodyguard with no education could recognize the disease. Only, Pa-pa was grateful for the diagnosis. He and my mom were unhappy together. If she died, he would be spared the scandal of a divorce. As for Mr. Shiflit, if he became

107

a war hero in Cuba, he wouldn't have to go to Yale, like Pa-pa, in order to climb the ladder to success.'

"Well," Scampy continued after taking a deep breath, "when Fredson returned from Cuba a few years after my mom gave birth to me, Pa-pa promoted him to chief of operations in Colorado. It was a really and truly big, secret job. Fredson went incognito . . . Pa-pa, who was having the Sun Palace built, had hired your father as its Director, but he wanted Fredson to be Head of Security, to protect my mother. Like Pa-pa said, 'Dr. Penhallow is a first-class nincompoop'."

"Actually," I said.

"You're sweet," Scampy said. "Pa-pa also wanted Fredson to keep an eye on our mine in Cripple Creek. As Pa-pa said, 'The day will come when the Wobblies call for a national strike.' He suggested that Fredson join the Guard and get on friendly terms with General Case in Denver, 'an idiot,' Pa-pa called him. 'We'll need the Guard to break the strike.' . . So, nephew, what you didn't know about Fredson, he was supposed to assume Chairmanship of Corporation, and Pa-pa encouraged him to join the Army in the Philippines where he could continue to become a hero worthy of the Chair . . . Now, nephew, are you ready to learn what Fredson told me about your being, like you say, 'kidnapped' in Cripple Creek? I'll betcha never guessed what the commotion was all about."

"O.K.," I said. "I figured Daddy was so crazy about Pia he wanted to have her in the house all to himself and me out of the way."

"Close." Scampy shook her head as if to say Silly Boy. "Pia was the fly in the ointment all right, but: Pa-pa never went with your father on that hunting trip into the backlands of Colorado . . . When he and your father arrived in Denver with their entourage, Pa-pa suddenly announced that he had urgent business to attend to, would your father carry on, all expenses paid? Your father and the hunting party took off, while Pa-pa, for whom Fredson had secured a private Pullman car, returned to Colorado Springs. The car was shunted off to a quiet downtown siding. It was very luxurious with a bedroom, a dining lounge, a bar, a kitchen, a cook and a maid. A love-nest on wheels.'

"Remember, Fredson pimped for Solomon the prophet? He could do the same for my Pa-pa, couldn't he? His relations with General Case were so cordial he could come and go from Cripple Creek as he pleased . . . He had Pia summoned from Los Tristes and introduced to Pa-pa in the Pullman . . ."

"Wait," I said. "How did Shiflit know that Pia was willing to ditch Daddy for an old tycoon?"

"She's a gold-digging nymphomaniac, I guess," Scampy said, glancing at the ceiling. "As soon as Fredson got back from the Philippines and resumed his job at the Sun Palace, he discovered your father's affair with Pia and saw an opportunity to accomplish three things at one blow. One, he had a mysterious score to settle with Captain Dare. Two, since Mom was dying, Pa-pa was looking for a mistress. Pia could audition for the job. Three, Pia was tired of being at the beck and call of your father without receiving a dime. Once she got a rich man into the sack, she could realize the dream of her life: have a Y.M.C.A built for coalminers."

I didn't entirely follow and said so. She hadn't revealed how the "commotion" had come to involve me.

"For Fredson," Scampy explained, "the cream of the jest was to convert your home into the love-nest. It was all very well to please his boss by renting a luxurious Pullman car, but why not give Pia the pleasure of taking possession of your mother's whole house and not to have quickies with your father in his stinking lab? Your dumb daddy was away hunting. Alphie and I were booked into Antlers Hotel. That left you, you and Ruby. He had to get rid of you both. Once you left the house for Cripple Creek, and Ruby, as I'll explain, was ordered to leave the premises, Fredson installed Pa-pa and Pia alone together in your house on Wood Avenue.'

"Pa-pa spent a week being—pardon Fredson's Army slang?— pussy-whipped."

Scampy's use of bawdy words had been one of the surprises of our relationship without relations. Probably to high-society folks she as a debutante had come across as refined; privately at my digs in Paris, she liked to pretend she hated stuffiness. Because she had been privy to Shiflit's partly true confessions, she was able to shed some light on my own destiny. Shiflit and the Pinkerton dicks had, one way or another, improvised upon or failed to execute the Halloween plot to have me killed, Shiflit by adding his firing squad hoax and by telling Alphie and Scampy that Daddy wanted me to remain in Cripple Creek to have my so-called "ambition to be an artist" drummed out of me by means of Shiflit's military discipline, and the Pinkertons, Gott and Mush, by pistol-whipping instead of shooting me. The aggravated arrogance of these clots had, in Shiflit's story, turned a simple homicide into a dropped clanger.

Ruby, Shiflit believed, had been easily warned off the premises. Some of the young Guards from the sanitorium had donned uniforms of hospital workers and arrived at the house to warn Ruby that it had been "quarantined until further notice due to Dr. Penhallow's lab experiments." They had given her a lift home in a buggy and along the way tried to impress her with the gravity of the situation at our house: Daddy's deadly germs, they declared, might escape and wipe out millions. Ruby promised them she would stay at her Shooks Run home until she received further notice.

"Let me get this straight," I said to Scampy. "Aged twelve, I am kidnapped after facing a firing squad and being locked in a bull pen together with anarchists who drink the blood of their enemies. I am pistol-whipped, robbed, and hurled out of a moving train in the middle of nowhere. I am accused of raping the daughter of a tycoon with my finger, even though wild horses couldn't have striped you of your jodhpur breeches, and of plotting the murder of my mother who is herself accused of being a slut, doubt thrown upon my legitimacy. Then, of necessity, I work in a coal mine alongside an innocent man accused of committing atrocities in war—and all because a polygamy pool pimp and Corporation goon arranged to have a tycoon, whose beautiful wife was dying of tuberculosis, *pussywhipped*, as you so delicately put it, by my father's mistress who dreams of building a Y.M.C.A. for coalminers."

Scampy frowned. "Fredson didn't murder anybody. Did he?"

"Are you still in love with him?"

"No."

"Then I'll answer your question when we're old, auntie, eating prunes by candlelight."

I had leftover questions myself. After debating whether to burden Scampy with them, I decided to rely upon the great tough-mindedness she prided herself on having.

"On second thought," I said, "Shiflit was a murderer in the Philippines before he returned to New York and then came to Cripple Creek and Colorado Springs with the Guard. Dare told me everything about it in '04. He was blamed for Shiflit's murders. But, for now, I'm curious about my father. Do you mean that, when Daddy went off hunting, he expected to find me safely home from Cripple Creek upon his return? In other words, he never conspired to have me kidnapped and killed? He was innocent."

Scampy said nothing. I plunged on. "From what you say Shiflit confessed to you, it's obvious Daddy believed Pia was in Los Tristes during the hunt, though in fact she was in the Springs auditioning for your father until Daddy was about to return, whereupon she dashed back by train to the ranch. Then, but not until then, he was persuaded by Shiflit's allegations against me to banish me from home. Is that what you mean?"

"Oh, nephew," she sighed. "Alphie and Fredson cooked up the finger-raping story for one reason: to deter you permanently from returning home. What better way could Fredson think of to achieve that than to have Alphie swear to the truth of a makeshift legal document? Who was more likely than your poor dumb father to believe anything—that your mother had a fatal disease, that she cheated on him during their honeymoon, that you were not his son, and even that you and Captain Dare had been having a pansy affair in the middle of the desert? You, nephew, were an evil little bastard who of course was planning to murder his mother and get her money! Your father's plot, so to say, became yours."

"Permanently," I pursued. "You said 'permanently' in relation to Shiflit's scheme to have me deterred from returning home. What was the scheme? He wanted me out of the house. My temporary absence should have sufficed. Why did it have to be permanent?"

"Oh," chirped Scampy, "I forgot to tell you. One night in New York I overheard Pa-pa and Fredson laughing together over a scheme involving murders. I didn't think they were serious. Anyway, after Pa-pa was satisfied with his research into Pia, Fredson wanted to have no one in your house except your father and Pia. Then he could have them both murdered, and Captain Dare would be arrested for the murders, jealousy the motive . . . I asked you if Fredson ever murdered anybody. You said no. Then you changed your mind and said that he murdered lots of people. If you had asked me if he had ever wanted people murdered, I could have said, 'yes, Sue Puh,' long before we have to eat prunes by candlelight."

I looked at Scampy and wondered why I was feeling attracted to her. "So," I said more to myself than to her, "Daddy and Pia were to be murdered in order for Shiflit to get revenge on Dare. That was the real purpose behind the plot to have me go to Cripple Creek and, later, killed."

Scampy scowled. I certainly was curious as to why she would marry Shiflit when he had blatantly revealed plans to kill Pia and Daddy and to frame Dare. I cleared my throat, acting the role of a scold.

"When Shiflit, for once, was transparent," I said, "didn't you suspect you were marrying a killer?"

"There you go again," Scampy replied, pouty-lipped. "When Pa-pa screamed that he wanted to 'kill' Rockefeller, Morgan, Vanderbilt, Carnegie, and any other competitor, he was just ranting, right? When Fredson gives me his cock-and-bull story, am I supposed to take him seriously? I could wrap him around my little finger."

"The way you wanted to make love with me until we discovered you're my aunt?"

"Well," she said, meeting my gaze, "a glance at small details in the life of someone like yourself not conventionally perceived as even existing in the grandiose historical view shows what true history is actually made out of." . . .

≈≈≈

Some of what I didn't know about Dare, years later I learned from him and from Mum.

Shortly before our arrival at Homesteader's, he had been listening intently to everything I said about Mum and my determination to liberate her from the Sun Palace. As it had to me, so it seemed to him that her life was in very real danger in a real Bluebeard's castle. Even if she proved strong enough to resist infection from patients with TB, her spirit was being broken. To what I said about her being in danger of being murdered, Dare could embellish from his own experiences with Shiflit. Although he kept an open mind about Woodbridge, an antiunion Corporation Chairman who also owned mines and a TB sanitorium was unlikely to care much about either workers or patients. Dr. Penhallow, Director, probably had absolute authority over Mum.

So what could he, Dare, do to help Mrs. Penhallow? She might as well be in the penitentiary in Cañon City for all the effort that had been spent by Corporation on preventing patients from escaping: high walls, security guards, limited visitation rights, rules against communications. Given the likelihood of close cooperation between members of the medical profession and those of the legal one—Dare had been warned about professional skullduggery by his father, Dr. Randolph Dare—a doctor's socially shunned patient could not escape from institutionalized care without his consent. Therefore, if Mrs. Penhallow escaped from the sanitorium without her doctor's—and her husband's—authorization, she could be proclaimed a fugitive from Law, hounded throughout the United States, captured and locked up in an asylum. Dare couldn't be sure of the fate awaiting Mrs. Penhallow, but his experience of the military justice system in the Philippines had inclined him to believe that the Law was usually drawn up by and often abrogated by the powers-that-be.

In developing any strategy Dare usually worked his way through from finish line to starting line. Based upon his knowledge of the persistence of Shiflits and Woodbridges of the world, he concluded that Mrs. Penhallow must flee the country and live abroad. Using the psychological jargon just coming into vogue, he often said of himself, "You have to be paranoid enough." If she would agree to take up residence at the house he owned in St. Aignan, France, she would be safe from pursuit, whereas, if she took refuge with her mother in New York, that apartment would be among the first places to be watched by emissaries of those powers-that-be. Next, in order to get her safely to a seaport, he had to consider limited transportation options, horseback initially, trains thereafter. Whether they traveled eastward, Denver-Chicago, Denver-Kansas City, or Denver-Albuquerque-New Orleans, or westward, Denver-Salt Lake City-Sacramento, they might be apprehended if they traveled alone and unarmed. Shiflit was familiar with his tactics; Shiflit could get in touch with a national network of Guards. Transportation would nevertheless have to be by rail. If they could get to the Great Lakes at Duluth or Detroit, then cross the border into Canada, they could book a transatlantic voyage from Montreal, Quebec, or Halifax.

The obvious problem with rail transportation would arise when police or Pinkertons boarded trains to arrest them. Here his Union affiliations would prove useful. His Union brothers would have to come along as bodyguards. Conductors and porters, if unionized, could assist them in eluding pursuit. Still another strategy would be to bluff people into believing Mrs. Penhallow was his wife. The biggest problem was Mrs. Penhallow herself. From all indications she loved her husband and submitted herself to his every wish. Would she consent to leave the sanitorium? Would she trust a stranger to help her escape? Would she, disastrously, insist on going to rescue Tree? Everyone would then be captured.

While his experience as an ex-patriot, a college student, a rancher, a miner, an officer, a veteran and a labor organizer had taught him various survival techniques, not the least of which was saving documents of all kinds, when it came to his understanding of women he was, he believed, a donkey. Out of loneliness, pity, physical attraction and a desire to settle down and start a family, he had married an uneducated young woman with whom he had little in common. His romantically perceived exploits as a footballer and soldier notwithstanding, he had actually been a virgin when he married Pia. Just because he had been unhappy in marriage, was he not indulging in a near-middle-age fantasy about another man's wife, a woman he'd never even met?

He had a plan for saving Mrs. Penhallow. He would wear his mothballed Army uniform, trusting that security guards, who, as he, were soldiers, would be impressed by military rank and authority. He would show them a letter signed by Dr. Penhallow, one declaring a certain patient of his to be "cured" of TB and in need of no further treatments. He had in his desk at home precisely such a letter, one written on Sun Palace stationery. Instead of mentioning Pia by name, Dr. Penhallow had referred to her as "your wife." If the "y" in "your" were erased, the letter would read, *our wife is cured.* Use of the pronoun plural would be consistant with the Englishman's pompous style of speech. Moreover, Dr. Penhallow had neglected to date his letter. In sum, the letter originally authorizing Pia's discharge from treatments could be forged to authorize Mrs. Penhallow's release from the sanitorium.

It had often been observed of Dare that he was cool under fire. Sudden surprises, twists of fate, a volte-face or prospect of defeat he met with calmness and resolution, whereas, if he were forced to choose between an *éclair* and a *gâteau*, he was apt to get tongue-tied with indecision. When he burst through the blue door of his ranchhouse, his emotions were under control, his nerves ready to confront any enemy. One glance around the living room had smothered his rage. Pia had cheated on him. Dr. Penhallow had cheated on wife and son. Shiflit, who had tortured Tree, had him kidnapped and, he thought, murdered, had obviously not turned over a new leaf. The subornation of Gwilym and the plagiarized legal mumbo jumbo had added a touch of farce. When Tree, banished, bolted, Dare, for all his own flaws and folly, had already decided upon allegiance to honor. Although others might be too shameless to wear its badge, it was not his righteous duty to condemn them. It was his obligation to himself, however, to heed a personal thing, a code to live by. His father had it. His father's life had been suffused by an indestructible attitude of reverence for life and by a grieving for human misery. And now there must no longer be for that father's son further denial of fitness to wear the badge of honor. He must strive to live by its demands as an antidote to cheapness of soul.

His spirit was already putting his plan into play. Brushing Doc Penhallow aside, Dare strode into the soiled bedroom and from there into his study. From his desk he collected documents, among them the Doc Penhallow letter. From a cedar chest he removed his old uniform. These items bundled up, he dashed back through the living room, shouting over his shoulder in order to foil attempts to follow him, "Wait here until I bring the boy!" From the house he ran to the barn, almost tripping over his happy dogs, and as sorrels swerved into sight in a cattle-moaning meadow, he instructed Dawn Antelope to cut the telephone wire, to send the Army ponies loose into pastures, and, in the morning, to collect Natural Selection from U.S. Livery. Then he mounted the roan, spurred it. If the little foxes believed he was hunting for Tree, they might stay in the house and get drunk. In particular, Pia needn't wait years for a divorce. By the time he returned from, he hoped, France, she might have dumped Doc Penhallow and be pleading for reconciliation. Divorce, though, was in his cards. He was having no trouble making that decision. He would not grant her title to the real estate, but he would give her ample alimony. That would be the honorable thing to do.

He caught the train. As it rumbled into the night, he, staring out a window, observed for a few moments the steeple of a country church. It was gleaming in last rays of setting sun. The sight struck his heart a blow sharp as a *bolo's*. Once upon a youth in France more than twenty years ago he'd been anxiously peering out the window in the *rez-de-chaussée* of his parents' fourteenth-century townhouse in St. Aignan and observing the nearby church steeple transformed by setting sun into a golden-yellow integument for the thrust of hope into the heavens. Just then, the priest who had given last rites to his mother upstairs came and put his hand on the boy Kyle's shoulder, the wordless gesture speaking of the passing away of one who would always be slim and pretty, not a bald, emaciated, huddled mass of cancer-riddled bones, always the giver of caresses and kisses, always the beautiful voice singing joyous songs, not a morphine-tolerant screamer. Numbed, the boy had continued to watch as the light faded from the steeple. Might he have helped his mother? Had he hastened her death with neglect even though she was the one who had insisted that he continue his schooling? Dispossessed forever of the sound of her rustling skirt the boy Kyle had cherished hope he would never see a steeple in a setting sun again. But the man, Dare, seeing one such steeple in Colorado and emerging from swirling mists of yesteryear, envisioned an end to that old, nagging grief, and a convergence of his soul with another soul . . .

Ruby had a Kodak.

Ruby also had in her house on Shooks Run a dark room where she developed pictures. If I had known that the relationship of Mum and Ruby was not just that of employer and servant but of conspirators, wouldn't I have had my eyes opened earlier than they were to a reality like that, in one of my favorite analogies, of stars in daylight, invisible but there, covered but constant? With no more technology than a small box camera Ruby had collected a gallery of pictures of those persons who came to our house, especially anyone having an appointment with Dr. Penhallow. If her suspicions were sufficiently aroused by a stranger's appearance at the front door, she would endeavor to take a picture during the visit. She had managed to snap, for instance, Mrs. Pia Dare and Dr. Penhallow in a passionate embrace. Ruby gave such pictures to Mum.

And so it happened that on the morning of my trip with Scampy and Alphie to Cripple Creek, after Shiflit's security guards dressed as medical personnel declared the house "quarantined" and packed her off to Shooks Run, she muttered to herself, "Kodak time." That very evening, in spite of the pain of her osteoarthritis, she sneaked back to the house with camera and waited in the bushes outside an open window. After a while she saw Pia—"sho back by pop'lar de-man," Ruby muttered to herself—and heard the whore-woman shrieking jubilantly as Mr. Alpheus Woodbridge ripped her blouse. "That a quar'teen, I is a pillow of salt." She snapped a picture.

It was in Mum's possession within twenty-four hours. Having met Woodbridge at the ceremony when the Sun Palace was opened for business, she identified him at once and warned Ruby to stay away from the love-nest. If Woodbridge caught Ruby in the act of taking pictures, he would believe he was going to be blackmailed. He had power to do her harm, even to kill her.

The incriminating pictures of Daddy and of Woodbridge caused Mum's heart to come to a standstill. Their philandering was cruel and insulting enough. To befoul her home and her dignity was more than she could tolerate. She must escape confinement in the sanitorium and in marriage—or die in the attempt.

Not long after Mum had been dumped in the sanitorium, Ruby took advantage of the fact that she was in some white folks' eyes invisible. All she needed to do to gain admission to the sanitorium was to dress in a starched white uniform splattered with tomato ketchup and gravy and the security guards assumed she belonged to the staff, either chattel employed for washing dishes and scrubbing floors or part of the crew assigned to incinerating putrid matter and corpses. No one bothered to stop her or ask for identification, albeit she took the precaution of appearing at the gates only when a Guard lieutenant with an old cheek wound and black mustache was not on duty. The regular guards were just skylarking kids. If 180 pounds of great-hearted and intelligent life strolled past them, as she did three or four times a week on her way to visit Mum, what they apparently saw was skin. Paradoxically, it was invisible . . .

Anna Maria Dautremond Penhallow sits by the window of her private room in the Sun Palace Sanitorium. It is two in the morning and cold. The window is open. She smells Death. The odor comes from the two-hundred-foot smokestack which is emitting smoke and cinders as some of the last of that week's patients who died of TB are incinerated. By staying up at night, sometimes all night, and by dressing in street clothes as if she expects a gentleman caller, she takes full possession of her senses away from daily routines. Although she is usually enraged by the fact that she cannot see a full sky, she does see gallows humor in her surroundings. How many patients have figured out what the smokestack signifies? How many have pondered the omnipresence of death? Or realized that this hospital, when lit up at night, resembles a sweatshop or a mill? Probably they, the lungers, have seen these writings upon their walls but lost the will to resist.

When she was a girl living on Washington Square, she and her mother had played a game known as Dumb Supper. According to the folklore, one could get by means of Dumb Supper a glimpse of her or his future mate. One could sweep the floor, set the table, cook a meal, put it on the table and eat it in silence, then open the door and wait; the guest who came to the table, actually an apparition, would be the future Intended, and a supernatural wind would blow out the lights. Or—and this was Anna Maria's preference in the game—instead of expecting to see a ghostly visitor or perform foolish acts such as walking backward while serving the dinner, she would simply bow her head over an empty plate in order to see in it her future husband's face. Since she never did see him, she would giggle and throw herself into her mother's arms, still loving the game because it was sweet, preposterous, and sassy.

Lately, late at night, she'd been playing Dumb Supper. From the dining room she had borrowed a plate, a slice of bread, and a sherry glass. She filled it with water and covered the plate with a slice of bread. Glass and plate she then placed on the windowsill.

When she was ready, she would drink the water, eat the bread, and bow her head over the empty plate.

As happened lately, one of Ruby's pictures, one Mum was fond of, had been taken of me as I was shaking hands with Captain Kyle Deville Dare for the first time, that occasion when he had returned from the Philippines and come to the house dressed in uniform, that time when I had run to her bedroom and recited lines from Dante.

This night, after a surprise visit from Mrs. Elizabeth Woodbridge, she has reason to fear for her life. This night, too, as she sits by the window, she has already eaten the fairytale dinner but delayed bowing her head. There have been, as always, disappointing results—no face at all, no glimpse of her future mate. She sees the smokestack, the lit-up hospital windows, the illuminated gate guarded by soldiers. She bows her head. And, this time, she sees a face—that of Captain Kyle Deville Dare. No sooner has she identified her Intended than a commotion at the gate draws her attention. A horse and buggy are waiting outside the gate, steam from the foot-stomping horse's nostrils making magical bubbles in wet air. She recognizes a tall man in an Army officer's uniform who, having shown some paper to a guard, is striding through the gate and, it seems, looking up at her window . . .

Chapter Seven

I arrived at the AT&SF depot only to learn that I had missed my northbound mail-train and that the next one would be at four o'clock in the morning. I was determined to take it, in the meantime wander about the city. I could buy a pouch of Bull Durham, roll a cigarette, and blow smoke rings at old ladies.

As I walked back to Main, a light snow was slanting in. Panhandlers and thinly clad prostitutes—Dare's "cranes"—squatted under or leaned against lampposts. Workers and shoppers in winter hats and overcoats scurried in and out of brightly lit buildings. On the ballroom floor of the Imperial Hotel a waltz was in progress; at open windows from which spilled the *rum-pa-pa rum-pa-pa* of string and wind instruments dancers appeared, jewels glittering. Under the marquee of Josca's Opera House an elegantly dressed lady stepped from a buggy into mud up to her ankles. From inside the swinging doors of the Tap'er Light Saloon came a crooner's cloying lyrical equivalent of a wet dream:

Ay! ay! ay! ay!
Canta y no llores
Porque cantando se alegran
Cielito lindo, los corazones.

Some of my schoolfriends had sung that song on the Cinco de Mayo. Further along Main, outside Cousin Jack's Dancing,

Liquoring, Vittling & Gambling Establishment, I peeped through a window on the inner side of which curtains of red plush hung with ball fringes were parted. Beneath Chinese lanterns aswirl with tobacco smoke, gamblers leaned over tables upholstered in green baize. Dancers—swarthy men with heavy mustaches and short-cropped hair, fat women with loose expressions on painted lips—stomped feet while a hillbilly singer accompanied by a fiddler nasal-twanged:

> *Oh-h-h! A monkey settin' in a pile of straw*
> *A-winkin' at his mother-in-law!*
> *Turkey in the straw, Haw! Haw! Haw! . . .*

Among candle-lit tables and booths waiters dressed up as Cornish miners carried trays of greasy steaks and foaming beermugs.

Would a grownup man catch a fool train to please his mommy? A mug of beer, a steak with a side of oysters, a polite conversation with cranes, and I could blow out my five dollars like a pneumatic tire on tenpenny nails. But with axle grease rubbed into my scalp I would look a sight! That giant guard from the Pluck Me, who had greeted me so courteously when I was dressed as a scarecrow, was now a putting-off-er. When he finished masticating offal, he wedged a toothpick into his maw and dislodged a morsel as slimy and chewed as Jonah puked up from the belly of the whale. I decided to return to the waiting room at the depot. I could warm myself by a potbellied Franklin stove.

I was passing by Josca's Opera House when from inside it came a tenor's voice. I don't remember whether it was *"La donna é mobile"* or the cold-hands tearjerker, not then knowing one opera from another, but he reached for—and grasped—a dimension of life beyond ordinary humanity's closed door. Previously, chilled by Daddy's mockery, I had rejected a calling to become an artist. I had a few talents but doubted if I should ever put them to a test. The tenor's voice penetrated my soul, though, and lit up the path that my dreams of self-fulfillment might seek to take.

A little while later I was in the waiting room and laying my head down on a pillow I had contrived to make out of a couple of bricks. The rest of my body I stretched out on a hard wooden bench. In case a policeman came and poked me with his nightstick, presuming me to be a bum, I covered my face with an old newspaper, indicating that I was an authentic gentleman who had just chanced to fall asleep in a public place. I did fall asleep, warmed by the stove and lulled by the steady *tick-tick-tick* of a telegraph transmitter operated behind a barred cage by a uniformed agent with a green shade at his brow. I dreamed a horrid dream about Daddy aborting me with an ice pick while I was curled inside Mum's womb. Suddenly I was jolted awake by the hooting, hissing, and screeching of a train being brought to a stop outside the waiting room. By the big depot clock it was 1:05 a.m. Snow was blowing through cones of light. Presently there were mobs of passengers out on the platform and inside my waiting room. Many of them jabbered in foreign tongues while they waited for luggage or queued up to do business with a ticket agent. When finally these passengers left my room empty again, I noticed some camera men still out on the platform. By the way they were gesturing and cursing and rubbing hands impatiently I assumed they were reporters who had been expecting someone famous to arrive and been disappointed. Soon they departed.

Thanks to the bricks, I had a crick in my neck. I sat up and put in some thought. It indeed would be folly to take the four o'clock to Colorado Springs. Perhaps if I could get to New York and Ganny's apartment on Park Avenue, I could overcome her resistance to helping Mum while I rose in society, played football at Yale in order to impress Woodbridge, and married Scampy. I had to keep my five dollars in reserve. I remembered a newspaper article describing three ways for hoboes: hide in boxcars, make the blind, or ride the rods. The boxcar way had advantages of comfort, but if fate put you in bad company, you could be robbed and murdered. If you chose to travel "by the blind," meaning the end of the baggage car through which none of the train crew passed between station and station, you would be reasonably safe from molestation; however, you would be constantly subjected to high winds, freezing rains, smoke, cinders, and dust. That left the rods. These were located beneath carriages and were recommended as good hiding places. If you fell off the rods the wheels would grind you into hamburger.

I decided to seek the advice of experienced hoboes. Where was I more likely to find them than out in the railyards? Ticketless migrations were bound to be occurring out there at any hour, I surmised, due to the number of miners leaving Los Tristes in order to seek work elsewhere.

While I was making plans, two young men entered the waiting room and ambled over to the stove to warm hands. They were miners of the Glass-Eye Gwilym type, bearded, stocky, scruffy and disheveled, faces pale and in-grained with black spots of coal. I considered seeking their advice. However, before I moved from my bench, I noticed that they were pointing at me and whispering. So intense was their scrutiny that I had to imagine myself as an easy mark. I should, I reasoned, avoid eye contact, back away slowly. If I were followed, I would run back to Main Street and get lost in the crowd. If I were not followed, I could relax my vigilance, recognizing that they were no more interested in me than they were in their dirty fingernails. Affecting casual unconcern, I left the waiting room and walked as far as the Commercial Street bridge. Then I turned around. I hadn't been followed from the depot. I couldn't be absolutely sure I was safe, however, what with snow falling thickly and blowing in a gale-force wind. I headed for the yards.

Roughly a mile from the depot there were dozens of boxcars strung out in an alluvial fan of tracks. I didn't fancy climbing aboard a car if it had been shunted aside. Its destination would be too uncertain. Nor did I fancy cars with names such as Lackawanna, Burlington, Chesapeake, Norfolk or Gulf. There was no telling where a car with unfamiliar place names might end up. Spotting a water tank illuminated by electric lights, beside the tank a concrete bunker, I plodded toward them. Surely veteran hoboes would wait in that bunker until an engine was stopped at the tank in order to take on water. When I reached the bunker, I saw behind a burlap bag which fluttered over its entrance the glow of a fire. I parted the burlap bag.

They didn't look surprised, the two men in the bunker who had also been those miners in the waiting room. Smoking pipes as they squatted around a small campfire, they had somehow twigged it that I would be coming their way. I beat a retreat as I had done previously, backing out slowly, making no sound save the squeaky crunch of boots on powdery snow. When I reached the water tank, I looked over my shoulder. The stiffs were coming toward me at a shambling gait! I turned to run but twisted my foot on a tie and sprawled on my back. The stiffs came and stared down at me. Snowflakes bit my hot face.

I heard snowcrunch behind me.

"Eve'nin', Mother," one of the stiffs said in deferential tone, touching a finger to cap.

"Boys," a woman's voice replied. It was a low, slow, solemn voice, hers, with a slight brogue. "I spose noo the little two by fours were waitin' for me at station?" She seemed to be clucking in her throat as I turned to study her. She was a tiny old lady underneath an umbrella, wearing in the blizzard only a black dress with lace at the throat and wrists and with a bonnet which bore resemblance to a porcupine tied in ribbons. She had bunched-up white hair, a finely wrinkled face, behind glasses keen eyes. She and the "boys" were in cahoots.

"They was fit to be tied, Mother," said one of the stiffs as he knocked ashes from his pipe. "Conductor let you off O.K.?"

"Mile back."

"We striking?"

"Here to find out."

"We ain't got nothin' to lose no more, Mother," the stiff said. He was bowed over his boots as if embarrassed to have spoken his mind to this woman who didn't really look powerful or famous enough to have lured reporters to the depot.

Dropping at her feet a bundle wrapped in a black shawl, the lady named Mother placed hands akimbo. "I wish I was God Almighty!"

125

she declared vehemently. "I would throw down something some night from heaven and get rid of the whole bunch of blood-suckin', sanctified cannibals who are driving the people to become dog-eat-dog bloodhounds!"

She took notice of me. "What have we here? This the lad named Tree? Why's he layin' in the snow? Get up, boy, before you catch your death of cold!"

I stood up, hopped on one foot, put weight on the other foot until I was satisfied it wasn't sprained or broken. I had to recognize I was growing happy about the mouth. The stiffs had been looking for – and out—for me. As for the lady who called me Tree, she had come directly from the Association of Fairy Godmothers.

"Cap'n Dare called us at Union H.Q. from Col'radder Sprangs," said the stiff who had been quiet. "He said he was in such a tear to catch his train that he'd left the Penhallow boy, goes by Tree, in the dark. Would we track him down and turn him over to you? . . . We didn't mean to spook him."

Mother said something about a call she, too, had received from Captain Dare before she left Denver. Looking me up and down she said with kindly inflection, "Well, son, if you want to die, come with me. Be so good as to carry my knick-knacks."

She thanked and dismissed the stiffs. I picked up her bundle. It was heavy, clunky. How, I wondered, could anyone so frail-looking as Mother lift it, let alone walk a mile carrying it in a blizzard and she without winter clothing while the wind under her umbrella was threatening to turn it inside out? As we began to walk together, she spoke to me as if she were, indeed, manifested out of the fairy godmothering dimension. "Isn't it funny, Tree?" she remarked. "I live in the United States, but I do not know exactly where. I spend cold nights in miners' hovels, sleepin' on a bare floor with my handbag for a pillow. I sleep in my clothes, not knowin' what's to happen to me next. Am I gonna get beat up or kilt? Am I gonna be de-ported by some two-bit governor in the pockets of Corporation? Slander and persecution, they follow me like black shadows. I guess my address is like my shoes: it travels with me . . ."

Half an hour later we were pausing in front of the Imperial Hotel. I had grim feelings about myself. I wasn't cut out for a hobo. The old lady had the guts to be a vagabond, but I didn't. If she tossed me aside as an encumbrance, I couldn't blame her because I wasn't worthy of her care. I wasn't a child prodigy. I wasn't a good-looking man. Almost an orphan now, I wouldn't have selected me if I were cleaned and polished and put on display for adoption at an orphanage. I had fool notions of making something of my life and marrying the daughter of a tycoon but they were not likely to become reality. Still, why had Dare cared for me so much he had had me tailed and towed into safe harbor? Maybe, after all, I wasn't too damn bad.

If there's a time on the clock deemed particularly suited for melancholia, it's two o'clock in the morning the day before Halloween. Throw into the circumstance a deserted street in Podunkville during a blizzard and a couple of church bells tolling the fateful hour as if to announce the end of the world, and you had best stay away from swords. You may feel impelled to fall on one of them. We entered the hotel lobby. A couple of old gentlemen in the corner were spitting in brass spittoons and dealing cards to one another, no doubt to decide which one of them would be first to go up to the top floor and throw himself out the window. I didn't see any Pinkertons. They'd gone home to their rat-holes and put Winchesters in their mouths.

I peeped over Mother's shoulders as she signed the register. "M. Jones, Chicago," she wrote. The clerk's eyes seemed to become open and very clear like those of murder victims in a street. He didn't ring a bell for a porter or offer to lug Mother's bundle upstairs. I suspected he had a delicious glass of potassium cyanide waiting for him in a back room. Carrying her bundle, I followed M. Jones, Chicago, upstairs to a second-floor corridor and the numbered door of a room. Her key fit the lock. M. Jones, Chicago, took her bundle from me.

"Wait here," she said. "I won't be long."

A girl in a ballgown and a young gentleman in a tuxedo rushed,

127

giggling, past me and down the stairs. Their pumpkin would be waiting for them in the street under a black sky sprinkled with twinklers.

About this time—nicely past two—a penny about the size of a steam locomotive's wheel dropped in my brain with a thud: M. Jones, Chicago, was Mother Jones! I'd read about her for years. She was the greatest labor organizer since Jesus!

And the door opened and there she was, dressed in an old calico costume that had probably been worn at a cotillion in the Garden of Eden when Eve was introduced to society. Mother Jones had wrapped the black shawl about her head. She carried a torn carpetbagger's case. She opened wide her bright blue eyes and said, "How do I look, young man? Do I look like a peddler?"

She still looked like the ink sketches and photos of her that had appeared in a million papers. I had learned from Mum to equivocate when a lady such as Mother Jones sought a gentleman's opinion about beauty and style. "Smashing," I said. One of Daddy's English expressions seemed appropriate.

"Well," said Mother Jones with a surreptitious glance about the corridor. "I like to go to the company-towns in disguise. I don't want the mine guards and sucks to suspect that I'm fixin' to raise hell . . . My case is full of pins and needles, swatches of fabric, knives and forks, notions and samplers . . . And one more thing, changin' the subject . . . Captain Dare told me your father has been bamboozled by Alpheus Woodbridge, no less, and has banished you from home . . . Don't you worry. The Union is lookin' after you now. There'll be a fella to knock you up in the morning, as the English say in their peculiar idiom."

She gave me the room key and lowered her voice. "When I lost my husband and our four little children to the yellow fever epidemic which was sweeping through the city of Memphis in '67, I sat alone through nights of grief. No one came to me. No one could. Other homes were as stricken as mine. All day long, all night long, I heard the grating of the wheels of the death cart . . . Remember what they say in the mines when they test the roof lest it collapse and crush them without a moment's warning: tap 'er light."

She set off at a brisk gait. I didn't catch up with her until she was descending the stairs. "Mother Jones!" I said, my voice breathless. "Thank you! God bless you!"

I'll admit, in my white Anglo family showing emotion had been discouraged by everyone but Mum. Gushing, as I was, and allowing tears to lurch in my eyes, as I was, were especially frowned upon. But to wish God's blessings upon another person was considered absolutely ridiculous. On the Christmas Eve when Ganny was visiting us, Mum had asked me to read aloud the last part of Dickens's *Christmas Carol*. When I got to Tiny Tim's God-bless-everyone bathos, Ganny cried, "Oh dear, I may vomit!"

Out the hotel window a Colorado morning of sunny blue skies and fresh mountain air was going about its business of being sensationally beautiful. Rolling out of bed, I rushed to the window, stuck out my head. Snowmelt dripped on it. Small birds were deciding to postpone migrations to Mexico until there was a reliable weather forecast. Indian summer? Rich odors of baking bread, piñon smoke, and horse manure came up to me from the muddy street. Whipped by gusts, drooping cottonwood branches released snowclumps on happily shrieking children who were chasing dogs away from a steamy garbage pile. Horsedrawn carriages rattled. An electrified trolleycar clanged. Men in shirtsleeves were unloading beer barrels from a wagon. I closed the window but kept the yellowed curtains parted so that I could relish my good fortune in being alive in a room fit for royalty.

Daddy would have complained about this room. The plaster ceiling had been generously shot full of bullet holes by some drunken galoot with a passion for home improvement. Hanging on pinkpapered walls were mildewed prints of locomotives with cow-catchers. The polished brass bedposts could have been perpendicular snakes perpetually digesting tennis balls. The

Imperial, moreover, had provided me with free toiletries. Using the enamel wash-basin and a bar of scented soap, I cleaned the grease and blood from my scalp and rubbed brilliantine into my hair. On my previous stay at the hotel, while Daddy was out every night curing Pia, I'd been left alone in the windowless basement accommodations he had booked. It featured a pisspot. Folded on hangers in a *trastero*, Mother Jones's clothes were soggy and reeked of sweat—but, because she was out traipsing for miles in pneumonia weather, sharing the peoples' squalor in a dispossessing land, they might have been regarded as unpleasant but added a special value to the room. She had left her umbrella behind, too, understanding that people in shantytowns might consider an old peddler with an umbrella to be uppity.

Rat-tat-tat!

The knocking on the door had to be, I hoped, the unionist, not the police and not the manager demanding payment. I opened the door to a gentleman in the corridor who was tall, grizzled, burnt-umber-skinned, wearing a black frock coat and a Lincolnesque stovepipe hat and peering at me with fierce but melancholy eyes behind spectacles.

"Tío Congo," he said, accompaning the introduction by tipping the hat. His voice was as solemn and measured as that of God in the King James Version. "Master Tree Penhallow, I presume?"

I stepped aside to let him in. Removing hat and ducking under the lintel, he went and seated himself in a chair by the window, folded legs and arms. "I don't beat around the bush," he deep-throated. "I spoke with Mother Jones early this mornin' and yesterday with Worthy Brother Dare over the telephone. You will be pleased to know that he has helped your mother to escape from the sanitorium and is escorting her to New York. To elude the wrath of the vengeful and blind, he and other brothers are serving as bodyguards. At the present time he, she, and your grandmother plans to take passage for France, safely conducted to Worthy Brother Dare's childhood abode thereabouts. In the meantime you are to lodge at his expense with Doña Luz at our boarding house. I takes you there after you, at my expense, have breakfast at Cousin Jack's. I trust that these messages will redound to your complete satisfaction?"

I was dumfounded. I sat on the edge of the bed, said "gee" to myself out loud. Not wishing to seem rude, I asked the first question which popped into my mind. "Why do you call Captain Dare 'worthy brother'?"

" 'Worthy Brother' is what I calls him," Tío Congo said, placing hand over heart. "He done joined the brotherhood of enlightenment about doors . . . Consider a door, how it divides. If you are on the inside looking out, you are excluding the outsiders. Conversely, if you are on the outside looking in, you are excluding the insiders. After a while, the insiders and the outsiders cease to comprehend the connections between them. They show each other, so to speak, the door. What is the solution? The only solution is for all-s the insiders to come outside and become outsiders, or for all-s the outsiders to come inside and become insiders. In short, no doors, man, no doors. Worthy Brother Dare and I have arrived at this universal philosophy together. Do I make myself clear?"

"Yes," I said. "Stuck in Life, we go mad until we finally realize we're in the same boat, but on the other side of doors there's relief."

Tío Congo looked at me dubiously. "I wonder what wrong with you," he said. "You tryin' to sass me? You ain't Boss Man?"

"Boss Man?"

"You don't know about Boss Man?"

"I'll not be mocked," I said.

"You play Boss Man. I play Boy."

"You mean it's a play?" Tío Congo's vernacular I enjoyed.

"I brung you the hat and coat," he said, " and we get you the whip and mustache. You don't have to say nothin'. You just naturally sassy, ain't that right?"

He was tease-smiling at me. "I don't mean to be sassy," I said.

"O.K. Let's see how the costume fit."

The frock coat was many sizes too large for me. The stovepipe hat came down around my ears. As soon as I had the costume on, though, I was glad to have been selected to act in the play. The door-stuff? I didn't know where his idea had come from, but it really did seem peculiarly bully. Since, I had concluded from books I had read, all people were physically and spiritually connected, they ought to be on the same side.

"Ecclesiastes 4," he let out like a preacher, divining my thought. *"Two are better than one because they have a good reward for their labor, for if they fall, the one will lift up his fellow, but woe to him that is alone when he falleth, for he hath not another to help him up . . ."* He was standing and stroking his beard in a quizzical manner before he finally clapped hands and exclaimed, "Perfect! You the meanest Boss Man I ever saw 'ceptin' the Laredo Desperado." He pronounced the next to the last syllable *ray* to make a rhyme: *La-ray-do Despe-ray-do.*

I took off the costume, returned it to him, and said I was worried about Mother Jones. "You spoke with her this morning? You saw her? Is she all right?"

"You have a heart," Tío Congo said with a slow nod and sat down with heavy sigh. "She worry everbodies, son. Cain't argy with her. Cain't tell her to lay down her sword and shield. She workin' for the Union, she be workin' for the people . . . Worthy Brother Dare, now, he calls me at the Union H.Q., and they brung me the message at Doña Luz's, to see you all right, only I don't knows where you at . . . About four o'clock this mornin'—we-all's fixin' to start the day—Mother Jones come to the house, like you know, dress like a peddler, and knock on the door . . . Already she been walkin' in the snow like to three mile from town. She on her way walkin' another five mile to the St. Mabyn's company-town . . . Doña Luz, she woe out as usual. Miss Golly, she combin' her momma's hair to make her feel good there in the kitchen where the wood stove is keepin' them warm before they starts breakfast . . . Well, Miss Golly answer the door and, I'm told, give Mother Jones the *abrazo* while Doña Luz dash upstair to put on a fresh apron. She wake me up. I join her downstairs for a spell. Mother, she tell me where you's at . . . Lots of folks think Mother is like Jesus. He was trampin' vagabond, too, didn't own no mill, didn't own no mine, didn't want for chi'rens to work for 40¢ a day, wanted to bless 'em, wanted to show 'em the light . . . Only, Tree, *only* I wonder what wrong with those Pharaoh people!"

Beads of perspiration appeared on Tío Congo's brow. He had to wipe it with a big linen handkerchief. I could count on the fingers of one hand the number of people who, I believed, really cared about me, but it seemed with the appearance of Mother Jones and Tío Congo that the arithmetic of my other hand would have to be employed. When I considered that Mum and Dare were traveling together and probably taking passage for France, the matchmaker in me was glad that Daddy and Pia would be divorced. I wanted Anna Maria Dautremond, maiden redux, and Kyle Deville Dare, bachelor redux, to kiss each other a lot and get hitched.

Cousin Jack's, where we went for breakfast, was crowded with miners who were, as Tío Congo put it, "coming off the graveyard." Quite a few of them greeted him as "buddy" and clapped him on the back. A waiter led us to a private booth and handed us a greasy menu. Some miners clinked glasses and bellowed, "Here's to crime! Long live prostitution!" Seated on a stool at the bar was a life-sized wax cowboy dressed up in Texas hat and leather vest and packing a six-shooter. He had been painted as ill-shaven and icy-blue-eyed. His eyes didn't blink, and his life-like body spooked me with its stillness.

"Laredo Desperado," Tío Congo whispered. "He's fooled plenty of folks. Notice how he's smiling? That's so's you scairt into getting another round of drinks . . . Pickhandle for me and a high-collared for Boss Man." Tío Congo's order was aimed at a waiter who also scribbled down what we would have for breakfast.

When the drinks arrived, "pickhandle" came in a small unlabeled bottle with a cork Tío Congo removed with crooked teeth. My "high-collared" was a beer imported from St. Louis.

"Tap'er light," he saluted.

"Tap'er light." I wasn't planning to fix my wagon, but I wasn't going to be on the wagon for the rest of my life, either.

133

Tío Congo's first swallow of pickhandle brought tears to his eyes. He smacked his lips. "Fine, mighty fine. Now take," he declared, "ten pounds of meal, ten pounds of sugar, three cakes of yeast, water and something for flavor—evaporated peaches will do. Cook the mixture, jug it. You can brew a gallon for fifty cents and sell it to the mine guards for fifteen dollars. When they're stone-dusted out of their minds, you go underground and sign up the boys for Union, nobody the wiser. Your mine owners back in New York, they may not be the devils Mother Jones make them out to be, but they is ig'rint for sho. They believe the boys don't want to mess with no Union. They think the boys are so proud of their independence they just love workin' twelve-hour shifts for nothin' and payin' to live in hovels. Funny thing is, soon's Union calls a strike, tens of thousands of them sposedly nonunion miners come out, tell the owners go to hell . . . Back when I was organizing, I liked that moonshine trick. Trouble was, word got around that Congo was a damn-fool organizer! You put organizer and cullud man together and you got dynamite!"

A couple of miners speaking in a Mediterranean language approached us. "How Mudder Jones?" one of them asked Tío Congo. Finding his King James Version form, he thundered, "Though the Pharaoh-worshippers may cry, 'Crucify her! Crucify her!,' the promise of the prophet will be fulfilled! The new Pentecost is a-comin'! The new Pentecost will come when every man shall have accordin' to his needs! She here, brothers, she here! A gret day is a-comin'. That the way with God's love. It's waitin'! It's waitin'!" Tío Congo dropped his voice and ended suddenly: "Because God is love—that all He is."

The miners, looking pleased with this bromide, disappeared into the crowd. The waiter served us plates of bacon, fried eggs, hominy grits, pancakes, hash browns and coffee. I didn't wait for Tío Congo to finish mumbling a blessing but shoveled food into my mouth before he could say, "Jesus's name, Amen."

Tío Congo shook his head at me. "You been rolled out thin for Boss Man . . . Now, he fat. He ain't livin' on the wind. He livin' off the fat of the land. To Boss Man, people is cattle and swine, but him, he live in a bed of roses and bask in the beautiful sunshine so's he can walk into Heaven. Boy, though, he the one that made that rose garden. Instead of getting some flowers, he get beat up, and that's the name of the play: *Kangaroo*. Didn't I done tell you about *Kangaroo?*" He slapped his forehead. "Don't tell me I done forgotted!"

"*Kangaroo?*"

"Sho," he said, wincing. "Pologize. Doña Luz, she's fine lady. Her and Don Fernando done raised a fine family. Everbody calls me '*Tío*' on account I lost my own family and gets one back as 'Uncle' . . . Now, where was I? Doña Luz . . . She cain't stand for nobody layin' around. Too many chores, too many people, too much sorrow. Don Fernando's dyin', spend mos' time in bed now. So. Worthy Brother Dare told me you-all's need some rest. So. How you gonna rest when Doña Luz, her man is dyin'? She see you restin', she put you on the road-gang! So. You tell her you workin' already when you ain't workin' because you the Boss Man in *Kangaroo*, gotta learn your lines even though you ain't got no lines . . . Now, you and me have the important parts. Miss Golly do the Bucket part. President do the rest. President is a draft horse. What do you think?"

"It sounds like a great play."

"You ain't joshin'?"

"I like the horse. His name."

"President is a real front of a horse," he said. "The one in Washington is just the rear end. That's a joke. I done me some actin'."

"You were an actor?"

"Sho."

"What did you do?"

"Shakespeare. . ."

He was in Chicago in a park near Lake Michigan, he told me. A young man not yet married, he scraped together a living by giving impromptu performances of speeches from Shakespeare that he had memorized when he was growing up in Virginia. One day a carnival came to the park. He spent hours watching a small merry-go-round. What impressed him was the way a draft horse turned the circular platform that made wooden horses go up and down on painted poles. For years he forgot about the merry-go-round. He married and settled down in Buxton, Iowa, in a community of Negro miners. Happening one day to see his fire-boss about to light a match down in a gassy mine, he lunged at him with a mucker and knocked the box of sulphur matches out of his hand, breaking his superior's wrist and preventing an explosion which could have killed hundreds of miners. For "insubordination" he was severely beaten and evicted from his company-owned house. After many years of working in mines scattered throughout the West, he was rewarded by Union in Indianapolis with the job of organizer and sent to the coalfields of southern Colorado. All was going well. He made a good salary. His wife worked as a seamstress and laundress in Los Tristes. Together they saved enough to buy a two-story house with six rooms and to provide each of their three little girls with a room of her own. One night, when he was working late at the Union office, his house was blown up and set on fire. His family was buried in the rubble. The murderer, an ex-con from Texas who was a mine guard at the St. Mabyn's and also member of the Guard, was brought before a military tribunal and acquitted. Tío Congo became a boarder at the big house owned by Don Fernando and Doña Luz.

"Way back from the big house, past the corrals and pastures and near where the sandstone bluffs begins to rise from the plain," Tío Congo explained, "I used to go and set a spell with the miseries. It was natural amphitheater, that spot, 200-foot cliffs risin' on three sides. I was already thinkin' of puttin' in some bleachers and makin' a baseball diamond for kids. It might could also be an outdoor Shakespeare theater. One day I notices in the exack same middle of that amphitheater a piece of a barn door layin' there rottin'. I figure maybe it blowed there during a torne'da. I went and looked, movin' the door aside. What do I see but a shaft goin' down on an old wooden ladder. I clumb down that ladder. I'm in a small room, got shelves stocked with cans and candles. What it was, was an old hideaway from Injun attack.'

"Well, right there the play comes to me in the mind's eye. First, a draft horse goes round and round this hole. There's a steel headframe over the mouth of it. The headframe has a pulley wheel. You loop a chain over this wheel and puts a bucket on that chain. The horse makes the bucket fall down the shaft, collect some coal, shoot back up with it and gets the bucket to tip the coal back into the shaft. Like that merry-go-round in Chicago, you got you a continuous make-believe mining operation, only you got to have someone down in the old hideaway, fillin' the bucket. That's Bucket. Miss Golly play that. O.K.?"

"What?"

"O.K?"

"Yeah." I was so appalled by the story of his family, how they were blown up in his house, that I hadn't been concentrating on staging. I did have a vague idea that the "operation" was meant to be endless. A full bucket was forever drawn up and its contents forever dumped back in the hole from which coal had supposedly been collected.

"Now this where you come in," Tío Congo went on. "Before President—that's one of the horses on the farm, or did I tell you it's a farm?—before President goes round and round the hole, Boss Man, wearin' the hat and coat and carryin' a whip, pops out of the hole, followed by Boy who ain't got no shoes or shirt, his body greased up and shinin' on account of sweat. Boss Man whips Boy. Boss Man chains Boy to President. Boy is chained facin' the horse, his back to the direction the horse gonna move. Boss Man cracks the whip. President goes. Boy has to run back'ards to keep from being trampled to death. He limps, coughs, staggers, slumps, and fine'ly, when Boss Man halts President, Boy leans back in his chains like the Crucifixion. Now the climax.'

"Union," Tío Congo leaned forward and said in a whisper.

"Union," I repeated almost unconsciously. My jaw was droping. The Laredo Desperado, the waxen dummy at the bar, had just

137

moved! With one arm raised, he had tilted back his Texas hat; with the other arm he had extracted a cigarillo from a vest pocket and was twisting around on his stool in order to have the bartender light a match. Cigarillo lit, the Laredo Desperado exhaled smoke, swiveled about. He was staring at Tío Congo with blue eyes made to kill.

"Boss Man," Tío Congo was saying, "let Boy go from the chains. Boss Man drives Boy, whipping him, back down the shaft. Suddenly up Boss Man pops from the shaft, pursued by Boy—because now Boy has him a big sign which reads UNION! When he cotches up with Boss Man, he beats him over the haid with that sign. Boy says to spectators, 'We have the same rights to fight back as did them rebels of 1776!' Then he mounts President and rides around like Buffalo Bill! What you think?"

I hadn't taken my eyes off the Laredo Desperado. He had slipped from his stool and was dancing spur-jingling feet toward us.

"Mr. Congo," I said.

"What you think?"

"Mr. Congo." Finally Tío Congo saw what I saw: the Laredo Desperado had stopped next to our booth, cigarillo dangling from lips, eyes firing ice bullets at Tío Congo who stared directly back at the Laredo Desperado and said in measured, KJV voice, "The sheep must learn to eat wolves."

Whereupon the Laredo Desperado walked slowly away and Tío Congo ate breakfast.

Not long afterwards we left Cousin Jack's and went to U.S. Livery to collect Tío Congo's horse and buggy. I be dog, Dawn Antelope, as we arrived, was just leaving the stables, mounted on a pony and guiding Natural Selection with a rope. I flashed on to the way it must have been, Dare's leaving the roan in town in order to grab the train. As for Dawn Antelope, we exchanged glances but no words. I considered asking him what had happened to Daddy, Shiflit, Pia and Gwilym, but curiosity, which killed the cat, just wasn't my runneth-over cup in spite of the way people liked to talk stories to me.

As we were crossing the river and headed north toward sandstone bluffs, I did, though, blurt out pent-up questions. "Why does the Laredo Desperado pretend he's a dummy? Why does he hate you so much?"

Tío Congo shook his head sadly. "The evil are not so," he said. "They are like the chaff which the wind driveth away. Maybe's you-all's too young to notice, but evil folks play clown to show everbodies, 'Lookit me, cain't cotch me.'" . . . The Desperado, now, he was in the calaboose in Texas. Up here, he's a suck and a mine guard, likes to set still as death around bars, doin' his scary, not missin' a thing. Folks think he dead as Billy the Kid, but he, mostly, ain't never died . . . To answer your second question, he hates me because I'm a black man he ain't kilt yet."

While I was mulling over this reply Tío Congo cleared throat and declared to snow-drifted fields,

> "When we are born, we cry that we are come
> To this great stage of fools."

"*King Lear*," I said. "Act Four, Scene Six."

Tío Congo once again glanced at me with expression of doubt. "I know'd there was somethin' wrong with you," he said.

"What," I pressed, curious in spite of myself, "did you mean when you said the Laredo Desperado hadn't killed you yet?"

" 'Pends," he replied. "Like I say, some say he hates cullud folks, but others say he wants to kill me on account of my organizin' . . . Why do you think Mother Jones got off the train a mile from the station? It wasn't reporters she was dodgin'. She gets death threats all the time . . . If you're organizin' for Union, someone out there is bound to be down on you. Maybe he's got a gun. Maybe he'll stop you in the street, pretend that you draws a gun on him so's he can kill you in 'self-defense' . . . Maybe he's such a coward he lays sticks of dynamite under your house to blow you and your family to hell!"

"Is that what happened?" I asked after a pause. "Are you saying the Laredo Desperado did it?"

Tío Congo seemed to be looking a thousand miles away in the sky. "I lost my best friend when I lost my wife. I lost my chi'rens, too . . . He the one. But who really did it? Take any trail. Sooner or later you arrives at the door of the rich mans in New York, the one who hates Union. Corporation done it. Mr. Alpheus Woodbridge done it."

Chapter Eight

A Chinook wind was melting snow except in the higher
elevations of the Sangre de Cristo, but the ice on our muddy
road was solid. Mother Jones had walked on it about three
in the morning. She could have broken a leg or a hip and frozen to
death. Few people even knew she was in Los Tristes. Tío Congo
had not been expecting her at his boarding house. The more I
thought about her, the more I realized she had actually risked her
life for me. Dare had asked her to help me, and she sent Tío Congo
to collect me and have me safely settled at Doña Luz's.

I asked him to tell me more about the place where I would
be living until Dare returned from France. We were going, he
explained, to a *ranchito* which had belonged to the Medina family
for more than a century. When Don Fernando's people had come up
the Chihuahua Trail to ancient Chimayo in northern New Mexico
Territory, his great-great-grandfather had been granted lands by
the King of Spain in what was now the New Mexican *llano* and in
southern Colorado. After the Mexican War ended in 1848 Anglos
had tried to ignore such royal grants. The original Medina *hacienda*,
comprising vast hectares, a villa, and a small army of *vaqueros*,
had dwindled in size to the present *ranchito* of a hundred acres for
raising cattle and sheep and for planting gardens and orchards. The
original adobe villa had been burned down during an Indian raid.
Nothing remained of it but a palisade of mud bricks poking up from
a cow pasture. Tío Congo, himself, in order to contribute to family

income, was selling dairy products in the coal-company towns. The present Medina house was an ungainly, two-story whitewashed frame structure in the Mexican style with a second-floor balcony the length of one side and curved iron bars fronting windows and entrances. Numerous bedrooms once intended for couples in the habit of breeding large families had become accommodations for boarders. In addition to the main house there were stables, barns, outhouses and a wash-house. The *ranchito* depended for survival more upon income from members of the family who worked in the mines than upon subsistence-level farming.

"Doña Luz is one fine lady deservin' of the old *hacienda* way of life," said Tío Congo. A sorrowful look clouded his face. "She's got fourteen mouths to feed almost all by her lonesome. That ain't countin' you and a couple Irish stable hands. Why, her iron stove is so big it could do the cookin' for a hundred folks on an ocean liner! And the dinin' room's like one I usta see at a college in Virginia. Ceiling's low. She has her a couple wagon wheels slung over the table, and candles in the wheels. That's plumb pretty. Only guess what that lady has on the table all for a bunch of stiffs like me? Table cloth, that what, starched damask table cloth, napkins to match. She got her real silverware, meanin' polishing time for the girls, and she told me the chinaware is from England and glasses from Germany. If that old table ain't set right by Miss Golly and Miss Carmencita like it's for rich folks, Doña Luz raise all kind of hurricanes! . . . One more thing."

Tío Congo leaned sideways to spit, went on. Don Fernando, determined to pay off his father's gambling debts as a matter of honor, had gone to work in the mines as a young man. Now in his forties he was dying from black lung disease. Unable to suck enough oxygen to climb stairs, he had the living room for his infirmary and also for his studio. To keep himself, as Tío Congo put it, "happified," Don Fernando was painting pictures. The living room was crowded with his canvases. "Seem like," Tío Congo said, "he need that color to make up for all those years he spent in blackness so black no self-respectin' devil in Hell would tolerate it . . . That's another frazzlement for Doña Luz: she has to order canvases and brushes and oils and frames and easels from Kansas City so's he can empty his haid of things that look like a cow done pissed in snow."

Doña Luz had "a *mestiza* strain in the Andalusian," one introduced to her family in the wild mountain hinterlands north of Santa Fe before the Pueblo Revolt in the late seventeenth century. No one in her family had ever gone beyond the "third reader" in school. She, however, not only had finished high school in Santa Fe but also had graduated from a Normal college in Oklahoma and come to Los Tristes to teach pupils, ages six-to-twelve, in the St. Mabyn's company-town school. Because the school's tall cedars were being strangled by myrtle vines, a "handsome *vaquero* and *caballero*" from the honored Medina family had volunteered to come, climb the trees, and trim dead branches. He married her. They had four children, eldest, Adonio, known as "Nono," the next, Aladino, both now veteran miners. Sixteen-year-old Carmen, known as "Carmencita," and thirteen-year-old Golondrina, known as "Golly," had defied Doña Luz's wishes for them to stay in school and were helping with chores.

"It's part of good manners out here not to be curious about folks' past," Tío Congo said about the boarders. Rusty and Curly, "just boys from Back East," were "typical bindle stiffs roamin' the West like tumbleweeds," five others were immigrants "hopin' to get rich and go back to the old countries," Orlando from Italy, Milenko from Zagreb, Willito from Mexico, and two from Greece, Nick and Kiki. "We-all-s get along," Tío Congo said, "on account we don't talk too much. You got three kinds of English with them miners: survival English for the mines, decency English for the house, and cussin' English for brothels, bars, and baseball. . . You got you a problem, son, same's me: poetry. You better lay low in the Shakespeare bushes. Someone's like to believe you got a cobweb in your britches and whup the tar outa you. Bad enough as it is."

"What do you mean?"

"I mean Doña Luz," Tío Congo replied. "Worthy Brother Dare guarantees boardin' and lodgin' for you. Mother Jones puts in a good word for you. *But.*"

"But what?"

"Doña Luz thinks ever' natural-born white boy from north of the Arkansas River has violated the treaty of Guadalupe Hildago, meaning you must of stole the land from her in 1848. Number two, you're an outcast, number three, you're a pauper, number four, you're a greenhorn, and, number five and worst of all, you're just about a teenager, meaning don't mess with Miss Golly. You ain't a cunger, is you?"

"Cunger?" Repeating his word, I grabbed at its meaning: conjurer.

"If you got the witch power, you cain't he'p yourself, man. I knows that. I'm plumb glad to claim you as my friend. But the man with the witch power is got to give it to a woman. That's the Lord's truth, and Miss Golly is a woman, or almost. Of course, to get your power she has to sleep with the Devil ever' month at the time of the wanin' moon. Don't stick around when the moon is bad. Zat right?"

"That's right," I said. I had no idea what he was talking about.

Tío Congo's advice about Doña Luz was for me to show deference toward her rebellious, restless, and dissatisfied spirit. Hating settled life, he explained, she wanted it to have a purpose, a goal. Women in particular fell into the trap of living all days as the same, marrying, having babies, going on their knees for scrubbing, staring blankly into the road ahead. There had to be more to life than that, even though men, once married, settled down to work and family as if these were enough, hardly noticing that women in the house "had the miseries."

"That lady has a fire burnin' inside her," Tío Congo said in a tone of admiration. We were crossing railroad tracks and approaching what looked to be the *ranchito* he had described. "When we's young, we set on the back porch of a summer evenin', dreamin' adventures. When we is settled down, our dreams are forgotten . . . That lady wants everbody to grow up different from the people who live only to work. Trouble is, Don Fernando is too sick to work. Miss Carmencita and Miss Golly quit school. Nono and Aladino are making good money in the mine, but what happens if they have to go out on strike or get kilt? Doña Luz is workin' herself to the bone to let people see the importance of dreamin' big, but nobodies goin' nowhere nohow."

While I was listening to Tío Congo, an image of Mr. Lily, my schoolteacher in Colorado Springs, popped into my head. He was speaking to us kids in the auditorium. I expected to be chloroformed by his voice because it had squeaks in it of the domesticated mouse variety. On that occasion, too, since he was from Maine and was speaking about sailing, he was addressing an audience of landlubbers born in the Rockies with no knowledge of that subject. "One hand for the boat, one hand for yourself," I had heard Mr. Lily say just as I was about to visit Xanadu. I kept listening to his message in spite of myself. We all lived in a crowded ship in dangerous waters. Lest we be swept overboard, we had to hang on to available ropes and masts. If we the sailors contributed nothing to the ship, it would founder. But also if we ignored our survival instinct and cared only for the ship our journey would be boring. Mr. Lily's message surfaced now. Dare was paying my keep. Mum hadn't raised me to do manual labor, but Doña Luz's "ship" was in need of "sailors" willing to pitch in. I had to strip off the vulgar, easy, indulgent bourgeois self in order to grow and make my life my own.

Tío Congo drew the buggy to a halt outside stables. Two thin, ill-shaven men in filthy overalls immediately began to load the buggy with large cans of milk. I swung down to ground. Tío Congo, who remained seated with the reins in hands until the buggy was loaded, finally whipped his horse into a trot and rattled out of sight. He had done his job getting me fed and delivered and now had better things to do than worry about an invader, an outcast, a pauper, a greenhorn and a teenager.

"Need any help?" I asked the Irish stable hands. "Got an extra shovel?"

They looked at each other in mock amazement. "Shovel?" one said. "Wot's a shovel? Appen he fancies a mooker?"

Having no wish to pick a quarrel about shovels and muckers, I decided to rest until my labor was appreciated. I went to the back door of the house and stood looking in at a large kitchen which smelled of floor wax. A small woman was bending over a big stove, stirring a pot. She was wearing a soiled apron and had her hair piled high on her head, her gown a flowered cotton print, a black silk shawl draped over her shoulders. She was talking to herself. "There'll be no more sorrow here," she was vowing vehemently. "God and I can do anything . . . To think Mother Jones went out this morning . . . Weather wasn't fit to be out in except for crows and Methodists . . . *¡Cristo rey!*"

She saw me. Her trim figure, finely cut nose, and dark eyes under dark eyebrows gave her a youthful, classy appearance. The wistful, tired face, clenched lips, and big-veined hands of a forty-year-old lady, however, seemed to belong to a charwoman in her fifties. She studied me as if I were the sorriest *gringo* on the planet. When I took off my hat, Mum having taught me that a gentleman does this for ladies and houses, she relaxed and said without any apparent tone of underlying resentment, "I see there's good grain among the chaff. *Bienvenido, señor* Tree. Please excuse my not having on a clean apron. We'll get Golondrina to show you around the place."

I mumbled thanks, relieved that the Treaty of Guadalupe Hildago was not yet going to be presented as evidence against me.

Doña Luz—this lady had to be she—looked me sternly in the eye. "I don't need to tell you," she said, "we're holding to the right around here. There is a time when a girl blossoms into a woman and there is a time when a woman becomes very nervous."

"Very nervous," I repeated as if I'd been hypnotized.

"When she's very nervous, she wants to get married."

"Yes, ma'am."

"We don't waste our lives around here. We learn."

"Yes, ma'am."

"If you see Golondrina becoming very nervous, you're not to pretend you're blind to consequences, understand? 'The eye that does not see bespeaks the heart that does not feel.' Don Fernando says that. He is my husband. In our culture the man is like a god."

Not wishing to pick a quarrel about cultures and gods, I placed a hand over my heart and put highfalutinness into my speech to show her *Discreción*. "Please convey to Don Fernando my greeting and solicitations and the honor accorded to me by his reception of a poor *gringo* into his beautiful home through the grace of his beautiful wife. Truly, my heart is full of feeling."

Doña Luz looked at me as if I might be daft, but I thought I detected an *¡olé!*—a "bravo"—in a smile coyly hidden behind a mask of tyranny.

Hitherto I've made scattered references to Spanish language and culture in the American Southwest. In what we would now call elementary and junior high schools Spanish had been part of my curriculum. I had a smattering or "bonehead" grasp of it. Spanish culture was virtually the same from what had once been the Louisiana Purchase all the way to Tierra del Fuego. The Purchase meant acquisition by the United States of some trans-Mississippian lands, and Anglo conquests from Texas to California had been more or less completed about forty years before I was born. Finally—in contradiction to stereotyping of peoples "south of the border"—those of us raised in the West knew there was a refinement among Mexican-Americans which in certain quarters was clearly of a superior kind, pretensions of greedy Yankee conquerors notwithstanding.

Tío Congo, then, had been right. The deference he recommended I show to Doña Luz was actually what I already extended to Hispanic peoples generally. I was the *gringo* in land that was theirs since before the Pilgrim Fathers landed in New England. In trying to adapt myself to the ways of the Medina family, I may have been clumsy and insensitive, but I did understand the importance of *honor* and *discreción, familia* and *machismo*. For instance, in order to be properly admitted as a boarder, I had, I knew, to be evaluated by the male proprietor. Don Fernando was dying and

Doña Luz was the power behind the throne, but he could still add to my collection of banishments.

Doña Luz led me down a dark and chilly hallway and knocked on a pitted oak door. We were met by the sound of violently raspy coughing, one intermixed with a braying, high-pitched wheezing. Not having heard its like since my last visit to the Sun Palace, I writhed inwardly at Don Fernando's suffering. When the sound subsided, Doña Luz rushed into the living-room-cum-infirmary-cum-studio, approached a four-poster bed, and threw her arms around a strikingly handsome man there with a shrill cry of "*¡Pobrecito!*"

I glanced away. High-backed leather chairs and thick black oak tables had been shoved into a corner to make room for easels. Although the room was cold—Tío Congo had warned me that smoke from fires and candles tortured Don Fernando as did fried food, scented soaps, and ladies' perfume—there was plenty of sunlight pouring in through barred windows and being reflected in mirrors with gilt frames. Apparently the intense smells of turpentine and oils which permeated the room were not poisons but aphrodisiacs for an artist. I stood at a distance from where he was sitting up in that bed canopied with white linen. Even a cursory glance told me that his paintings were fanciful. A scarlet bull with uprolled eyes of a saint and a chile pepper for a penis was charging an enormous orchid with pubic hair. Against a black background the red explosion of a volcano was throwing pairs of white dice into the clouds above a village in which peasants wearing *sombreros* were beseeching the heavens for succor.

Doña Luz came, tilted her head toward the bed, and said, "Don Fernando would like to speak with you. He tires easily. Don't be long."

We approached the bed together.

I still half expected to see a Sun Palace lunger with feverish eyes, trembling, chalk-white lips, and hollow cheeks, and I did, but Don Fernando's shoulders were still broad, eyes still bright, his flowing dark hair and neatly trimmed mustache just beginning to be edged with gray. The row of gold teeth he showed when he gripped my extended hand was like nothing I'd ever seen before.

"Welcome, *señor* Tree," he said warmly. "Never mind the *vieja*, the old woman, here. She likes to boss the men around, is that not true, *mi corazón, preciosa mía?*"

Doña Luz looked at her husband adoringly and sighed the kind of sigh which expresses a feeling of being blessed.

Don Fernando spoke directly to me as if her presence was barely to be tolerated. "You have observed my gold teeth? One winter, my horse slipped on the ice. I fall off and hit my mouth against a stone. Along comes this *bruja* here, this ugly old witch, and she makes the fire. Sacred Heart of Jesus, the fire thawed my face and made my teeth fall out! And what does she say? She said, 'Go get yourself some solid plated gold teeth. At least everybody will think you are worth something even if it's only in your grave.' What a terrible woman she is! She has no heart!"

Doña Luz placed a hand over her heart. "You have to develop a hard heart," she said to the ceiling, "to live with an artist."

"Luzita," said Don Fernando without looking at her, "I wake up this morning so happy in my heart."

"You always say that." She flushed pink as she spoke.

Don Fernando, with a wink toward me, cried, "There, you see! She insults me when there is only kindness and happiness in my heart!" He turned his gaze to Doña Luz. "I am so glad that I am going before you. If you were the first to go, I couldn't live without you. But you are strong. Your soil may not be the best, but Hell doesn't show through."

"*Tesoro,*" Doña Luz murmured, placing her hand on top of Don Fernando's. His pale hand was smeared with paint of many colors. She aimed her gaze at him, her words at me, saying quietly, "A year ago he could slowly walk six miles a day. Six months later he could manage just two miles. Then he had trouble walking from room to room. Now he spends most days in bed but rises to paint when I'm not looking . . . Stubborn as a mule! Every evening I would fight back tears as I watched him crawl up the front steps after a day in the mine. He would sit on the front step, catch his breath, crawl two

149

steps, and sit again. He tried to hurry, believing I wouldn't see him."

"I knew I'd pay for breathing all that dust," Don Fernando said in his raspy voice. "I just didn't think it'd be this quick . . . You don't think too much about your breathing when you go into the mine, but once it gets bad you realize you made a mistake. By then you already have the black lung. It's too late. You get dust in your throat. It's dry, scratchy. You vomit because you can't get enough air. You start aching between your shoulder blades, you cough so much."

"He came home," Doña Luz said, "got in his chair and fell asleep. I'd have to wake him up to feed him dinner. He'd go right back to sleep. His hair was wet with sweat. His face was red as a *ristra*. He would gasp as if he'd been punched . . . One night his chest hurt so badly he thought he was having a heart attack. The next day our doctor said his heart was fine but his lungs were all but destroyed. Our children were called together and told he loved them. He wanted nothing left unsaid. When he is painting, he loses all sense of time."

"Tesorito," said Don Fernando. He tightened his grip on her hand. She leaned in. They kissed. I turned and wandered among the paintings. Not all of them were as fanciful as the two I had glimpsed from a distance. There were still lifes of fruits and flowers, landscapes of adobe houses against red and gray-purple mountains highlighted by orange sunsets. Several paintings were impressions of Pueblo Indian ceremonials. One of these showed parti-colored, shawled figures kneeling in a little white-washed church while a procession of women carried the Virgin and San Gerónimo out from an adobe pyramid while two strings of naked young men were dancing in a plaza.

I paused to gaze at Don Fernando's paint box. When I lifted it in my hands, my spirit seemed to plunge into the colors. Even if I studied and achieved some knowledge of art, I would probably never cross the mystical line between capable work and great work. Nevertheless I thirsted for this work and knew I would not erect a brick wall to prevent me from undertaking it. Mastery might elude me, but, like Don Fernando, I would strive to make beauty my own.

"I see you like my paint box." Don Fernando's voice interrupted my thoughts. I went to stand at his bedside. Doña Luz had left the room.

"Yes, sir, Don Fernando. You are a wonderful painter!"

"Oh," he said, "I don't say or think I am doing masterpieces. If a thing is not done, I am joyful because I love doing it. Do the great works of art come to us as amusement only, or do they change your nature and give you a vision? Excuse me."

A fit of coughing convulsed him. Before me, clenching gold teeth from pain of coughing, sat, in reality, a young man, young and dying. His fit over, he shrugged as if to apologize. "Isn't it funny," he said, "we can't see the big hoop the sun goes round on? I once heard an immigrant boy from Finland ask that question. It was so beautiful, his believing that the sun goes around the earth on a hoop. You see, he was profoundly right. There *is* a big hoop! Sometimes after a rain you can see that hoop in the sky, all different colors . . . *Pues, amigo* . . . Luz has gone to fetch Golondrina, that she may introduce you to your new home . . . I am going to paint for a little while. I have to get across the quality of this beautiful day on canvas before the sun goes down . . ."

The girl in the kitchen was white and resembled in her dress the Mexican schoolgirls at home on the Cinco. She, as they, favored the bright red skirt, the white bodice, flowers in long dark hair, arms and legs bare. Golondrina also wore fine black leather *botas*. She fixed me with a domineering glance, then flung me a sly smile. Perhaps, I thought, she takes pleasure in seeing a boy at a nonplus.

"Tío Congo had to put off the milk deliveries because of you," she said.

Not wishing to pick a quarrel, I said nothing.

"Did he tell you who we are?"

"Yes," I said. "Your family has been around since Peter, Paul , and Moses played ring around the roses."

"You're funny." She swept me with a scornful look. "Did you really run away from home?"

"Actually," I said. I wanted to get on her good side.

"Neat," she said. She stared at me a while longer. "I hate my brothers," she said.

'Why?"

"I dunno. I hate school."

"But you're helping out at home," I said. "Nothing wrong with that. Do you want me to talk funny?"

She giggle-smiled. "Talk funny."

"Yessum, I be dog if'n you ain't the purdies' gal I ever done see in them thar hills, Miss Golly."

"Right nice a-yawl, honey," Golly shot back. "Whyn't we go spit in the pie-yanna?"

She was fast on the draw. Trouble was, I was figuring, if I fell in love with her, would I have to forget Scampy? I followed Golly out of the kitchen and into the yard. "Tío Congo," I offered to Small Talk, "wants you to play the part of Bucket in his play."

"That," she said, scornful again. "I know some words that rhyme with Bucket. The boys in the stables say them all the time. What's your favorite cuss word?"

"I dunno," I dodged after some self-censorship. "My daddy says 'Judas Priest'."

"Your daddy is sad," she said. "Tío Congo is really sad. That play is nothing but a dream. I suppose he told you about his fraternal organization?"

"Is that what he means when he calls someone 'Worthy Brother' so-and-so? He mentioned a brotherhood."

"Well, the Knights of Piss, or whatever they're called, refused to admit Tío Congo into their brotherhood because he's black. To get even, he dreams up his own fraternity, deciding who he will admit. Ask me, he's lived in his make-believe world ever since they blew up his house, killed his wife and children."

"He told me about the Laredo Desperado," I said but stopped myself before explaining what she probably knew already, that

152

anyone connected to the Union, and I assumed that the Medinas and the boarders were all members of it, was in constant danger.

We rounded the house and went to sit in rocking chairs on the front porch. The American flag there was fluttering in a breeze. Railroad tracks gleamed about a hundred yards away.

"Tío Congo's a Jefferson," Golly said.

Not having the foggiest idea what she was talking about, I waited for her explanation.

There were former slaves in Albemarle County, Virginia, she began, slaves believed to be descended from President Thomas Jefferson. Although Congo was raised in Prince Edward County about seventy miles away from Charlottesville, his owner regarded him as a "Jefferson" and gave him special privileges. One of these was to teach the "boy" to read and write and then to recite passages from Shakespeare and the Bible. As the owner was a professor at one of the oldest colleges in America, and as the "boy" lived in a whitewashed cabin just off campus, close enough to the professor's antebellum brick house to do housework and yardwork there easily—and to pursue his studies there at night without much fear of detection—no one suspected that laws forbidding the teaching of reading and writing to slaves were being broken. Golly went on, saying it was the custom of Virginia "gentlemen" attending the college to go hunting and drinking all night in the surrounding wilderness, returning to campus at dawn in time to stack rifles outside their classrooms before resuming studies. It was on one of these occasions that some "gentlemen" who were passing by the professor's house at dawn overheard a booming voice reciting Shakespeare by candlelight. Upon closer inspection of the house they saw Congo in the kitchen with the professor and came to the conclusion that "both should be legally hanged." However, because the "gentlemen" were Virginians and sportsmen, they left a note on the professor's door, advising him that he had twenty-four hours to hie himself and his "boy" out of Virginia, whereupon owner and slave saddled horses and later turned up in western Pennsylvania. There the professor freed Congo and decamped. Congo began a coalmining career as a trapper boy. Whenever he was asked if he had a surname, he mentioned that he had been told he was "Jefferson," but he didn't try to explain a direct link to the President of that name.

Whether Tío Congo was a "Jefferson" or not the story of his owner irritated me. Injustice accounted for most of my irritation, but something else was bothering me. I just couldn't put my finger on it. If Tío Congo was admired and respected, as he clearly was, by Union leaders, by Mother Jones, by Dare, and by the Medina family, his probable blood-relationship to a slave-owning President might have influenced people's opinion of him, but he had earned respect on his own. Had the professor risked his life to educate a slave "boy" because a Jefferson deserved privilege, or was there a less benevolent reason?

"I really like your father," I said, changing the subject, not expecting much of a reply. Golly, as I was discovering, was a streaky storyteller.

"Once a miner, always a miner," she said. "And a miner's life ain't worth five cents. Know what I mean? I don't want to be like my mother, getting married, having kids, working myself to the bone. Know what I mean? If there was another miner as wonderful as my father, I might change my mind because he is intelligent, not like my brothers . . . My father? He was promoted to fire boss after four years. One time when he was in charge of a mine at night, he left for a minute, putting a *gringo* in charge. The *gringo* lit a match. The mine blew up, killing nine men. Another time when a mine blew up, the explosion crippled my father's feet for a couple years. The mine owner paid the hospital bill, nothing else. My mom had to sell off some of our land to pay folks to sow and harvest. She also bought Papá an expensive pair of red boots to cover his bad feet and show everyone he is a *caballero*. My father went back to the mines because somebody has to inspect the roof. It only takes a piece of rock to get loose, and everything collapses, and damp, or gas, is the worst for blow-ups . . . My father worked in Utah, used to be forty-feet coal there, high coal, and when they pulled the

154

switch to blast out the shot inside, that mine blew up, killing three hundred men. It was a trap mine, a gassy mine. If you haven't got ventilation in there, you have to put up canvas to get some fresh air in and all that dead air out. And the black damp is a gas that's just dead air, no air at all. You better get out of there, mister! Or you're going to die!'

"I tell you one thing, buddy, it was tough. When my grandfather died, he owed a Texas cattleman thousands of dollars for gambling. One thing you better know about Papá: honor is all. He has sacrificed his life to honor, he martyred himself to beat the devil. Papá decided to pay off that debt if it took him the rest of his life. He went to the mine. He started at the age of thirteen, outside, picking rock out of the coal. Then he went on the tipple. When he was fourteen, he went underground, opening canvas doors for the trips, going in and picking up loads and taking empties . . . He broke a leg, too. He got caught between the bumpers. He was in a hurry. He went to couple a car blind. It got him.'

"How many years has it made since my mom was a young girl without a care in the world? After she married, she had to steel her heart every minute while my father was down in a mine, steel her heart because she's thinking the mine whistle's gonna blow, my father killed, nothing left of him but a grease spot seven miles underground . . . If there's a strike almost everybody's ruined. Know what I mean? If there's a strike, though, my family's lots better off than most families. We take in boarders. We run dozens of cows in the barn. Tío Congo sells the milk, five cents for a pint, ten cents for a quart. With a little measure he figures the difference between a nickel and a dime. . . I guess I'm supposed to show you the place. Then I have to help Mamá in the kitchen."

"Wait," I said. "You left something out of Tío Congo's story. Do you remember what it was? Was that professor always so kind and noble?"

Golly looked at me with what seemed to be respect. 'Yeah," she said, rising from her chair. "Tío Congo's a game fish. You got to play him along because he doesn't like to whine and complain and put people in a bad light . . . There was a reason the professor was teaching him to recite from Shakespeare and the Bible. And it wasn't because Congo was a 'Jefferson' but because he had a good memory and a great voice, and these were worth a bunch of money . . . The professor sold Congo's services at outlying plantations. Congo had to go wherever there was a funeral and someone was needed to preach a sermon. If he couldn't preach, he could sure rattle off some Bible and throw in a little Shakespeare for good measure. For every funeral service, Congo earned a dollar—not for himself but for the professor. . . You're right. The professor was preaching equality while making a profit off slavery, but in the end he did right, setting Congo free."

We toured the *ranchito*. I'd seen farms before, most recently Homesteader's, but Golly's guidance was increasing my appreciation for the sheer amount of labor involved in farming plus sending men to the mines. I was a sucker for picturesque red barns, mustard-brown haystacks, yellow wood piles, sheds made of scrap lumber, tar-papered stables, a rounded adobe *horno* for baking bread, glazed blue Mexican pots and sheep moving in slow white patches. Doña Luz, then everyone else, rose about four in the morning. Men returning from back-breaking work—comparable to being bent under a kitchen table to swing a pick for twelve or more hours—retired to bed after bathing themselves and eating supper, but the women were seldom finished with chores before midnight.

Golly on the *horno*: "Mamá bakes twenty pounds of flour after it is rolled into dough, yeast added. After removing the red-hot coals, she puts the dough into the *horno* to get cooked."

Golly on cows in the barn: "We make cheese and churn butter from leftover milk."

Golly on the well: "We used to, before I was born, have to hitch up a wagon, go and haul our water from the river. After my brothers went into the mines, my father took out a loan from the bank so we could get a well drilled. Not counting watering the livestock, we have more than a dozen people needing water to drink, water for laundry, water for baths in wash-tubs. We have to heat laundry and bath water. The pit clothes are caked with mud and coal dust every day. The sheets and towels and table linens have to be washed every day and most of those, plus regular clothes, ironed. When we put the pit pants on the clothes-line to dry, they get frozen stiff ... We don't have an ice-house. We sling the perishable foods on strings and lower them into the well."

Golly on the outhouses: "Them's two-holers. You have to use Monkey Ward catalog papers quick's you can, or, woe's me, your butt gets frost-bit. When I was a tiny girl, I almost fell into the chloride of lime."

I asked her if she missed school.

"Reckon," she said with a wistful smile. "I miss baseball. The hot corner is best. Know what I mean? You have to keep your glove close to the ground. You have to look the ball into your glove.'

"I'd really like to do what Mamá did, finish school, go away to Normal. Like I said, I don't want to get married. I would rather lick the horseshit out of the stables than lose a baby to diphtheria or scarlet fever . . . Sometimes I dream of being down at the river with a boyfriend. There are thousands of fireflies there. He scoops up a fistful of fireflies and spreads them over my face . . . My Mamá needs all the help she can get. I scrub floors and dust the shelves and wash the lamp globes. I fill the lamps with coal-oil. I set the dinner table. I help wash dishes. Carmencita chops wood and heats water and gathers eggs and goes down yonder to the tracks to pick up lumps of coal. I help her put the chickens in the coop at night where the foxes and coyotes can't get to them. We stir the vats of lye soap. We help Mamá with spinning and carding, and she's learning us needlework ... Did you know, she used to set up Saturday nights sewing so's we could have things to wear to next week's school?   The man down to the store saves her all the flour sacks he has after putting the flour in big barrels and shaking the sacks out and stacking them up. Mamá will go down to his store and have her a stack *that* high of flour sacks. She makes us underpants from them. Did you know we have MORE PILLSBURY'S BEST printed on our behinds?"

Golly continued to talk as we strolled. "She gets so tired, my Mamá. Either midnight or before four the next morning I make her set in her rocking chair in the kitchen while I comb her hair. She has beautiful hair. After a while, I go, 'Mamá, why don't you just close your eyes and stay warm by the fire?' I slip her shoes off. I comb. She sleeps. Couple minutes. Then she's up. Fries mountains of eggs. Stirs up pots of mush. Boils a gallon of coffee. That's just breakfast. She won't let the men leave for the mine until they each one has him a lunch bucket filled with a meat sandwich and a fruit pie and an apple and a jar of water or ice tea."

"Doña Luz never sleeps," I said by way of appreciation.

Golly's face brightened. "Mom thinks there's something aristocratic about *not* sleeping . . . If there was an old-fashioned Mexican dance going on in town, reels and lancers or a Spanish *flamenco*, she'd be floating away in a *caballero's* arms in her imagination, tangling her legs and belly against him in a cradle waltz, and she'd be off like a shot!"

The wash-room was like a long military barracks with coal-burning stoves spaced about twenty-five feet apart, pipes of corrugated iron thrust through low ceilings. I'd seen a sketch of a barracks like that in my *Book of Knowledge*, but this building had 4-foot-by-2-foot-by-3-foot wooden tubs, instead of bunks, aligned in a row. The walls, tar-papered for insulation, were hung with mirrors for shaving, hooks for clothing and towels, and webs of ropes for drying laundry. Dozens of kettles full of water were kept close to boiling point on the stoves. Based on Golly's description of Doña Luz's regulations, I easily imagined how the troops of miners, soot-blackened as chimney sweeps, had to pile up filthy clothes for Carmencita to wash, had to bathe themselves in individual tubs full of the water heated by Carmencita, and had to dress for dinner in clean clothes laid out by Carmencita. In addition to chopping a chunk of a cord of wood every day for the kitchen stove and indoor Franklin stoves, Carmencita had to keep four wash-room stoves stoked with coal every day, had to empty tubs of about 100 gallons of water every day, had to fill the tubs with about 100 gallons of hot water every day, had, every day, to scrub, mangle, hang out to dry, then iron the mounds of clothes, sheets, blankets, tablecloths and napkins, had, every day, to light enough candles for a Mass, mop floors, and still had, every day, to convey the impression that she, like Cinderella, had unique shoes and a coach-and-four and was ready for a night on the town.

"My sister wants to get married," Golly said, shaking her head. "If there's one thing worse than marriage, for her it's working for our Mamá." Golly paused, studied me, went on. "I said I ain't never going to marry, but, to be honest, I might hitch up to a rich old man so's I can make something of myself, like my Mamá says."

It seemed, I was thinking, that dreams really were a necessity. Tío Congo had a play he would never produce. Don Fernando had his painting, Golly had her swarm of fireflies, Carmencita had a Prince Charming she would never meet. Doña Luz wanted to live in the style of Queen Victoria, Mum wanted freedom, Daddy wanted a sex-machine, and me, I wanted to be an artist. I made a noise in my throat and said in my father's authoritative manner, though I scarcely knew what I saying, "We have three lives, Golly —family life, work life, dream life. You seldom have all three at the same time. Most people have family and work lives and allow their dream life to wither and die. Your mother is right about that. If you absolutely must have the dream life, you may have to sacrifice family life and the work life that earns a livelihood. What do you think?"

Golly again showed she liked me, excitement in her eyes and voice. *"¡La cueva de los olvidados!* The Cave of the Forgotten! It's my name for the underground hideaway where I go to be alone and happy . . . Come on. I'll show you."

The Cave of the Forgotten, she explained, was discovered by Tío Congo near the sandstone cliffs. On the way up there she would also show me orchards and gardens.

Golondrina, meaning "swallow," was more and more becoming lovely as her name. There were a billion pretty girls, a few of whom I'd met, including Scampy. What was the difference between a pretty girl and a lovely girl? I was learning something, something new, at least to me. Loveliness manifested itself from within. Golly and Scampy were lovely.

The *ranchito* had over twenty acres of *acequia*-irrigated orchards and gardens in addition to pasture land. Most produce had already been harvested—cabbages, tomatoes, beans, potatoes, white corn, wild spinach, apples and chokecherries. A few chile peppers and pumpkins remained.

"Every year before Halloween," Golly was saying, "we invite all the little kids from the company-towns to come with a grownup and choose a pumpkin to take home to make squash pies and jack-o'-lanterns. You should see a kid no taller than a wheelbarrow trying to carry a big pumpkin! My brothers roast the chiles. They sell them below market price. I make a few *ristras* for my brothers to give away to their bosses . . . We've got *yerbabuena* and *ocha* for colds and other illnesses, and cloves to relieve toothache. We make our own shampoo from *amole*."

As we were scrambling up a rocky slope toward the bluffs, she told me more about *la cueva de los olvidados*, the Cave of the Forgotten.During Indian raids on *ranchitos* of the Purgatoire region, her great-great-grandparents had dug a hideaway about six feet beneath the surface of the earth, supporting sod with the thick *vigas* of the ceiling and leaving one entrance about the size of a well. When Tío Congo discovered the hideaway, this entrance had been under rotten planks, enabling snakes, rats, and scorpions to have winter quarters. Golly had constructed a concrete animal-and-water-proof frame around the entrance and placed on top of it a 6-foot-by-4-foot steel trap door secured by a Yale lock. She kept the key to the lock on her necklace. Once the door was flipped, one climbed down an 18-foot ladder of *latillas* to a room measuring 15-foot-by-15-foot with a height of ten feet.

Entrance opened, Golly disappeared down the ladder and presently had candles lit in the cave. I descended the ladder slowly, wary of rotten rungs. Tío Congo had been right about furnishings and shelves, but Golly had transformed the place to suit her own needs and tastes, a pallet with pillows and woolly blankets, a powder-keg table with Mexican tin candle holders, and shelves not stocked with food but with books. The floor was still hard clay. She had plastered walls with a mixture of flour, water, and newspapers, whitewashed them, and pinned up a recent map of the United States (no territories in dispute), a copper-colored photograph of a bullfighter, and a picture-poster of ballet dancers painted by, she informed me, a Frenchman named Degas. Her most remarkable treasure, also mounted on a powder keg, was a new clockwork gramophone.

In those days, at least in my school in Colorado Springs, we were given instruction in dancing. Actually, the word *marching* would be more accurate than *dancing*, for, to a gramophone recording of the *Marche Militaire* we were taught formations for a "cotillion" and introduced to the "dance card." Although girls were allowed to dance only with other girls, they learned ballroom steps in two-quarter time, whereas boys, who were not allowed to touch girls in school and who in any case were notoriously unteachable in the dance, seldom progressed beyond shifting weight from one foot to the other. Boys were expected to bow to girls and request the honor of dancing with them, though not at school. On rare occasions when parents had money enough to employ a band, parlors large enough for tea-dances, and duchess-faced chaperons enough to referee hanky-panky with the aid of gold-rimmed spectacles, frosty blue eyes, and peacock-feather fans, the sweaty palms of boys could, finally, make contact with the sweaty palms of girls, one arm apiece lifted in a gesture of surrender, one arm apiece distantly pressing flesh between hip bone and lower back. A few of the tallest boys were able to peer down through a girl's blouse and later tell us unlucky ones how uncouthly made were the boobies.

A girl's dance card could determine her future life. If she were popular, she had the misfortune of having to choose among too many suitors. Later she would be inclined, according to my calculations, to marry the tall, handsome, silent rich boy without realizing he was destined to become a drunkard and a bully. On the other hand, if the girl were unpopular and not a single partner would sign her card, not only would she be humiliated from having to sit and watch others dancing, but also her future had the words *wallflower* and *spinster* written all over it. Some wallflowers, even if in their teens they resembled the hound of the Baskervilles, blossomed into princesses, but spinsters, unless they became nuns, teachers, whores or writers, usually stayed at home at their fathers' expense, had a glass of sherry before bedtime, and went gradually bugs. Such was my education in the mysteries of dancing. I preferred to sit out most dances in the company of the wallflowers, bringing them refreshments, signing their dance cards to take home and show their parents but excusing myself from dancing because I was comforting the heartbroken ones when they puked on their silk dresses with the narrow white necklines.

As soon as I had finished inspecting the place, Golly put a record on the gramophone, wound it up, glided into my arms and stirred my petrified legs into a semblance of motion. The music crackled as if violins were being dipped in a hot greasy skillet. My feet gathered rhythm before I could think of myself as a clodhopper. Only when the record sputtered to an end did I remember Doña Luz's warning.

"Are you," I asked Golly in a couldn't-care-less tone, "feeling very nervous?"

She glanced up at me, frowning. "No," she said. "Why do you ask?"

"Nothing," I said. 'That's hunky-dory. Did you like school?"

"You asked me that already. I said I like baseball. Remember?" She went and, having again wound up the gramophone, placed another record on it. A tinny tenor's voice burst into the cave.

After this record, too, sputtered to an end, Golly said, "I liked school O.K., know what I mean? The teacher gave us a test on the Middle Ages. She asked, 'What was a flying buttress?' A boy wrote, 'A flying buttress was a bird in the Middle Ages.'"

Golly was really fast on the draw. "What do you want to be when you grow up?" I asked.

"I already told you, Tree!"

162

"Oh," I said. "Sorry." I couldn't remember all that she had said, but she dreamed of going to college.

"Look," she said, calming down. "All that the girls at school can think of is getting married. They have strands of colored yarn twisted into the *medallitas de San Blas*, blessed by the priest, and tied about their throats. Me, when I grow up, I'm going to be a spinster!"

When we returned to the house, Golly excused herself to help Doña Luz in the kitchen. I went upstairs to the room assigned to me, a small one in monastic style, a pallet with white linen sheets and a crazy-quilt comforter, a powder keg for a table, candles in bottles, *trastero* for personal belongings. The walls were cloth-covered, the cloth nailed to studs, newspapers stretched over and glued to the cloth; a sky-blue oilcloth had been nailed to the ceiling. An early afternoon sun printed geometric figures with bars on wooden floors. Since none of the boarders' rooms had doors—a fact that supported Tío Congo's metaphor about a lack of doors equaling the inclusiveness of humanity—I could see that each room was similar to mine. I could also see that each room was tidy—a sign of respect for Doña Luz.

Although I intended to stretch out on my pallet for only a minute, having removed hat and boots, I fell deeply asleep. I was wakened by the shrill whistle-blast of a nearby train. I was momentarily tumbled about by an avalanche of sensations, anxiety about Mum's escape, desire to kiss a girl, curiosity about the miners, pity for a man who was coughing and dying in a room directly beneath mine. Sunlight no longer slanted through my window. The sky outside had darkened. During the first week of November, 1903, I reflected, I had found a *familia*, a home, and a new life.

For a while I could hear from outside the house the boisterous sounds of men in the wash-house. Then up the stairs they clumped. Candles were lit in their rooms. Fits of coughing, clearings of throats, exclamations in foreign tongues and deep-throated chucklings: the sounds of my new environment resonated with a faint collective memory of hunters and warriors.

Before long, they crowded into my room and introduced themselves. Milenko the Croat said, *"Kako ste?,"* translated by *Nono*, Golly's brother who looked like a black-bearded santo, as "How are you?" A gaunt-looking man with a handlebar mustache, Milenko showed me a flute in his hand and played a couple of riffs on it. *"Zurla,"* he said.

"Flute," Nono said.

"Flute," I said.

"Floo-ta," Milenko managed, grinning at me.

Orlando the Italian was a stockily built young man with a round, clean-shaven face and a head of wavy dark hair. Nono, hairy arm around Orlando's shoulders, said, "Orlando loves my sister Carmencita."

"To learn the language you have to sleep with your dictionary," Orlando said with a shrug.

Nono pulled an eyelid down with a forefinger to indicate Orlando's craftiness. "He wants to be *mi hermano*, my brother, to get my land."

Orlando shrugged. "Is problem? *Chi ha prato ha tutto.* Who got land got everything."

The Greeks, Nick and Kiki, the Americans, Rusty and Curly, the Mexican Willito and Golly's other brother, Aladino, another *santo*-type, shook my hand but had nothing to say. When Tío Congo appeared at the head of the staircase and announced that dinner was ready, we trooped downstairs to a large room smelling of candlewax smoke and glittering with silver, china, and glass wares set on a heavy refectory table covered with damask. Once we were seated at table, Doña Luz, Golly, and the fat young woman who had to be Carmencita came from the kitchen and placed before us pots and platters of abundance, fried steaks, boiled potatoes, beef tomatoes, pumpkin squash, apple sauce, chilies, *frijoles, arroz* and *queso*. Golly filled glasses from a pitcher of milk and gave each of us a hot roll. She still had a flower in her hair, as did Carmencita the axe-wielder and water-heater of legend, who, though fat, was softly rounded and big-bosomed. The three ladies joined us at table. Doña Luz called for silence.

"It makes me suffer in my body," she began, "when a soul is satisfied to merely exist. There is no purpose in living from day to day. I want to know from anyone here who is willing and able to speak to stand up and tell us what you learned today."

I swam my eyes about the room. Cupboards were *armarios* and shelves were *estantes*, but I hadn't seen any at home as artistically carved as these. Pictures of saints framed in tin and glass were hung on white plaster walls.

"What have you learned today, *m'hija?*" Doña Luz asked Golly.

Golly stood up, glared at her brothers. "Today I learned," she said, "that there is such a thing as a *caballero* who has, unlike some persons I know, intelligence."

She sat down to whoops of applause. Doña Luz looked at me disapprovingly. Suddenly, as if she had just understood Golly's insult, she started laughing, "*¡Cristo rey!*" After a while she turned to Orlando. "What have you learned today, *m'hijo?*"

Orlando, standing up, said, "Today I learn new word: *dusk*. I hear this word. I like this word. Dusk. Is beautiful word."

"What does *dusk* mean, Orlando?"

"I not know," Orlando shrugged. "Is problem?" He sat down.

"*Señor* Tree," said Doña Luz. "Would you care to speak?"

I stood up awkwardly. Encouraged by friendly nods, I made my first-ever speech, saying, "Today I have learned that I want to go to work. Also today I have learned that I must become an artist like Don Fernando." I sat down to applause. Golly's gaze upon me was warm.

"Anyone else before we eat?"

Tío Congo, nodding toward Doña Luz, slowly rose from his chair and studied the faces lifted toward him. "Today," he intoned in his King James Version baritone, "I learned from Mother Jones at St. Mabyn's that the conditions under which our people are forced to live are not fit for beasts of the field. Upon her return to Indianapolis tonight, she will recommend that District 15, southern Colorado and Utah, join our brothers to the north and come out on strike. . . I wonder what went wrong with those people."

When he sat down in the ensuing silence, Doña Luz asked, "Union or Corporation?"

"All-s the people," Tío Congo said, shaking his head sadly.

Doña Luz stabbed with a silver fork at the meat on her plate. "We might as well starve striking," she said, "as starve working."

Chapter Nine

On Monday morning, November 9, 1903, Colorado miners joined some 100,000 workers nationwide and refrained from going to work. Immediately the coal companies evicted hundreds of families from their homes in company-towns. In Los Tristes wagons loaded high with furniture came streaming down the canyons followed by long files of men with trunks on their shoulders and of women and children with pushcarts filled with bedding, clothing, cooking utensils and cherished odds and ends. Streets were soon clogged with thousands of people with nowhere to go. Some unmarried miners managed to leave town to seek employment with independent or unionized mines. Most miners seemed unable to fathom that their jobs in the Los Tristes mines were gone forever. The Union provided them with 63¢ a day. The specter of poverty was like a mist blurring the bewilderment and resentment in the eyes of miners and their wives.

Misery embarrassed me. While Golly and I had been dancing in the Cave of the Forgotten, I made a stupid remark.

"You've got a house with a mother, father, sister, and brothers, I'm half-orphaned," I said even though I was well-fed, warm, boarded without charge to me and spared lousy chores. My principal duty was to keep Don Fernando entertained. Having no reason to complain, I deserved to clapperclaw myself as a suck-egg clot, but I was too proud to apologize to Golly.

Trains serving St. Mabyn's via a spur continued to rumble past the ranch at intervals throughout the day and night. Burned brake grease stank in my nostrils, ungreased axles screeched shrilly enough to shatter eardrums. Most trains hauled coal down the canyon or empty cars up it. Some coaches which were headed up to the company-town were bringing scabs. According to Tío Congo, these scabs hadn't rested since leaving European ports and passing through inspections at Ellis Island. Inexperienced, unaware they were replacing strikers, they were still unforgiven by local inhabitants for being "damn foreigners." As often as I could, whenever I believed scabs were passing our way, I ran to the tracks and beat a frying pan with a hammer. My protest wasn't as loud as a jailbreak, but I believed it would find favor with my new family.

Unlike members in most coalminers' families, those of us at the Medina ranch continued to be fortunate. We could weather any storm. Nevertheless at Doña Luz's command we did tighten our belts. With Nono, Aladino, and the boarders available to run the farm, the Irish stable hands were dismissed. Carmencita and Golly walked the five miles to and from schools in town. Baths went unheated during weekdays, and washing and ironing duties were reduced.

Our main effort on behalf of strikers was to distribute beef, mutton, eggs and milk free of charge directly to those scattered about in the mountains. When the St. Mabyn's mine operators offered Doña Luz a small fortune to have these products delivered to them rather than to strikers, she let them know where they stood in her estimation, declaring, "I'll not be a war profiteer." Once in awhile when Don Fernando needed a long rest, I accompanied Tío Congo in a delivery wagon. Way up in the mountains, living in canvas tents, old prairie schooners, and shelters cobbled together out of powder kegs and scraps of galvanized tin, were little colonies of the dispossessed. Hollow-eyed and bearded men in coveralls, gaunt women in filthy garments, and half-naked children without shoes seemed to manifest themselves out of the thick woods, receiving gifts one minute, disappearing the next, acting as if they were doing *us* a favor. Tío Congo respected their independence. To him they were like "hillbillies" in the Appalachians, proud descendants, he claimed, of pioneers and slaves. "They like to knock about footsloose," he said with his gentle laugh, "restless as mule colts being weaned. They don't kow-tow to nobodies. They don't axes anybodies to help them in a war. But they's mighty plumb glad to see my spring wagon, fo' sho.'"

War was the word. In Cripple Creek I had been a spectator of a civil war. In Los Tristes I was *in* one.

One cold dark evening in early December, after we had all finished eating our *chile con carne*, Doña Luz touched her Dresden glass with a fork and said she had an important announcement to make. "Now, you all know Governor Peabody is a shill for the coal companies," she began. "He sits in his mansion in Denver and does whatever they ask him to do . . . Killing us, that's the latest."

Having been an avid reader of newspapers, I knew that state governments in Colorado and elsewhere were dead-set against recognizing labor unions. Now, according to Doña Luz, Governor Peabody had openly declared war on them. All strikes, he was saying, were equivalent to "war, rebellion, and insurrection against laws which assure protection of liberty and property." Deportation of strikers was "humane, preventing riots and bloodshed." Strikebreaking by military intervention "protected the right of workingmen to be free of dictatorial leaders."

Peabody's words as quoted by Doña Luz were so absurd I exclaimed, "Bull feathers!"

Everyone at the dinner table seemed amused by my outburst, everyone except Doña Luz. She frowned. "Sorry," I muttered.

Doña Luz resumed. "The governor has declared war on us. He has authorized the Guard to kill us . . . I have no quarrel with the Guard in ordinary times. Most militiamen are honorable and courageous, not a few of them coming from mining families like ours. But these are not ordinary times. The Guard has been infiltrated by a lawless gang. If you don't count the college boys and the veterans of the Philippines War, you've got cowboys, ex-cons, former gunmen and other scum wearing the uniform, the same kind that wear badges as deputy sheriffs . . . Let there be no illusions about where we stand in this war. To those who are supposed to enforce the Law, you are just tumbleweed wheels surrounded by barbed wire. The Law cannot be trusted to protect you. It serves criminals. Our land is occupied by an enemy calling itself the United States. It pretends that we have no respect for liberty and property, that any assembly of two or more strikers is a riot, and that our leaders are dictators obstructing our right to be enslaved . . . We must do everything in our power to demonstrate that we are loyal Americans with peaceful intentions. Resist the soldiers, the deputies, and all the other riffraff, and they'll kill you . . . Any ideas how we can protect ourselves? Tree? You go first."

I thought she might be trying to humiliate me, but I had in fact pondered the matter of protection for some time. I agreed with Doña Luz about a policy of peaceableness and nonresistance except when self-defense was our only choice. In particular, Don Fernando, after the manner of frontier times, had hanging on pothooks above the front door a hammerless Savage rifle. If the wrong soldier of the Guard or a deputy sheriff were to see that rifle, he could use it as a pretext to herd us all into a bull pen.

I rose to my feet. "Ah," said Doña Luz, schoolmarmishly, "a Daniel come to judgment . . . His father is employed by Mr. Woodbridge, owner of St. Mabyn's, who wants us to do an air dance. How, Tree, can we protect ourselves?"

There was a silence broken only by Rusty and Curly, who were noisily scraping their plates. Was I really going to propose a policy of nonresistance to this lot? The Greeks, Nick and Kiki, and Milenko the flute-playing Croat had very likely been involved in the Balkan wars. Nono and Aladino might want to fight for the return of all the land south of the Arkansas River to Mexico. Tío Congo seemed to be a wolf lying down with sheep, perhaps an insurrectionist at heart.

"I think," I said after clearing my throat, "we should get rid of the rifle."

"The rifle?" Doña Luz, pronouncing the word as *wry-fool*,

seemed to be mocking me.

"Yes, ma'am."

"Why, *m'hijito?*"

I explained my reasons, adding, "I think Miss Golly should have the rifle. When Miss Carmen has to stay at school, Miss Golly walks home alone. If she takes the rifle to school, she can protect herself."

Golly piped up after a silence, "I know where to hide the rifle." I understood from the squinty-eyed look she darted in my direction that we could play with the rifle in the Cave of the Forgotten. I sat down.

"Well," said Doña Luz, "hoo-rah for you . . . You have spoken with a wisdom beyond your years, *m'hijito* . . . Golondrina, hide the Savage before alpenglow . . . Tree, while your intentions are commendable as regards taking a gun to school, your thinking is like the fat lady in the sideshow, all bottom and no top . . . We do not take guns to school. We do not want the consarn dickens to do with strangers. If you see a stranger on our property, remember he is protected by the Law, but you and the property are not."

That night as I was preparing to sleep, Nono entered my room. His *santo*-like black beard reminded me he was a *penitente*, as Golly had told me he was, trying to explain why she "hated" him. After he flagellated himself in a *morada*, she had to cleanse his bloody, lacerated back and put ointment on it. She wanted her brother to leave the *penitentes* and obey the Church's laws condemning them.

"Hey, *gringo*, you done good," I was relieved to hear Nono say. "You carin' for my little sister like that, ya know?" He paused to punch air like a prizefighter warming up. *"Mira,"* he said, "ya don't know, but the miner, he's workin' underground, he's worried about his wife and kids sunnyside. Ya know? Maybe he got a pretty wife. Know what happens? Some sonsuvabitchin' mine guard, like, she's alone, he busts into that house and has his way with her, ya know? You don't read stuff like 'at in the papers. Too immoral, they say. Unfit for publication, they say. It happens, *mi hermano*, alla time, alla time. Hey, that mine guard, he warns the lady, puddle your panties at your feet or your old man's goin' down the mountain mutterin' to hisself. She goes to the Law, they say she's a whore. The husband goes down the mountain, talkin' to hisself. The mine guard gets off scotfree. Oughta be strung up, ya know? Keep an eye out for Golly. O.K., buddy?"

We shook hands. Me being called *gringo*, "white man," wasn't, to me, an insult and *hermano*, "brother," felt good. As long as Golly didn't get nervous, I would protect her like a brother.

Blow me down, a couple of days later one of the milish sent to protect us from dictatorial leaders showed up at the ranch. The rape and murder he was going to commit to prevent bloodshed would have been unfit for publication.

I was alone in the house with Don Fernando. Doña Luz, the brothers, and the boarders had gone to a Union meeting at Josca's Opera House. Tío Congo was delivering gourmet dinners to his hillbillies. Carmencita and Golly had walked to school.

It was really and truly fun to be with Don Fernando. I loved watching him paint on canvas and listening to him talk about art, his voice raspy but enthusiastic, golden teeth gleaming in candlelight. He let me hold his paint box while he mixed colors and wielded a palette knife as if he were caressing icing on a cake.

On this particular afternoon he was showing me photographs of paintings by masters. Extremely tired, he lay propped up in bed with the photographs in his lap. His fingers were like dead-white twigs at the 11,000-foot timberline. I was near the bed, standing near the low oak door.

"The masters," he was saying, "breathed life into these works by exploiting underpainting and colors. A hitherto unknown brilliance, depth, and impression of great vigor and spontaneity resulted. We can observe some of these qualities in Jan van Eyck's *Adoration of the Lamb* and in El Greco's *The Cardinal*, but Rembrandt's *Lucretia* is best. His boldness and ingenuity are to this day unequaled, not even by the experimentalists who call themselves 'Impressionists.' Note the atmosphere of mystery in *Lucretia*. The glazes superimposed with the keen blade of the palette knife ride roughshod over the maze of the impasto, and yet the painter started off with a fully loaded brush!"

I wanted an explanation of technical terms, but he closed his eyes and sank at once into deep sleep. Just then, I heard glass—it could only have been panels in the front door—shattered in an explosive clink. The bolt on the vestibule side of the door make a *schnicking* noise as it was unlatched. I heard the door creaking open, then thumping of boots on old boards. As my heart throbbed in my ears, he appeared, a six-foot-sixer and 250-pounder by any measure, the biggest monster-osity since Jack climbed the beanstalk. Ducking his massive head under the lintel, he stood swaying above me, breathing heavily, cap scraping ceiling. The stripes on his tunic and the service revolver in his hand indicated he was a sergeant in the Guard. The paunch on his stomach, the purple veins on his bulbous nose, and the reek of a malt vat on his breath pointed to his being one of the riffraff, not a regular militiaman.

His name was Shorty. I learned this a few days later when I read in the papers about GUARDSMAN BELIEVED DROWNED.

"Hi! I'm home!"

Golly, according to my instantaneous calculation, was calling from the kitchen and would soon dash into the hallway. My brain was floundering in emotional quicksand, voice immobilized. The bovine vacuity inscribed on Shorty's face began to change into noodledom and then into an expression of rapture akin to that in old paintings depicting a saint like Augustine rejecting carnal sin. Shorty backed out, I peeked out. In the hallway was that lovely girl with blue ribbons tied to her pigtails. She seemed to be trying to read Shorty's mind a few seconds before he became Train No. 97 going down grade, making ninety miles an hour. Luckily, she was fast on the draw, realizing she had been spotted stealing home from third base. As Shorty steamed toward her, she zigged, zagged, dodged and ran, Shorty on her heels, I behind Shorty. Racing through the kitchen, she upset a pot of beans on the waxed floor. When he tried to tag her, Shorty slipped and ended up windmilling his arms. For a few moments there, I thought she might score, win the Series.

She never had a chance. So I convinced myself as the three of us raced up the slope toward the Cave of the Forgotten. Out of the corner of my eye I saw Shorty's horse hitched to a post in the front yard. Instead of deserting Golly and Don Fernando by stealing that horse, I kept running, oblivious to the fact that Shorty would kill me before he ravished and killed her, who didn't have time to get the Savage in the Cave. Even if she reached its entrance she would have to fumble for her key, insert and turn it in the Yale lock, flip the heavy steel trap door aside, descend the ladder, find the rifle in the dark and fire one round of live ammunition through a rusty bore at an armed, moving target.

But he stopped running. And studied me. I was about twenty paces away from him when I, too, stopped. I was, I realized, easy meat. While Shorty was pondering my fate, Golly was flipping the door of the Cave and descending the ladder. Suddenly she stuck fingers in her mouth, whistled. Shorty was distracted. I quickly put another forty yards between us. Then he, as the French say, improved his toilet. He tossed cap and tunic on the ground. He loosened his galluses. He tucked the revolver into his pants. When he was satisfied with his charm, he sauntered over to the Cave, descended the ladder, and, I soon learned, took a bullet between the eyes. This effect, which was preceded by the muffled crack of a rifle shot, became, in turn, a cause. Golly popped up out of the Cave, flipped the door, padlocked it. There was no one in our occupied land we could go and talk to. I went and picked up the cap and tunic and, without pausing for conversation with the girl who had saved me, herself, and her father, walked deliberately down the slope, mounted Shorty's horse, and rode off to an isolated spot about six miles downstream from Los Tristes. There I hitched the horse to a willow by the banks of the Purgatoire and tossed cap and tunic into bushes. I jogged home so as not to be late for dinner with the family.

I couldn't sleep that night. I was kept awake by the horror of confronting the sadness of necessity. Golly and I stood innocent before the ultimate bar of justice. She killed in self-defense and saved three lives. Law, however, could not be trusted to clear her of wrongdoing. I, an accessory to the killing when I drew a red herring across the track leading to the ranch and Golly, had been trying to save her from the Law. But no matter how innocent we were, our lives had been changed. Already at the dinner table Golly had shown signs of remorse. My own conscience was pricking me. We were haunted. Lying was becoming inevitable. If we told the truth to Doña Luz or anyone else in the family, we put them also at risk. If one of us were to confess to the family or to the Law, or even to heap blame upon the other, there was no telling where the matter might end. I'd lately had enough experience of falsehoods and rejections to distrust everybody. In the unlikely event that even Golly made me a scapegoat, I could plead, for both of us, special circumstances, one, we were juveniles, two, not being strikers, we were not rebels. While this line of reasoning seemed promising because the conditions of warfare were not directly relevant to our situation, the fact of the matter was, a uniformed noncommissioned officer of the Law had been killed, the killing covered up. The Law would show no mercy to us for that.

The more I thought about the situation, the more attractive became a return to the people to whom I had belonged. Daddy might not protect me, but Mum would, Ganny would, money and influence would. Had I sworn any allegiance to Dare, Don Fernando, Doña Luz, or to the Union, itself? No, but I liked Miss Golondrina Medina with an awful liking.

I rolled out of bed onto my knees but didn't know how to pray, so I rose and dressed for the cold weather and went for a walk. I had no intention of going to the Cave of the Forgotten. Willy-nilly I was drawn to the spot. The corpse, I realized, would have to be moved. The Cave was not "forgotten" by Tío Congo, who wanted to stage *Kangaroo* in and around it. What if he suddenly demanded entry into it? Wouldn't every vulture in Los Tristes soon be circling in the sky above the Cave, every coyote howling nearby? On the other hand, I hadn't seen the body; I had only assumed it was in the Cave. As long as I didn't have to identify it, I could deny knowledge of its

175

existence, couldn't I? I could explain the business of the horse and the clothing. Having found a riderless horse in the front yard, a soldier's tunic wrapped around the saddlebow, I was going to Los Tristes to the sheriff's office to leave the horse when it threw me to the ground and bolted away.

"Hi."

Golly's voice startled me out of my flirtation with flight and into a brief moment of jim-jams. I could barely make out her figure approaching me from the direction of darkly visible cliffs.

"Hi," I said, intentionally sounding almost bored.

"I know what you're thinking," she said. She was close enough for me to see a pale face. "You're thinking you're half-orphaned," she said in a sympathetic tone.

"I'm sorry about that," I said.

"That's all right," she said. "You're free to go back home, back to the *other* side of the railroad tracks, the good side, know what I mean?"

"I don't know what you mean," I said.

"Yes, you do, Tree," she said, sounding exasperated. "I appreciate your helping me, taking the horse away. You don't have to do anything more. And I ain't a snitch. What's coming gonna come, nothing I can ever do about it."

"We have to move the body," I said.

"You ain't offering, and I ain't asking," she said. "I'm a-doin' it soon's I can. Never wrassle with a girl who has a Yale lock. *Mierda!*"

She had a plan, she said. At the first opportunity, whenever everybody went to town for a Union meeting or funeral, she would return to the ranch alone. By tying President, the draft horse, to the corpse, she could drag it out of the Cave and up to a spot under the cliffs where gravel and rocks, loosened, could bury the corpse ten feet deep in what would look like a natural slide.

Instead of deserting Golly and her family, I felt more than at any time committed to them. I could hardly give myself high marks for having helped a girl who trusted me and would carry the full load for us, but I owed her, owed her a lot more than an apology for self-pity, a lot more than thanks for saving my life. I owed her love even though I didn't know what I felt about her.

That night at the dinner table Golly cried a strange cry, strange to everybody but me and her. She was sitting straight up, motionless, not touching her food, not making another sound. Tears were streaming down her cheeks. She didn't try to wipe them off. "What is it, child?" Doña Luz asked.

"I love everybody," Golly said without a sob.

Doña Luz came, embraced her, and said, "Of course you do, *linda*, of course you do."

A few days before my thirteenth birthday, Don Fernando suffered a stroke and lost his eyesight. Realizing his time had come, he summoned everyone to his bedside. When we were all assembled there, he was sitting up, a red bandanna around his eyes, a *caballero's* pair of red boots on his feet. His box of colors he clutched in those dried hands of his. He embraced his children, told them he loved them. He told Doña Luz he wouldn't kiss her until she fetched for him the pleasures she had denied him. She asked Orlando to find an old packet of cigarillos and a full bottle of blue agave tequila from Jalisco. "No problem," he said. When he returned with the items, Don Fernando said he'd changed his mind. Kisses, he said, were better than smoke and alcohol. He gave Doña Luz a big *abrazo* and kiss. When she told him she had sent Milenko to bring a priest, however, Don Fernando flew into the semblance of a rage. "You, *usted*, you, Luz," he roared, "are the Devil's sister! Why do I need a priest? I already know where I'm going. And I'm not going to confess any sins!" After a pause, he lowered his voice and grinned. "I relent on one condition: all the nudes I have painted must be displayed on the easels when that old *maricón* pretends he brings forgiveness." Don Fernando, I knew, had never painted any nudes.

Doña Luz, hearing the priest arrive in Milenko's buggy, went to the front door to greet him. I was glad that Golly had swept up the broken glass, but the panes had not yet been replaced. I hoped Doña Luz was too preoccupied to make inquiries. When the priest entered the house, I went to sit in a rocking chair on the porch.

No matter how often I had seen the American flag displayed above the steps when I ran to the tracks and hammered a frying pan, I hadn't really paid much attention to its significance. It had been thumbs down on patriotism in my family. Daddy, who was not a citizen, liked to make jokes about "the colonies." I just stayed indoors on the Fourth of July, watched fireworks from a distance, and let my imagination take me to faraway places. Now looking at Don Fernando's flag, I remembered that he and Luz came of old stock, she an American before there was an America. Their land had been taken away from them by the Mexicans, the French, and the Yankees. In a sense they were losing it yet another time to an alien and rapacious culture. Yet they showed the colors. They were proud to be Americans. They understood we were all in the same boat. The truth of brotherhood hadn't fully hit me before.

The priest smiled at me as he was leaving the house. Maybe he was an old *maricón*, but I respected and nodded to him. Doña Luz and Golly came out on the porch and waved to the priest until Milenko had driven the buggy out of sight. Then Doña Luz turned toward Golly and me and asked, "How did the glass get broken? Why haven't I been informed?"

"Oh, that," Golly said quickly. "Tree forgot to tell you. He was down by the tracks when a train carrying replacement workers happened to slow down. A mine guard with a rifle fired at the house, didn't he, Tree?"

I'd never seen a mine guard in my life. "Yeah," I said. "He was angry. I was beating the frying pan."

"The bullet hit the door," Golly hastened to add. "Tree was going to tell you. He was embarrassed. If he hadn't been aggravating the mine guard, nothing would have happened."

Doña Luz glanced away, half closed her eyes, finally said to distant trees, "My early education was brief. It ended abruptly when my teacher was hung from a sycamore tree outside the schoolhouse for stealing a horse. I had to teach myself to read and write from scraps of paper I found lying around. I took them to a pharmacist in Santa Fe. He helped me make sense of them." Doña Luz paused to scan our faces. "I guess the moral of this story is, don't hang the teacher."

Golly and I exchanged a furtive look. Since Doña Luz had been a teacher, maybe she was saying we shouldn't try to deceive her.

"Don Fernando wants to see you now," said Doña Luz, dropping the matter of the glass.

"Me?"

"Yes, Tree. He wants to give you a birthday present."

I followed her into the house. When had I given away my date of birth, and to whom? The answer came to me. One day Don Fernando had asked for my date of birth because we were discussing matriculation rules for admission to the Académie Julian.

Everyone was still gathered around Don Fernando's bed.

"Tree has graced us with his presence," Doña Luz announced. She stepped aside so that I could approach the bed.

Don Fernando's golden smile caught candlelight. "Take my hand, *m'hijito*," he said. I took his outstretched hand. It was cold and dead-white. He did not let my hand go. "Ah," he said, "the true artist . . . These others, they think I am blind. They don't know that an artist sees perfectly well without the benefit of eyes. An artist sees the unseen, hears the unsaid . . . The imagination's a swift, the heart is a starling. These birds are kind to us. *Pues*. See with the sight of our birds this box of colors . . . Go on, touch it . . . When I was a young man in the mines, I felt a great indifference to what I had to do, but when I held this box of colors in my hands, I knew it was my life. Once I owned my life, I became completely free and at peace . . . I want you to have this box of colors. *¡Feliz cumpleaños!*"

He released my hand and pushed the box of colors toward me. *"Muchas gracias,"* I managed. Leaning over the bed, I threw my arms around his neck. He hadn't been shaved. I kissed the salty sandpaper of his cheek, slid back, and clutched the box. "Will you come, sir, to my first exhibition in Paris?"

"*Sí, sí,*" he replied, frowning as if it had been a slight discourtesy my question. He smiled and said, "*De acuerdo.* When you weary of painting naked women in Paris, come back here to watch our mountains turn red."

He died that night.

Nono told me that Doña Luz bathed the body and wrapped it in clean cloth. He and Aladino had put the body in a coffin they had made, nailed the lid down tight, and delivered the coffin to the family church in Los Tristes. There the coffin with Don Fernando's red "*caballero*" boots on top would be displayed for several days, after which period the Union would conduct the funeral. So it came about that we all went to town in phaetons, passing through streets where homes were gaily decorated with wreaths and with *candelaria* for the Christmas season. After the ceremony at the church, we all except for Golly joined a procession of a thousand men walking to the Mesa Miners' Union Cemetery overlooking the ice-bound river. Each man in the cortege carried a sprig of evergreen to leave in the open grave after the coffin was lowered into it. After the burial ceremony we assembled in Josca's Opera House.

I had expected to hear eulogies about a miner whose life had been cut short. Instead, what I heard from Doña Luz was a speech not about Don Fernando but about the ways of our lives. Rising in her black dress, black silk shawl wrapped around head, and setting her teeth firmly, she strode on stage and came to stand behind a flag-draped podium. There might have been as many as a thousand people in the audience.

"I really don't think you've done anything to merit such punishment as having my speech flung at you," she began at an unexpected pitch of levity, "but that is one of the afflictions that goes with my inability to serve as a substitute for Mother Jones. She can't be here, but I have her permission to speak to you in her words."

She paused for a chorus of groans to subside.

"I'm not Mother Jones," Doña Luz continued, "but I'm gonna speak with her words even if I don't have her tongue. The tongue I have for you is cold tongue. If anybody chooses to stay here out of respect for my Fernandito, that's deep enough for me."

A ripple of laughter settled back into rapt expectation.

"It is freedom or death, and your children will be free!" Doña Luz's voice, now raised to a level of wild indignation, was greeted with shouts of, "That is right, sister, that is right!"

"We are not going to leave a slave class to the coming generation! The next generation will not charge us for what we have done. The next generation will charge and condemn us for what we have left undone!"

"That is right! That is right!" the miners roared.

"If it's strike or submit," Doña Luz implored, "why, for God's sake, strike—strike until you win!"

Again she paused. Miners lunged from their seats, raised fists, released a torrent of angry words until they finally fell back and grew quiet.

"Rise up and strike!" Doña Luz went on. "If you are too cowardly to fight for your rights, there are enough women in this country to come in and beat hell out of you. If it is slavery or strike, I say strike until the last of you drop into your graves, as Fernandito has done. We are going to stand together and never surrender.'

"You men, you great, strong men have been enslaved for years. You have allowed a few men to boss you, to starve you, to abuse your women and children, to deny you education, to make peons of you. What is the matter with you? Are you afraid? Do you fear your pitiful little bosses? I can't believe it. I can't believe you are so cowardly . . . I tell you this. If you are, you are not fit to have women live with you!'

Following another ripple of laughter and subsidence into silence, Doña Luz glared at the miners and lowered the pitch of her voice to one of solemnity. "Now," she said, "we are here today as the outcome of an age-long struggle, and it has crossed the oceans to you. It is about to crystallize. The ship is sailing. It calls for pilots to come aboard . . . I want to say to you that all the ages of history have been ages of robbery, of oppression, of hypocrisy, of lying, and

I want to say to you tyrants of the world that all the centuries past have been yours, but we are facing the dawn of a new age.'

"This, my friends, fellow workers, is indicative of what? No church in the country could get up a crowd like this, because we are doing God's holy work, we are breaking the chains that bind you, we are putting the fear of God into the robbers. All the churches here couldn't put the fear of God into them, but our resolution has made them tremble.'

"Now, my boys, we are facing a new day. We are in the early dawn of the world's greatest centuries, when crime, brutality, and wrong will disappear, and man will rise in grander height, and every woman shall sit in her own front yard and sing a lullaby to the happy days of happy childhood and to the noble manhood of a great nation that is coming. She will look at her mansion, and every room will be light, and there will be peace and justice.'

"I see that vision today as I talk to you. Oh, God Almighty grant—Oh, God Almighty grant—Oh, God grant that the woman who suffers for you suffers not for a coward but for a man! God grant that. God grant, my brothers, that you will be men, and the woman who bore you will see her God and say, 'I raised a man'!"

Doña Luz found a seat on the stage, sat down. The audience yelled, "Right! Right! Right!" After silence was once more restored, Tío Congo, who had been waiting in the wings behind a curtain, walked at a kind of lordly pace to the podium.

"The Epistle of James," he intoned deeply while raising his eyes to the ceiling. From where I was sitting I could see he had no Bible before him. After a very long pause, he thundered: " *'Go to now, ye rich men, weep and howl for your miseries that shall come upon you. Your riches are corrupted, and your garments are motheaten. Your gold and silver is cankered; and the rust of them shall be a witness against you, and shall eat your flesh as it were fire."*

Chapter Ten

S oon after delivering her speech based upon conversations with Mother Jones, Doña Luz seldom emerged from her bedroom except to spend time alone in the converted living room and studio where Don Fernando had died. The daily operations of the farm she left to Tío Congo and her sons. Carmencita and Golly, on holiday from school, took on the cooking and housekeeping chores. The rest of us seemed to be treading water, waiting for a Christmas which, instead of being a pieceways ahead on the 1903 calendar, suddenly arrived. We were not prepared for it.

I had mixed feelings about Christmas anyway. My birthday fell on December 18th. As far back as I could remember, I wanted that day all to myself and didn't want to postpone its celebration until the 25th, which, after all, belonged to Jesus. To solve the problem, Mum relegated Christmas to the status of an anticlimax and gave me all my presents on the 18th. Once I had my fill of gifts, I did what I could to give presents on Christmas Day to members of the family. Mum and Ruby came first. I made for them, to choose an example, little purses crocheted out of stray pieces of wool. Daddy, however, presented a difficulty. First of all, like Scrooge, he considered Christmas to be humbuggery. He refused to give presents; those he received he mocked or rejected outright. Secondly, he had a Christmas joke, one he cracked every year: the Holy Ghost made Joseph a cuckold. As for Ganny, who had spent the Christmas of

1901 with us, her disgust with religious sentiments of any kind had not been confined to the season of the winter solstice but spread in equally toxic amounts throughout any year. Of course, as I've mentioned before, she outdid herself in 1901 when she threatened to vomit after I read Tiny Tim's blessings in *The Christmas Carol*. I think I gave her, that Christmas, an empty tin can in which she could soak her false teeth every night. As for Daddy, the only present of mine he seemed to like was a back scratcher. One of the shark's teeth, found in a cutbank in the Garden of the Gods, I had glued to a coat hanger in order to create that back scratcher, and Daddy had scratched himself contentedly with it for hours. The thing was, having no allowance from him, I couldn't shop for presents but had to make them myself. "It's the thought that counts," Mum always said.

Most of the time, I should add, a Christmas at home in Colorado Springs was quite pleasant. Every year Ruby fetched for us from Shooks Run a small juniper tree which she and Mum proceeded to decorate and surround with the boxes wrapped in colorful tissue paper. Every year Mum took me, weather permitting, to a church service where we could sing the carols and thrill to the sound of bells.

According to Golly, her family, too, had celebrated Christmas Day with presents, a feast, and pieties. It was, she said, the only time in the year when Don Fernando puffed on a cigarillo and swallowed a glass of tequila from Jalisco.

This Christmas of 1903 Tío Congo had taken Carmencita and Orlando to visit with Italian friends in town, their father, editor of *Il Lavoratore*, needing cheering up since deputy sheriffs had smashed his printing presses. Nono, Aladino, and the miners played cards upstairs. Milenko made *tamburitza* sounds on his flute. Golly rose early to prepare breakfast. When we all except Doña Luz had straggled down to the dining room, we were not expecting anything festive. In fact, Golly apologized for not serving us "pancakes layered with blackberry preserves, gingerbread cookies, and *huevos rancheros*." We assured her we were grateful for our cups of

Arbuckle's black coffee, which was viscous as molasses, our plates of bacon which was cold and greasy as an Eskimo's skillet, and fried eggs with the pale hue and texture of putty. We thanked her for the heat from the kitchen stove, even though she had forgotten to put firewood in the banked embers of the Franklin stoves. Only Nono upbraided Golly for this oversight. She ran crying into her room. At that point I slipped into the kitchen and washed and dried the dishes. I knew she was suffering from guilt about that Shorty's death. After I had done the dishes, I fetched firewood from the stack by the back door and started fires in the Franklin stoves in the hallways upstairs and downstairs.

We'd had sunlight and blue skies for several days. By mid-morning the sun had gone out. Snow was beginning to fall. Windgusts were sweeping over the mountains.

Golly was in the vestibule trying to seal the damaged part of the front door with newspapers soaked in starch. Because I had been presented for my Jesus-free thirteenth birthday Don Fernando's box of colors, I thought he would be proud of me if I put them to good use. I entered his room, placed a large stretched canvas on an easel, opened my box and, with a hand numbed by cold, primed the canvas with white lead.

It had been my habit to spend many hours a day with Don Fernando, listening to his lectures on art, serving him his trays of food, assisting him with ablutions and just keeping him company. Not only was I learning about art, but also I was discovering in myself the joys of work. After he died, I helped Doña Luz turn the room into a sort of shrine. We made the bed with clean sheets and pillowcases and covered it with an embroidered comforter. On the dresser we aligned the shaving kit and silver-backed brushes exactly as they had been before; we stocked the bedside table with books and candles. In the *trastero* were the neatly pressed suits, the *sombreros*, the polished shoes. Nothing had been moved, not easels, paintings, canvases, jars of turpentine and linseed oil, or brushes.

Standing before a blank canvas, I realized I had no subject worthy to be drawn in honor of my master. I didn't hear Doña Luz enter the room or notice her until she hurried past me with a breakfast tray in her hands. She had covered her nightgown with a buffalo robe and her head with the black silk shawl which reminded me of European peasants depicted in my *Book of Knowledge*. On the tray were thoughtful gifts from the Wise Men of the Orient: gingerbread cookies, a fruit cake, one cigarillo, a box of sulphur matches and a bottle of blue agave tequila from Jalisco. She placed this tray on the bed exactly where Don Fernando had lain. After closing her eyes, clasping hands, and moving her lips in prayer, she took a match and lit a candle. If she had called out, "Breakfast is ready!," I think I would have dashed to the Arctic, breaking the world reindeer record for the 100-yards. I was entranced by the ceremony: in light of Mexican culture, it represented an acceptance of death as part of life. Right there, I found my subject. I would try to portray against a background of bright colors, alizarin crimson, say, and cadmium yellow, a jolly skeleton, cigarillo clamped in titanium white teeth, a bottle raised on high. I would entitle the painting *Salud*.

She was about to glide past me again when she pivoted on bare feet, tilted her head at me, and said in a sweet but gaga tone, "Trigonometry."

I hadn't a clue why she was mixing trigonometry, the study of angles, with Christmas unless she had mentally regressed to her time as a teacher.

She looked at me as if I were the one going bugs. "What are you doing in this room? Who said you could use this room? This room is not to be disturbed! I know you. I've seen you making eyes at Golondrina. I'll not be deceived! I know what's going on! Sacred Heart of Jesus, you'll not be smooching in his bed! Leave this room at once and take your dirty picture with you!"

"Dirty picture?" I queried myself silently. The canvas was white as Christmas in Antarctica.

"I feed you," she continued without let-up. "I wash your stinking underwear and your filthy sheets! What do you do? Nothing. You may bang on a frying pan when the train goes by. You may tell

Fernando your smutty jokes. You don't do a lick of work . . . Touch
my daughter, Mr. Fancy Pants, and I might-nigh beat the life out
of you! Do you think I give a damn for your Treaty of Guadalupe
Hidalgo? Exhibition in Paris, Mr. Fancy Pants? Why don't you
go back to where you belong? You can live with that gold-plated
scoundrel, Mr. Alpheus Woodbridge. You'll have paved streets and
electric lights and ladies in pastel satin."

Somehow I remembered that I was a paying guest in her house.
"Has Captain Dare paid up my room and board?" I asked. I think
she was as surprised as I by my cheeky riposte. She blinked eyes,
dimming their candlepower, and wrinkled her brow. "Everything,
sir," she said in sweet voice. "Mr. Dare has paid for everything. Tío
Congo saw Worthy Brother Dare in town just the other day. He's
staying at his ranch, you know. He'll be coming to live with us as
soon as he has straightened out his business affairs. I'm sure he'll
be delighted to see you . . . Merry Christmas, dear."

The news of Dare's return released Shorty's ghost into a
metaphorical potty. As long as Dare was around, Golly and I had
in reserve someone we could turn to in case of problems with the
Law. I was about to shower Doña Luz with a big Tiny Timmer in
gratitude for her news when I overheard her out in the vestibule
berating Golly with some leftover codswallop. "If, girl," Doña Luz
was saying, "you can't keep that boy off you, I'll be hanging asafetida
around your neck. He's lice!"

That did it. Stepping out of the forbidden room and encountering
Doña Luz in the hallway, I asked her, nice as pie, if I could please
borrow a horse in order to go to town to greet Mr. Dare.

"Of course," she said, her pie nicer than mine. "Dress warmly."

A little while later I was borrowing from Nono a heavy sheepskin
coat, wooly Angora chaps, a knitted wool cap and a pair of miner's
thick leather gloves. Milenko loaned me his wellingtons padded
with sealskin. Dressed for a blizzard I weighed so much I figured I
might need to be winched up to my horse's saddle, like Henry the
Eighth. Presently out in the stables I hoisted myself onto President.
The draft horse would be glad as I to avoid working for Doña Luz

on Christmas Day in the morning.

We hadn't been gone more than half a mile before we were caught in blinding blasts of snow. Like any old politician, President turned tail to whatever direction the wind was coming from. We must have spun around a dozen times before I found the road where snow had blown patches off on it. After what seemed ages I heard but could not see directly in front of us the river. Then lights began to poke through mists, and soon I was threading my way through streets covered with one-to-four feet of drifting snow. A wreath with jingling bells rolled and bounced like a hoop along Main Street. The town was deserted. The Imperial Hotel had lights on but no creature stirring there. A single fat Santa Claus, icicles spiking from white beard, was ringing a bell outside the hotel. Unlike the Laredo Desperado, he really was a fake, the bell connected to an electric gadget in a hotel window. I wondered if people had given the wooden peddler any money in the pot at its feet. They had not, but the thought would have counted.

The storm had abated by the time I reached the evergreen ponderosas at the rim of the mesa where I could look down at Homesteader's. Snow had piled to a depth of five feet or more out in the fields where buffalo and cattle were like motionless gingerbread cookies. Over against the side of the ranchhouse a tall man wearing a sheepskin coat and Stetson was shoveling out a hole. I could see him only from the waist up. He was Dare, though. Just seeing him again, safely back from France, really did make the world seem right again.

A few minutes later I alighted from President, led him into the barn where there was an empty stall next to Natural Selection's and tried without success to take the saddle and bridle off, my gloves being so frozen I couldn't grip anything. Noiselessly, Dawn Antelope appeared by my side, removed saddle and bridle, and covered President, who was snuffing happily, with a wool blanket.

Dawn Antelope pointed a bent finger at the ranchhouse and

said, "Mebbe dynamite." I got the idea. I wasn't to move toward the house. At any moment it might explode, taking Dare, like Tío Congo's wife and children, with it.

Nothing godawful happened. Dare had crawled beneath the foundations of the house to a spot where the bedroom was above his head. There he had found sticks of dynamite stuck between boards. Holding them with one hand, he used his free hand like a fin to inch himself out into the pit he had shoveled. From there, stumbling, he had gone to the frozen fishpond into which he had broken a hole, had tied the dynamite to a heavy stone and pitched what he later called "the nuisance" through the hole and had let it sink.

For an hour I'd been sitting with him and drowsy dogs in the living room at a distance from the blazing fire in the fireplace, thawing out slowly, my toes and fingers itching and burning at first, my stomach warmed deliciously by another Glass-Eye Gwilym cocktail: half hot coffee, half whiskey.

Dare had chuckled. "Don't get the idea," he said, "that you have to have a drink every time we meet."

"Not to worry," I said. "I can't stand the stuff except when I'm Lazarus returning from the dead. Tap'er light."

"Wise guy," he said with poker face.

The day after he had abandoned the ranch to Pia, Daddy, and Shiflit, pretending to leave in search of me as he galloped on Natural Selection to catch the northbound train, the story of the dynamite had had its beginnings. While the inhabitants of the house were sleeping off the effects of their party, Dawn Antelope had gone into town to pick up Natural Selection at U.S. Livery. When he returned to the ranch, he found it deserted. Daddy's hired carriage was gone; the ponies which Dawn Antelope had sent scattering into meadows were gone. Someone must have observed his running-off of the ponies and his departure. So Dawn Antelope believed.

Suspicious, he went over the grounds near the house and came upon tracks of a horse he had not previously identified. These led him to the cottonwoods by the pond. There, hidden from the house by a thick juniper hedge, were trampled buffalo grasses and soil, and there just beneath it he had discovered wire. This buried wire, he discerned, led directly toward the house. He cut the wire at that point. From old friends who had been in the mines he had learned enough about explosives to suspect the purpose of what he had stumbled upon, a detonator to be attached at any time to the wire behind the hedge, dynamite attached to the wire under the house. Tío Congo's tragedy had long been known to him, as had the name of the Texan responsible for it, Jefferson Jones, the ex-con who liked to frighten customers at Cousin Jack's by posing as "The Laredo Desperado." Dawn Antelope didn't think anyone would attempt to blow up the house until Dare came back from France. Pia and Daddy had occasionally taken up residence. She had consulted with Dawn Antelope about matters pertaining to ranching expenses. He didn't think either she or her lover knew anything about the dynamite or were in any danger from it.

"I know you're good friends with the Union," I said to Dare after he told me the story of the dynamite. "Mother Jones helped me a heap after you left, saying you called her. A couple of Union stiffs were looking for me at the depot. Tío Congo calls you 'Worthy Brother,' and Doña Luz melts at mention of your name . . . guess, someone from Corporation, someone like Lieutenant Shiflit, is down on you."

"Reckon," Dare half-smiled. "There are plenty of Corporation goons hereabouts who don't care much my helping the Union, and you can buy dynamite at the Pluck Me . . . Your father and my wife are welcome to stay here. Whoever's down on me, as you put it, won't blow them up. Me, I'm moving my freight over to Doña Luz's . . . That's another thing: unless you're set on joining your mother and grandmother in France right off the bat, I'd like you to be my buddy in the St. Mabyn's."

"Aren't they just bringing in scabs?"

Dare half smiled again. "I see you're catching on fast . . . Here's the deal. We're going in as nonunion. We *hate* the Union. Got it? We want to be spotters for Corporation and get Union boys sent down the mountain. Only, on the q.t.—otherwise we're hamburger. We'll finger the antiunionists and get *them* sent down the mountain. Can you swallow that?"

The title, "buddy," conferred upon me a bunch of glory.

"Anna Maria, excuse me, your mother," Dare went on, "says it's all right." He stood up, paced in front of the fire, came and squatted on the floor where I was seated in his Morris chair and looked me squarely in the eye. "Everything's aboveboard between me and your mother. Someday after each of us is divorced, if she'll do me the honor to listen to me, I'd like to have a talk with her. In the meantime we'll be writing letters, thinking of one another at ocean's length . . . Now, I know she wants you to join her at St. Aignan where she and your grandmother have bought a house. You could go to my old school, the École Supérieure, and from there the Sorbonne, Oxford, Cambridge. *¿Quién sabe?* You see, your mother's a wise woman. Before you go lallygagging down the academic path, she wants you to make peace with your father. I'm not saying—she's not saying—you have to forgive him. Her words, not mine: 'Tree has to take his father off the hook.' Make any sense to you? We'll talk about it at another time . . . By the way, she wrote you a letter."

The thick envelope containing Mum's letter still had a lavender scent after a journey of 5,000 miles, the lavender bringing to mind the Provence of Vincent Van Gogh. Mum's cursive blended with Don Fernando's black and white reproductions of Van Gogh's paintings. For the first time I really yearned to visit France.

The letter, addressed from St. Aignan early in December, consisted of thirty foolscap pages, the sheer number of which constituted both a treasure and an apology for the long-delayed terms of endearment.

I have that letter now before me so many decades later. Its style at first is jejune, reading like a schoolgirl's report about a summer's holiday. She hadn't corresponded with anyone for a long time. Her life had been spent in virtual solitary confinement. At her school in New York City she had been taught penmanship and correctness, how to send expressions of gratitude and condolence, how to exhaust the vocabulary of happiness on Christmas cards and of whimsical flirtation on Valentine's Day. To be oneself in letters, clearly and forthrightly, sharing the authenticity of one's person with another, was an act of compassion and was, therefore, omitted from the curriculum. So it was in this letter and in the letters that followed throughout the spring, summer and fall of 1904 that she was learning to break through the crust of conventions in writing as she already knew how to do in intimate conversation. When she was a girl and then a young bride, with whom, after all, could she have offered gifts from her heart? Ganny, though Mum loved her, was indeed, at times, a moral imbecile. Daddy, when he traveled, would never have blown himself to the expense of a postage stamp. Didn't Daddy have relatives in England? He did, a mother, and we knew her name: Mrs. Irene Penhallow. And that was all we knew about her except that she was, to quote Daddy, "supported by a rich American in the style to which she was accustomed." We, Mum and I, were forbidden to make further inquiries about Mrs. Irene Penhallow, this mother-in-law and grandmother. The Rich American assumed in our imaginations the status of a myth, someone as mysteriously concealed from the light of day as the true author of Shakespeare's plays and sonnets. Mum believed that the anonymous American had been supporting an abandoned mistress because she raised his illegitimate son. She wrote no letters to England.

She began, after "Darling Tree," "Happy Birthday," and "Merry Christmas," to describe the history, the customs, the rivers and rabbits of Touraine.

*The Province of Touraine lies a little west of the center of France. Its climate is what the French call **doux** or **charitable**.*

In winter it is about like that of Virginia. The thermometer very rarely goes below freezing and then only for a few days at a time.

Touraine is watered by the Loire, the Cher, the Indre and many smaller streams. It was the favorite place of residence for the French Kings from Charlemagne to Louis XIV. At first they built strongly fortified castles as they needed to protect themselves from their fierce neighbors and powerful, quarrelsome vassals who, in their turn, built equally strong citadels. These castles were built on sites chosen for defense on hills overlooking the rivers and valleys. At their feet grew up small villages and towns, built against the rock and walls to gain protection from the fortress.

*Foulques Nerra was the greatest builder of castles, François Ier of pleasure palaces, whereas Louis XI, Henri IV, and Cardinal Richelieu were the greatest destroyers of the **châteaux forts** in their attempts to reduce the power of the barons and to increase their own. What escaped their hands was further destroyed during the Revolution.*

It has been said of Touraine that it is a land that has been run, directly or indirectly, by women. It is a land of the wicked Isabelle of Bavaria, of the saintly Jeanne d'Arc, of Agnès Sorel, of Anne de Bretagne (wife of two kings of France), of Louis de Savoie and her daughter Marguerite, of Claude, his wife and of the many mistresses of that king, of Diane of Poitiers, of Catherine de Medici, of Marie Stuart, la Reine Margo, Gabrielle d'Estrées and of many more. Some swayed the kings for good, others for evil. But all of them left indelible traces on the history of Touraine. It has also been the land of many celebrated authors, of Balzac, Rabelais, George Sand and others who have all loved it and written about it.

St. Aignan, the village of Mr. Dare's youth, has already had a vital effect on our hearts and imaginations. Let me try to make you acquainted with it and with some of our delightful friends.

As one approaches St. Aignan from the right bank of the

Cher, the château and the towers of the magnificent church dominate the town with most medieval effect. St. Aignan is one of the quaintest and most picturesque little towns in Touraine, with its winding streets and old houses of wood and stone, of the fifteenth and sixteenth centuries, with strange gable-ends and dormer windows, decorated with delicate carvings and corbels, which are all so unexpected and full of charm and which make it so easy to reconstruct the past in one's imagination and to enable the visitor from the New World to realize how this little town is simply saturated with history.

Let me tell you about a luncheon we had with the peasants. An old peasant, known to everyone as 'Père Bricole' because he declares that he has just **'un tas de bricole'** *in his wheelbarrow, 'just a little of everything,' lives with his wife in a two-room hut. The old couple have one room, and their rabbits have the other. One day Ganny and I walked down there to the hut to buy some strawberries. The two old people were at their dinner and wanted us to share it. We set a day when we could have* **déjeuner** *with them. Our servants begged us not to do anything so crazy and predicted we would die of ptomaine poisoning, but go we did. We found the table set and ready for us. The place was nothing but a hovel, and yet everything was as clean as could be. Even the napkins had the old dame's initials embroidered on them in red. This was our menu: snails cooked in white wine, eaten with long steel knitting needles, then rabbit done in red wine. There was white wine to drink with the snails and red to drink with the rabbit. I must say, I felt like a cannibal to be eating a rabbit with all its brothers and sisters looking on, for the door leading into the room occupied by the rabbits was open. The meal ended with goat's milk cheese and preserved fruits, and it was all very good indeed.*

Ganny has bought us a house! We couldn't continue to be beholden to Mr. Dare as guests in his and his parents' lovely house, so we went to see every house we heard was for sale. One day a friend told us of a house in the very center of St.

Aignan that was about to be sold at auction and advised us to look at it. As soon as we visited it we knew our search was over: we had found the very place we had been hunting for! Mind you, Mr. Dare tried to persuade us to remain in his house forever, such is his kindness, but he was not altogether displeased with our decision to live in St. Aignan beyond the reach of some violent fools in America.

When the late owner of the house died, about the time of our arrival in Touraine, the house was left to one relative and the furnishings to another, so it had to be sold at auction. When a piece of property is to be sold at auction it is done by the 'three-candle' method. Three small candles of equal length are stuck on a board; one is lighted, and the house is declared to be for sale at a certain price. If the candle burns out without raising a bid, the second candle is lighted, and, if there is no bid by the time that that, too, has burned out, the third candle is lighted. If that one also burns out without a bid, the property is declared not sold. If there is an uncontested bid on any of the three candles, and they have all three burned out, the property goes to the only bidder. If, however, a bid is made during the burning of any of the three candles and it is raised by a second bidder, a new set of candles is lighted, and so on until three have burned out uncontested.

My heart almost stopped beating when our first candle was lighted, and I heard your Ganny's voice bidding in her New Orleans French, for I was sure that every man in that crowded room wanted the little house as much as I did. Of course, I had not as yet become acquainted with the French passion for attending auctions. Then the second and the third candles were lighted and burned peacefully out without another bid. I breathed again as I realized that the house was actually ours! Now, we've bought furniture and hired servants, and I do so wish I could show you your upstairs room! **Comme on dit, au plaisir de vous revoir.**

Oh, I so hated to have Ganny spending my father's tainted

*money! When a little more than a year from now I inherit my
share of it, I shall no longer give it away to your father for his
research. Perhaps I should buy and set free all the rabbits in
Touraine. What do you think, dear? I do so wish I had the man
in the family to come and advise his 'Mum.'*

Mum's letter continued in this vein for some time. "Man in the
family"? Coquettish conventionality? Given the fact that she had
been for so long isolated from the world and had now as her sole
companion the imbecile of New Orleans, not to mention she was
living in France, she was bound to be susceptible to silliness. It
was as if—and I had this thought at the time—she wanted to regain
the person she had been at eighteen before she married Daddy,
but also, as I read between the lines, she was in love. I knew the
feeling of love. With Scampy's photograph still in my wallet, a trifle
scratched and faded due to wear and tear, the picture itself that
of a Snow Fairy who was beginning to look a little young for me,
I realized I had been clinging to puppy love. I loved Golly now, as
Romeo his Juliet, incandescently.

About halfway along in the letter Mum stopped being
conventional. The death-in-life of the Sun Palace I had twigged, her
escape from it I had not, escape with a man she had never met
before. Had Dare brought her up to date on my adventures?

In a passage coming after Mum cannibalized a rabbit while
its brothers and sisters were looking on, she amazed me by
her knowledge not only of Daddy's affair with Pia but also of
Woodbridge's affair with her.

*It is Mr. Dare's opinion that Mrs. Dare, who left him to
become your father's mistress, is looking for the main chance
and will abandon your father for another, richer man. In such a
circumstance, much as I regret any pain I may cause you, I shall
not be taking him back, though he crawl to me in sackcloth and
ashes and protest his love for me in the usual deathless terms.
While I was in New York I engaged a firm of lawyers to begin*

divorce proceedings. I also changed my Will.

I have known for a long time about your father's infatuation and affair with Mrs. Dare, known from the time she first set foot in my house. Everyone who comes there is secretly photographed by Ruby, who has a Kodak and shows me the pictures. I tell you this because I do not take divorce lightly. I refrained from making an issue of the affair, expecting your father to lose interest once he realized what a fool he has been. Since, however, he forced me to enter the sanitorium where he had complete control over my life, I determined to free myself from him, should opportunity arise, as, now, it has so risen.

Further, I have evidence, as Mr. Dare has not, that our home has been converted into a love-nest for Mrs. Dare and Mr. Alpheus Woodbridge. Therefore, indeed, we may expect at any moment to learn that your father is betrayed. He will then be turning to you for a shoulder to weep on. His cruel and absurd actions against you he will try to discard as if they never happened. You who have largeness of heart may then act toward him as you see fit.

Mum here and thereafter in her letter was her true self, letting me know who she was, how she felt, and why. She trusted me. She was coming closer and closer than, perhaps, she should have done to revealing not only why she trusted Dare but also how and why there had come into her possession a secret so powerful it had placed her life in danger and now my own life.

Mr. Dare arrived at the Colorado Springs station about one in the morning. After taking a carriage to a livery stable near the Sun Palace, while retaining that carriage and driver, he there purchased —not hired but purchased—two quarter horses with Mexican saddles, these to be kept in readiness for him upon his imminent return. At the livery stable he also changed his attire from rancher to Captain in the United States Army (appearing as I had seen him once before in one of Ruby's photographs).

He then was driven to the gates of the sanitorium. There he was stopped by National Guardsmen who use their off-duty time from Cripple Creek to serve Daddy's Head of Security, none other than Lieutenant Fredson Shiflit, whom you know. Mr. Dare showed them an official letter written and signed by your father and pronouncing a certain person—me in place of Mrs. Dare—cured and immediately to be released. I believe Mr. Dare has mentioned to you the existence of such a letter, if not the forgery he had made of it. At any rate, Mr. Dare effected my release, a fairy-tale escape. Really, I was so glad he didn't have to climb up to my tower, pulling on my hair. Ladies who give their uncut hair to 200-pound gentlemen are very apt to become bald, and gentlemen who climb towers by this method are certain to be disappointed. I heard a tapping on my door. There he was, quite handsome if I do say so, blushing so much I thought he would never get around to introducing himself (I already knew who he was) and stating his business (I already imagined what it was). He had the most adorable look on his face but was tongue-tied.

I asked him, "Would you like us to escape, Captain?"

He replied, "Yes, ma'am, Mrs. Penhallow, we have to get the hell out quick."

"And what is our destination, Captain?"

"France," he said.

"Would you like to use the bathroom?" I inquired.

He shook his head and asked if I were an equestrienne. I informed him I'd won a blue ribbon for riding at school. He said, "Splendid, perfectly splendid."

And we went. Fortunately, I'd already put on some woollies, as it was quite cold, and now that I knew we were going to France I congratulated myself for having been so perspicacious and provident. We alighted from the carriage at the livery stable and mounted and rode off on our quarter horses. It was about seventy miles to Denver; however, we must have traveled ninety before we arrived at Union Station, Mr. Dare deeming it prudent to avoid the thoroughfares and navigate our way at the base of the mountains and by the stars. Especially in the elevations over 7,000 feet, such as in Greenland, Colorado, it was rather cold. As you and Ruby know, though, I've been long accustomed to running in cold weather at high elevations. Your Old Lady did pretty darn well for herself. In Denver Mr. Dare had some telephone calls to make concerning your welfare, and at the station we were met by six of his friends in the mining trades, two of whom helped us to see our horses removed to safe pastures, the other four, big, burly fellows wearing dungarees and derbies, prepared to travel with us as armed guards. Mr. Dare was proving himself prescient at every step of the way. Later on in this letter I shall explain why I was agreeing so readily to his plans for my safety.

Someone from the Union in Denver had already purchased for all six of us first-class Pullman tickets to Indianapolis, avoiding Chicago altogether. We did observe on the platforms in Denver and in Omaha a congeries of shady-looking characters who were, Mr. Dare said, " a species of vermin called detectives," but, if they were seeking to arrest us, as they undoubtedly were, we had bribed a conductor and settled in to our sleepers out in the yards hours before departure time in Denver, and in Omaha the conductor prevented any snooping around. During this journey to Indianapolis Mr. Dare and I at last had time to improve upon our acquaintance. You may be sure he has formed an extremely favorable opinion of your mind and character. As he is a gentleman of quite refined sensibility, a bit diffident but good as gold, I was very pleased with his report and, of course, extremely proud of you and confident of your ability to cope with adversity.

Mr. Dare's gift of laughter is imbued with sorrow. He playfully thumbs his nose at the world of laws and conventions yet envisions no escape except in evolutionary time, the emergence of a new world of consciousness.

One of our precautions against discovery and arrest was to invent names for ourselves, pretending we were newlyweds returning to our home in New York. For our surname Mr. Dare chose Marlow. He explained that this name has literary associations for him. For given names we needed to mix the ordinary with the off-center, our theory being, plainness, like Mr. and Mrs. Bill and Betty Smith, gives the incognito away. I decided upon Prunella. Mr. Dare, laughing, decided upon Murd.

"Murd?" I frowned. "I've never heard of such a ridiculous name. It doesn't suit you."

He smiled wistfully as if at a loss to explain himself. "Murdstone," he said. "Character in David Copperfield. First four letters of 'murder.'"

"Mister Marlow," I protested, "why in heaven's name would you associate yourself with murder?"

"Because, Mrs. Marlow," he replied, shooting me a look of distress, "when people die, I think it's my fault."

"Well," I said. "It's how we live that matters."

For an address for Mr. and Mrs. Murd Marlow, I chose 26, Washington Square. It was my place of birth, now demolished.

Then there was the matter of a wedding ring. When our train crossed over the Mississippi River on a bridge, I opened a window and threw your father's ring into the drink. That he had purchased it, a stolen ring, from a drug addict on the Ponte Vecchio had once charmed me—all that glisters is not gold—but no more. "Murd, dear," I said, "I'll buy myself a ring in Indianapolis."

"I have just the job, Prunella, honey," he said. Keeping a straight face, he dug into the tiny watch pocket in his trousers and removed the most beautiful ring I've ever seen, a clear, European-cut diamond about 1.3 karats, priceless, really. He slipped the ring onto my finger—and off again. "Le voilà," he said with mock dignity. If it hadn't been for his burlesque manner, I might have believed he was making a proposal.

"It's beautiful, Mr. Marlow," I blurted out, quite beside myself with unexpected emotion. "It must have a special meaning for

you since you carry it about on your person like a talisman."

"Precisely," he said after a pause of astonishment. The ring, he explained, had been his mother's, purchased for her in Paris by his father, Dr. Randolph Dare. After his parents died, Mr. Dare did in fact carry the ring about his person as a talisman with magical powers, especially in the midst of battle. "I want you to wear it, Mrs. Marlow, when we're in New York. It will keep you safe."

We spent several days in Indianapolis in separate rooms at the hotel. Mr. Dare abandoned his uniform, rancher's outfit, and gun at the Union and purchased for himself the three-piece suit, high collar, and cravat of a traveling salesman. For me he purchased some clothing in equally bad taste, purple with pink ruffles. We both had haircuts, he sacrificing curly blond locks, I dark tresses. With a bowler hat he now looked, as Ganny would later exclaim, "perfectly hideous," while I will pass for a tart at the Moulin Rouge. Of more importance than these trifling attempts at disguise was our conversation over "long distance" telephone with Ganny. As soon as she learned that I have left your father for good and was accompanied by **un homme tout à fait beau et gentil**, she was eager to arrange for our stay in New York and for her own **décampement** upon short notice.

It seems Ganny told you a "fib" about her slave-based pelf, believing you were too young several Christmases ago to know the truth, namely, our fortunes are intact whether we choose to accept them or not. For myself, come next year's inheritance, I shall have to save some of it for living expenses and for your education. I trust that, when the time comes, you will place yourself at the service of your fellow human beings and ignore windfalls.

"You lied to Tree," I admonished Ganny.

"Nonsense," she said. "If we didn't lie to children, there would be no religion."

Mr. Dare advised Ganny over the telephone to have all

her valuables removed to safe deposit and all her furniture to storage, leaving her Park Avenue apartment empty. She was to reserve rooms for "Mr. and Mrs. Murd Marlow" and for herself at a small hotel off Fulton Street, to purchase steamship tickets, to have her trunks deposited ahead of time with the company, and, above all, should anyone inquire about "Kyle Deville Dare" or "Mrs. Penhallow," to deny any knowledge of their whereabouts. Ganny, of course, was delighted with all the fuss and derring-do.

From Indianapolis we went by Pullman to Baltimore and from there by ferryboat to New York. Such a long time since I had seen sky-scrapers, the bay, steamships! For the first time Mr. Dare explained to me his extraordinary precautions with respect to Ganny's apartment. "It's Shiflit," he said. "He has some mysterious connection with Mr. Alpheus Woodbridge and Corporation. Corporation goons will likely be on the lookout for us in New York, and what more probable place for finding us than your mother's apartment? We've been lucky so far, but I prefer to leave nothing to chance . . ."

The day before we embarked on a steamer bound for Cherbourg, Mr. Dare and I put to the test his speculations about Ganny's apartment. Taking an empty suitcase with us, we went and nonchalantly surveyed our surroundings. Sure enough, a beefy fellow in a drab beaver hat seemed to be observing us! So we proceeded up the elevator to Ganny's fifth-floor apartment and entered it, using her key, but instead of departing by the way we came in, we opened a window, descended to an alleyway on a fire escape, and returned to Fulton Street. We had left an impression with the "spotter," as Mr. Dare called him, that we were going to spend the night together with Ganny in her apartment.

I can tell you this: Mr. Dare's speculations proved not only true but also far more deadly than I could have imagined. The next morning the **Times** *reported that a fire had destroyed the fifth floor of that apartment building on Park Avenue! Although* residents had been safely evacuated, the whereabouts of one of them—meaning Ganny—had yet to be confirmed by police.

Let me add, Mr. Dare and I very much doubt whether your father was the least bit involved with this attempt on our lives. After all, for him to receive my inheritance in 1905, as he believes he will, your Old Lady had to remain alive and kicking. *Donnez-moi ça.*

Mum finally arrived in her letter at the Deadly Secret she had been withholding.

The night before Mr. Dare came miraculously to liberate me from the sanitorium, I happened to make the acquaintance of Elizabeth Woodbridge, the wife of Mr. Alpheus Woodbridge and the mother of their two children, Alpheus, who is mentally disturbed, and Felixine or "Scampy," both of whom you know. The Sun Palace was built expressly for the care of Elizabeth, once her disease had become terminal. As you may have noticed, the sick and the elderly in this country are often whisked out of sight to die alone while court-appointed lawyers, doctors, and others consume the estate or while, as in this case, a spouse is looking to fill the anticipated vacancy with a vagina. I do not know exactly why Mr. Woodbridge chose Colorado Springs as the site for his sanitorium, other than the fact it is rapidly becoming a resort famous for treating lungers, and I do not know exactly why he chose your father as Director, though Mr. Woodbridge wanted Lieutenant Shiflit of the Colorado National Guard to serve as Head of Security and, especially, to keep careful watch over Elizabeth to prevent her from talking.

She is still a beautiful woman. Her lustrous black hair falls freely to her shoulders. Her dark eyes, though feverish, sparkle with intelligence. Take note that her father, who was one of Mr. Woodbridge's Bones crowd at Yale, is Vice-President of Corporation. Also take note that Elizabeth, as I, was married at eighteen, no sooner having come out in New York society than

*her father's secret society "brother" and boss pounced on her.
"You don't resist Mr. Woodbridge," Elizabeth confided in me.*

*When "Lady" Woodbridge was incarcerated in the Sun
Palace, we lungers (in my case a pretend lunger) were wildly
curious to know more about her. Married to one of the most
powerful men in America, she had to be, we imagined, too good
to mix with us **hoi polloi**. We were not surprised to find that she
was confined to her private room with an armed guard posted
at her door, day and night. These arrangements, we assumed,
were intended to keep **us** out, not **her** in.*

*Now, I have no wish to sow further discord between you
and your father. His foolishness you have observed for yourself,
painfully so, and I fear he will persist in it. However, whether
you know it or not, any evidence to the contrary, he is fond of
you and, I dare say, proud of you. Well, everyone to one degree
or another is stuck, closed, obstructed, shut in, out, or off.
Occluded would be a good Shootout word for our condition.
Your father occludes shame. He is ashamed, deep-down; he
will not admit that shame spins the plot of his life. But I know
him very well. He is ashamed about his identity. His mother,
Mrs. Irene Penhallow, may very well exist and may be, in his
eyes, low-class. His father is unknown. His birth makes him a
bastard. For this reason I want you to take him off the hook, if
you can, remove this difficulty, bring him some peace of mind,
perhaps effect a reconciliation. Consult with Mr. Dare about
this matter (this matter only, not anything else in this letter).
Take Daddy off the hook.*

*Your father, in an effort to please "Lady" Woodbridge,
told her I was living (!) in a room "down the hallway, second
door on the right." In his own way, I suppose, he believes I
am worthy enough to be Elizabeth's companion. Further, he
is so insensitive to the feelings of others, especially those of
women, he probably fails to notice that Elizabeth is a prisoner,
a humiliated prisoner. Is it any wonder that she would want to
seek me out as her confidant?*

It is two o'clock in the morning. Her guard has deserted his post. She slips out of her room, tiptoes to my room, raps softly on the door. Having seen her when Mr. Woodbridge and family brought her for admittance to the sanitorium, I recognize her. "I must speak to you in confidence before I die," she says. "Do not light a candle or raise your voice above a whisper, or they will find us together, and I fear for the consequences," she says. "Every word of mine, every glance of mine, every whim—all are reported to my husband. Listen," she says.

Everything is allowed to Mr. Woodbridge, she tells me. He takes a perverse pleasure from knowing he can get away with anything. He protests undying love for her but subjects her to his every command and caprice. When she first married him, he would leave her locked up in their mansion and vanish for indefinite periods of time. His visits then came to be her whole life. When she pleads with him to stop destroying what he claims he loves, he holds a lighted cigarette against her cheek, repeating, "I love you, I love you," while her face is burning.

He has had many affairs in his youth and anonymously supports a bastard son and his mother. But he wants a legitimate male heir to his fortune and to his chairmanship of Corporation. Elizabeth presents him with a son, but "Alphie" is perceived by Mr. Woodbridge as "unfit" to inherit such power and responsibility.

"See the scar on my cheek?" Elizabeth asked me. "Mr. Woodbridge promised to light another cigarette unless I gave him another son—by another man."

He evidently is impotent, Mr. Woodbridge. If she will become pregnant by another man and give him a healthy son, he will raise that son as his own. If she refuses this demand or tries to run away, her father will lose his job. She consents to the scheme.

There is a seventeen-year-old prizefighter recently arrived in New York from Utah, an insolent fellow who comes to Mr. Woodbridge's Sunday School sessions at church, Fredson

Shiflit by name. He is paid to have intercourse with Elizabeth while Mr. Woodbridge observes the couple from behind a one-way glass partition. In time, she gives birth to a daughter, Felixine or "Scampy."

Now for the first time, son or daughter, it doesn't matter which, Mr. Woodbridge has met his match.

The country bumpkin from the West, like Mr. Woodbridge, himself, has no shame. Blackmail is threatened. Exposed, neither Woodbridge nor Corporation will survive the scandal. He pays Shiflit off. Shiflit disappears from time to time to play soldier, but he always comes back, sometimes to serve as coachman, always as a blackmailer. It is in Lieutenant Shiflit's best interest to make certain that Elizabeth never reveals their secret.

"When Scampy grows up," quoth Shiflit, "I intend to make her my wife, Mr. Woodbridge, and you will not only encourage the business but also make me your heir and Chairman of the Board, Corporation . . . In the meantime I will agree to deceive Scampy into believing you are her father."

Mr. Woodbridge, Elizabeth told me, had no objections to a future incestuous marriage. He admired Shiflit for his cheek and considered his future son-in-law well-suited to carry on the family business.

There you have the secret as it was divulged to me by Elizabeth. You have yet to understand why I unhesitantly agreed to accompany Mr. Dare out of the sanitorium and as far away as this village in France. Why could we not have delayed our flight, rushed to Los Tristes, and brought you along with us?

In the wee hours of the morning of what would turn out to be my last day of captivity in the Sun Palace Sanitorium, Elizabeth, poor dear lady, Mr. Woodbridge's "last dutchess," if you will, tiptoed out of my room. I watched her go. The hallway was dark. At its end, next to her room, I saw no armed guard. Yet, suddenly, the chandelier lights were switched on! Bless me, there in the hallway were two uniformed Guardsmen, one

206

of whom was grabbing Elizabeth in an ugly fashion, throwing
her to the floor and putting a boot in her face. The other was
slowly coming toward me, his hobnail boots on the marble
floor going **click, click, click***. You have seen that officer's face*
for yourself, the black mustache, feral eyes, scar.

Lieutenant Fredson Shiflit stopped, glared at me. His lips
twitched.

He knew that I knew. I backed away, closed my door, locked
it. His bootsteps faded.

Love,
Mum

~~~

The letter I received from Mum on Christmas Day, 1903, differed
greatly from most of the stories with which from time to time
people have burdened me. A secret report with the potential to
push Humpty Dumpty off his wall, it had been entrusted to me
for safekeeping. That her life was in danger, I had often imagined.
Now the danger to her proved to be real. Shiflit knew what she
knew: Elizabeth Woodbridge had passed the Secret along to Mum.
By passing it along to me, Mum was taking the precaution to have
it preserved should anything happen to her.

Dare invited me to stay at the ranch for a few days after Christmas
while he tidied up his affairs and we prepared ourselves for going
to work in the mines. The snow having melted, I rode into town
on President and had Mum's letter locked in a safe deposit box at
the First National Bank. So important was the letter, I opened an
account with one of the dollars Daddy had left to me.

We, Dare and I, again discussed his plan to get us hired on at
the St. Mabyn's by pretending that we were haters of the Union and
that he was eager to be a spotter for Corporation. "Mother Jones
may have jumped the gun on this one," he remarked after a deep
sigh. "Strikers in our District 15 are being abandoned by those in
the fields north of Denver. The fellas up there have been coaxed to

return to work, having achieved nothing, and our fellas, as you've seen, are closer to starvation than they were before. Not only that, but the miners with the most skill and the best understanding of trade unions, that is to say, the English and the Welsh, have been deported, their places taken by the inexperienced scabs and antiunionists. In future, I guarantee you, there'll be more gassy mines, more explosions, more widows than ever before. The Union will have to call the whole thing off. The National Guard will be leaving, but the mine guards and deputy sheriffs and detectives will be freer than ever to do as they please. We have to plan for the next strike. Next time we'll have solidarity. Next time the Union will have tent camps in which to house strikers and their families evicted from the company-towns . . . Here's where we come in."

The plan was, as I've said, he would pretend to spot Union members and sympathizers in order to get them fired when, in fact, he would be spotting antiunionists and getting them fired. My job would be to teach non-English-speaking scabs to cuss out the Union while secretly pledging loyalty to it.

We went to the Pluck Me. After getting me outfitted with clothes and gear for mining, Dare took me over to Union H.Q. It was little more than a shabby, smoke-filled suite of rooms occupied by men wearing unbuttoned vests and delivering rapid-fire messages over a battery of telephones. That, as it turned out, was what we had come for, to have a telephone line strung between the office and the Medina ranch. Everyone seemed glad to see Dare. When he introduced me as his "buddy," a couple of armed, cigar-chewing bullies clapped me on the back and offered me a choice of snuff, whiskey, or crackerjack. I chose crackerjack and hoped no one would consider me a Little Lord Fauntleroy with a velvet suit and lace collar hidden underneath my new pit pants and denim shirt.

It was Dawn Antelope's custom every year the last week of December to return to his 1,000-year-old ancestral home, Taos Pueblo, New Mexico Territory, to participate in their sacred Deer Dance. "Them big doin's," he had told me, by which he meant, as I supposed, what Dare had told me about Indian ceremonialism, that it often had the aim of keeping the world in harmony. That was deep enough for me. Dare and I had the ranch to ourselves unless Pia and Daddy, whom he called "The Claim Jumper," should decide to come down and spend the holidays.

It was during this time that Dare taught me how to shoot a Winchester, how to rope a maverick, and how to prepare for dinner a quail full of buckshot. Also at this time he arranged to have his herd of cattle and buffalo auctioned off so that he could concentrate his attention on what he called "the coalmining war."

One more thing, the letting-Daddy-off-the-hook bit: we had a little time, evenings before the fireplace after dinner, to discuss Mum's insistence upon it. She had shared her theory about Daddy with Dare as well as with me, and it went like this. First, although Daddy had an English mother, Mrs. Irene Penhallow, address unknown, she was probably not a married woman and possibly never had been. He was the *bastard* son of a union between a girl of uncertain class and, probably, an anonymous but, fortunately, supportive Rich American. Presumably the Rich American had arranged to have this accidental mother pensioned off for life and the son educated up to and including Guy's Hospital. In return for this settlement Mrs. Irene Penhallow must have agreed to keep undisclosed the Rich American's identity. Second, Mr. Rountree Penhallow had grown up with a hidden sense of shame. In England he had but a limited future, such was the stigma attached to his birth out of wedlock, and so he had been particularly anxious to light out for the States. Third, because Daddy was deeply and secretly ashamed, he indulged in scapegoating, pinning the lable, *bastard*, on me in order to rid himself of it and shifting the violence he felt onto me, readily believing Shiflit and Alphie when they claimed I had raped Scampy. Finally, Daddy's attitude to women was influenced by his lack of a respectable mother. He enjoyed watching militiamen shoot up a dressmaker's dummy. He persecuted Mum, controlling her at every turn, debased his female patients by encouraging cousining and torturing them with *Nearer My God to Thee*, and cracked jokes about feminine body-parts. Did he, dreaming of killing his mother, cast that dream off on me, making me out to be a matricidal maniac? The shoe seemed to fit. Since he was blind to what he had been doing, my job was to open his eyes.

"What do you really think I can do, sir?" I asked Dare.

"I might be wrong," he replied, " and any drilling you do may end up with a dry hole, but in my opinion you have just to be yourself . . . Try writing the Claim Jumper a letter once a week for as long as it takes to get a response. Expect nothing. Don't beg, plead, pander or whine. Don't dwell upon the past, and don't refer to your mother or to anyone in the family. Cool off the terms of endearment. Show you care simply by the act of communicating. Show you respect him by avoiding reproaches. Ask him but don't tell him or command him . . . What will you write about? Your new life. Your work in the mines. People you observe. Use the power of implication to enable him to put himself in your shoes and get out of himself. Then, gradually, he may come around to accepting you, regarding you as a worthy person, a loving person, someone to trust and be proud of . . . Once he realizes that he is accepted by you in spite of what has been inflicted upon you, 'the whips and scorns of time . . . the proud man's contumely . . . the thousand natural shocks that flesh is heir to,' he may accept you. Acceptance is the spur."

"*Hamlet,*" I said. "Act Three, Scene One."

"Pedant," he said.

Following Dare's advice once I became a coalminer, I wrote Daddy a letter once a week, giving him the new telephone number as well as my postal address. He never responded. I kept on trying to break through to him. I even risked a prose-poem about mining, the kind of literary pretension he was almost certain to deride.

I have gone inside the earth for coal, it began. Blackness of the mine, lightless, soundless, motionless, formless as death, lacking the feeling of space and far from the fields of felt time. How can I tell you of eternal night? Here the sun never rises,

never sets. Here the wind never blows, the birds never sing,
the aspens never tremble, no rose ever blooms. Instead of
rivers, stones, instead of meadows, bones. The pointed flame
of my lamp brings twinkles to crystals. The cottony filaments
of fungus on timbers catch my flickering light. Coal glistens.
There is a musty odor like that of clay floors in a sodbuster's
hut. There is a reek of oil, of smoke from old explosions, of dust
you don't think too much about breathing because it is killing
you quietly. Picks and shovels are clinking, mule-drawn cars
are rattling, echos are blotted out. The white damp will smell of
violets. Beware. The black damp will drum in the ears. Beware.
The rumbling roof pings to the hammer's tap or sounds hollow.
To load a car, I strip to the waist, lifting each shovelful four feet,
turning it, dumping it, hour after hour, breaking with pick the
blocks of coal too large to lift. I am wet with sweat. My skin
is smeared black, my muscles go into spasms, my blisters are
broken, in-grained with dust, my fingers stiffen into twigs. A
sudden burst of cold air from the ventilating tunnel turns my
skin clammy. Cramps, like small boa constrictors, squeeze
my flesh. I go up the shaft in a cage, from the belly of earth
I emerge. The mountainside aspens are whispering. Smoke
coils into stars. Lights of the company-town harvest my face.

The strike, as Dare had predicted, had to be called off.
Throughout southern Colorado there was widespread bitterness
about the intransigence of Corporation and mine owners, their
refusal to recognize the rights of workers to organize. We in Doña
Luz's household, as usual, fared better than most. Because the
supervisor at the St. Mabyn's had been a friend of Don Fernando
in spite of the Medina family's well-known dedication to the Union,
he allowed Nono, his brother, and the other boarders to return to
work there, while Dare and I, as planned, were hired as vehement
antiunionists, he a spotter paid an extra $30 a month. By the summer
of 1904 Carmencita and Orlando were married and living in the
St. Mabyn's company-town, thus leaving the heavy chores more

than ever in the hands of Doña Luz, Tío Congo, and Golly; the Irish stableboys were rehired. There were now few cattle and sheep to be cared for, most of them having been slaughtered in order to keep Tío Congo's "hillbillies" alive, and the number of dairy cows was reduced to four, enough to supply us with milk, butter, and cheese but no longer adequate for a business in the company-towns. All of us with the exception of Golly, whose schooling was cut short at the age of fourteen, were, relatively speaking, prospering.

Dare and I regularly received separate letters from Mum. The French postage stamps and the odors of Provençal lavender elevated us in the eyes of the family to an exotic level. The fact that we read these letters in the privacy of our rooms also made us objects of wonder and perhaps of envy: we had lives beyond the boundaries of the farm. The introduction of a telephone proved in this respect a godsend. Primarily installed so that Dare could conduct business with the Union, it also served to open a window on the world for Doña Luz and Golly. When they were in the kitchen and talking on the telephone, Doña Luz to Carmencita and an expanding flock of friends and relatives, Golly to schoolgirls no longer lost, their faces reflected the weather, sometimes cloudy, usually breezy, once in a while exhilaratingly sunny.

When I wrote my letters to Daddy, I no longer held back feelings but closed with "Your loving son, Rountree," the name I hated. I gave him that.

He telephoned me on December 18, 1904, my fourteenth birthday. Before talking with me, he asked Doña Luz, who answered, if he could speak with "Captain Dare." He and Dare spoke with one another. Because I had never received a telephone call from anybody during 1904, I had given up the habit of expecting one. I was upstairs in my bed, enjoying a day off from work, when the telephone rang in the kitchen. I expected no birthday greeting or presents. Doña Luz was as nice as pie when Dare was around but glared at me when I was alone, evidently still believing I was guilty, one, of treason due to Daddy's being employed by Mr. Alpheus Woodbridge, and, two, of lust for Miss Golondrina Medina—which was true even though she was as set against marriage as fervently as an Amazon.

Burrr-ring burr-ring. The telephone, as usual, made a sound so jarring to the nerves that it seemed to compete with a mine whistle's blast for urgency: FIRE IN THE HOLE! I overheard the usual fuss in the kitchen, the cessation of ringing, then, far off, Dare's voice. After a while, instead of yelling for me from downstairs, he stomped up the stairs and down the hallway to the entrance to my room. "Tree, it's for you," he said a bit breathlessly. "It's the Claim Jumper in Colorado Springs. He's coming down to Homesteader's for Christmas in order to meet us . . . Here's the deal: Mrs. Woodbridge has died at the Sun Palace. Upon learning the news, Pia deserted your father and went to live with Woodbridge in New York. The Claim Jumper wants me, me of all people, to persuade Pia to come back to him! Just be nice to him. He sounds almost suicidal, but I think you've taken him off the hook."

A minute later I was in the kitchen preparing my mouth and ear for a long-awaited but dreaded conversation. Out of the corner of my eye I saw Golly pointing to a cake on the table, then to herself. *Baked it for your birthday*, her lips said silently.

"Hullo."

"Rountree, dear boy," Daddy said, voice half buried in static. "Pater here. Judas Priest. Long time. Just thought I'd give you chaps a tinkle . . . Captain Dare and I are planning to have a little *tête-à-tête* at the ranch on Christmas Day. I wonder if you'd fancy coming along? Do come, and happy birthday, that sort of thing . . . Did I tell you the one about the licensed victualer and the navvy? Well, the navvy approached the licensed victualer in the pub and said with a cheeky look, 'What will you do, Mr. Bugalugs, if I leap over the bar and rape your daughter?' And the licensed victualer replied with remarkable presence of mind, 'Charge you corkage, old boy.' The navvy had the mickey taken out of him, eh wot? How's your mother? Bit of all right? To think of all I did for her! The devil tyke it, and all that . . . Ringing off."

"Wait, please," I said. Daddy's tone, though false and bitter, wasn't snide and hectoring. He seemed to know who I was and where I was, an inch away on the magical, if primitive, wire. "Are you all right, Dad?" I wanted to come directly to the point.

"Kipper's knickers. Fit as a fiddle."

"When you met Mum in Florence," I blurted out, "did you throw Muggins over the *loggia* balustrade?"

"Of *course!* " Daddy replied on a rising inflection as if he'd never heard such a silly question. "Gorblimey, the bloody four-legged defecator bit me! You have to put rabid dogs down, you know . . . Any more questions? I dare say you have more up your sleeve, eh? Don't be timid."

Just be nice to him, Dare had warned me. "Well, Dad," I said, "I do have a question, if you don't mind, sir?"

"Get the bloody hell on with it then," he said.

"My grandmother," I said. "You've never told us anything about her. Irene. Is that her real name?"

"I should bloody well hope so."

"Is she alive?"

"So far."

"Where does she live?"

"London."

"Where in London?"

"Frognall Gardens."

"So she lives in Frognall Gardens, London, and anyone can locate Mrs. Irene Penhallow there . . . Does she live with her husband, your father, my grandfather?"

"She's very well taken care of," Daddy said.

The line went dead.

The palm of my hand felt sweaty on the receiver. I wondered whether we had been cut off or he had hung up on me. Either way, I was glad about his call and glad I'd grasped a couple of nettles. Placing the receiver back on the hook, I glanced at Golly, who was spreading icing on my cake. She caught my glance, lowered her gaze. I turned and went out of the kitchen and up the stairs to Dare's room.

He was sitting on the edge of his bed and punching a fist into his palm in a gesture of frustration. "The Claim Jumper," he said quietly as if to himself. "I'm flabbergasted. He seems to believe that my claim is *his* claim. Pia is a perk, my ranch is free lunch. Now that she has flown the coop to live with the tycoon, he thinks I can haul her kicking and screaming back to his chemistry lab . . . He's welcome to her. He's in love with her. She's better off with him than with the great balls of fire, Woodbridge . . . When he asked for my advice, do you know what I said, just to give him a straw to hang on by, some peace of mind? I said, 'Doc, you must offer to marry her.' I swear I didn't tell him that to be self-serving." Dare once again slammed fist into palm.

"Self-serving, sir?"

"I want to marry your mother," he said. "And there I go encouraging the poor guy to marry my ex-wife as soon as she's no longer my claim. I save alimony payments."

"It's O.K. with me, sir," I said.

His gaze at me was one of relief. "I feel very, very sorry for your father," he said.

"I do, too, sir." I said. Until I said it I didn't realize how true my feeling was. Daddy didn't deserve love. To feel it for him was sappy. Still, I couldn't refuse to love. I turned my head in order to keep Dare from seeing me fight back tears.

A few days later on Christmas Eve he took the buckboard and sorrels and went to Homesteader's, Dawn Antelope having left for Taos Pueblo. Daddy was expected to arrive at Homesteader's next day. There was no snowstorm this time, the weather being unseasonably warm, the skies sunny and blue. The plan was, after the Medina family had celebrated Christmas in the morning, I was to ride Natural Selection to Homesteader's for the reconciliation with Daddy.

All went according to plan until a moment when I brought Natural Selection to a halt on that ponderosa-shaded mesa with the vista of Homesteader's in the foreground and the vast plains spreading out for almost a hundred miles to the east, the river running through them. Even as once before I had seen Dare digging a ditch next to his house—digging for dynamite—so now I saw him out by the barn splitting firewood with an axe, the *thump-glop* of each stoke reaching my ears a second later. Not seeing a carriage or horse by the fishpond, I reckoned that Daddy either hadn't come or that Dare had picked him up at the station.

Then it happened.

Seconds, minutes, hours, days, weeks, and years would pass, and for the rest of my life I would be experiencing again what I saw, then heard, the deafening KA-BOOM exploding under the house, the ranchhouse an orange ball of flame, the fire expanding, the smoke already beginning the coiling, black and greasy, to the thousand-foot altitude where its shadow would become a conquistador's giant sword black-slashing the earth, I already knowing, because of what had happened to Tío Congo's house, the wrath against leaders of men, and because of what Dawn Antelope had done to prevent another wrath, that Dare, save for a kind of providential urge to make firewood, was meant to die. Because I knew already about the wrath, I glimpsed out of the corner of my eye the distant figure of a cowboy galloping away on a pale horse. But as people came running from town, I spurred the roan down the switchback road to the barn where Dare, whipping the sorrels out into the meadows in case the barn and other buildings caught fire from brands hurtled skyward, would be telling me, anguish in his eyes, how my father, mere minutes before the explosion, had asked for forgiveness, tears streaming down his red nose and smearing his pince-nez with so much mucus he was virtually blind, the room growing cold before the scorching heat, cold as any stone.

Chapter Eleven

One day in October, 1904, while Dare and I were working in the St. Maybn's, I learned more about him, my future step-father, than I'd ever known before.

If Dare had been a miner all his life, which he hadn't been, he might have seemed much older than thirty-six. A miner in those days would start out as a breaker boy aged about ten and end up barely able to breathe by the age of forty. Now the physical labor involved in mining was doing Dare good. You would think he belonged to the pits. His body had been molded by low tunnels and by pick-and-sledge undercutting work at the face of a drift. His shoulders and arms had thickened with overlapping muscles. And he had a natural air of command. When we were paired in a room underground, nobody dared bunch in our corral or tried to prevent us from keeping an even turn. Checkweighman, notorious for cheating miners in order to increase Corporation's profits at the scales, exhibited deference to Dare, weighing in a ton of coal from one of our cars at exactly a ton.

In thick blackness our pit-lamps burned with brilliant white light. By the time we had put in the first six of our twelve hours picking and mucking we were hungry and thirsty. Up at the workface Dare had finished the hard, skilled job, lying on his side and swinging his pick up to undercut the seam. Me, I had the easy jobs. Growth stalled, I hoped only temporarily, at five-foot-two, I could still stand up under the roof of rock. With my No. 2 banjo mucker, I had loaded yesterday's blasted-out coal on to the cars, filling middles with slack, chunking up along the car-walls with large lumps. While Dare got ready for a shot in the afternoon, I did some of the dead work, collecting timbers and wedges and preparing bottom for brushing so as to lower tracks for Cuddy, the mule. Just before lunch Cuddy came into our room dragging his chain and whickering with joy at sight of me. His driver, Andy, a boy younger than I, got the cars connected while Cuddy butted me with his muzzle and munched the apple I gave him. Where he rubbed roof on his way through miles of tunnels to the cage, he had leather pads to protect the hide. These were wearing out so that it was rubbed raw and getting infected. When Cuddy was driven out of our room on the long journey to the cage, to the checkweighman, to the tipple and to the train that would take our coal to Woodbridge's steel mills, and Andy's flickering light was sucked into utter darkness, all that could be seen by the light of our pit-lamps was a cloud of coppery-smelling dust, an installment on any coalminer's death-plan: black lung. Dare in his canvas pit pants, blackened face with white-encircled eyes like a raccoon's, sweat streaming from his naked torso, looked, as usual, like he should be dipped in a hot springs in order to get his shine back on. I must have looked the same to him. On break, we went and fetched the water buckets we had hung on props and the lunch pails which were where rats couldn't get to them, then crawled to a pillar-room where roof was ten-foot high. I drank my water slowly, relishing each swallow. It was fresh and ice-cold and tasted so much like happiness that I wished I could run the mile out of the room to the cage and up it into sunlight and roll on warm earth like a puppy. We dug black hands into our lunch buckets. As usual, Doña Luz had packed each of them with two meat sandwiches, a slice of fruit pie, and an apple (this last being what I would save for Cuddy the next day). We ate and were quiet for a while.

We began to hear rats scurrying in the gob to feast on spilled oats and refuse. We also began to hear what the old-timers call "working" of the roof. It made a rippling sound like that of mountain water over pebbles but graduated to a crackling and rolling like thunder. It was good to know our rats were as happy as bedbugs in Bethlehem. If the roof were going to collapse the rats would already have abandoned their dinner of dung, would already have skedaddled from their manger accommodations. Our roof had not yet decided to crush us into hamburger. The thing we had to fear was silence. In a mine it induces panic.

Maybe that's why Dare stood up, stretched limbs, and, breaking silence, began to tell me the story of his adventures with Shiflit in Cuba and on the island of Samar in the Philippines.

American soldiers had been massacred in the village of Bagapundan on the island of Samar, and soldiers under Captain Dare's command had been sent there in retaliation for this defeat. Lieutenant Shiflit, second in command and pretending to act on orders from Dare, had eighteen natives executed by firing squad. When American newspapers learned of the atrocity, Dare in Manila was blamed for it by Shiflit and faced the prospect of a court-martial. That, in summary, was the story. It was not, however, the whole story, all blacks and whites as in a coalmine.

From their years together during the Cuban revolution Dare had come to rely upon Shiflit as a fearless warrior and trustworthy subordinate. He was stunned when, in Samar, Shiflit usurped his command, had eighteen innocent boys executed, and then testified at the pre-trial inquiry that he had reluctantly acted upon orders from Dare. Because the atrocity had come to the attention of "anti-imperialist" newspapers in the States—Dare portrayed in them as THE BUTCHER OF BAGAPUNDAN—officers at the inquiry seemed more concerned about a scandal than they were about the facts.

Dare had been for several days prior to the attack on Bagapundan quite incapable of exercising his authority in any form whatsoever. He was deathly sick and practically unconscious from effects of malaria and pneumonia. The officers seemed to discount this fact as an inconvenience. According to Dare's narrative, as told to me in the mine, "My commanders were ill-educated veterans of the Indian wars, their own hands not unbloodied at the Sand Creek Massacre in Colorado, and their minds so inhospitable to reason that they could easily have been persuaded to believe that babies are found in hollow stumps, laid by a buzzard, and hatched by the sun."

Officers of the committee of inquiry had already decided that he was twisted as a plug of tobacco.

"My first mistake," Dare said, "was to use the word *usurped* in describing Shiflit's misconduct. Anyone who has ever read Shakespeare understands the word and the way evils are unleashed upon the world when the authority of a properly constituted monarch is taken over by a blindly envious or blindly ambitious subordinate. I mentioned this Shakespearean idea of order to the committee. There was, unfortunately, a member of it whose head had been permanently lodged up his tail since the Civil War. This elderly gentleman from the South thought that Shake Spear was a Lakota war chief. He interrupted my testimony to ask, 'Would the Cap'n, suh, kindly explain what *you syrup'd* has got to do with a hill of beans? Is you sayin' that Loo-tenant Shitless done been in charge of *mo*-lasses? Yo argyment gets wusser and wusser.' Well, the old boy wasn't *that* silly, for in a way he was right: I made my argument worse than it was when I mentioned the black butterfly.'

"It was like this. Three days before our company reached Bagapundan, I watched in hypnotic horror as a black butterfly alighted on my left hand. Delirious, I decided the best way to rid myself of this sign of bad luck was to shoot it—and my hand—off. I restrained myself in the nick. Suddenly I seemed to hear from out of the jungle the terrifyingly primal, spine-tingling bugling of conch shells. In reality, this sound often announces an enemy's attack. I felt as certain that I had heard it as if I were to inform you, right now in this pit, that I can see the moon rising. In other words, I was so sick I had gone temporarily bugs. The officers didn't believe me.

I can't say that I blamed them."

Early in 1902 a company of officers and men had arrived in Bagapundan from Manila, a journey of 500 miles by boat, having been lured there by *insurrectos*, Filipinos hostile to the American occupation. That company was bushwhacked and slaughtered, only a handful of survivors left to tell the story. The newspapers in the States, comparing this defeat to that of Custer at Little Big Horn, demanded payback. Dare's company of fifty infantrymen was shipped out to Samar and bivouacked in a village just thirty miles up the coast from Bagapundan. He was sent orders to re-take Bagapundan, orders in the form of a telegram from his CO in Manila.

Though feverish with malaria, Dare prepared for the assault. Fair-complexioned prostitutes were placed off-limits. The sergeants were sobered up. In need of supply-carriers Dare hired eighteen native boys and paid their families the extraordinarily generous sum of ten dollars in advance as warranty for their safety. These boys were no sooner in camp than Shiflit and others began to call them "Goo-goos," a term used by Americans throughout the Philippines to refer to native peoples. On the eve of departure for the assault Dare sent a telegram to his CO requesting that a Navy vessel steam for Bagapundan to relieve the company after the attack.

He personally doubted its success. For one thing, the *insurrectos* in Bagapundan probably outnumbered his men by a large margin. For another thing, the *insurrectos* would have captured arms and ammunition from the massacred soldiers of the garrison. The usual American superiority whereby .30 caliber bolt-action Krag-Jorgensens were pitted against spears and the long knives called *bolos* would in that event be lost. Shiflit, for example, had already been shot in the face by a Krag in an earlier engagement. Dare sat down with Shiflit to devise a strategy for the attack. In his opinion, the company would have to spring a surprise in order to overcome slim odds. He favored a five-day forced march through thick jungle. Shiflit favored a simple route along the seacoast. To Dare, that plan was reckless. Natives offshore in the outriggers called *bancas*

221

would spot the company on the beaches and warn the *insurrectos* in Bagapundan of the imminent attack.

Having ruled against Shiflit's plan, Dare began to study a map of Samar. Happening to glance up from it, he saw enough contempt and loathing in Shiflit's gaze to make him wonder whether the real subhuman goo-goo lurked, masked, in every soul, including his own.

"Back home," Shiflit said, "I'm taking over Corporation and can do anything I want." It was the strangest *non sequitur* Dare had ever heard.

He became very ill on the first day of the march. Matters were slipping beyond his control. Food supplies were mysteriously disappearing. What was left of them would not last for another four days. That night he had the supplies stored in his tent. According to his inventory at dawn, some of these supplies, too, had been pilfered while he slept.

The second day of the march was that of the black butterfly. The company had been snaking along beneath enormous ferns and towering dipterocarp trees, fording swollen rivers, being relentlessly tormented by mosquitoes and leeches. Dare called halts. During the first halt, thanks to his being a student of American medicine, he ordered the sergeants to put salt in all canteens of water as a precaution against heat exhaustion. He called another halt in order to empty his pockets and take inventory of his quinine tablets, a snotrag, the CO's telegram and a watch, this a gift from Dr. Randolph Dare, his father who had been a physician in France before raising cattle and a motherless son in Los Tristes. Watch in hand, he lifted burning gaze to the sky and saw fluttering down "from a patch of clear blue sky barely big enough to make a Dutchman a pair of pants" a black butterfly. It settled on the watch. Studying the butterfly as if it were a specimen of iniquity, he slipped from its holster his Colt .45 caliber double-action revolver, aimed it unsteadily at the butterfly, and squeezed the trigger—almost. Sweating profusely and somehow managing to relax trigger finger, he returned the revolver to holster and rationalized inaction on the basis that the stump of his hand would have been almost instantly devoured by leeches.

"The watch, itself," Dare said, "must have been the restraining influence. It had come to me from a father whom I adored."

Angered by Dr. Dare's sudden death, Dare had swerved from the promise of a college degree and the inheritance of a prospering ranch in order to prove that honor could be passed from one generation to the next and that what he regarded as neglect of his mother hadn't hastened her death by cancer. He wanted to put himself on trial. He wanted to interrogate himself before the possibly foul tribunal of his soul. He became a soldier.

He had lifted the watch toward his lips and gently blown the black butterfly away. He thought he heard the bugling of conch shells.

Dare gestured to the roof of the mine as if to mock himself. "If you believe you are in the vanguard of progressive evolution, you would do well to listen to the sound of conch shells from time to time. It resonates within and conspires against your presumption of humanness . . . The sound which I thought I was hearing ceased abruptly as if slashed by an invisible *bolo*. I was on the verge of forming my men into skirmish lines against an enemy attack, but I was imagining things. I had, though, become acquainted with the real sound of the conch shells on a recent occasion. We were attacking the rebel leader's stronghold in the mountains of Samar . . ."

Dare's voice trailed off. He bit into his apple, threw the core to the floor where it raised the insidious dust. Until that moment I had not realized how distressed he still felt well over a year after his return home, how impelled he was in telling his story. It seemed to be coming to him in pieces, time sequences mixed, some details overlapping as he quarried out memories which had been lurking heretofore beneath the surface of consciousness.

He cleared dust from his throat. "After we captured the rebel leader's stronghold, Shiflit ordered the execution of some old folks and little brown children. Should I have had him arrested on the spot? My orders were to take no prisoners. He had usurped my authority for the first time, but how could I hold him responsible for doing his duty?"

At the hearing before the committee of officers who were deciding whether to have him court-martialed, Dare admitted to feeling no great fondness for the natives. Because they had been enslaved for centuries under Spanish rule, however, he not only sympathized with their rebellion but also considered them allies rather than insurrectionists. We were, after all, occupying their country. He had no sympathy for the perpetrators of the Bagapundan massacre. Its participants, if judged to be inimical to American interests in a criminal manner, must, he believed, be brought to justice. For those guilty of pilfering rations, as he suspected the supply-carriers of being, some form of punishment would have to be applied, perhaps docking of wages once the mission to Bagapundan had been accomplished. Of course, as he explained to the officers, Shiflit's execution of the carriers on suspicion of pilfering could not in any circumstances be justified.

"My guess was this: the officers of the committee thought it was pretty bully to exterminate 'Goo-goos' . . . Unconsciously, perhaps, they approved of Shiflit. We are the good guys. The evil we might do to the bad guys is divinely sanctioned. Evil, therefore, is good . . . I've seen my men yelling and firing and charging at 'Goo-goos' as if they were jack rabbits. So what if we were occupying their homeland? Why weren't the dirty little water-buffalo buggers settled on reservations?"

Dare came and squatted on his haunches beside me. "Listen," he said in quiet voice. "Your father banished you as a matricidal maniac, a bastard, and a rapist. You, his legitimate son, wouldn't dream of such violence. Our situations—false accusations, perjured testimony—are to some extent similar. Unlike you, I have nightmares about what I have actually done in the line of duty and about what was done by Shiflit in my name, though I never gave

224

him authorization. I allowed myself to come under his spell.'

"He was a hero. Our men believed what he told them: he was an instrument of God's wrath. For instance. . . during one engagement a giant aboriginal caught Shiflit off-guard, disarmed him and was about to decapitate him when Shiflit picked up a *bolo* which lay next to a dead *insurrecto* and plunged it into the giant's stomach to come out the back. This is the 'hero' who had the supply-carriers murdered. This is the 'hero' who had old folks and little brown children murdered. This is the 'hero' who tortured a native with what is called the 'water cure.' . . . Did I pretend to myself that his behavior was not my problem? Did I chalk it all up to the crutch goddess—Law, necessity, expedience, fate, destiny, whatever you choose to call her when you're trying to put your nightmares to rest and redeem your honor?"

Dare fell silent again. I already knew about some of his nightmares. At another time when we were at the boarding house, he had told me the story of an ambush in which his company had overcome slim odds and earned victory without a single American casualty. Invisibly inscribed on black walls the nightmares passed before my eyes in a matter of seconds . . . *swarming bands of insurrectos howling and brandishing bolos as they leap out of concealment in the jungle . . . Krags put to work . . . Bodies piling up like puddles of suddenly melting snowmen . . . The half-Chinese, half-Tagalog mestizos are clothed for combat in white pajama-like shirts, white cotton pants . . . Aboriginals have long matted hair made glossy with animal fat. Aboriginals wear antings antings, amulets of pottery shards and boar's teeth, in order to become invincible . . . Mestizos and aboriginals have eyes as wild and glittering as those of dogs when the moon breaks through clouds . . . Dare empties his revolver again and again . . . Bodies melt again and again, bolos clattering around them . . .*

"As you know, Shiflit," Dare resumed, "in addition to his duties with the Guard as a strikebreaker in Cripple Creek, is somehow connected to Woodbridge's Corporation and is Head of Security at Sun Palace Sanitorium. He's held in high esteem. In Cuba he hurled himself into every fray. He had horses shot out from under him. Later in California he sought me out and had himself assigned to my command because he believed I would promote and decorate him. He was . . . valorous. And yet unfit to be flea-catcher in a prairie dog town. He thought he perceived in me a person who secretly approved the use of torture and shared his idolization of brute instinct. Accordingly, he expected me to recommend him up through channels of command for medals, promotions, political office . . . or for those executive positions at Corporation . . . but I couldn't bring myself to do it. For that, he feels reproached by me and loathes my guts. He wants me dead. My very existence is a reproach to him. Am I giving myself credit for conscience? Perhaps. Perhaps I never lost it completely . . .'

"Our so-called 'enemies' wore pajamas, loincloths, sarongs. We wore floppy campaign hats, khaki trousers tucked into canvas leggings, heavy blue wool shirts. Get this! When in the 110-degree tropics, we American soldiers are ordered to dress for the minus 50-degree Arctic . . . We carried ditty bags, blanket rolls, Krags, double web belts with 200 rifle shells. We ate hardtack, bully beef, canned bacon and black coffee. Our enemies traveled light. They ate a rough rice, *palay*, a sweet potato, *camote*, and any fish, chicken, goat, pig or carabao they could come across . . . They are short of stature, tend to lose teeth, suffer from chronic malaria and gamble an entire livelihood on cockfights, while we have advantages of science, soil, and climate . . . and yet isn't it odd how much alike we are? Filipinos love their lands and families as we do. We, however, go into the depths of darkness without moral pit-lamps . . . as if God is made in *our* image, sort of pasty-faced with a smirk . . . commanding us to increase and multiply and subdue the earth . . . We blame the poor and the hopeless for lack of virtue. By this measure the only virtuous Americans must display white picket fences and marble-topped tables and Jenny Lind beds and rosewood dressers with swinging mirrors and large square pianos and bathtubs with clawed feet. We go to war for the sake of what our leaders call 'Anglo-Saxon progress and decency'—meaning what?"

"You asking me, Captain Dare?" I suspected he was close to being full of bull feathers.

"I'm asking you, Mr. Rountree Penhallow, Junior."

"No fair," I said.

"Bathtubs." Dare was half-laughing. "Anglo-Saxon progress and decency, the phrase, means imperial conquest and subsequent sales to the vanquished . . . of our bathtubs."

"I put my father's watch in my pocket," Dare said, rising and pacing again in the mine, picking up the story where he had left it on the trail to Bagapundan. "I studied my men. They were scattered behind me on the trail. Some smoked or chewed tobacco. One soldier was playing his harmonica. The sweet fool was expressing his desire to be back home in the land of cotton where old times are not forgotten. I don't carry the burden of Southern history, but that song seemed the most heart-breaking sound I'd ever heard . . . At the end of the column was Private Salvatore Riccatone, a young immigrant from Italy who had joined the Army in New York in order to send money to his folks in the old country. Now, it seemed, he had nothing to go to market with except time. He'd *really* gone bugs! I had him lashed to a bamboo *travois* with two supply-carriers detailed to drag him along with us. I was going to temporary duty him to a hospital in Manila once our mission had been completed . . ."

Private Riccatone, one night in the coastal village, had been on guard duty. Suddenly he let out a scream, fired shots in the air, and plunged into the jungle. He didn't go far. Shiflit tracked him down and had him rolled up in canvas and hauled, shouting obscenities in broken English, before Dare, who called for witnesses. According to their testimony, Private Riccatone had been observing a young woman as she emerged from her *nipa* hut with a torch and began to thresh a supply of rice. Her shoulders and breasts were bare. She wore a brightly colored sarong of thin cotton cloth, the dress split up the side to expose almost the full length of smooth brown leg. The sight of this woman had allegedly driven Private Riccatone mad.

"Them I-ties," a sergeant said with a sigh and a knowing headshake.

"Shoot the sumbitch," Shiflit said.

Dare tried to speak with Private Riccatone out of the hearing of others. He formed the impression that, mentally, the young soldier was no longer "present" on the island of Samar. He seemed indeed to be back in New York, seated at the window of a tenement building, watching snow falling.

"He was as pleased with the world as a Christmas carol," Dare was saying as he paced up and down in the mine. "There was obviously more to the matter than the sly glances of a half-naked girl . . . I thought of Melville, the *Typee* book, girls mere children of nature, 'breathing from infancy an atmosphere of perpetual summer,' but, to the best of my recollection, no one goes nuts over nipples in Nukuheva . . . The more I thought about Private Riccatone's snapping, the more convinced I became that it had its cause in an incident of extraordinary and brutal humiliation . . ."

When Dare's company first landed in Samar, the massacre at Bagapundan had recently taken place. Orders for the counterattack had not arrived. Dare's assignment in the interval was to track down Luc, the leader of the *insurrectos* who had planned the massacre. He with his band had disappeared somewhere into the mountains. From time to time they raided villages to spread terror, and one such village was Quinapundan. Suspecting that the police chief in that village was spying for the Americans, Luc had him bound to a stake in the plaza, his head wrapped in a kerosene-soaked American flag. It was set on fire. "I had sent Shiflit," Dare said, "with a patrol to gather intelligence about Luc's whereabouts, specifically to use normal interrogation techniques. So Shiflit was just then approaching Quinapundan. Upon entering the plaza he found natives with hands over their ears to muffle the screams of the police chief whose head was burning off. Shiflit arrested the mayor, *el presidente*, had him tied to a board, and gave him the 'water cure.' The mayor talked."

Luc had constructed a redoubt where mountains rose to more than 6,000 feet. From the coast it could only be reached through a jungle of screw pine, large-leafed rhododendron, climbing rattan, bamboo, palms and ferns, a jungle believed to be so impenetrable that Magellan in the early sixteenth century decided to sail around Samar.

After a forced march through this jungle Dare's company came within sight of Luc's redoubt. It had been timbered to create a parapet, this reached from below only by means of bamboo ladders. The parapet was protected still further by bamboo cages dangling from ropes made of a vine called *behuco*, the cages holding tons of rock which could be poured down upon anyone attempting to climb up the ladders.

"The sky was clear and blue, for me an augury of death ever since my mother and father died," Dare was saying. "From the parapet Luc's *insurrectos* spotted us little ants below them and began to sound those conch shells. . .'

"In Cuba I had sometimes fired Gatling and other machine guns. With me in Samar I had a Colt automatic gun. After assembling it and adjusting it for trajectory, I opened fire on the *behucos* and shredded them so that the cages with the rocks tumbled harmlessly down into the jungle surrounding us. From the parapet the *clap-da-dap clap-da-dap* firing of a Krag, obviously one seized at Bagapundan, had us pinned down. When a bullet split open Shiflit's cheek, he never hesitated for a second: he furiously led a charge up the ladders, reached the parapet, scrambled over it, and disappeared from my sight. The *insurrectos* were, strangely, offering no resistance. I heard no more rifle fire, no more bugling of conch shells, no more bloodcurdling screams.'

"All was eerily quiet while I broke down the Colt and prepared to lug it up a ladder. I then heard bursts of Krag fire. When I finally climbed a ladder and heaved myself over the parapet, I found my men standing around in a semicircle. In the middle of it stood

Shiflit bleeding profusely, Private Riccatone, his Krag at port arms, and on the ground the corpses of two old men, two old women, and three little brown children.'

"Luc and his band had fled, and a search of the area's huts had turned up those seven natives, plus three pigs, a dozen chickens, and a West Point ring. Infuriated by discovery of the ring, Shiflit, as he told me, had ordered Private Riccatone to execute the men, women, and children.'

" 'Prisoners expended while attempting to escape, sir,' Shiflit said. 'West Point ring belonging to the commander at Bagapundan recovered, sir.' Shiflit's excuses came to me as if from an enormous distance. I wasn't looking at him or at the corpses—but at Private Riccatone. That which might have appalled the devil, as Shakespeare has it, had been inscribed on his face. I knew, knew as certainty, that I could never again bear to see anybody humiliated as Riccatone had been, forced to act against conscience.'

"That night on the mountain, after the bodies had been burned in a hut, we roasted the pigs and chickens and feasted on them, vampire bats swirling in angry gyres above the smoke. At one point Shiflit, who told me when we first met in New York that he was raised in a small Christian community in a remote mountain valley in Utah, rose and preached. 'The Almighty,' he declared, 'destroyed Sodom notwithstanding the fact that there may have been a few just people in that community.' The flickering light of the bonfire gave to the black blood on his cheek, next to the black mustache, a peculiar prominence which, put together with his catarrhal accent and hornswoggling righteousness, gave me the sensation of being present with devotees of a mad religion . . ."

Dare paused, went on. "I took Private Riccatone aside and explained to him as best I could that he was not to hold himself personally accountable for the executions, that our orders were to take no prisoners. He wept. I hugged him as if he were my son. The stubble of his blond beard was like a cornfield in spring. Angelic, he could have posed for Leonardo.'

"Luc's band ambushed us in the jungle on our way back to

the coastal village. I've told you about that encounter before. We killed scores and suffered not a single casualty, ourselves—except, perhaps, for my nightmares.'

"Upon our return to the village I relaxed discipline. Soon, though, I received the telegram from my CO in Manila, ordering the attack on Bagapundan and repeating previous orders. *Kill anything that moves*, it read. *I want no prisoners. I wish you to kill and burn. The more you kill and burn the better you will please me.*'

"We are pausing on the trail to Bagapundan. I contemplate Private Riccatone strapped to the *travois*. I envy him his bliss. I, too, yearn for the land of Dixie, any land like home. Because he had been humiliated beyond endurance, I sense a vocation and swear an oath: I must take my stand with the humiliated. Another oath: I must change my life and take my stand against the violent of the world . . . I remember Homer's Achilles, the bitter wisdom of the greatest of warriors once he has fallen and become a ghost in Hades. O how he wishes he had been some poor country farm hand instead of a nobleman so deluded by the idea of honor and glory he had gone to war! At that moment I felt so disenchanted that I abandoned the plan for a surprise attack. I would follow Shiflit's proposal for a march along the seacoast, native spies in *bancas* be damned! In effect, I was unconsciously placing confidence in the very man whom I consciously not only refused to promote or cite for actions beyond the call of duty, but also intended to report for using torture. I had to breathe cool, salty air, cleanse myself in surf . . ."

There on the trail to Bagapundan he had removed his campaign hat and waved it in the manner of a cowboy at roundup. Soldiers and supply-carriers struggled to their feet. Sergeants bellowed orders. Soon the company was following its stumbling captain down steep ravines and around narrow ledges where any slip of footing could send an unlucky fellow falling and shrieking into the rainroar of a black abysm. The company arrived at the coast before dusk. The Stars and Stripes soon fluttered in seabreeze. Tents were erected around a central bonfire. Sentries guarded stacks of rifles, crates of ammo, rations, the Colt automatic gun. Too ill to swim, himself, Dare watched his beefy, sunburned men, many of whom were volunteers from the Rocky Mountains with little experience of oceans, whooping as they flung themselves naked into surfboomings beneath screeching seagulls. The sun sank like an enormous orange balloon into sea-dirge. Cicadas summoned the moon. The supply-carriers prepared food over fires and piled everyone's mess kit high.

Dare retired to his tent, teeth chattering. With trembling hands he lit a candle. He stretched himself out on his cot. Why hadn't he ordered quarter rations? Why hadn't he ordered supplies once again to be stacked in his tent? What if the company arrived half-starved in Bagapundan, found it deserted and the Navy vessel nowhere in sight?

"Captain, sir?"

Shiflit's tone of voice, as usual, communicated obsequiousness and patronizing contempt simultaneously. Dare turned on his side. Candlelight revealed Shiflit in the tent.

"Quarter rations from now on," Dare said. "I'm afraid, Fredson, the carriers may have been pilfering."

Shiflit rolled eyes. "Bullets are the only things the Goo-goos understand . . . sir," he said.

"How in God's name can the natives ever respect us or respect themselves if we continually refer to them as sub-human?"

"I'll post a sentry over supplies, sir," said Shiflit, ignoring him. "Native personnel looking for trouble will be shot. Sir. Shall I blow out the candle? Sir? I trust you'll change your mind and recommend the medal and promotion, Captain?"

"I think, Lieutenant," Dare muttered, fever rising, "I am quite capable of blowing out my own damn candle."

Shiflit glared at Dare through narrowed eyes before about-facing and sauntering out of the tent. Dare's mind tumbled to a loathsome judgment: sedition.

～～～

White light from our pit-lamps reflected off glistening minewalls and illuminated Dare's blackened face, white rings around eyes. He came and squatted down beside me again. "It's amazing, son," he said, "how many hurdles a man will put in his own path. I had just graduated from college when my father suffered a stroke and died—under a clear blue sky. We had, as you know, Dawn Antelope managing the ranch. I was in no rush to take management of it over."

Dare chuckled to himself, cracked a smile. "When I was in college, my teammates gave everyone nicknames. There was a blocking back from North Carolina. He knew of a place-name there, Kill Devil Hills, so wouldn't you know for a guy named Kyle Deville I'd be nicknamed 'Kill Devil'—Kill Devil Dare, like Iron Lung McClung and Pudge Hefflefinger of Yale. People thought I was a Hellfire Methodist! . . . Anyway, when I had been out there on the football field running and tackling, the crowd noises, the roars, the tumult seemed a long way off, but now, after college, I felt curious about people, wondering who they were and what I could do to build a bridge to them. I went down in the local mines for a spell. If there was a patriotic duty to be done in this world, I didn't think it fair to leave others to do it for me. However, contradicting myself, I decided to light out for New York, figuring to corral me a job as a war reporter in Cuba, turn one for the *vaqueros* . . . Nothing doing in that line, but I drifted into the company of some Cuban recruiters, those fellows with felt *sombreros* and cigars. *Amigo,* they say, you comprehend the artillery and machine gun, we feex you up big, my captain, *verdad,* no bulla-sheet, most damn fun you ever have with your pants on . . . I memorized manuals, everything from belt action to Kentucky windage and received a telegram, unsigned, instructing me to appear at the Cordlandt Street ferry at such-and-such a day and time. Did that. Met Shiflit, a cocky hellraiser who said something about a girl in Utah who got an abortion. God evidently told him what to do: abandon her, to hell with the girl who aborts your child, ride the rails east.'

"We crossed the river to Jersey City. From there we took a train to Charleston. Some more idiots joined us there. In order to avoid

Pinkertons working for the Spanish government, we took a slow train to Woodbine in Georgia where we boarded a tugboat for Cuba. I received a commission all right: captain in artillery. For a year I helped blow the crap out of forts. Spanish troops captured me one night in a cantina. Since I wasn't in uniform and had no ID, I pretended I was a tourist, treated the boys to rum and rounds with the percentage girls, slipped away to Havana, came home, got married on the spur."

While Dare was taking a deep breath, I cringed at the thought of what was coming: more self-abasement. He slumped and said, "I don't blame Pia for trucking out on me during and after my tour overseas. I hardly knew her. Her daddy was a pit boss in one of the mines I had worked in. You've seen her: poorly educated but gorgeous. I tired of marriage, of raising cattle. General Funston was calling for volunteers to join him in San Francisco and go fight in the Philippines. Now, at last, I thought I could serve my country. I deserted her."

I said nothing. I wanted to say but didn't, "Pia was no Penelope." He straightened up on a sigh and gave me a tight smile. "You're going to be all right, Tree . . . When I was younger than you, my mother died in St. Aignan, the French village where my father, who was American and well-off, was assisting local physicians as a free service, not only because my mother was French but also because he believed foreign culture to be *comme il faut* for an American lad. Once she died he realized he couldn't stand it over there any longer, too little freedom, too much confinement in tradition and space. The competence I had gained in Latin and European languages would stand me in good stead: it's one reason I'm back in Los Tristes where immigrant coalminers speak more than twenty languages . . . In case you haven't guessed it, Tree, and I'm risking my life by confiding in you, I'm organizing for the Union . . . My father brought me to his Homesteader's Ranch. Let me tell you: the sizeable scale of the West invited me to feel an expansion of self such that I sometimes yielded to a belief in unbridled freedom. I loved the joke about the young couple who went out to milk the cows, and their children came home with the milk. At the same time, due to my upbringing in Europe, I could see that the West was starting to build all the cities it could handle and that social cooperation had to be in the cards.'

"Here's the catch: unbridled freedom can make you insensitive to the suffering of others. After a while, you don't recoil from the uses of power. You may be a hero. You may be a man of iron. You may be the fastest gun in Cloud-Cuckoo-Land. And all of a sudden you turn into Fredson Shiflit. He has a kind of apocalyptic hatred of people of all stripes. There's about as much humanity in him as in an abandoned cemetery.'

"Emergence and convergence: that's the future. We emerge out of self-centered selves and converge in an in-the-same-boat spirit with others."

Bull feathers, I was thinking, even though I shared his "in-the-same-boat" philosophy. I had a short fuse when it came to preachiness. Nevertheless, the more I reflected on what Dare had just said the more I realized he was showing his care for me and trusting me in that in-the-same-boat spirit. I might not like his being philosophical, but he might actually be wise. Still, intelligent and grownup as he was, he needed me, needed my support—a strange reversal of my boy's role and one of my Never Befores.

"Tell me again about the massacre," I prompted in toughened voice.

He shot me a look of pain but relaxed as he spoke. "I've been circling subjects too long, haven't I? . . . It was like this . . . Bagapundan had no military value, not even a harbor. The village consisted of a church, a convent, and a town hall, mildewed masonry courtesy of Spain. About a hundred huts surrounded a plaza. Our commanders in Manila had originally had no intention to establish another garrison there. Moreover, they didn't know what Luc had done, how he had had all the friars and the nuns and the police chief murdered and had installed as mayor a little fellow who wore a white cotton suit and a black stovepipe hat. This mayor, this bizarre mimic of Abraham Lincoln, paid no attention to the accumulation of garbage, dead animals, and excrement but sent an envoy to Manila begging our commanders for troops to protect the village from what he called 'pirates.' Our commanders, thinking the mayor was on our side and secretly giving us a signal that the war was coming to an end, sent to Bagapundan a company of seventy-four officers and men under command of a West Pointer, Captain Priggs.'

"Captain Priggs and company were set ashore from dories, which then returned to our Navy vessel. In one of the dories were crates of English textbooks and boxes of petticoats and camisoles. As you may know from your reading in newspapers, the late President McKinley coated the pill of Empire with a policy of 'benevolent assimilation.' Accordingly, Captain Priggs believed that a distribution of female underwear and *McGuffey's Eclectic Readers* would bring the evolution-disadvantaged natives up to date, benevolence-wise . . . He had the Stars and Stripes run up from the church belfry. He converted the town hall into barracks for the enlisted and the convent into officers' quarters. A large mess tent was erected in the plaza. A regular schedule of meals and drills, all announced by the bugler, was instituted. Thus prepared for friendly negotiations, Captain Priggs invited the mayor over to the convent and addressed him as follows: 'See here, Mister *Señor Presidente*, unless your sweet-assed little gals cover up their shame with these-here *regalos*, my men are going to tricky-tricky-boom-boom them, savvy?' With a sweep of hand he pointed to the boxes of petticoats and camisoles. Doffing hat, the mayor bowed to those treasures and promised to have them distributed to the topless gals of Bagapundan. Next, Captain Priggs held his nose and pointed out a window toward the garbage, the dead animals, and the excrement, whereupon the mayor, after genuflecting and heart-patting, promised to round up laborers *muy pronto* for the great clean-up . . . as soon as the cholera epidemic, then devastating the countryside, had been brought under control.'

"Weeks passed. Hut windows had curtains made out of petticoats. Camisoles on *cette île triste et noire* proved to be very useful for the gathering of coconuts.'

"One evening the sentries reported to the captain that large numbers of women bearing coffins were entering the church. Inside a coffin, the only one opened for inspection, lay the body of a dead child. There were copious cries of lamentation: '*La calentura! El cólera!*' Had Captain Priggs thought to have all the rest of the coffins opened, they would have been found to contain not bodies but *bolos*. Had he thought to have the mourners' veils parted, they would have been found to disguise the faces not of women but of men.'

"At 6 a.m. next morning, as the bugler sounded call for chow, the mayor showed up in the plaza with *obreros*, he in white suit and black stovepipe hat, they with shovels and pitchforks. Our boys, sleepy and unarmed, moseyed over to the mess tent and sat down to eat. Twenty minutes past the hour the First Sergeant, who had finished his breakfast, went to wash his mess kit in the barrel kept full of steaming hot water by a native woodchopper who tended the fire under the barrel. The woodchopper was standing next to the First Sergeant.'

"Church bells suddenly ring out—*clang-bong-da-ping-ling, clang-bong-a-bong-rung*. The woodchopper splits the First Sergeant's skull with an axe and pitches the body head first into the barrel. Bolomen burst from church door. Under a clear blue sky they chop sentries to pieces and run to the barracks to finish off the enlisted. The laborers from the countryside cut the mess-tent ropes and, using *bolos*, shovels, and pitchforks, hack at the struggling mass of bodies underneath the collapsed canvas. Back in the town hall a few of the boys are able to put up a fight with Krags and baseball bats. They kill the mayor. At the convent the captain jumps out of a window but is overtaken in the plaza and beheaded. An *insurrecto*, to get at the captain's West Point ring, chops off a finger.'

"Survivors, most of them badly wounded, stagger to the shore and scramble into *bancas*. One Private Wingo notices that the

Stars and Stripes still fly from the belfry. Though injured himself, he takes three volunteers with him to rescue the colors. He and one volunteer return to the shore with the flag in their possession. After several days at sea, during which period seven more men die, Private Wingo among them, five *bancas* reach safety at Basey. At the infirmary there, another eight men succumb to wounds, leaving a total of twenty survivors out of the original company of seventy-four officers and men ..."

As I listened to the chilling tale in its horrifying detail, I could well understand why the massacre had led to demand in the United States for payback. "Tell me about the payback," I said. "It haunts you."

Dare stood up. His pit-lamp was like an eye from which a beam of light penetrated darkness. "Early on the morning of the third day," he said, folding arms and shaking as if malarial chill had returned, "Shiflit found me virtually unconscious on the cot in my tent. I was nevertheless able to insist that we continue with the mission. If we returned to the coastal village where we had been bivouacked, we would have found there no medical assistance, whereas, all being well, a Navy vessel would be awaiting our arrival in Bagapundan, complete with sick bay. Lest our supply-carriers come into harm's way during the attack on Bagapundan, I decided to forgive their pilfering. I specifically instructed Shiflit to have them paid off and discharged from further duty so that they could return home before the attack began. I neglected my own rule: put everything in writing and save all documents. I made one further request: I was to be strapped to my cot, as Private Riccatone was lashed to his travois, two carriers assigned to carry or drag me along the coast.'

"I remember little of the march. Once in a while I seemed to hear gentle voices speaking in, I suppose, Tagalog. My throat would be moistened with canteen water. My carriers cooled my brow with icy seaweed. Did I drink some Chinese herbal remedies? Later, the Navy surgeon claimed that I did—that I could easily have died without them, without, in other words, the kindness of the Filipinos.'

"Days. Nights. I have little recollection of them in my brain-fog. When I briefly regained consciousness and opened my eyes, I was being dipped—baptized, as it were—in an icy, soughing surf, my limp body carried in the arms of a young man with the beginnings of a blond beard. It was Private Salvatore Riccatone. At one point I thought I heard rifle fire followed by machine-gun fire but didn't learn until later that we were in Bagapundan, Shiflit and the company in the village, Private Riccatone and I near the shore. Indeed, later, when I was aboard the Navy vessel, it became clear what had happened: the carriers assigned to us had released us from our bonds, had attempted to flee into the jungle, had been captured by Shiflit and eventually with the other fourteen carriers tied to stakes, blindfolded, and murdered."

"Riccatone?" I interrupted in surprise. "After he participated in the attack on Luc's redoubt, his mental breakdown must have come, caused by Shiflit's command that he murder the villagers . . . You said humiliation had driven him bugs. For you, it was a turning point. You could never again bear to see anyone humiliated. That is why you're working for the Union at risk of your life."

"Hang on," Dare said. "First, Bagapundan . . . It was abandoned, no *insurrectos*, no villagers, only a few emaciated dogs scavenging in the garbage. The First Sergeant who had been killed while washing his mess kit was still in the barrel. Soldiers killed under the mess tent were still clutching knives and forks. In the plaza the bugler had been buried up to his neck, evidently while still alive, his mouth propped open with the bugle; to his mouth, it appeared, a trail of sweet stuff had been sprinkled from the jungle. Armies of ants, following this trail, had played *Taps* very slowly upon him. Captain Priggs was found in the church, in two parts. The torso had been bundled up in petticoats and camisoles. The head had been placed on the altar so that it peered, as it were, at the body of the child who had died of cholera. This obscene and blasphemous parody of a father-and-son, God-and-man relationship was unmistakable in its anti-American intent. The captain's eyes had been gouged out and stones stuck in the sockets, replicating some hideous Paleolithic god . . . The rest you know: the murders. But

I didn't tell you what Shiflit did before the Marines landed from the Navy vessel. Gathering my men around him, he told them that the Almighty has no use for people who would teach us Americans to imitate 'abominable things.' He told them, in other words, that Captain Dare would be punished for having authorized, in His holy name, the summary executions for pilfering rations. After delivering this edifying sermon, he had the bodies strewn about the plaza, photographed, lugged into huts and set on fire. Then he, personally, turned the Colt automatic gun on the masonry buildings. Why? Riddled with bullet holes the buildings would seem to bear mute witness, as did the bodies, to a fierce firefight waged during the great siege and capture of Bagapundan. These buildings he had photographed. As a final touch, he had the mayor's body, white suit and black stovepipe hat now festooned with flies and leeches, strung up from the church belfry in the attitude of delivering a Gettysburg Address in Hell. Shiflit had this little Gothick scene photographed, too . . . Remember, when the folks back home believe that the Kingdom of God is being created by the military, there's room for a Shiflit at the top."

Pacing back and forth, Dare paused to look me in the eyes. "When I surfaced from coma, which had returned, we were all of us bound for Manila. My sergeants came to the sick bay and told me the story of Bagapundan and pledged, unasked, to keep their lips sealed about Shiflit's crimes. These, they obviously believed, had been authorized by me. I kept them in the dark.'

"I decided to go straight to our commanders in Manila as soon as I could and tell the whole story about Shiflit, accepting responsibility for all that had happened under my command even though I had never authorized torture and executions. As for Private Riccatone's antic disposition, I feared he would be charged with cowardice in battle, for which the penalty could be death. I had him examined by the Navy surgeon. Together we drew up a document to the effect that Private Riccatone's extreme fatigue, not a desire to shirk duty, had temporarily disabled him. His fealty, I judged, outweighed his folly . . . Private Riccatone's good intentions led to a relatively mild comeuppance for misconduct. In Manila, he jumped ship and went straight to the authorities. Why on earth would he do that, Tree?"

"To go to the military authorities would have been suicidal," I said.

Dare opened a smile on blackface and said, "The 'authorities' to which I refer were not, to his mind, military ones. They were newspapers. An immigrant in New York, he believed that American newspapers always tell the truth. He didn't reckon with those bully for Empire. He told his story to an American news agency that promptly went with it to the military commanders, one of whom, my CO, suggested to the general in charge of our operations in Samar that the private might be persuaded to retract his charges. Private Riccatone refused to do so. He was immediately given two years in the hoosegow for conniving at the publication of an article containing so-called 'willful falsehoods.' And there the story might have ended had Shiflit not overplayed his hand.'

"One morning while I was recovering in hospital, I received a visit from a major in the judge advocate branch of the commanding general's staff. I was, he advised me, going to be investigated by a committee of inquiry about the murder of eighteen boys in Bagapundan. The major showed me an American newspaper. Its headline read, THE BUTCHER OF BAGAPUNDAN—meaning me—and it ran a story in which Shiflit blamed me for having authorized, quote, 'murders too unspeakable to be described by the pure of heart,' end quote. I told the major what I've told you and did the same when, eventually, I appeared before the investigating committee.'

"When Shiflit testified against me and came under cross-examination, he changed the time for my alleged authorization for the murders. It had happened, he swore, back when I was in full possession of mental faculties, back at the beach. There, he swore, I had ordered the execution of the carriers for pilfering. Thereafter feeling, quote, 'much troubled in heart,' end quote, he had prayed until God told him what to do, namely, carry out my orders. Shiflit burst into tears and appealed to heaven. 'I have sinned, Lord, I have sinned!' He shed more tears than Niagara has falls. The committee never asked to see documentation for these alleged orders.'

"Well," Dare went on, " I didn't know about God, but somehow through all that tour of mine in Samar I had kept a waterproof bag in a pocket, a bag which contained my CO's telegram, which read, *Kill anything that moves, I want no prisoners, I wish you to kill and burn, The more you kill and burn, the better you will please me.* I introduced into evidence this little hymn to benevolent assimilation. The officers looked at my CO, an old Indian fighter, then looked at one another, nodded in agreement and told me I was dismissed, all charges dropped for lack of evidence that the atrocity had ever happened. The news agency would be advised that the story of 'The Butcher of Bagapundan' had been enemy propaganda. Of course, as was strongly suggested to me in private, I could resign my commission and go home, honorably discharged. I affected to be riled up at the suggestion. What, gentlemen? Questioning my honor? Well, okay. Throw me in the briar patch.'

"Shiflit wanted to sell the photographs he had taken in Bagapundan, the ones illustrating his glorious victory there and presumably securing for him that strange executive job at Corporation. Unaware of what Private Riccatone had done, he went to the same news agency in Manila. He was immediately queried about the massacre. With great presence of mind, I must admit, he confirmed it. Otherwise the 'Butcher of Bagapundan' phantasmagory would not have been leaked."

The silence of the mine seemed to close us in.

Dare broke the silence once more. "I'm sure you've wondered why Shiflit is my nemesis. Is it only because I refused to recommend him for promotion in the Philippines? Remember, I revealed to my superior officer that business of his use of torture? Remember, he used the 'water cure' to force the mayor of a village to reveal Luc's whereabouts?'

"A man would be thrown down on his back, whereupon three or four men would sit on his arms and legs and thrust into his jaws either a rifle barrel, a carbine barrel, or a stick as big as a belaying pin. Water would then be poured onto his face and down his nose and throat until the man divulged information or became unconscious. He would be drowning but could not drown . . . I had heard about this method of torture but never witnessed it. It is said to have been employed during the time of the Spanish Inquisition. Our enemies, it was said, were using it.'

"When, performing my duty, I informed my superior officers that Shiflit, against our military traditions, let alone humanity's, had employed the water cure, I succeeded only in making Shiflit my enemy for life. The officers, instead of giving him a dishonorable discharge, chose to have *me* investigated."

So concluding the story, Dare half-crawled back toward the workface. He began to sledge up a prop, sitting on heels and rocking on knees. He repeatedly swung the sledge against the prop until the cap piece slipped into place and the timber leaned toward the face at just the right angle to be driven more firmly once coal from his afternoon's shot had been blasted out. After a while he came back to our room where he had talked to me as never before, trusting me with his secret life of atonement. Wiping sweat out of his eyes, he pointed to a spot well back from the workface. "See that equipment there, son? I'll need the augur and the tamping bar, and bring me those squibs and the needle, would you, please? Leave that powder keg to me . . . Hang on."

He took from his cap and slowly lifted his pit-lamp, holding it high above his head and against the torturous water-cure trickling of the roof. Some fire-damp in the hollow of the rock burst into tongues of soft blue and yellow flame. He sure gave a body comfort with the one "eye" of his pit-lamp's penetrations of darkness. He fixed in my mind the fathering I could rely upon and at the same time brought his Spanish proverb to remembrance, the one he had quoted that time he and Glass-Eye Gwilym saved me in the Comanche Grasslands of the Great American Desert.

I cupped my mouth and declared with the bravado of a grownup, "Hey, Kill Devil! You're the one-eyed man! 'In the country of the blind, the one-eyed man is king!'!"

243

He turned and stared at me for a moment. *"En casa del ciego, el tuerto es rey?"* A warmly playful, pleasured smile of bright teeth spread across his blackened face. "At ease," he said, "you prince of the sad people."

Sad people.

That was a joke between us, a literal translation from the Spanish of the name of the city of Los Tristes: Sad People. I, for one, had grown so used to thinking of those of us who lived in or near the city as "sad people" that, after a while, I began to think of people everywhere as *los tristes*, and there was more to the story than that. Dare's father had discovered the full, original name of the city or the region, *la puerta de los tristes*, "The Door of the Sad People." Legend had it— the librarian at the new Carnegie Library had been my source—that this name could be found in a plaza in Granada in Spain. Perhaps a conquistador from Granada had brought the name to the New World.

Chapter Twelve

We had tried, Dare and I, to save Daddy. Dare had had experience in pulling dead and wounded from battlefields and collapsed mines. He hoped that Daddy might still be alive, perhaps pinned down by the *vigas* that had crashed to the floor of the living room. We fetched buckets from the barn, filled them with water from the fishpond, and flung the contents onto flames. With a hiss one tongue of fire licked Dare's left hand. On another trip to the pond a couple of dozen townsfolk showed up with their own buckets forming a line between the pond and house. After a while, though, we all quit fighting the fire. Disregarding the pain in his hand, Dare went around thanking people. One man apologized for having arrived too late to be of service.

"Cap'n, I done heard the explosion from a mile away. When I seen smoke quilin' itself into the sky, I said to myself, by grab, that's Doc Randolph Dare's Homesteader's! I'd of come sooner if'n my dog had howled with his nose in the air."

"Obliged," Dare said.

Me, hearing the word dog, I wondered if the shepherds had followed their master out of the house when he went to chop wood. I spotted them over by the barn, barking at a horseless carriage.

We had company. The dogs were not interested in the departure of the townsfolk but in the horseless carriage stirring up a cumulus of dust and engine smoke and bringing men in raccoon coats.

"Union," Dare muttered, frowning. "I told them about the dynamite party Dawn Antelope put the kibosh on. Now they've heard-tell of the real thing, they'll want to take pictures and sink fangs into Woodbridge."

"Does Union provide district officers with tin Studebakers?" My tone was sarcastic.

"Dues, Tree, may disappear during a strike," he said. "I can't say I stomach luxury for bosses, let alone exploiting my ruins of a home for publicity purposes, but I'll let it all go. A vehicle is a necessity. We have thousands of square miles to cover, and Corporation has us out-equipped, out-gunned, out everything, even outlaws and outhouses. Let me handle this, son."

He went and talked to the Union men after they parked the Studebaker by the barn. One of them was already taking pictures of smoking ruins while Dare talked with his boss, whom I recognized as a Greek named Orestes, a roly-poly *político* with a waxed, curlicue mustache. Heedless of Dare's pain, Orestes was raising his voice to what seemed an abusive level. I went and stood by Dare's side, figuring Orestes better beware the man and me, too.

"The sheet I no givin', Captain Dare, whudya say," Orestes was yammering, "you ain't goin' unner ground no more! You takin' my place like pretty soon. You dead don't do Union no good! Corporation's got your number. Soon's old Jeff Jones tells them robbers you still kickin' ass, they'll be layin' for youse again, you betcha. You organize in the open, now on. They no more touchin' youse . . . Hiya, kid. Sorry about ya old man. God rest his soul." Orestes greeted me, crossed himself, spat. Then he again addressed himself to Dare but in softer tone. "Shiflit's in town again. You and the kid gotta scram a-fore he gits here with them deputies . . . Who gonna b'lieve you no blow that claim jumber to hell outta jealousy? Youse tell me that. Far as I, Laredo Desperado done did it. We want him gnashin' his teeth in Hell for a million years. If he ain't got no teeth, in Hell teeth will be provided."

246

I studied Dare, waiting for words gathering behind his lips. "Orestes," he began in low, slow voice, "thanks for the tip about Shiflit and Jeff Jones's teeth. I'm sorry about Doc Penhallow. He did me a favor, claiming Pia. Jealousy isn't in my cards. If anyone wants to indict me for a murder I didn't commit, they'll know where to find me . . . Leave a couple of men here to prevent looting till I come back tomorrow . . . If you want to feed some oats to that tin contraption of yours, help yourself."

We had the sorrels hitched to the buckboard, President in tow, and Dare on Natural Selection gripping reins in his good right hand. We didn't say anything on the way home, if *home* was the word. We were probably thinking the same thing: Shiflit had an ace in the hole. As long as Corporation controlled the government in all its branches, Dare could be indicted for murdering my father, would automatically be found guilty in any courtroom in Los Tristes, and probably sentenced to death. Upon arrival home he had his hand washed and dressed by Doña Luz. Me, figuring Golly was doing soul-time in the Cave of the Forgotten, I went there and found her. We talked quietly together for a spell. I allowed her to see me crying.

Dare, who had gone to town to see a doctor, returned with an EXTRA edition of the local English-language newspaper. Next morning around the breakfast table, five of us, he and I, Doña Luz, Tío Congo, and Golly, perused it while we drank our Maxwell House.

The front page photograph of the ranchhouse in ruins put Los Tristes on the map up there with *The Last Days of Pompeii*. Even that historical romance was nearer to truth than the report of the fire. According to the "news," several jackrabbits, which had been looking for a comfy home during the holidays, had jumped up the flue of the chimney of Homesteader's ranchhouse. Unwittingly, Dr. Rountree Penhallow of Colorado Springs had set the jackrabbits ablaze when he lit a fire, whereupon, falling down the flue, they had run helter-skelter and torched everything in the house. Dr. Penhallow was survived by his wife, Mrs. Anna Maria Penhallow of St. Aignan, France, who was last seen in the company of the ranch's proprietor, Captain Kyle D. Dare, and by a son, Rountree Penhallow, Jr., of Los Tristes. Dr. Penhallow was best known as Director of the Sun Palace Sanitorium in Colorado Springs, a subsidiary of Corporation of New York. Mr. Alpheus Woodbridge, Chairman of Corporation, when reached by telephone, wished it to be known that he was making all the arrangements for the funeral in Colorado Springs, after which he would be coming by special train to Los Tristes in order to explain his plans for employee representation and for building a Y.M.C.A. as a gift to the community. "We will meet not as strangers but as friends," Mr. Woodbridge was quoted as saying. "It will be in that spirit of mutual friendship that I shall be glad to gather with my employees to discuss our common interests. It will be a red-letter day for me when I can see for myself how thoroughly satisfied with their labor conditions are my friends in the mining and steel industries."

No one spoke until the "news" had been absorbed. Dare, carefully placing his coffee cup in saucer, remarked in an imitation-blasé tone, " 'Proprietor'? I've gone up in the world."

"Jackrabbits don't climb up no chimbleys." This from Tío Congo.

"Nothing funny about setting animals on fire." This from me.

"It's mostly about Woodbridge, not about Tree's father." This astute and forgiving remark from Doña Luz.

Dare asked us to consider the obvious: no local reporter could have had so much information at his fingertips, let alone have spoken directly to Woodbridge, nor would Woodbridge have divulged to anyone outside his retinue his plans for the funeral, so-called "employee representation," and a Y.M.C.A.

"Shiflit," I proposed, recalling the whimsical cynicism he had employed in concocting allegations against me.

"What's the by-line?" Dare asked.

Tío Congo peered through spectacles at the paper. "Damon Romero," he said.

"Damon Romero died two years ago," Doña Luz said.

All of us exchanged looks. "Then it's Shiflit," Dare said, wiping his mouth with the back of his bandaged hand. "No one will believe the jackrabbit nonsense, and there are plenty of witnesses who heard an explosion. But people will remember the innuendo about me and Mrs. Penhallow and suspect I killed her husband while she was abroad. Some will believe that 'employee representation' means Union recognition. It's a fraud. As for building a Y.M.C.A., philanthropy flavored with religion is Woodbridge's stock in trade. The Woodbridge Foundation gives millions in charity every year, not, however, to the workers who make the money for him in the first place. Does anybody care about that Robin Hoodlumry, stealing from the poor to give to the rich? I'm blowing off steam."

"Please go on," said Golly in sweet voice. "We all care. We ought to get rid of Woodbridge and keep the Foundation."

I think in that moment I thought I loved her. I didn't have the right words for her in the right place, but I felt in her a generative power of authenticity. Dare must have felt it, too. He resumed speech with fervent intonation. "I don't know if Woodbridge reveals his real thoughts to Shiflit, but let's take him at his word. He wants to be friends with his workers, and he believes they are satisfied with their conditions, their problems arising from the interference of outsiders—like Mother Jones, like me. As long as he remains ignorant and delegates authority to local managers who tell him only what he wants to hear, he will believe he has discharged his full responsibilities as a leader and stockholder. I know enough about his public and professional performances, including appearances before Congress, to see in him a sad man who must carry great burdens. That said, I also know there are millions of good people, including you, Doña Luz, and you, Tío Congo, who dream once in a while of going after Woodbridge with a slanted gun.'

"When you meet him, Tree, as you will, try to accept him with kindness and understanding."

≈≈≈

Almost three years would pass before, in London in 1908, I discovered that Woodbridge was Daddy's father and my grandfather. Had I ever dreamed, which I hadn't, of being grandson to that Rich American, I would have likened my chances to those of winning the lottery. That analogy was weak, though, for the person who bets on the lottery wants sudden riches, whereas, whatever my entitlement, I had no interest in Woodbridge's money. I also had no desire to have him in my family. Ambiguously he had set Daddy up at the Sun Palace, then broken Daddy's heart jumping Daddy's claim to Pia. By recruiting Shiflit to impregnate Mrs. Elizabeth Woodbridge and then encouraging Shiflit to marry his own daughter, Scampy, Woodbridge had qualified himself as one of those monsters in Greek myth. I already had a lousy ancestor, Rufus Obadiah Dautremond, slave trader. Why couldn't a Rich American who had gotten with child an English woman, Irene Penhallow, have turned out to be a run-of-the-mill philandering jackass like Daddy?

When I met Woodbridge at the funeral for Daddy, he knew who I was. At that time, I didn't know who he was. That knowledge came in 1908.

The idea that Woodbridge would be making all the arrangements for the funeral struck me as odd. Was he suffering remorse over his acquisition of Pia from Daddy? Whatever his reason for barging in, he was denying me my grownup's responsibility. I had Mum on my side, too. As soon as I cabled her the news, she retired from post-marital cares with the alacrity of Henry the Eighth. After she cabled me back that I was to be in charge of obsequies, I proceeded to get in touch over the phone with undertakers, lawyers, bankers, insurance agents, clergymen and others, seeking advice as to what to do but getting nowhere. To the best of my knowledge, all that remained of "Daddy" could be poured into a shoebox. Still, I shopped around for the most luxurious casket in town, one to be weighed down with a cigar store Indian for an additional hundred dollars. I was just about to sign a contract to that effect when I happened to receive a call from the one person whom I should have telephoned in the first place: Daddy's lawyer in Colorado Springs, Mr. Waffling. He explained that Woodbridge had already made the necessary arrangements—an urn inside a casket, no cigar store Indian, shipment via rail to the Springs, funeral service at the Catholic church on Kiowa, burial in Evergreen Cemetery, ushers selected from the El Paso Club, obituary notices posted, and so on and so forth. All I had to do was come to his office for a look at the Will, then greet Woodbridge the day of his arrival.

I was in no hurry to meet with Mr. Waffling. In spite of Daddy's belated attempt at reconciliation, he must have disowned me. Since Mum was suing him for divorce, he would have taken revenge on her by changing his Will to omit her from an inheritance altogether. I considered it certain that he had squandered most of his wealth on Pia and would leave her the remainder. If, I decided, I went to the Springs a few days ahead of the funeral in early January, I could at least with Ruby's help rescue Mum's possessions from the house on Wood Avenue; perhaps, too, my books and toys could be collected and donated to the Salvation Army. So accustomed had I now become to living without many material things that "stuff" beyond bare necessities and Don Fernando's paint box didn't appeal to me.

In due time I acted upon my decision. Ruby's not having a telephone or the ability to read, I had someone from the lawyer's office visit her home on Shooks Run and advise her of my plans. Thus it came about one warm January afternoon she and I stood outside the house on Wood Avenue, noting how paint was chipping off, how the roof needed repair, how shutters had come unhinged and how weeds five-feet high surrounded the property.

"It's a fixer-upper," Ruby said.

"Aye," I said, "there's the rub."

The front door was unlocked. Upon entering the house, we were met by odors. Stale smoke permeated the air, not quite enough to cure Virginia ham but sufficient to send me scurrying to the clinic for surgical masks. While in the clinic I made a hasty inventory of Daddy's supply of drugs. Although it had been his custom to keep dangerous ones such as tincture of opium locked up, these were now on a counter, bottles empty. In the kitchen Ruby discovered not only piles of unwashed dishes green-gray with fungus but drawers full of horse manure and mushrooms. As for the master bedroom and adjacent bathroom, we found clothes, linens, and towels scattered about, all unwashed, and an infestation of cockroaches.

We exchanged knowing looks. Dismay and revulsion, all that Ruby and I were feeling, led to my immediate decision to leave the clean-up and sale of the property in the hands of the lawyer. Why should we clean up a house belonging to Pia? As soon as we had identified Mum's things for storage, we should go and never look back. After a few nights at the Antlers I would be leaving Colorado Springs—forever.

I hated to say good bye with such finality to Ruby but consoled myself with the thought that Mum, now free, would be returning someday from France and would be certain to see her old friend. Then another thought came to me: what if there were a way to leave Ruby something out of Daddy's Will? This thought led swiftly to another: what if there were a way to leave something out of Daddy's Will to Doña Luz that she might hire help and enable Golly to pursue her college education?

The next day I went to the law firm of Evans & Waffling on South Tejon Street across from the palatial El Paso County Courthouse. I was now glad that Woodbridge was taking care of the funeral business. Since I fully expected to find myself disowned by Daddy, I needed all my energy to cope with that humiliation. Evans & Waffling was on the second floor of a "pioneer" red-brick building, renovated with new floorboards and electric lights while still retaining such reminders of the past as brass spittoons, plush curtains, and the head of a taxidermist's buffalo. A pert-looking secretary welcomed me with a frosty look, announced my arrival by rapping on the door to an inner office, motioned for me to sit down next to a potted palm tree, and resumed her typing on expensive paper. I inspected the majesty of the Law as evinced by photographs of bearded judges who looked only too ready to grant Shylock his pound of flesh and by an oil painting of the courthouse, one inscribed, as I imagined, with the words from Hell, *Abandon all hope ye who enter here.*

"I guess Mr. Waffling is pretty busy," I ventured to say to the secretary after I had waited for half an hour.

The secretary made a long face and said in low voice, "He's talking on the phone with his mistress."

For another half hour I entertained myself by watching greenbottle flies, my insect cousins, buzz around the secretary's pomaded hair, but finally we heard the tinkling of a bell. Opening the door to the inner office, the secretary let me in to a high-ceilinged room, walls stacked with books which could be reached by ladders only, or so I supposed until I saw Mr. Waffling standing up behind his desk. He was at least seven-foot tall, though bent over with age, so bald that only a few strands of white hair hung over his ears like Spanish moss. His spectacles and watch chain glittered in the light thrown by a bulb dangling on a wire from the ceiling, and the wrinkled skin of his cadaverous head also gleamed. Other than these appearances of life, this defender of the Law, who was apparently, God knew how, cheating on his wife with a mistress would have been a good fit for Daddy's casket.

'Sit," he said. I did so at once, sinking into depths of a leather chair, pleased to have been reclassified from an ant to a trained dog. When Mr. Waffling sat down in his ladder-back throne, he studied me silently for a few moments before whipping off the spectacles and waving them back and forth as if he were hypnotizing a jury before pronouncing the death sentence. "Penhallow?" he said in a voice seemingly laced with contempt. "What have you got to say for yourself?"

"Nothing, sir."

"I thought so," Mr. Waffling said, shuffling papers on his desk. "That is good. It is my duty to inform you of the sorry state of your late father's stated estate, not intestate but estimated to be overrated before it was probated."

For the next hour he hemmed and hawed in a soporiferous tone while I yearned for toothpicks to prop up drooping eyelids. I thought I knew what *bulls* and *bears* were but had difficulty picturing them as grazing on Wall Street. *Futures?* Was there more than one of them? The word *commodities* got mixed up with *commodes*. I confused *mutuals* with *nuptials, dividends* with *long division*, and *liquid assets* with *diarrhea during potty training.*

"Almost nothing left," Mr. Waffling tut-tutted.

"Yes," I said, "Mrs. Dare, Daddy's mistress. I believe she cleaned him out. Did he leave everything to her?"

Mr. Waffling arched little white eyebrows. "To his mistress? Let us consider this word, *mistress*. What is wrong with it? It is abbreviated as *Miss*, meaning an unmarried woman without the honorific title of *Mrs.*, which is higher than a waitress or a teacher or a silly, sentimental girl. Now, one may argue that Miss also means a kept woman, does it not? But consider this: a married woman is also a kept woman. Neither *Miss* nor *Mrs.* has a vote. Unless she is independently wealthy, she depends for money upon an allowance from her husband. And he can put her in an asylum for the insane merely by appealing to the court. In other words, it is just as honorable to be a mistress as it is to be a married woman. For this reason I call my wife my 'mistress'. It horrifies me that any woman is treated as no more than a warm watermelon."

"Sir?" I liked what Mr. Waffling was saying about women but his candor surprised me. And his smile was so fleeting it might have been mistaken for another wrinkle except that his eyes had a moist, dreamy expression. "When we were boys in Texas," he said, "as soon as we discovered our manhood, we would find watermelons that had been soaking up sun and, with a pocket knife, carve a six-inch round hole in them . . . It took us a while to realize that a woman is a human being. Your father never realized this: his mistress was to him a warm watermelon."

While Mr. Waffling paused, I pressed on with my unanswered question. "Sir," I said, "I'm not interested in the market value of a hump with a warm watermelon but in the Last Will and Testament. Does Mrs. Dare inherit the estate, including the house? She earned her keep by staying coked to the gills on drugs and by filling kitchen drawers with horseshit, the better to cultivate mushrooms."

"House? What house?" Mr. Waffling demurred. "Dr. Penhallow's house was repossessed by the bank weeks ago and hasn't been sold . . . Let us get down to brass tacks."

He leaned over the desk. I lifted my dog's gaze to meet his. "Mr. Penhallow," he said, "as you are doubtless aware, when your father let go of a dollar, it squealed. Therefore, in death, since he would be indisposed to raise the energy for what you call a 'hump', he realized he would not desire to endow a warm watermelon. Ergo, he has left nothing to Mrs. Dare. Furthermore, because his wife had tuberculosis, he assumed she would predecease him. Now that he has predeceased her, as deceased he has ceased to write a codicil, though he never ceased to believe he would be predeceased by a wife who has ceased dying . . . My dear fellow, your father had no intention of capitalizing a corpse. He penned one Will. He has left everything to you!"

The shock of finding myself recognized by a very distant relative of mine, my father, didn't last long. Mr. Waffling, astonishingly as sympathetic as he was tall, agreed to draw up documents in which my intentions would be disguised as Daddy's. Ruby would receive $2,000 in cash "in gratitude for services rendered." Doña Luz would receive $5,000 in cash "for saving my son from homelessness and penury." Once these deductions were made from my inheritance, I still had enough money left over to support myself modestly and become an artist in France.

Not too damn bad.

The morning of the funeral I was down on the platform of the DRG&W station by nine o'clock just as Woodbridge's special train was pulling in. Hundreds of people, perhaps as many as a thousand, had already gathered there to get a glimpse of a tycoon. A band dressed up to look like French Zouaves was already playing *Hail to the Chief*, evidently in the belief that Corporation and White House were indistinguishable. When Woodbridge, surrounded by bodyguards, alighted from the train, the crowd, instead of greeting him with cheers and applause, just gawked.

He was palpably unreal, not at all like the man I had seen in Scampy's photograph album. Gone were the fierce mustaches in the style of Prince Otto Eduard Leopold von Bismarck in my *Book of Knowledge*. Gone, too, were the short-cropped black hair and the icy stare of an emperor. When he tipped his derby, he shook loose a flowing mane of silver hair, though his thin mustache was still dark, and, when he grinned, his teeth gleamed like pearls and his eyes, a pale shade of cerulean blue, conveyed perpetual amusement. He was wearing a black frock coat, a fawn waistcoat, striped trousers, satin tie, pearls at cuffs and collars, a boutonniere and black kid gloves in addition to the silk derby. Weight-lifter shoulders sloped to the tip of his biceps so that his chest pushed against the coat. Had I not been privy to the fact he was at least in his mid-sixties, I might have taken his appearance for that of a prince in his thirties. Rich men, I had heard, were supposed to be found guilty before they were tried, but Woodbridge, in person, seemed too great to be measured by fortune or by the Law.

He was friendly, expansively so. After shaking hands with various dignitaries he turned to the crowd and thrust both arms into the air. The crowd responded with a jubilant roar. The band struck up *The Stars and Stripes Forever*. As I was close to him, I heard him say to his bodyguards, "I do not want to establish the precedent of going about guarded." He then turned his attention to reporters with their cameras and raised his hands slightly as if he were catching a flyball. Immediately they stopped yelling and taking pictures. Parting their ranks, he walked briskly over to a group of men in overalls, shook hands and chatted with them, and declared, "Gentlemen, I shall remember our conversation for the rest of my life." When the band stopped playing, some of its girls in wide loose skirts began to scream hysterically. He went to them and kissed their hands before striding from the depot in the direction of the redbrick church less than two blocks away. The crowd fell in behind him, masses of little children behaving as if he were the Pied Piper of Hamelin. When we came to the church door he waved his derby high in the air and cried, "Thank you, Colorado! God bless America!"

He entered the church and disappeared from my sight.

I felt a bit of a supernumerary. Woodbridge was in complete control of everything. Then, too, Daddy having denied Mum a social life, I wondered whether there would be anyone in attendance at the service who had been their friend. Chances were, the church would be full of strangers, most if not all of them craning necks to catch glimpses of personified Success. The closer I came to church door, the greater was my temptation to jam hands in pockets of my new three-piece suit and slink off to Acacia Park where I could remind myself of two Americas, the rich and the rest of us. An organ was thunderously bellowing from inside the church. Bells outside were clanging. Anyone who was going to come had already come. The door was closed. I turned to leave.

Just then the door burst open and there holding it for me was Woodbridge. "Come along, Tree," he smiled. "I'm Alf. Delighted to meet you at last. Let's give the carrot-tops something to wet their pants about . . . There we are. The place is packed. I dare say, I didn't know your father was so admired in the community. You must be very proud of him. Our seats are in the front row. We'll talk there, shall we?"

Together we walked slowly down the aisle, Woodbridge nodding his head this way and that at people who chattered while the organ thundered on and, up front, cherub-faced acolytes and pale priests were having what, for all I knew, was batting practice. Either Scampy or Daddy or both, I figured, had familiarized Woodbridge with my features and nickname, but his recognition of me as the Last of the Penhallows elevated me to an American peerage. By the time we were seated side by side with, behind us, hundreds of people speaking in hushed tones about me, how noble I was, how proud my father must have been of me, how with Woodbridge's backing I was destined for greatness, I had almost come to the conclusion that I owned Colorado.

"See that, son?" Woodbridge said, gripping my arm and shaking me out of my vainglorious daydream. He was pointing at Daddy's casket. On top of it was a ruby-colored bottle and a jar of something pickled. "Rose-hip syrup and the pope's nose," Woodbridge explained. "Rose-hip is the fruit of the rose. The pope's nose is the fatty extremity of a fowl's rump. Your father was very fond of these delicacies. I had specimens shipped directly from New York from a shop specializing in English food . . . The very thought of eating it gives me the willies."

When I saw a twinkle in his eyes, I couldn't help but smile. It seemed inconceivable that a man of his eminence would have an uncanny, magnetizing charm. Treated on intimate, equal terms, I relaxed, feeling lucky to have been taken under the wing of the same man who had been ultimately responsible for clumsily bumping off my father.

An hour later, after bells, incense burners, prayers, eulogy, incantation of Latin and the lugging away of the casket, Woodbridge and I waved good-bye to Daddy's sudden friends and climbed in to a two-horse carriage for the trip to the cemetery. A fleet of phaetons bearing bodyguards and dignitaries followed us. On the seat beside us was a picnic hamper. Removing gloves and opening it, he gestured for me to partake of oysters, watercress sandwiches, apples and a bottle of sarsaparilla. "Tuck in before you bugger off, as the English say," said Woodbridge. "I suppose you coalmining fellows would prefer grain alcohol to sarsaparilla?"

"No, no," I protested, helping myself to a bottle. "I'm not a miner now, Alf. I'm an artist. I'm going to France."

He swallowed an oyster and licked fingers before speaking. "Of course. Your mother lives in Touraine. Lovely country . . . Tree, I'm sorry to say, the unionists are ungrateful for the opportunities I have afforded them, but I simply cannot accept their implication that I act unfairly. My managers know far better than my workers what my business requires. They are proven agents. I trust them. I trust them even when they are sometimes guilty of actions of which I, myself, am ignorant. Besides, matters concerning labor are unimportant compared to questions of sales, finances, and profits. You see, it is the duty of my managers to employ fair play in the hiring and overseeing of my workers, and they must be vigilant when it comes to the Union. Those who threaten our loyal miners and use incendiary talk are not, as I am, working in the service of humanity."

We munched apples for a few minutes. When his mouth was full, he, unlike Daddy, did not hesitate to talk while he was chewing. "I have an apple every night before going to bed. I keep a paper sack of apples on the sill outside my bedroom window. Good for the bowels." Swallowing, he resumed talk but seemed to aim it not at me but at the coachman's back. "I look at myself and say to myself, there's a man whose life has not been perfect. It has been human, too human. He feels the heartbeats of every man and has tried to be the friend of every man. He loves his fellow man. Still, there are some people who would destroy me. They are strong, they are powerful. On the other hand, there are millions who realize I have done more good than evil." Woodbridge looked at me sharply. "You're a handsome lad," he said. "Oh, by the way, my wife left me a daughter just about your age."

"Scampy," I said. "I met her when you were hunting. I also met Alphie, your son. I tried to entertain him. He had a mind of his own."

"Oh, he still does," said Woodbridge guardedly. "If only his mind were in his head and not up his tail. I've had to have him committed to a private nursing institution."

I was not altogether surprised to learn that Alphie had been committed. I recollected his presentation to me of the photograph of Scampy as snow-fairy, which I had been keeping in my wallet. It was now without sentimental value. A nymph who looked like Napoleon wasn't my type. The picture was wrinkled and cracked, its chemicals turning it into a sepia color. If Golly, when I married her, should find me in possession of this relic from yesteryear, I'd be in for a grumble I'd never forget, so why not give it to Woodbridge while the going was good? I did feel sorry for him. He had lost his wife. He had a stupid mistress. His son was bugs. His "daughter" wasn't biologically his. If I gave him Scampy's picture, I could do him a kindness and at the same time be shut of it forever. I reached for my wallet, fished out the photograph, handed it to him.

"I'd like you to have this," I said.

He put on his glasses, studied the picture, scowled. "I'm not interested in little girls," he said.

"It's Scampy," I said.

Again he studied the picture. "Oh," he said with a slight smile, "so it is. Where did you get this picture?"

I told him that Alphie had given it to me. He stared over his glasses and said, "You've been secretly carrying the torch for her. I shall tell her when I see her. You have given me a pearl of great price. Thank you very much indeed." He thrust the picture into a pocket of his frock coat.

When we came to the crest of a hill overlooking the cemetery, he ordered the coachman to pull over. The carriages which had been following us also came to a stop. I thought Woodbridge was going to admire the view of the mountains. Instead, he reached into his frock coat, pulled out a large pistol, and thumped it down on the seat between us next to the picnic hamper.

I looked at the pistol.

I looked at him, wondering if he, like his son, intended to use it.

He chuckled, catching my drift. "The damned thing has been rubbing against my spine . . . I thoroughly believe in severe measures when necessary and am not in the least sensitive about killing any number of men when there is adequate reason."

After a pause he chuckled again. "Young man," he said, "I've taken a shine to you. You will join me, won't you, on my train to Los Tristes? There, that's settled. And, starting tomorrow, I want you to show me around my mines and introduce me to some of the what-you-call-'ems, stiffs. I'll be at the Imperial Hotel. At the end of the week I'll be hosting a dance in the ballroom . . . I never wanted to get into coal and steel. They bring me less than 15% of my profits. Not worth my trouble, really, but I have a sacred duty to look after my workers' welfare, wouldn't you agree?'

"I'm going to tell you the secret of my success," he said, lowering voice to the pitch required for confidences. "Powerful men are chosen by God to create wealth. I am steward of a divine trust and must use my success for the right, to be worthy of it, to eschew wrongdoing and error. If I do wrong, I do not intend it."

Woodbridge prodded the coachman into action, sat back, and seemed to forget all about me. We and the others continued the trip to the cemetery, and, once there, the burial ritual began. People seemed to shun me, perhaps because I had pull with Woodbridge, an exception being Mr. Lily. He nodded in my direction in recognition of bygones at school. As best I could, I blocked out the scene before me and reflected upon the turn of events. Whatever people might think of me in Los Tristes, just because I was willing, as I was, to show Woodbridge around, didn't mean I was disloyal to persons I loved or to the Union. By falling in with his plans for me, I might open his eyes to what was going on in the lives of his workers. I might help to avert a repetition of suffering brought about by strikes. When it came to matters of freedom and justice, I philosophied to myself, someone had to create wealth, didn't he? Why not work for a transformation in Woodbridge's point of view, bringing it closer to Dare's, the convergence of the world through an in-the-same-boat spirit?

We returned to the railroad station after a brief stop at the Antlers to enable me to collect my things and pay the bill. It was Woodbridge, not I, who proposed this stop, an act of urbane, courteous consideration seldom seen in my neck of the woods and very much to his credit, I thought. A short while later, when we were in the parlor car having an English tea with scones—the train, *his* train, rattling and swerving at sixty miles an hour, steam whistle shrieking for crossings, wheels screeching around bends, four bodyguards in identical black suits sporting identical upside-down-V mustaches, and sitting glumly far from us—I looked out the windows and surveyed the land from a perspective new to me. Unlike that time when Daddy first took me to Los Tristes, now, instead of admiring the beauty of ordinary things and orienting myself to plains and mountains, I seemed to possess the land. Like Woodbridge, I exercised power over it as exemplified by the black, smoky towers of steelworks in Pueblo. Hitherto, armed with the righteousness of a victim, I had made common cause with the poor and oppressed. Even though I still considered them my brothers, now I wondered if they genuinely craved freedom. Ants in the antheap, and I had been one of them, wanted someone to rule over *them* and grant them an illusion of happiness. Persons in power, and I was now one of *them*, had to carry the burden of a sadness. A Woodbridge perceived, as only he could perceive, that he sold his soul for the sake of others.

As in Colorado Springs, so in Los Tristes the platform was crowded with reporters and spectators. When Woodbridge rose from the tea-table, I noticed that his pistol, a foreign model unknown to me, was now tucked back in to his trousers in the lumbar region. As he was putting on his frock coat, he dismissed the bodyguards, saying, "I told you I do not want an escort. Proceed to the Imperial. Young Penhallow and I shall walk there at our leisure. I am here to understand and to be understood, to gather facts and to win confidence."

As in Colorado Springs, so in Los Tristes the people were awestruck by Woodbridge's visit. He was spry and friendly, making little impromptu speeches, shaking hands, kissing babies and their mothers, chatting with workers. The crowd followed us as far as the Pluck Me where, at my suggestion, he was going to equip himself in a coalminer's outfit. Just as he was entering the supply store, he stopped, seeming to remember something, and went directly to the reporters, exacting two promises from them: that they would not intrude on his personal talks with miners, and that they would not divulge in their stories each night where he was going to be the next day.

During my week with Woodbridge, he and I appeared unannounced at mountain camps. Dressed in his clean new outfit, he spoke informally with miners and accompanied them down in the cages. As far as I could tell, there was no animosity toward him; on the contrary, he was idolized, his fame having spread to remote corners of the world. One evening at Josca's Opera House he promised a thousand workers and their families what he called "representation," one worker from each camp to be seated with management for discussion of grievances. The plan was a fraud, of course, just as Dare had predicted, but the audience applauded wildly, believing Union had been finally recognized. One afternoon there was a groundbreaking ceremony at a vacant lot. A Y.M.C.A. was to be erected there to enable workers and their families and friends to lodge, bathe, and swim in a Christian manner.

None the less my infatuation with Woodbridge was beginning to wear off a pieceways down the primrose path. My sober diffidence in regard to him had little to do with his publicity stunts. Now that I had received a small legacy I was determined to go to France within a matter of weeks. The more I pondered the significance of my breakaway, the more my feelings for Golly were becoming desperate. If I declared my feelings and left her, she could name a dog after me who would be good, but I would be worthless. If I proposed marriage, an institution she, I believed, abominated, she would turn the back of her hand to me. Besides, I wanted her to go to college before she settled down, exactly as Doña Luz hoped she would do. I decided to wait until she and I went to Woodbridge's ballroom dance. Unless I had a failure of nerve I would find a way to hold her hand.

Someone, presumably one of Woodbridge's trusted managers, had obtained the names and addresses of a hundred local citizens in order to send them engraved invitations to the ball. The words "formal dress," "black tie," and "champagne cocktails" had not been circulated in Los Tristes for a very long time, an invitation from "Mr. Alpheus Woodbridge I" had not ever. As far as anyone could remember, nothing like this kind of aristocratic procedure had previously arrived to eclipse the glittering of Cousin Jack's, the Tap'er Light Saloon, the whorehouses on the west end, Italian opera at Josca's and Mexican dances on Saturday nights. Previous balls at the Imperial had been supervised by reformed cattlemen who hated drink and women.

Meanwhile, life at the ranch had been transformed by the delivery of a letter from Mr. Waffling of Evans & Waffling addressed to "Sra. Medina" and announcing my father's bequest of a sum made real by a cashier's check. I assured the family that Daddy had sent me into "exile" as a test to see, as in the fable of Diogenes, if there were an honest person anywhere to be found, and I had found her. Even though I could tell from Dare's narrow-eyed look that he scouted my story, I trusted him to keep his peace. Dare had, after all, heard Daddy's deathbed conversion, as it were, and so it was conceivable he had changed his Will.

We rejoiced, actually, to see how far a little windfall could go. It went, as I had hoped, in the direction of a correct self-indulgence. Doña Luz hired a cook and a housemaid to sweep, do laundry, and build fires, thus relieving Golly of chores and releasing her back to school. She and Golly hired a seamstress to come from town and measure them for gowns for the ball. One more thing: if Doña Luz were harboring malice toward me for seeming to pander to Woodbridge, she apparently now believed that Daddy, in spite of working for Woodbridge, still had had a heart of gold. Woodbridge, himself, like Charles V and Phillip II of Spain, had a Roman numeral after his name. He must, therefore, have been, if not royalty, then a *caballero* too refined to have signed the Treaty of Guadalupe Hildago.

It was my conviction that Woodbridge was mistaking the workers' deference to him for a vote of confidence. Once he returned to New York his name would be remembered as a byword for tyranny. So when, the day of the ball, he clapped his hands and exclaimed to me, "Mr. Penhallow, there'll be a hot time in the old town tonight!," I realized he came from the country of the blind.

Me, if I had had the one eye to be king, I was still abdicating the throne and going into exile of my own volition. Every man's destiny was Odyssean, I believed; every man must go forth in search of himself and bring that achieved selfhood home to his Ithaca.

That night of the ball, Golondrina was blossoming in a silk gown of elegance, the long dark hair flowing to her shoulders, the quick step, the bright eyes, the warmth of a dreaming gaze dazzling me. The door of the sad people opened into realms of great beauty and mystery. Love and Art together could be reached beyond that door, and we would go there.

Woodbridge had arranged for a band that could play anything from bluegrass to a waltz, and all that night of the ball he led the way with buck-and-wing steps, with cakewalk stompings, with hoe-downs and fox trots, switching partners until every woman in the room had been held in his arms at least once and swirled into breathlessness. Perhaps, after all, he would be remembered for his charm rather than for his tyranny. He had, it seemed, won the heart of Doña Luz. A word from him and the bandleader produced from his group a violinist. Doña Luz, who had come dressed in traditional costume, performed, Woodbridge beside her, a *rat-tat-tatting* flamenco dance, the crowd hand-clapping and howling, Woodbridge crying, 'Bully! Bully!"

Two lovers fled away. When they came to a bridge over the River of Souls Lost in Purgatory, they bridged the strangeness between them. The young man remembered that the young woman had once dreamed of having a fistful of fireflies spread over her face. He bent down and scooped them up, though no one but he and she could see them, and spread them over her face where they twinkled like all the stars in the firmament.

I kissed Golly.

My first kiss.

PART III

Chapter Thirteen

When Joseph H. Sharp, Bert Phillips, and Ernest Blumenshein met in Paris in 1895 at the Académie Julian, they established a link between French and American art, one that would lead them to become pioneers of an art colony in Taos, New Mexico. The figural work at the Académie, the emphasis upon *plein-air* realism, and the sweeping techniques of Impressionism were channeled into a land of limitless space with a mystical quality of light, a brilliance and subtlety of colors, and a quiet serenity in Indian and Hispanic cultures. After a couple of years of study at the Académie Julian, I, too, gravitated to Taos and in a sense apprenticed myself to those masters who had gone before me both in Paris and in Taos.

Blumenshein has described as bleak and gray the Académie as he first found it on the Rue de Dragon. It was, apparently, an inspiring *atelier* where painters were expected to observe, persevere, and concentrate. He passed under an arched entrance to a courtyard, turned and climbed a dark, winding stairway of stone steps, and groped his way along a very dim hall. He had, as I suppose, a sinking feeling in his heart. But then he opened a tall door and there before him was a huge, high-ceilinged room "blue with light and smoke." As his eyes became adjusted to the change, he glimpsed above the heads of a crowd of students a nude woman posing with arms outstretched; twenty feet away from her on another stand was posing a man stark naked. Unlike the École des Beaux-Arts, the Académie admitted women. There they were. These women and men from all over the world were, to Blumenshein, "a jolly lot, insolent, disrespectful, proud to defy most of society's conventions," some wearing large, flowing black neckties and smoking cigarettes. As high as the hand could reach, the walls were plastered with palette scrapings. Because cold air was bad for the models, the studio windows at the top of the walls were closed. A big coal stove kept the place heated.

The basis of academic study was drawing from the live model. Nudes enabled one to demonstrate knowledge of anatomical structure and virtuosity in painting the tactile surfaces of and variations in skin tones. When Sharp, Phillips, Blumenshein and others later came to Taos, they were prepared to capture some of the infinitely beautiful effects of changing lights in the high, dry mountain climate, as well as to portray Pueblo Indians as warm and gentle, not the "savages" of popular sterotypes. For example, a young Indian seated before a glowing fire would be given glowing skin tones. Like some of the French Impressionists, American artists in Taos and elsewhere in the Southwest sought to evoke feelings of vastness and peaceful isolation.

In 1908 at the age of seventeen I enrolled in the Académie. Among its most famous students prior to that date were Marie Bashkirtseff, Pierre Bonnard, Edouard Vuillard and Henri Matisse.

My steamship arrived in Cherbourg in early spring of 1906. Met there à bras ouverts by Mum and Ganny, we went by rail to the tenth-century village of St. Aignan where they had a room awaiting me in their "new" house. My growth, apparently, was miraculous, my features extraordinary. While my vanity certainly hoped that there might be some truth in Mum's descriptions of me, I seemed to myself to be the same awkward scapegrace I had always been. When I looked at myself in mirrors, I saw a homely coalminer who was maidenly conscious of little to shave. Mum, herself, was the one who had blossomed. Away from Daddy, she had always been pert and sprightly, but he with his demands for instant obedience to a raised eyebrow had managed to shrivel up her natural vitality.

Now, though, she had recovered the person she must have been before marriage. At thirty-five she exhibited a kind of nobility, infusing from a depth of feeling a rapture of caring. Perhaps that was why she generously endowed the world—and her son—with a gift of life already fulfilling itself. And part of her transformation was doubtless due to Dare. I didn't know but I suspected that his wildly romantic scheme to free Mum from captivity and escort her to safety in France had had much to do with therapy for her before it proved friendship and a bond.

Daddy's death had also helped to remove tensions between Mum and Ganny, in particular those associated with Grandpa Rufus Obadiah Dautremond's trust fund. If and when Mum attained to the age of thirty-five, she was supposed to inherit half of his estate which in the meantime had been left to Ganny. Because Mum wanted no part of money derived from the slave trade, she had drawn up a Will giving all to Daddy; that Will she had revoked before she embarked for France. But Ganny, supposedly, had invaded the fund and reduced it in value to almost nothing to avenge herself on my father for slighting her in Florence. I hadn't been long in St. Aignan before the truth came out: not only had Ganny lied to me about reducing the fund, but also she had invested it so wisely that Mum's inheritance in 1905, her thirty-fifth, had tripled in value.

As soon as I had opportunity, I scolded Ganny for lying to me about Mum's inheritance. "I realize," I said in a nervous tone which sounded priggish, "that Daddy may have deserved to get his comeuppance. I give you credit for having driven home for me an excellent lesson in economics, namely, that I must earn my own keep in this life and have no great expectations, but I lost the silver spoon in my mouth eons ago and resent your attempt to save my soul."

"Pishtash," said Ganny, ever the sophist. "It is bad luck to give away an empty pocketbook. To break that spell I need have filled it only with a penny instead of a fortune. Instead, your mother has her cake and can eat it too. She has deposited the originally tainted money in a French bank until such time as she can give it outright to a victim of slavery. The remainder of the fortune—two-thirds in fact—she has in all good conscience reserved for herself. If you have a problem with usury, that is your own affair. If you're going to be an artist and try to live off the wind, you'll soon come clinging to my knees."

I hadn't been long in St. Aignan before Mum hired tutors to prepare me to become a day scholar at the École Supérieure. As it was the very school Dare had attended, I respected its tradition of teaching subjects for which I had, I thought, no earthly use, such as Latin, the history of kings and dates of battles, algebra and calculus. I swatted up those subjects and eventually entered the École Supérieure. As an American I found myself pigeonholed as *un grand enfant*—a big baby without history, so innocent I was dangerous. I was given by my cruel and competent teachers a pass. I could sometimes skip their classes and attend those of the art teacher, Madame Batiot. Although I continued to study Latin, French, Natural Philosophy and the like, I did so half-heartedly but I was mysteriously ranked by my masters among the real scholars in those subjects. Before Madame Batiot I stood properly evaluated. I seemed to her to be a clot irrespective of my country of origin.

In winter I rose before dawn to paint any subject I could find before going to school. In summer I hurried home to slip in another few hours of painting before the light failed. In the course of two years I piled up at least a hundred paintings in oil and filled dozens of sketchbooks. I submitted everything to Madame Batiot, confessing to her my ambition to go to the Académie Julian. "We shall see," she always said, meaning "Not if I can help it." She, herself, had studied at the Académie. Her standards were as high and ogreish as those of the Parisian masters, Bouguereau, Jean-Paul Laurens, and Benjamin Constant. Still, in 1907 she accompanied Mum and me on a tour of museums in Paris and secured us permission to view private collections of Van Gogh, Cézanne, and even a young Picasso. I had seen a few works of masters in New York galleries. Not until that visit to Paris did I feel

272

Like some watcher of the skies
When a new planet swims into his ken.

What was I painting in St. Aignan? Shall I speak of the tulips
in our garden-terrace built on top of the old city walls? What of
the horse-chestnut tree, the feathery white clematis, the ponderosa
tomatoes? I could see over our old gray wall rows of red tile roofs,
a chateau high on a hill above the river, and towers of the church
which had distressed Dare as his mother lay dying. I painted
those subjects. I needn't forget having painted the old women in
their quaint bonnets, little black shawls, and sabots, nor the old
farmers in blue smocks and corduroy trousers. And there was
Père Rollo, our gardener whose portrait I painted. He had been
sexton of the church and regarded as an exemplary citizen. When
the Curé began to find that the funds in the box for the parish poor
were falling off, he never thought of the old sexton but had the
gendarme pass the night in the church to see what was happening.
In the middle of the night someone entered the church, and the
gendarme clapped his hand on the shoulder of Père Rollo, who
exclaimed, *"C'est le Diable!"* It then transpired that Père Rollo was
in the habit of entering the church at night and fishing coins out
of the offering boxes with a whalebone from his wife's corsets, on
the tip of which he put some glue. I also painted a portrait of the
Town Crier, a little man with a little drum. He beat the drum before
delivering his message, sometimes a new command of the Maire
to tell us, for instance, that our pavements must be swept before
morning or to notify clients of the milk vendor that his price had
gone up. A First Communion procession called for a large canvas.
Each little girl wore the costume of a bride, being dressed in white
muslin with a veil and white wreath, white gloves and shoes. All the
boys had new suits with white arm bands and wore white gloves.
The procession of communicants passed through the town from
the school to the church, led by the Curé. Once in the church the
procession was led by the "Suisse," or beadle, in his gold-braided,
scarlet coat, plush knee-breeches, long white silk stockings, black

three-cornered hat and long brass-tipped staff of office. Also calling for large canvases were scenes of the *vendange*, the grape harvest. All through the summer the grower and his family would work in the vineyards, tilling the soil, spraying the vines, and watching the grapes develop. He wanted sun and no rain during the latter part of July and August to increase the sugar content of the grape and to combat mildew, and he wanted just enough rain in September to fill out the grapes and make them juicy. When thunderheads rolled up, he sent rockets into the clouds on all sides in order to prevent hail. These rockets were spoken of as the *contregrêle canon*. When the moment for the harvest came, all hands were solicited for service, wandering bands of gypsies and even children especially set free from school. The pickers were each provided with a basket and scissors. As soon as the baskets were filled, they were emptied into wooden hods carried on the backs of men. These hods, in turn, were emptied into barrels, which were then loaded into carts to be carried back to farms for pressing. The screw of the press would be turned by two or more of the strongest workers. The juice would run in a ruby stream into barrels which, when filled, were emptied into great vats to ferment. For many days the tonnes would be left uncorked, as the fermenting wine would burst them if they were closed too soon. When I painted these scenes, I felt happy as a Rabelais proclaiming the Oracle of the Bottle. Indeed, whenever I set up my easel near one of the farms, some pretty girl was bound to bring me a glass of the old vintage to taste. I was willing to sacrifice myself to the custom.

On the whole my years in France were happy ones. Privately I yearned for *mi tierra* and Golly, the landscape of my soul and she, I thought, its mate. At first, hardly a week would pass when we did not exchange letters. Hers, to my melancholy eyes, were written in a classic cursive as much of a joy to look at as to read. Her style was, I believed, her character largely based on simple sympathy.

I loved her through her letters and tried to take the utmost care to be and remain faithful to her in word and deed. How fortunate I was that she understood me, what I was aiming for! I was taking a journey into myself in order to emerge as a grownup and bring that achieved selfhood to the relationship. How many girlfriends, let alone parents, would perceive the necessity for a man to pursue such a dream? How many inchoate men would abandon their dreams and settle for female values of home and family? Had Golly tried to hold me back or found another partner, I would not have faltered on my path, but I would, I believed, have harvested sorrow.

She was doing extremely well. The bequest to Doña Luz from, as everyone supposed, Daddy, had enabled Golly to return to school. Her work there was so remarkable she was placed in a stream of students who could be counted on to go to college. By 1908 she matriculated first at a college in Silver City, then at a college in Denver. More about that later.

Dare, too, was doing well. Not long after my departure he had replaced Orestes as district manager of the Union. As many as 10,000 miners and their families were directly or indirectly dependent upon his leadership and that of his second-in-command, Mr. Jefferson, formerly known as Tío Congo. The ranchhouse was rebuilt and enlarged. When his divorce from Pia was finalized, Dare kept the ranch but paid her, according to his own request, a generous alimony. In 1907, he came to St. Aignan, and Mum accepted his proposal of marriage on condition that he wait until I graduated from the École Supérieure.

That condition was for me the rub: I wanted to be beholden to no one, not even to a mother for whom the call of care was conscience personified. The solution to the problem as I conceived it was for Mum to accompany Dare back to Los Tristes at once, leaving me with Ganny until I graduated. After graduation, if I were denied admission to the Académie Julian, I would have to investigate art schools in Boston, New York, or Philadelphia. Or, if I absolutely must be self-taught, I could just take the whole of the American West as my province, inspired by the fact that Shakespeare's Oxford and Cambridge had been a stage and Melville's Yale and Harvard had been a whaling ship.

My senior year (as I called it) I sought Madame Batiot's advice. Her smiling headshake seemed to say it all before she spoke: I would never become another Michelangelo, but I might become a poor man's Masaccio. She was being kind. Masaccio, too, was beyond my range. I did have, Madame Batiot allowed, a capacity for realizing space in which people and objects were proportionally depicted. I was friendly and ready to oblige; I was teachable. Best of all, because I was an American, she argued, I had "no taste in anything." Therefore, I could ignore tradition and aim for "novelty," and the Devil would take care of his own.

To my astonishment, Madame Batiot recommended me to the Académie Julian, and I was accepted. Without further ado I bid farewell to Ganny and St. Aignan and lit out for Paris. Of course, Mum had already been persuaded to return to Los Tristes and marry Dare. Once I was in Paris, Ganny rented her house to tasteless expatriate Americans and returned to New York, this time to Fifth Avenue, her Park Avenue apartment having been destroyed.

In Paris I found cheap accommodations at a small hotel on the Rue des Beaux-Arts. I had to climb four flights of rickety stairs to get to my room on the *troisième étage;* once there I could open casement windows with a view of pigeons and laundry and try to tolerate a student violinist across the street who was practicing, day and night, a Bach chaconne. I had a skylight through which sunny mornings poured, enabling me to paint without having to light a candle. According to the concierge, Oscar Wilde had perished in the hotel in 1900 and left his grandfather clock to her. Upon his deathbed, it was said, Wilde had protested, "Either the wallpaper goes, or I go." Looking about my own papered room, I could see that he had a point.

I was at that time reading Wordsworth's *Prelude*, especially about his residence in France. When he exclaimed,

> *Bliss was it in that dawn to be alive,*
> *But to be young was very heaven,*

I saw his point, too.

One evening in the fall of 1908 I was in my room trying to recover from making, all day, charcoal sketches of a fat nude *odalisque*. I was getting weary of studying body parts, male and female, and would have preferred to paint them transmogrified into something that would stimulate the imagination by implication, into pistil and stamen of an exotic flower, for instance. I, then, was in a sour mood when the concierge, gasping, rapped on my door and announced, *"Monsieur Pen Allo, une jeune fille . . . est arrivèe . . . qui a dit elle vous connait . . . Elle s'appelle Woooo Bridge."*

My skull felt as if I were listening to a thief's breaking in to a house in which I was alone.

"Woodbridge, *madame?*"

"Ah, oui, bien sûr."

"Merci, madame."

There was something else, the concierge continued. The girl had a companion, an older woman, also an American, *"tout à fait désagréable."* Workers had delivered steamer trunks to the foyer, blocking entrance to the hotel. It was necessary for me to come at once.

"Merde." I girded up the old loins, opened the door, and followed the concierge as she limped down those stairs which might have been swiped from the set of *La Bohème*. Usually, whenever I passed through the foyer, I would consult the time on Oscar Wilde's grandfather clock, an antique made of inlaid wood, standing about five feet high, its pendulum ticktocking pleasantly. Now the clock was hidden by a large woman who had the cottage-loaf hairdo,

battleship bosom, and cushiony buttocks of that odalisque. It took me a moment to recall that this woman's smirk had once been a Mona Lisa smile. Some six or seven steamer trunks festooned with stickers of ports of call were indeed blocking entrance to the hotel. Squeezed in among them was an adorably cute brunette, face pudgy and apple-cheeked, bangs still falling over forehead, Napoleonic style. Before I could admit to myself that female anatomy had miraculously become beautiful again, Scampy rushed into my arms and stuck her tongue into my maxillo-mandibular. The kiss sucked out my masculine reasoning faculty like a rubber plunger used to clean out clogged drains. Finally able to break off the embrace, I pointed to the clock.

"It belonged to Oscar Wilde," I said.

Scampy shook her head in mock-disbelief. "You haven't changed," she said.

"She ain't got a buffalo nickel," Pia croaked in cigarette-husky tone. "I'm tard of her not payin' shit. She don't even know how to order a cuppa coffee in English. Well, buster, she's all yers!"

Pia flung a trunk aside and herself out of the hotel.

Dear Mum, I wrote to her in Los Tristes a couple of weeks later.

I apologize for my tardiness in replying to your letters. Although I've been writing Golly, telling her about my riotous fellow students, describing Parisian life, and jotting down impressions of London, from which I returned last week, only to you can I reveal what is truly going on. As soon as I had one **frisson nouveau** *to tell you I had another one. I should point out that I'm in excellent health, that Laurens, himself, paused to compliment me on a brushstroke. I've got a Solomon's choice to make which would be easy if I were Solomon.*

Let me put the matter to you in the abstract. Suppose one of the richest men in the world, upon growing impotent wanted

*a male heir to assume control of his business enterprises and
had been frustrated in previous attempts, having only a son
so mentally bugs he has been institutionalized. Suppose, too,
that the tycoon wants not just any old male heir but a man as
ruthless now as he had been. Although he never hesitates to
use scandalous methods to obtain his ends, he is in terror of
being found out and exposed. He would be, he believes, ruined,
and his Corporation, which behaves as if it is above the Law,
would fall like Humpty Dumpty. Now, our tycoon, one day,
happens to find exactly the man he is seeking. He promises to
pass control of Corporation on to this protégé on one condition:
the protégé must serve as a stud to the tycoon's wife until she
conceives a child. Protégé accepts the deal, realizing that the
tycoon, growing daft, is making a strategic mistake. One, if the
child is male and thus first in line to inherit what has been
otherwise promised, protégé can blackmail tycoon into keeping
his word. Two, if the child is female, protégé has two options:
blackmail tycoon into keeping his word, or marry the girl—his
own daughter—to legitimize his position as a member of the
family in a line of succession.*

*What happens is this: the tycoon's wife gives birth to a girl,
who is then raised to believe the tycoon is her biological father.
Meanwhile, her biological father (of whose blood relation to
her she is totally ignorant) is often at her home, and the tycoon
(to avoid being blackmailed) encourages her to think of the
protégé as a suitable mate. The scheme works. When the girl's
mother dies, she has only her "father" upon whom she can rely,
and, since she is accustomed to thinking of successful men
as naturally and necessarily venal—a condition about which
the protégé, now her suitor, seems humbly to confess—she at
the age of seventeen, in a high-society ceremony, marries the
designated future Chairman of Corporation, the bride even
being given away by her "father."*

*Then the wheels come off. On the very first night of the
honeymoon her biological father, now her husband, ties her*

down and rapes her. Instead of submitting to further criminal humiliation, she runs away and has the marriage annulled. What then? The tycoon disowns her and sends her off on a round-the-world cruise, expenses to be paid by his mistress, who lives off alimony from a recent divorce. The tycoon, of course, expects his "daughter" to be driven into such poverty she will agree to his demands, namely, that she re-marry his former son-in-law, the protégé, still the heir apparent. Had the girl told him about the rape, things might be turning out differently, but she has not revealed the truth to her "father," nor has he revealed it to her.

*Here's the rub. The girl would rather die than bow to her "father's" demands, but there is a boy, now coming of age, who lives in Paris and whom she believes is and always has been in love with her. To Paris she comes. There, her "father's" mistress abandons her, and she is completely at the mercy of the boyfriend. He surrenders his bed to her. He sleeps on the floor. He is an artist and has a limited budget, but he is providing her with everything. If he marries her (as she wishes), she apparently has no plans to contribute to mutual welfare. Her boy-husband must hire servants and, **malheureusement**, nannies. There is one more turn of the screw.*

*The artist is exasperated with the outcast. Once upon a time he kept her picture in his wallet but gave this picture to her "father," the tycoon, who then told her it was proof of the artist's undying love for her. Convinced that she and the artist are meant for each other, as previously noted, she clings to him. Not only does he love someone else, but also his means for supporting her in "the style to which she is accustomed" are limited. Chastely they are living together, but what if the artist's girlfriend back in Colorado (where she is matriculating at a college) should learn of this **ménage à deux?** What he really dreads, however, is that the outcast will have a nervous breakdown. Although she pretends to be "tough-minded," she is in a very perilous psychological condition. If she is abandoned by the artist, she will have no one to whom she can turn* *either at home or abroad. She is sensitive and intelligent but seemingly incapable of taking care of herself. For instance, she has never had to wash her own hair. Imagine what she might do to herself—or to the men who virtually enslaved her—should she discover that her biological father married and raped her.*

Now, the artist knows that he has a grandmother living in London. His father was her illegitimate son by an unknown Rich American, and he has her address. Other than that, he, the artist, knows nothing, and he has been so absorbed in his studies that he has made no attempt to introduce himself to this "lost" member of his family. In order to escape the clutches of the outcast he reveals to her his plan to go to London for a few days, leaving her in his room with money to feed and entertain herself. Boy, does that cause a row! No way will she permit him to leave her alone. The concierge will evict her. And besides, his grandmother's address, "Frognall Gardens," is vague. Why not , the outcast proposes, communicate with her before going off on a wild goose chase? Remember, the outcast is intelligent. A cable is dispatched. By some miracle, the superintendent of an institution replies, stating that "our patients" are allowed "visiting hours" at such-and-such a time and, she was sure, the person who had been "in our home" would be "delighted" to meet "a grandson she never knew she had."

The artist and the outcast travel to London together. In the course of their visit with the grandmother, the outcast sees a photograph of the grandmother's Rich American and recognizes him as the tycoon, the man she believes is her "father." In short, she believes she and the artist's father are siblings. The artist, therefore, must be her nephew! Although the artist is nothing of the kind, since he, not she, is related to the tycoon, the "relationship" spares him the threat of marriage to the outcast.

She, however, is as adamant as ever that they live together, pretending they are "aunt" and "nephew." They will be, she declares, as chaste with one another as, say, William and Dorothy Wordsworth. They will make a home together in New York. Servants will do all the work. Sans sex themselves, they will have ample partners, and any babies will be like a side order of fried potatoes.

Hully gee, Mum, what can I do?

Mum cabled her reply a fortnight later:

I am so glad to have a son like you, someone who has the humanhood of which your Wordsworth speaks in his Prelude. Of course you've been doing the right thing! Your "abstract" is transparent. What Elizabeth Woodbridge told me and I revealed to you in a letter is potentially dynamite, should the truth actually ever come to Scampy's attention. You are forced to play for high stakes, her very life. She might well survive a discovery that her "father" is not her biological father, but if she learns she has been married to and raped by her true biological father, she might well, as you have surmised, do violence to herself and even to others. As for your "Solomon's choice," the problem is solved. Methinks the lady needs money of her own, and it so happens that I have it and want to get rid of it. Having inherited capital from a slaver, I want it to be of benefit to someone whose men, as you put it, "virtually enslaved her." I can very well understand Scampy's predicament. Therefore, please escort her to my bank in Paris where the manager is already advised to present her with a check sufficient to support her for the rest of her life irregardless of the monstrous machinations of your charming grandfather. As Scampy believes you are her blood relation, you must somehow insist upon it, saying to her it is your clear and absolute duty to set her up, adding just a little white lie, that Elizabeth, her dear mother, had me swear to protect and endow a half-orphaned daughter, and that she is not to thank me for doing what her mother would have done, who loved her.

Harrow House, the institution to which Mrs. Irene Penhallow, my
paternal grandmother, had been committed, Scampy and I found
in a surburban area of London near Hampstead Heath. A redbrick mansion in Georgian style, it rose in the middle of several
acres of lawns and gardens which were surrounded by a high brick
wall embedded with gleaming shards of broken glass. Anyone
attempting to climb over the wall from inside or outside was likely
to suffer as a result, for instance, so lacerated by glass as to leave
behind for jackdaws to nibble a finger or sex organ.

At gates we were stopped by uniformed guards who checked our
identities. When I informed them that we had been invited to visit
by the Supterintendent, Miss Florrie Natters, they gave her what
they called "a tinkle on the blower"; after that, they doffed their caps
to us and bowed to Scampy in an obsequious manner. She and I,
as we entered the grounds, exchanged looks which said, Pleased to
Meetcha, Me Lord, Me Lady. We strolled along gravel paths under
copper beeches, passing massive flower beds and pausing to stare
at cast-iron cherubs which were continuously urinating a stream
of water into lily ponds in which swans were, it seemed, posing
as notices for pubs. Just outside the house, at the foot of a marble
stairway, we glimpsed a fenced-in graveyard with concrete, not
granite, stones. These had no names, just numbers.

"The stigma of insanity," Scampy replied sotto voce to my
puzzled expression. "They have stones like these where Pa-pa had
Alphie put away."

Had Scampy not barged into my life, I would not have entered
into correspondence with Miss Florrie Natters, and, if Miss Florrie
Natters had not been candid, I would not have, before visiting
Harrow House, picked up clues about Grandma Irene. Luxurious
appearances notwithstanding, the place was an insane asylum.
Even a woman who gave birth to an illegitimate child could, it
transpired, be considered in certain circumstances "insane."

From hints in Natters's correspondence I had already inferred that such had been the "case" with Mrs. Irene Penhallow. She, I was told, was "wildly excited" to be meeting her grandson, "the first in her family ever to visit her." Daddy, evidently, had known where his mother was, known she was, in his words to me, "well taken care of," and known that families with money and pull could persuade doctors and lawyers to abandon almost anyone to oblivion, and he had taken or had been given her name. He had none the less shut her completely out of his life—and Mum's and mine—and apparently made no inquiry as to the identity of the Rich American.

Suddenly out of the house and down the stairs there came charging toward us a phalanx of functionaries, some dressed as nurses, secretaries, and cooks, others nondescript, all led by a little rotund woman with spectacles, one arm holding down a bird's-nest bonnet, the other arm waving at us frantically as if we were members of the Royal Family.

I had long ago learned from Daddy to mock the comportment of Royals: stand erect, clasp hands behind back, smile without parting lips, and, when speaking, use only received ideas and mumble. I readied my "royal" self accordingly, but the woman ignored me and flung herself at Scampy, singing out in exuberant falsetto, "Miss Woodbridge, O jolly hockey sticks, O lovely die, what a gright honour you bestow, gricin' our 'umble abode!" She paused to press chubby hands against her heart as if to test its exhaustion. "It is, young lighdy, scion of Alpheus Woodbridge, such a veddy-veddy gright pleasure to 'av you 'ere, a bit of aw'right. Your father has bean our grightest benefactor these many years! Amighzing! A mon wi' all the world at 'is command, yit niver 's 'e 'sitighted to tyke notice of us 'ere in old country among our ivy-mantled towers! Niver! O, large is 'is bounty, and 'is soul sincere!.. I do go on. Allow me to interduce meself, if I migh be so bold: Florrie Natters, Super... And this gentlemon, I presume, is Pen Allow, Junior, son of the bastard, so to sigh? Charmed, I'm sure."

Before I could mumble "Gray's *Elegy,*" Natters with a flourish motioned for her hand-clapping staff, as I assumed it to be, to return to their bed pans and typewriters. Then sidling just behind us, she escorted us to the 'Ouse and 'Ome. Scampy and I again exchanged looks: Me Lord, Me Lady. We both climbed the stairs with hands behind backs following Natters who opened for us an oaken door with a lion's-head knocker right out of *The Christmas Carol*. Into the chill and dry-rot odor of 'Arro 'Ouse we went and presently into an oak-paneled office with a coal fire glowing in a grate and a large window offering a view of the graveyard, the wall, busy roads and countless row-houses with chimneys belching smoke.

I was still stunned by the Woodbridge connection. So numerous were his charities, I reckoned, he had somehow been extending them to insane asylums in London. I wondered if Grandma Irene had been immured while still sound in mind and body. If Irene had been and still was healthy, shouldn't Scampy use her remaining influence with Woodbridge to have the poor woman released from imprisonment, given a pension, and provided with a thatched-roof cottage in the Lake Country far from the madding crowd?

The three of us took seats by the fire.

"I noticed, Natters," I said, "that your graves have no names. Very economical, I must say. Unpretentious."

Natters rolled eyes behind spectacles. "Breaks me 'eart, them grighves," she said. "What can Natters do? I'm only a bird in a gilded cage. Bangers an' mash an' a pint o' wallop on Guy Fawkes, i'n'at right? No offense, Miss Woodbridge, beggin' your pardon as is the richest girl in th' world, I dare sigh, but the rich gits all the grighvy—'ow be we on without song? It's the bloody rules. Would you care to see me register? I 'av nighmes to the numbers, I do. Iv'ry die I sigh to meself, 'Natters, you 'ave a sighcred duty: you keeps the souls as 'av pighed the price of existence, pighn, sorrow, an' death.' Mind you, after the poor dears pass awigh, Natters gives 'em a number but keeps th' register up to date. I've got me own number riddy. Nobody knows me 'istory . . . A rum do . . . I do go on."

"Natters," I broke in, "you've been very kind . . . absolutely lovely, and I'm sure Miss Woodbridge will be giving you a nice recommendation to her dear Pa-pa . . . She's silent now. Took a vow of silence. Hasn't worn off yet. But . . . I do wish to make a few inquiries before we see my grandmother. Was she married?"

"O yis," Natters replied as if offended, "married proper. It was a gentleman soldier give his life in India. Iv'ry patient 'as a record. The Pen Allows lift a record of Irene when she coom many years past."

"The Penhallows?"

Natters nodded gravely. "That was before me time. They sid she was really crighzy, the poor dear, fallin' prey to temtightion, an' her lift with 'er innocent baby, 'is father deservin' the 'igh jump, pardon th' expression."

"Tell me about the father and the baby."

She looked at me with an eye-flutter. " 'Appen it was tup," she half giggled.

"Tup?"

"The 'Oly Ghost in the ram for all a body knows. Narry a nighme in the record, narry the slightest ´int, iver, from our Irene."

"But," I pressed, "I was always told he was a rich American who left her but supported her ever afterwards?"

"A fighry tighle," Natters said. "The Pen Allows pighed the necessary, iv'ry month, iv'ry year, and lift a fund to go on with pighin' after they passed awigh, which they did . . . The baby? They took 'im. Raised 'im. Sent 'im to Guy's 'Ospital, as you know, bein' son of the bastard, so t'speak."

There was a pause while I gathered speculations. Finally I said that the Penhallows of London must have been Irene's in-laws and that they must have gotten her locked up in order for them to kidnap her baby legally, to all of which Natters raised no objection. Someone, probably the Rich American, had conspired with and paid off the Penhallows from the beginning and had probably, through them, provided Irene's support. To that, too, Natters raised no objection. "She wasn't crazy one bit now, was she, Natters?"

"Well," she replied after another roll of eyes, "ask Natters and I'll till you. Irene niver slept in the light of the moon. She just gave 'er 'eart away . . . Lust, lust it were, not luv, drew 'im to 'er. Whativer luv 'e bespoke, 'e lied. It vanished with 'im. Your Irene, now that's another story—gave 'er 'eart to the bloody 'ypocrite to this veddy die. Like a god, she worships 'im an' 'im not fit to touch the 'em of 'er kit . . . Were it at 'is command she coom 'ere? I believe it so. She obighed, she obighed, an' niver 'as 'e written 'er a word, niver in more than forty years 'as 'e uttered a word of comfort. 'Er soul 'e 'as tyken, the unforgivable sin, 'er 'eart broken, yit in it she keeps foriver that which for 'er was 'is sweetness . . ."

"Thank you," Scampy said, ending her silence. I thanked Natters too, rose, and gave her an embrace. There were tears, I could see, in her eyes.

"Go to 'er now, bliss you," she said. "Just 'old 'er 'and. Let 'her know that 'er 'ope 'as coom back to 'er in another's form."

We followed Natters down a long hallway where patients were wandering about aimlessly. Entering a drawing room furnished with card and tea tables, plush chairs, and Victorian bric-a-brac, I found, seated by the fireplace, Grandma Irene! She had a petite figure sheathed to the neck in black silk. Her gray hair was pulled back and parted down the middle, reminding me of a sketch I had seen of Emily Dickinson in my *Book of Knowledge*. She wore a pearl necklace and ruby ring for, I reckoned, a wedding ring. Had I been a painter of madonnas in the Spanish style, I might have portrayed severity in her long face, but, in truth, there was none. She was a Raphael, perhaps a Donna Velata with luminous vitality and dignified bearing. In her lap lay a small framed picture and what seemed to be a keepsake folder tied by a pink ribbon.

Irene stared at Natters, then gasped, "Oh. Florrie. I didn't recognize you, you're so old and fat."

Her features melted at sight of me. She lifted her arms wide to enclose an embrace. I leaned over for it. She hugged me with fierce strength and murmured unintelligible sounds of joy. As we separated, she ran fingers over my face. I looked into her eyes, the bright sky-blue of them. There seemed to be nothing mad in them.

She motioned for me to sit beside her on a chaise longue. When I did, she linked her fingers in mine and wouldn't let go. Scampy took a seat near us. I introduced her as "Scampy."

She held out her free hand to Scampy, who lifted it to her lips.

"Scampy?" Irene queried, smiling and tilting her head.

"It's a nickname," Scampy said. "My mother named me Felixine."

"I like the 'Scampy,'" said Irene in a decided tone. "I hope she's your fiancée, Tree . . . She loves you, you know . . . You must both fly away! Don't delay for a single minute! Now, where should you go? They said the West Indies are very nice, though I've never been there . . . islands basking in the sun. You'll be very happy. Everyone, I have decided, deserves to be happy!"

Writing my letter to Mum after Scampy and I returned to Paris after our visit with Grandma Irene, I was trying to recollect in tranquility, as Wordsworth had advised, the spots of time so recently experienced. To be sure, having Scampy living with and totally dependent upon me didn't lend itself to a poetic formula although I was beginning, mysteriously, to get used to her. Irene's instant, charmingly loopy perception of Scampy as my true Intended had hit me like the proverbial bolt from the blue.

I was too angry for tranquility, angry not at Scampy but at myself for being unable to explain to her the terrible truth of incest, angry at Woodbridge for having been so cruel to my lovely grandmother. Her unrequited and undying love occupied a sacred space, one in which forever dwells the natural spirit of life.

Not while we were with Irene at Harrow House but while we were leaning over the railing of a Dover-Calais packet during a gale, trying not to throw up, Scampy heaved out the identity of Irene's lover: Woodbridge. Whereas I had already stumbled upon the truth, Scampy was confirming it. The framed daguerreotype picture of a beardless, dark-haired young man wearing a fur coat and fur hat, a three-masted ship in the background, had been shown to us by Irene.

"I wasn't totally taken by surprise," she said. "We in the family always knew Pa-pa had a bastard son somewhere. When Natters greeted me like a princess and disclosed that Pa-pa has been supporting that institution for as long as anyone can remember, I was already putting two and two together. The daguerreotype did the rest. You know my old photo album, the one I showed you at the Antlers Hotel, the one with my picture in it that you kept in your wallet? Well, in it is that same scene up in Alaska in the 'sixties, Pa-pa in the foreground at a different angle from that in Irene's picture. My first consideration was not that you are Pa-pa's grandson but that his charity was bogus . . . Yeah, maybe he feels guilty about what he did, but he tossed Irene overboard—excuse sea metaphor. He could have set her free instead of burying her alive . . . I can forgive him for making me marry Shiflit. I can forgive him for disowning me before he knew the facts. I'll never forgive him for what he did to your grandmother after she gave birth to his child." Scampy, hair whipped by the wind, cried, "He makes me want to puke!"

"The 'richest girl in the world' is not allowed to vomit," I said.

"Drop dead, son of a bastard," she said.

My thoughts had their own gale-force wind, bits and pieces tossed wildly about but settling into place. I'd been keeping score on Woodbridge for a long time. Scampy's revelations about him and Shiflit had been added to it. Now that I was stuck with him on my family tree, I saw him exposed to light more than ever. Yes, he had set Daddy up as Director of the Sun Palace, yes, he had buried him, yes, he might have learned from the Penhallows about rose hip syrup and the "pope's nose," yes, he would have bribed the Penhallows on condition that Daddy never be permitted to visit his mother—but these gestures, like his charities, lacked admission of responsibility, lacked remorse and redemption. And there was something else.

"Remember," I said to Scampy, "what you told me about the first meeting between your Pa-pa and Shiflit, the K.O. Kid, in a church, how he accused Shiflit of being an impostor? Well, he was an imposter, himself, yclept St. John Beauchamp, for God's sake!"

When I had asked Grandma Irene directly to reveal the name of the man in the daguerreotype she was showing to us, she had answered without the slightest hesitation, "St. John Beauchamp," pronouncing it *Sin Gin Beechum.*

"Why have you never revealed his name to anyone before?" In asking my question I wondered if she were, after all, a little daft, inventing a story.

Irene squeezed my hand and said with quiet smile, "Don't be a little goose. If your father had bothered to come and visit me, I would have told him the truth quick-sticks. Since you are the first of my family to visit, and since intuition tells me this lovely girl is destined to become your wife, the truth will out . . . Compared with St. John's vast experience of the world, my life was meaningless. I swore to him upon my honour, no ignominy would befall him from any lack of vigilance on my part. I have been true to my pledge. I set him free. I was ready to do anything for him. Never a word have I heard from him again. If you see him, dear hearts, do love him for my sake."

She showed us an inscription on the daguerreotype. "For my darling Irene, devotedly, St. John," it read. The man staring at the camera had voluptuously cocky eyes. Then Irene showed us and gave to me the off-print of an article by "St. John Beauchamp" in a scientific journal specializing in botany. He had evidently collected specimens of flowers in the Yukon Territory.

"This is for you, Tree. Oh, St. John was so terrified of being bored or possessed! He hated conventional society so, he was always seeking risks! He discovered a gold mine in the Yukon and came to London in order to find bankers willing to invest in it. The Penhallows were bankers in the City, you see. That's how we met. I was still in mourning for my husband when my father brought St. John home for a dinner party."

I didn't read the article until we had returned to my digs in Paris. I paraphrased Woodbridge's —"St. John Beauchamp's"—article for

Mum, noting that he had been, once upon a time, as intrepid as any romantic hero.

"Mum," I wrote, "I am beginning to understand what Dare meant once when he remarked that we are all emerging into a new world of convergence. That is, we must emerge out of a world of slavery and imperial conquest, of wealth for only a few, of excessively masculine codes, and of subjection of the earth. I suppose that sounds stilted coming from a seventeen-year-old smart aleck, but I'll trust you to know what I mean. Now let me tell you about your former father-in-law, the one who has been trying to have you, Ganny, Dare, Tío Congo and untold others murdered . . ."

The man named Woodbridge who traveled and wrote and became suddenly rich and begat an illegitimate son, all under the name, St. John Beauchamp, journeyed from Nantucket on a whaler down the coast of South America, through the Estrecho de Magallanes, and up the coasts of Chile, Peru, and Mexico to San Francisco, where he booked passage to the southeastern coast of Alaska and finally arrived in Yakutat Bay. "I do not need anybody to take care of me, and I do not want to take care of anybody," he announced on his way to Yukon Territory. He joined forces with three gold prospectors and hired a retinue of Thlinket Indians to help them get through the snows of Chilkoot Pass. By looping deerskin bands across their foreheads, the porters pulled the loads but were compelled to rest every two or three hundred yards. When the porters demanded more money, Woodbridge shoved the muzzle of a cocked Winchester into the face of their chief. Thereafter the Thlinkets chose to stay with him until they reached the Pass. At the beginning of the great watershed of the Yukon, over 2,000 miles distant from the point where it pours into the Bering Sea, the four travelers trudged for many days between granite hills covered with snow until the lake ice beneath their snowshoes began to soften. Then they stopped to build a flat-bottomed skiff out of spruce trees, which they whipsawed into boards and nailed together.

Weeks later, they launched this sailboat into the melt-swollen river and barely survived its being crushed like an eggshell against canyon walls, such was the velocity of the river's rapids. After one five-hundred-mile stretch, they picked up tributaries, the Teslin and Little Salmon, the Pelly and others. At Forty Mile Creek the gold prospectors bid Woodbridge good-bye. Alone he sailed for eleven days into eastern Alaska to the confluence of the Yukon and the Porcupine. Securing the boat on land for the winter, he followed a party of Tinneh Indians going upstream on the Porcupine for two hundred miles, wading in freezing water for most of the way. At an abandoned Hudson's Bay Company trading post, Woodbridge settled in a log cabin and prepared himself for a long, dark winter above the Arctic Circle. Soon, however, the Tinneh let him go with them on another two-hundred-mile trek to Peel River in the valley of the MacKenzie, the mercury 40 degrees below zero. The fur-clad men and sixteen dogs covered twenty miles a day. "When we halted for the night, we used a sled to clear snow away from a selected spot and threw down caribou skins. The sleds were then arranged to enclose and protect us from the wind. My companions would gather wood and build a fire at the foot of their bed. After supper we rolled up in our fur robes to sleep, with the dogs creeping on top of us for warmth. When we awoke in the morning it was 50 degrees below zero, and the air stung like the cut of a whip-lash. Rising before us was an apparently unbroken chain of spotless white mountains, the northern extremity of the Rockies, within fifty miles of where they slope down to the Arctic Ocean." When he returned to his little cabin on the Porcupine River, he had traveled on snowshoes another four hundred miles. With the coming of spring once again, he set off alone in the skiff to cover, by paddling, the 1,400 river miles between him and the Bering Sea, seeing no evidence of human beings during the entire journey. From time to time he made a botanical survey, but he was really looking for gold and found it in the great northwesterly bend of the Yukon, naming his find "St. John's Mine." To keep from going mad from loneliness, as he paddled he talked to himself and sang Yale songs, especially when he ran out of food, the dried caribou he had slaughtered, bellowing,

> *Gaudeamus igitur*
> *Juvenes dum sumus*
> *Gaudeamus igitur*
> *Juvenes dum sumus,*

meaning, "Let us rejoice therefore while we are young." Finally one day he guided the skiff into Norton Sound on the Bering Sea and went ashore in the town of Kotlik to arrange passage with a whaling fleet headed back home. The whaling crews were playing cricket on the snowy shore.

Chapter Fourteen

While in London we had stayed in separate rooms at a small hotel just off Bloomsbury Square, visited museums, and attended an amateur performance of *Man and Superman*. During the later Channel crossing, when Scampy revealed the identity of "St. John Beauchamp" as Woodbridge, we discussed Shaw's play. Was Woodbridge a "superman" liberated from conventional morality and permitted to do anything he wanted? Woodbridge, Scampy argued, was in the public eye indeed a sort of superman. Even if operations of Corporation were in violation of antitrust statutes, the Woodbridge Building, a skyscraper then under construction in midtown Manhattan, was welcomed as emblematic of the thrust of man into godhead. Just as awe-inspiring was the Woodbridge Foundation. Widely regarded as inspired by patriotism and piety, through it Woodbridge gave vast tracts of land to the nation, built hospitals and universities, and supported innumerable charities. He had founded Woodbridge College in Denver as proof of his dedication to the cause of women's education. Having, myself, met Woodbridge at Daddy's funeral and served as his guide in the mines, I could attest to his charm and force of character. His youthful audacity in pursuit of gold in Alaska would in any boy's imagination have earned him a ticker-tape parade.

With Scampy for companion in London and in Paris, I was able to retain some purchase on reality. Woodbridge seemed to have self-knowledge and conscience. He was just another human being, just another one of us sad people.

I was beginning to feel wonderfully at ease with Scampy.

She being eighteen and I almost so, we actually tended to relegate Woodbridge to ancient history. I pretended I was painting his portrait, that of an old bum posing naked at the Académie Julian, a punished pink penis drooping in futility. After Scampy returned to America, I drew verbal portraits of Woodbridge and Shiflit for Golly, my trusted girlfriend, revealing their withered humanity in complete detail.

Golly and I had been corresponding regularly for more than two years. My letters had lashings of terms of endearment, albeit I neglected, as being taken for granted, any proposal of marriage. She responded with pages of local and family gossip and signed off with "love" and a cartoon of a smiling sun. Golly's letters gave me reason to hope she could change her opposition to matrimony. Then, too, our kiss, because it loosened a bicuspid, held out promise of future wild embraces. Though I had to feign modesty, she had to have some gratitude toward me, a touch. I had been her accomplice in a homicide. By virtue of the fact that I had secretly orchestrated, by means of an apparent bequest from Daddy's Will, the welfare of Doña Luz, one that enabled Golly to continue her education, I had become a philanthropist, myself. Now in 1908 that investment had, to Golly's credit, borne fruit: she had not only graduated from high school but also matriculated first at the Normal School in Silver City, New Mexico, and then, of all places, at Woodbridge College in Denver, this transfer effected after she received my letter about the secret lives of Woodbridge and Shiflit! Perhaps I deserved a little credit, myself, for planting in her mind the name of a liberal arts college founded and funded by my newly discovered grandfather! Instead of wasting her sweetness on the desert air at a teacher-training school in Silver City, she could concentrate on subjects up my own alley, art, literature, and history. Even if I didn't deserve a single pat on the back, I wanted to believe that Golly and I were betrothed.

On the night of my eighteenth birthday, which I celebrated alone in my digs in Paris, I leaned out of my window and counted nine stars. Each time I looked for but couldn't see Golly up in the firmament, and the reason was clear: I didn't deserve her one bit. In telling Golly the truth about Woodbridge and Shiflit, I had neglected to confess to infidelity.

Before Scampy left Paris she and I had, once, made love together.

Usually "Aunt" Scampy and "Nephew" Tree retired for the night without so much as a peck on the cheek, she to my bed behind an improvised curtain, I to a pallet on the floor where I was surrounded by her steamer trunks and by my paintings of nudes. However, after Scampy collected Mum's windfall fortune at a French bank, we decided to celebrate at an expensive café on the Boule Miche. We ordered *canard rôti à l'orange* and carafes of *vin ordinaire*. Suddenly free of Woodbridge and Shiflit, she could plan her own future, she was telling me. Instead of going to a "finishing school," she would enter nurses' training at Presbyterian Hospital in New York.

"I admire you for that decision," I said. "I think I know how you feel, serving people instead of acquiring things. I don't ever want to feel myself dependent on material things. To have wealth and luxury beyond what is enjoyed by most human beings is an offense against them. I don't see that I have any right to riches except in so far as an endowment may be necessary to my full development." I paused to cup my hand atop one of hers. "In other words," I went on quite unaware of pomposity, "I don't live in the slums for I'd probably soon die of pneumonia, but beyond moderate comfort I don't want to feel that I'm having any physical advantages that everybody can't have . . . It isn't a question of duty but of happiness. I am uneasy when there are any more barriers than necessary between me and the working stiffs . . . Now that I've got that off my chest, I want you to know, when I asked Mum for advice about your situation, while I suspected she would want to tide you over, so to speak, I didn't dream she would become Lady Bountiful . . . Well, today you've learned you have capital in a French bank transferable to Lazard Frères in New York. And here's what I have to say about all that: write Mum, as I know you will, a letter of thanks and tell her about your plans to become a nurse, but try not to feel beholden to her beyond being yourself, because that's all she wants. It is important to realize where Mum stands in this matter. She has asked me to tell you a 'white lie' that she promised your mother to look after you if need should arise, but, the truth is, she owes her life to Elizabeth Woodbridge. If your mother hadn't warned my mother of the danger she was in at the Sun Palace, Mum might not have run for her life within hours of their meeting. In a sense no 'white lie' is involved. True, no promise to see to your welfare was actually made. Mum wants to serve as your mother and is very much obliged to you for accepting her gift. It's a mutual thing, a gift outright and uncontaminated, not at all like my new grandfather's so-called 'philanthropy' whereby he becomes a celebrity, tries to massage his guilt and to adjust his lousy relationship with the Almighty."

Scampy squeezed my hand. "I have a confession to make, my . . . 'nephew'. . . I do have one family relative in New York. I would have swallowed pride and gone to him had your mother not tided me over so bountifully. He's my mother's father, Hamilton Eliot, Grampy Ham. Without Grampy Ham, I really would be, as you believe, down and out. The problem is, he's First Vice-President of Corporation and has a fortune and an untarnished reputation to lose should he be given the sack. I've feared having to toss him on the horns of dilemma. If I had flung myself at his feet and begged to be taken in, Pa-pa would not have hesitated to ruin his former father-in-law."

After dinner we strolled along the banks of the Seine, sparkling lights of the city a-tremble on barge-rippled waters. We went home to "our" little hotel. Although the violinist across the Rue des Beaux-Arts was practicing the chaconne in torture-flat-major, this night, for some reason, I would have booked him into Carnegie Hall. When I gazed out my window, wondering whether, if I had counted nine stars, I would "see" Golly, I "saw" Scampy. She undressed and went to bed. I closed the window, stripped, lay down on my pallet and tried to go asleep. I had a palpable sensation, like an electric current rushing through my body, of communion with the woman not ten feet away from me.

"I want you," I heard her say.

It's one thing to thresh old straw, another to be a snitch. The historian in me, as I was writing my letter to Golly, knew the difference. For instance, Mum's long letter to me from St. Aignan, the one revealing Elizabeth Woodbridge's Secret, I had locked away in a safe deposit box at the First National Bank, Los Tristes. The information it contained was scandalous enough to destroy Woodbridge. And yet I gave that letter's Secret away to Golly along with other secrets. I could claim in my defense that we were going to be married upon my return to Los Tristes in 1910, but I had crossed a line.

When I mailed the letter, trees along boulevards were surrendering leaves to autumnal breezes. By the time I received Golly's letter in response, winter had arrived. Usually one allowed a fortnight to pass to effect delivery of mail to Silver City and another two weeks for a reply to reach Paris. She was busy with her studies to become a teacher, I allowed. When her envelope in the shape of a birthday card was handed to me by the concierge, I ran upstairs to open it. I read, in part:

> *I've transferred to Woodbridge College in Denver. I was getting sick and tired of the spinsters and dragons out in the treeless desert near the Mexican border. They say Mr. Woodbridge visits the college at commencement time. Maybe he can help me get into law school. With some make-up work I can still graduate in 1912, know what I mean?*

As much as I applauded Golly for pursuit of a liberal arts

education with ambition, rare for the times, to seek admission to law school, just as I applauded Scampy's entrance into nurses' training, Golly's birthday card struck several, for me, discordant notes. Surely not all the teachers and trainees at the Normal were "spinsters and dragons." Moreover, though I could accept in anyone a degree of manipulative skill, Golly's seemed out of character. Was she really going to Woodbridge College in order to ingratiate herself with its Founder and use his pull to advance her career? Finally she upbraided me for a "lack of sensitivity" in regard to Pia. While it was true I'd made fun of Pia in my letter, the joke had been on the human race: I was son of a bastard, and my grandfather, in turn, was a billygoat who until recently had been shacking up with his son's mistress. Golly had a defense lawyer's argument. If Pia hadn't married Captain Dare—so it went—she might have remained a coalminer's daughter and begun a dreary descent into poverty, child-bearing, sickness and premature death. Dare was her ticket to freedom. If he hadn't deserted her to go fight in the Philippines War, she could have kept the home fires burning. Alone and besieged by Dr. Penhallow she yielded to the affair, which then provided her with "the opportunity of a lifetime, to leapfrog into a love-nest with a gentleman worth hundreds of millions." Why, Pia had done very well for herself! She had alimony from Dare. She had pried loose some Woodbridge money for construction of a Y.M.C.A. facility in Los Tristes. To complete her triumph, as Golly put it, Pia, following an all-expense-paid cruise around the world, was free to play the field in Europe. Meanwhile, "From what you say about him, Mr. Woodbridge has a weakness for chicks—and now he's going to get it in the neck from some chick."

Cynical she sounded, but, I decided, she was laughing at the world the way Dare and I did.

We continued to correspond, though less frequently than before. In one of her letters dated in June of 1909 she mentioned that she had met Woodbridge in person when he came to her college to deliver the commencement address. She found him, she remarked, "as charming as he was when he tried to dance the *flamenco* with Luz," and he had asked her to join him and the Dean for afternoon tea at the Brown Palace. I wondered whether she informed the old goat of her virtual engagement to his grandson.

Following a four-year period of exile abroad, I returned to America in July of 1910. When my ship docked on the Hudson, Ganny was there to meet me with an extravagant proposal to advance my career. If I would leave with her the scores of paintings I had brought with me from France, she would have them framed and arrange to have them put up for sale at a friend's gallery. This friend would also serve as my agent for future works, anything "western" being currently in vogue. I agreed to the deal and was interviewed by a reporter who pronounced in his published article "a nineteen-year-old prodigy from the Wild West has sharpened up a bit in Paris." I spent a week touring town which was bursting with energy, masses of people swarming everywhere, motor cars *hoogah-hoogahing*, jazz bands blaring, jackhammers spluttering, skyscrapers, including the Woodbridge Building, obliterating the human dimension. I could hardly wait to go to Los Tristes and see Golly who, last I'd heard, would be spending summer vacation at home.

Actually, she was in New York, herself.

As my train was pulling into the Los Tristes station, I scanned the platform for a sight of her. Mum was there (now Mrs. Dare with Dare's mother's talismanic ring), Dare (wearing a three-piece suit and fedora), Tío Congo, now Mr. Jefferson (also in three-piece suit and fedora), were there, Doña Luz and sons were there.

Golly, however, was nowhere to be seen. I had in my pocket a small diamond ring I had found at a shop on the Rue de Rivoli during my years of sharpening-up. I intended to give it to her.

Once the hugs and kisses were over, I continued to crane my neck in hopes of seeing her. I was nervously fingering the box containing the ring.

"You sho happyfied!" Mr. Jefferson exclaimed as we shook hands.

To have inquired about Golly's whereabouts would have mortified me and everyone else. An ice-breaker came in the form of an invitation from Doña Luz to have us driven by Nono in her new Ford to their ranch. Although Mum was throwing a party in my honor at Homesteader's where I would be staying, I gathered by the way she and Dare were casting eyes downward that Doña Luz had first go at me. Whatever awaited me at the ranch, it had to do with Golly. Probably, I told myself, it's a surprise fiesta, she with flowers in her hair. I accepted the invitation, only requesting Nono to deliver me later back home.

The Ford rumbled along the old dirt road. Nobody said anything. When we arrived at the ranch, scattering chickens as Nono parked the car, Doña Luz grabbed me by the arm and marched me into the house and into the living room where the old furniture had been restored to places near the hearth. The room was no longer a shrine to Don Fernando. Its formality filled me with foreboding, as did Doña Luz's solemnity. Instead of her usual flower-print dress she was wearing a black one, as if for a funeral, the black silk shawl wrapped around her shoulders on a hot summer's afternoon, suggesting that no fiesta was in the cards. She motioned for me to sit beside her on a sofa. There she cupped my hands in hers to show we were now dearest of friends, studied me with moist eyes, cleared throat, spoke softly.

"Golondrina isn't going to college any more," she said, "and she isn't coming home no more. I don't know what got into her. Maybe her going to that fancy college in Denver went to her head. She ran off to New York with that Mr. Woodbridge. They got married. I'm sorry, señor Tree . . . Sacred Heart of Jesus."

I felt pale all over. Typically, I bottled up my emotions, knowing that at a later, private time I would have a letting go. For the time being I was concerned that sorrow was almost too much for Doña Luz. Her face was looking as if it wanted to crumble.

"That *anciano* didn't have the courtesy to come in person to the *ranchito* to ask permission to marry my daughter. The *hombre* must promise to support the wife. It is a disgrace for the wife to be made to work to support the *hombre*. The *cabrón* have so many cows and chickens he don't have to promise to support nobody! *Mucho dinero*. Golondrina, she come alone to tell me. I don't have to stoop to that *anciano*, like, 'Señor, por favor, I am mother to this poor little girl you buy with dollar. Promise she don't work in the laundry, please.' No. Golondrina, she come alone. She says to me, 'Mamá, I'll skin your hide if you try to stop me!' Huh! And I say, 'No daughter of mine speak that way to me, *preciosa*. Don't get your knickers in a twist. Beware the *entrometida!* It is still in you. You marry that *anciano,* you like a slut to me. Your sister, your brothers no speak to you no more. You think you can fly over this house like the *bruja*, but I pray to San Juan. He protects me from the witches. Poof! You fly away like a bug!' I say this to my daughter I love, Golondrina, the swallow. Yes, she was a swallow. Now she is only a bug."

Doña Luz paused for a long time. I couldn't think of anything to say, not that thoughts weren't whirling in my mind. Even though, as I judged from the tone of her letters, Golly had seemed to have been changing for several years—even though she was the very "chick" who had lured Woodbridge into marriage—I found it hard to believe she would insult her mother. After killing Shorty, she had said she loved everybody. "Maybe," I said, "Golly wants to get the good out of the old man, not his money. Maybe she has sacrificed herself in order to redeem his character. Maybe she just pretended to insult you. She loves you."

"Don't think," Doña Luz said, squinting her eyes, "I don't know that evil old man is your *abuelo*, your grandfather. She told me. You want to believe my Golondrina is a saint gonna beat the devil. Well, you have a good heart. I put you in front of my class. Don Fernando, he thinks maybe you a big artist someday . . . *Mira*. You do not always get the right sow by the ears . . . Why you think I dance *flamenco* with that old goat? I am stupid? He pretends to be our friend. He fool nobody. Sure I let him try to dance with me—to

303

make a fool of this *señor* Treaty of Guadalupe Hildago!"

We talked for a little while longer. She gave me an *abrazo*. I went for a walk. When I reached the shade of the bluffs, I sat down and surveyed the grounds of the place where I had started a new life. The sun glittered on the Yale lock on the metal door of the Cave of the Forgotten. I remembered Golly's making, one time, a pun on the meaning of *lock*, the word for a *hold* in wrestling. But what Doña Luz meant when she mentioned *entrometida* as still being "in" Golly required some analysis. Fundamentally, as Golly had once explained, it meant *busybody*. In her family and in families of her girlfriends "busybody" was anathema. If a girl was an *entrometida*, she would be given a tongue-lashing. Apparently if a girl called too much attention to herself, craved something for herself, complained or in some other way veered from the ideal of a demure and obedient "lady," she had to have the *entrometida* lesson drilled into her. Golly, in marrying Woodbridge, had violated one of the basic rules of her culture but might, with the *entrometida* still "in" her, return to her senses and people. However—so went my train of thought—the seeds of rebellion had been planted in Golly by Doña Luz, herself, who insisted that no one "settle" for marriage and children only but should seek to live fully and make something of herself. Golly, I speculated, had examined her life as a woman, not simply as a "lady," and accordingly, for some as yet unfathomable reason, roped a tycoon into matrimony.

An hour later Nono drove me to Homesteader's. I knew from Mum's letters that the adobe ranchhouse had been entirely rebuilt, doubled in size and provided with modern conveniences, and I knew that half a dozen *casitas* had been added to the property for the accommodation of family and friends. The old smokehouse having been torn down, Dawn Antelope had moved into one *casita*. Mr. Jefferson had moved into another. I knew, because I knew Mum, she wanted me to make my home in yet another *casita* and not go off to Taos. What I didn't know, and what surprised me as Nono was driving down a newly paved switchback road toward the ranch, was that the land resembled a fortified military post. A fifteen-foot adobe wall now enclosed all the buildings and corrals. There were still a few horses and cows to be seen, the barn and stables, but a large part of the meadow had been converted to a base of supply. A quick survey yielded a row of motor cars, stacks of lumber, piles of brick, heaps of camp stoves, sandbags, and roll upon roll of what looked like canvas tents. Dare had once told me what he would need in any future strike, tent camps for miners evicted from company-towns. Was he preparing for another strike in spite of the disaster of 1903-04? At least he was protecting Mum from another dynamite party planned by Shiflit and executed by the Laredo Desperado.

"Do we have guns?" I asked Nono.

He shook his head. "Some of them Mediterranean stiffs got rifles for hunting rabbits, but I don't theenk many gun, mebbe forty, fifty pea-shooters all in all. Last time the milish was here, remember, they confiscated all the weapons they could find and gave them to the mine guards to kill us with."

"I remember," I said, thinking of the Savage with which Golly had shot Shorty. "There're two of your pea-shooters up ahead at the gate, look like Remingtons."

Nono stopped the Ford at the gate. Believing I recognized one of the guards, I approached him. Wearing a miner's gear, standing about six-foot-tall, my own height, he lowered his rifle at sight of me.

"Welcome back, Mr. Penhallow," he said, grinning from ear to ear.

"Andy?"

"Yes, sir."

"Long time. Last I saw you, you were skinning with Cuddy the mule. How've you been, buddy?"

He, still grinning, shuffled feet. "Got married."

"I be dog! Married!" Andy, I reckoned, though a full-grown, ruddy-cheeked man to look at, had to be no more than sixteen.

"First one's on the way."

"Well," I said, "congratulations . . . You workin' for Captain Dare?"

"Yes, sir."

"He treatin' you right?"

"Hunnert a month. Beats tar outta Baldwin-Felts."

"What's that?"

"Baldwin-Felts? Them's detectives. Come 'ere after the Pinkertons. Shoot first, ask later. They eat organizers for breakfast, 'specially when the organizer got machine-gun lead in him."

"You don't say, Andy. Any trouble here?"

"No, sir."

"It usta be just a couple of dogs and Dawn Antelope for security. He's still around, I hear."

"That Injun? He takes care the Overland, Miz Dare's car. He drives it forty mile an hour, howlin' like he's ready to scalp fleas . . . Dogs is gone, though."

I thanked Nono for the ride and fetched my suitcase. "So long, Andy," I said. Then, "Wait." Out of my pocket I plucked the box containing the diamond ring. I opened the lid of the box, showed Andy the ring, handed the box over to him. "I'd be obliged if you'd give this here to your lady," I said. "Tap'er light."

I spent many a happy hour at Homesteader's browsing through the library of books Mum had brought with her from France and New York, augmented by those from Colorado Springs after the bank sold the house. One day I was reading *A Shropshire Lad*, an English poet's therapy of resignation for stenosis of the broken heart.

> *When I was one-and twenty*
> *I heard a wise man say,*
> *"Give crowns and pounds and guineas*
> *But not your heart away . . ."*

In the next stanza the Lad reports that in spite of the wise man's advice he gave his heart away at the age of "two-and-twenty" and for this naughtiness had suffered "endless rue." Well, I had to laugh.

I had beaten the Lad to heartbreak by three years. Besides, I was actually quite lucky, never having had a "wise man" to tell me to give all my money away but avoid love or take out an insurance policy against the death of the heart. What a bunch of bull feathers! If you didn't risk giving your heart away—if you didn't struggle—you weren't Odysseus, you weren't really alive.

Having set my heart on taking the risks of being an artist, I went to the Pluck Me and once more transformed myself from a dandy to a cowboy. I even bought myself a Remington. Unlike Dare, I wasn't preparing to encounter violence. In my opinion, the "Wild West" had practically vanished. Even though patches of lawlessness still existed here and there, including the Corporation-controlled Law of Colorado, the West had been settled by farmers and engineers, by tradesmen, miners, even by lungers, certainly not by pathological killers with guns. I bought the Remington as a precaution, not expecting to pull the trigger. Also at the Pluck Me there were needed supplies to be assembled but no art supplies. To procure these I resorted to Doña Luz and got lucky: she agreed to give me—she wouldn't sell me—Don Fernando's primed canvases, paint tubes, brushes, bottles of linseed oil and turpentine, sketchbooks and easels. She insisted, too, on loading me down with a couple of crates of canned fruits and vegetables. To top it off she gave me a stray dog she had wormed and housebred, a part Lab, part Golden Retriever, part Whatever. He didn't fiddle-faddle but immediately adopted me as his lord and master. I named him Merlin.

Mum, Dare, and the others at Homesteader's soon realized I was plagued by the loss of Golly and by restlessness. I wasn't painting. I was feeling confined by a lack of open space. As a coalminer I'd paid my dues to the world of necessity. As a student in France I'd paid them to culture. I respected and admired what Europe had to offer me, but I had felt cramped and suffocated there from what I saw in every direction—the tyranny of habit and the ministry of despair. Ancient America lured me the way the sea lured Melville's Ishmael.

Main Street in Los Tristes had, alas, been paved with bricks, just as Dare had feared. Taos, I'd been told, had neither paved roads nor names for streets.

One day we, Merlin and I, set out via narrow-guage railroad spurs and eventually arrived at Tres Piedras, New Mexico, on the western side of the Río Grande. Although bandits, it was rumored, lay between us and Taos forty miles away, we boarded a stagecoach and finished the last lap of our journey without incident. The sunflowers were just going it all along the trail. When Taos loomed up ahead, patches of early aspens were yellowing the higher elevations of Sacred Mountain. Hidden from sight at the base of Sacred Mountain, as I knew from maps, was the pueblo. Protected on three sides by the Sangres and on the western side by the Río Grande, it had survived raids by warrior tribes, by Spanish invaders, and in 1847 by U.S. troops. At an altitude of 7,000 feet the whole valley was also protected from extremes of weather, pestilence, and industry. Here, I was thinking, one could give one's heart away to the land and have no fear of endless rue.

At the plaza I met an Indian trader, Dawn Antelope's acquaintance, and was able to rent from him some rooms in a flat-roofed adobe property which was old when Kit Carson's family had acquired it in the 1830s. I had one room for a bedroom, a central room for a living room and kitchen, and a third room for a studio. The floors were mud. The walls, two feet thick, had small windows; these admitted pale light. The plaster had been blackened by smoke from the *kiva* fireplace and by soot from kerosene lamps. The cast-iron stove had to be fed with wood and rubbed with thick black wax to keep it from rusting. Although the studio had a skylight, rain and snowmelt, as I eventually learned, asserted a right to leak through it. The bathtub in the bedroom was a galvanized tin tub which had to be filled with about a dozen gallons of boiling water in order to be of any utility. A sturdy bedstead reputed to have belonged to one of Brigham Young's twenty-seven wives had a mattress stuffed with corn cobs. For an "ice box," a well outside these rooms had to serve, and a one-hole privy furnished with wasp nests and Monkey Ward catalog paper was located out in the sagebrush. The lintel of my doors was so low I had to crouch like Quasimodo to go through them, and the hard, straightback Mexican chairs were ideal for inducing hemorrhoids and herniated disks. I was in seventh heaven.

But I cheated. The plaza just a stone's throw away had a general merchandise store. There I purchased a mattress stuffed with wool, Navajo rugs for the floors, eiderdown quilts and pillows, a crude Morris chair, a raft of kitchen utensils plus pots and skillets and kettles, glassware, metal plates and cups, steel cutlery, soap, towels, briar pipes and smoking tobacco, not to mention staples such as flour, sugar, and coffee. Once equipped to prepare all my meals at home, I, like any bachelor, fell into the habit of eating out twice a day at a cantina on the plaza. There I could get for a few cents enchiladas, beans, lettuce, tomatoes, tortillas and sopapillas, all smothered in chili peppers so hot they numbed my tongue.

Finally, because I didn't want to go to the trouble of owning and taking care of a horse, I bought a dilapidated wagon, fixed it up as a caravan with a canvas top, and made arrangements with a livery stable to rent a horse whenever I got an itch to go painting and fishing where they'd have to catch me to put shoes on me.

I had right smart of comfort. And I had Merlin. If I was in the mood for conversation or cussed out a painting in which my daubs were like dead leaves, that dog had the good grace to agree with everything I said. He inspired me to return to work and discover a way through difficulty. Like as not, the way would be lit with the suddenness of a flashlight explosion.

As Golly began to fade from memory, I gradually recovered my sociable self, mixing with locals at the cantina, visiting studios of other artists, sharing a pipe with elders at the pueblo, hiring some of the English-speaking, "away school" young men to serve as models. Some Indians of both sexes were as beautiful to me as angels of the annunciation. I wanted nothing to do with the "noble savage" or "vanishing race" school of painting in which were portrayed half-naked, be-feathered warriors astride horses, lances dipped as a sign of defeat, sun setting. The Pueblo and Navajo peoples of the Southwest, in spite of centuries of suffering, had endured, and, I soon realized, they had much to teach me and others about a sacred view of life and land. I painted some subjects of popular interest. My agent in New York sold a few of them. Who could resist, after all, the pyramidal shape of dwellings at the pueblo, the glitter of sun on the Río Lucero, the multi-colored costumes at a Corn Dance, or golden boys dancing to the soft beat of drums, the figure, noble indeed, of the *cacique* as he reads the mysteries of a billion stars in the palimpsest of inkblot nights? Who could resist the elephant's-rump shapes of adobe buttresses of the old church of San Francisco de Asis? Who could resist the riven abysm of the Río Grande Gorge?

But I weaned myself away from popular subjects and began to go on caravan expeditions in the high country between Taos and Santa Fe. Roads were faint trails, a few of them originally blazed by Coronado and his slaves in the early 1540s. As a horse tugged me into 9,000-foot elevations, Merlin would perform acrobatic, parabolic leaps in sagebrush in search of the perfect jackrabbit. The old Spanish villages huddled in blue valleys made such a dent in me that I would often stop and stand and paint my impression of them, using the actual subjects only for suggestion. I might be looking over the whole Río Grande valley, the sun warm and baking, way beneath me a village like Cordova nestled into a steep valley with the most unspoiled church and tiny plaza filled with groups of men sitting in the sun, burros, cats, dogs, chickens, children all there, a church bell summoning lines of black figures, snow mountains looming like a dream of the Alps. Then my painting would become as natural as breathing. I would be filled with a sense of peace akin to ecstasy.

The Taos years, 1910-1913, confirmed in me the joy and the necessity, even the evolutionary necessity, of the creative imagination. Although the masters at the Académie Julian had guided and inspired me, I wished to stand on their shoulders, not in their shadows. If I worked to become the best artist of which I was capable, I believed I might become good, though not as good as Leonardo. What others might think of my work mattered little. Did Paleolithic cave painters 30,000 years ago worry what the "crickets" of the 20th century in Paris, London, and New York would think about them in terms of Success? The whole business of Success seemed to me a poor tool for measuring creativity. Every artist, whatever the art, had to labor without guarantees of income, unpaid and unhonored but with destiny for incentive. The insatiable tapeworm, Art, demanded constant feeding and hated being interrupted by intruders—people, the preparation and consuming of food, drinking, sleeping, bathing, shaving, hair cutting, doing laundry, reading books, smiling. My work was sustained by the unwavering success of the soul. It reached out in hushed wonder in order to articulate a natural order.

To love and to create, I discovered, were the same thing.

"Lookit ouchonder, Merlin!"

One day in July of 1913 the temperature in Taos hit 100 degrees. Heat shimmered off dusty roads. In the great leafed-out cottonwoods that shaded the plaza and nearby streets no breeze was stirring. The town looked deserted. Anybody with a grain of sense was staying indoors, cooled by adobe bricks.

I'd had a good day. I opened my eyes about sunup, stretched, hopped out of bed, went to the studio and squinted at a canvas on an easel, ready for me to set to work. It was a large canvas, a canyon road I'd been ripping out, loving the long, low adobe houses with dark figures standing in doorways and a sweet glimpse of a little boy at supper before a glowing fireplace. For about ten hours I was submerged in the task of putting in final touches, now and then taking a pipe and coffee break. Finally about five o'clock windgusts from the Sangres could be heard violently swishing about in the cottonwoods. I went outdoors to make sure we weren't about to be hit by lightning storms. Although the limbs of trees were bending like mizen masts in a hurricane, a scene I had witnessed during my Atlantic crossing, the sky, far from darkening, was getting ready for one of those New Mexican sunsets no painter could capture without suffering a sort of snow-blindness. I decided to take Merlin for a long walk in the direction of Ranchos where I could get an unobstructed view of solar fireworks. Some time after seven o'clock we came to sit on the rise of a little hill. The "ouchonder," a usage I'd picked up from Texans at the cantina, consisted of hundred-mile vistas westward as far as the volcanic cone of Perdenal, with, in the foreground, barren prairie rolling toward the Río Grande. The rays of the sinking sun thinned out in Prussian-blue heavens to cadmium yellows, vermilions, and magenta.

But what caused me to cry out was a sight far off in the prairie. Catching sunlight it resembled a tiny crystal, but it was moving, so it could not have been a Mexican sheepherder's shed, moving so fast it was leaving in its wake billowing clouds of dust. I quickly realized it was a motor car. Just what it was doing in nowhere's middle was a matter of conjecture. Once in a while touring cars from Santa Fe or Albuquerque had been known to come snooping around Taos. If they didn't carry spare tires and gallon cans of gas and water, they were apt to end up abandoned in a lunar landscape, rusted carcasses buried in sand alongside skeletons of cattle. In the absence of roads a driver had to forget straight lines, the shortest distance between two points varying according to the number of washed-out arroyos. The depth of sand had to be less than the height of hubcaps. The driver of this particular motor car was a straight-line enthusiast. The car would come tearing along, a black chariot followed by dust-devils of its own manufacture. Then it would suddenly disappear from sight, and then just as suddenly reappear, defying laws of curves, zigzags, and quicksands. The driver, I decided, was a poor deluded flatlander from Back East determined to become an Indian, or bust.

We moseyed back to town in the lingering light of dusk. That a stranger might want to be an Indian—in Taos such strangers existed—was sentimentality at its most absurd. That someone could regard Taos Mountain, as I did, as Sacred Mountain was salutary. It wasn't an object "out there" but an aspect of one's mind and spirit.

It was the custom for the Taoseños to leave their doors open. When Merlin and I arrived back home in the dark, our door was wide open, the kerosene lamps were all lit, smoke was pouring out of the chimney, and a mountain of laundry was stumbling toward me on an ankle-length skirt with boots. Doing laundry was not my strength. Three or four times a year I would remember to seek the help of the local laundress. When everything from sheets to shorts came back fresh and clean and neatly folded, I would feel so restored in well-being that I wondered how I could ever have allowed myself to degenerate into such a slovenly lout. It was the same with hair, facial and cranial. Whenever I saw myself reflected in a mirror or a window, I was reminded of Glass-Eye Gwilym, swore to strop my razor and oil my scissors, and promptly forgot to take action. I knew what the problem was: one, I was, when painting, absent from my mind, two, I lived alone. That I gave myself a bath every Saturday night I considered one of the triumphs of modern civilization.

Now, I realized at once that a mountain of my evil-smelling laundry being carted away indicated I'd come into an extraordinary piece of luck: the company of a real woman. And when the mountain was dumped at my feet, there she was. She was dressed in a brown taffeta motoring outfit, long, dark hair tumbling to shoulders, cleavage of bosom nicely exposed, cupid's-bow lips, dimpled chin, and mischief-maker's eyes all exactly as they should be according to what seemed to be piled-up centuries of my dreams.

Scampy.

"Strip," Scampy said.

"I beg your pardon?"

"Strip."

"I refuse to be inducted into the army," I said.

"I'm not asking you to bend over and spread your cheeks," she said, "though a shave and a haircut will be necessary before supper, and, it is true, a new uniform awaits you in the barracks . . . I want everything you're wearing. Add it to this pile of rubbish. I've seen worse than this in hospitals unless you sleep and work in blood and shit. We're going to have a little bonfire tonight as a service to your country . . . Don't be shy. I've seen a million weenies from pink to brown to gray, professionally speaking, and you don't get a Nightingale pin if you blush . . . Oh, very well, I'll go inside and avert my eyes."

"I see you've already made yourself welcome," I said. "Nobody lives here but a poor painter. Alas, he lost his mind over a body-part several years ago and believes he's a frog. If you kiss him, who knows what will happen."

"I'm fond of poor painters," Scampy flung over her shoulder. "I fain would sit for a portrait. Kissing will have to wait. As if I didn't have enough to do, heating your stove, preparing his lordship's dinner, cleaning dishes, setting the table, boiling water, and all after driving your mother's car since breakfast . . . Did you think I walked here or fell out of the sky?"

'Wait," I said. "I saw you on the mesa, doing what you call 'driving.' Lucky thing, I warned everybody in the new State of New Mexico to run for the hills! . . . By the way, I'd like you to pose for me as one of the Graces, nude. You must be unclothed, for a Grace is without deceit. If you wish, you can strip off what you're wearing, right now. Add the rags to this lot you're incinerating . . . Anyway, my Grace, as Hesiod wrote, from your glance flows a love that unnerves the limbs. Shall I get you on canvas?"

"I heard you," Scampy said as she ducked her head to enter the door. "Don't be chesty, and don't get any ideas even though I've brought us a bottle of Chateauneuf du Pape. Tonight I sleep in your bed under the new sheets I bought for you. You sleep in your caravan. I'll be gone in the morning before you wake up and realize I'm kith but not kin."

"A riddle?" I parried, curious as to whether she had discovered we were not blood relations.

Merlin had been sitting quietly, cocking his head. One of us, he was perhaps thinking, is on an invisible leash.

~~~

She had no sooner graduated as a Registered Nurse from Presbyterian Hospital than she packed up her belongings and headed to Los Tristes to a job being held open for her at St. Anne's Hospital. She had been drawn to Colorado, she declared, for a number of personal and professional reasons. She had observed, when her mother lay dying in the Sun Palace, that quality nursing care was rarely available in the West except for the rich; in the mining towns such as Cripple Creek, where need was greatest, help was least likely to be found. It was Mum who had persuaded her to pursue her career in Los Tristes, and there was nothing she wouldn't do for my Mum. And Mum had given her one of the new *casitas* for her home. The two were on a first-name basis, Mum as "Anna Maria," Scampy as "Elizabeth."

All this was being explained to me as Scampy was preparing a late-night supper. While we had for several hours been doing chores—incinerating laundry out in the sagebrush, cleaning the apartment, getting my hair cut and beard removed, heating water for her bath, the two of us finally "dressed up," she in nurse's uniform, I in smashing new clothes she had bought for me in New York at Abercrombie & Fitch—we had spoken little. Now she was standing at the stove, cooking up a spaghetti Bolognese with meat, tomatoes, garlic, onions and mushrooms she had fetched from Los Tristes in a picnic hamper together with the bottle of French wine we were sipping.

"Why 'Elizabeth'? You've taken your mother's name?"

"I've taken her maiden name," Scampy clarified. "Elizabeth Eliot. The dean thought 'Woodbridge' might arouse envy or class hatred among my fellow probationers. I don't think of myself as a 'Woodbridge' anymore, just as my mom's daughter. Any more questions?"

"Lots, Miss Eliot . . . The aroma of your cooking is absolutely mouth-watering. I thought Pia said you didn't know how to order a cup of coffee in any language."

Scampy shrugged. "Pia was trying to belittle me in front of you. She pretends that people who read and write and think are totally incompetent . . . Elizabeth, my mom, was a wonderful cook. I learned from her before she became too sick to sneak into the kitchen. We had a chef and a waiter and a scullery maid. I learned from them, too. Cooking is creative. Unfortunately, not being an artist like you, I haven't been invited by the Metropolitan Museum to exhibit my spaghetti on the wall or to cast my *pâté de foie gras* in bronze."

"Next question, Miss Eliot. You borrowed Mum's Overland, Dawn Antelope's toy. Was he, perchance, riding shotgun with you?"

"Correct, Mr. Penhallow. How do you suppose I knew where to find you? He has taken the car to the pueblo for tonight . . . Do you want to know what we're doing here?"

"No," I said. "I think I'm in love with you, but I have to wait an hour to be sure it's not an infatuation. Besides, you're abandoning me in the morning with Dawn Antelope. I suppose you're running off with the old man. I knew a girl who did that with an old man."

"Super," Scampy said. She met my gaze. "And sweet . . . You and Anna Maria, your concern about me: not to worry. I'm not going off the deep end. I know Pa-pa forced Elizabeth to be impregnated by Fredson. I know Fredson is my father. I know Fredson blackmailed Pa-pa in order to marry me and become part of the family and take over Corporation. In other words, dear, I know the secrets, and they haven't killed me. When I married the man you know as Shiflit, I made a mistake. I corrected the mistake. I, too, have had some experience. So what? Pa-pa disowns me. Am I supposed to run back to him? Let me tell you why he sent me on a round-the-world cruise with Pia, giving her money, me not a cent in my purse."

Stirring the sauce, pausing now and then to sip from her wine glass, Scampy described the cruise in a literary and an operatic context: the pact-with-the-devil bit, Dr. Faustus and Don Giovanni so addicted to luxury and power that the very thought that these would be snatched away tormented them. Pa-pa expected Scampy to return from the cruise so spoiled and broken she would do anything he wished.

"Remember I used to say 'Sue-Puh' in a very affected way?" Scampy said. "*That* was spoiled. I don't see how you could tolerate me—and keep my picture. Let me tell you about the real Elizabeth Eliot, R.N., on that cruise. Wherever Pia and I went, ports of call such as Manila, Singapore, Calcutta, Cairo, Genoa, Marseille, while she was ashore flirting with anything in pants, I stayed in my cabin. I had nothing in common with our fellow passengers. I didn't dance, gamble, drink. Once in India I did join a group on a tour. While the others were purchasing trinkets, I talked with starving children and saw the ravages of pestilence with my own eyes. When we arrived in Marseille, Pia changed the itinerary. Instead of continuing the voyage to New York, she wanted Paris, the *belle époque*, all that crap, and, since she had all our money, I agreed. I knew from Pa-pa that you were in Paris . . . I owe you an apology."

"Whatever for?"

"I showed up unannounced at your hotel accompanied by a pussywhipping nympho and steamer trunks. Before Pia dumped me with you and disappeared with the remainder of Pa-pa's travel allowance, I'd made inquiries at the Académie Julian and found your address. It was rude of me to intrude on you and, even worse, I leaned on you. You were a brick. If you hadn't described my predicament to Anna Maria and if she hadn't become my benefactor, I might have done something I'd live to regret. Do you recall my mentioning that my grandfather, Hamilton Eliot, is First Vice-President of Corporation? He and Pa-pa were at Yale together in the Bones crowd, a secret society. They are pledged to one another in brotherhood. They are both supposed to be gentlemen who live by an absolute code of honor. Well, when we were together in Paris and London, I was destitute, but I could have cabled Grampy Ham for money. Upon arrival in New York, I could have gone to live with him. I mentioned this matter to you in Paris but need to stress it now. He's not very bright, but he's as honest a soul as ever lived, a punctilious businessman. Can you imagine what Grampy Ham might do if he were ever to discover—as I discovered post-

Paris—that my mother sacrificed herself to Pa-pa's conspiracy with Fredson because Pa-pa was threatening to ruin her father, Grampy Ham? Consider this: if I had turned to Grampy Ham for help, I would have had to explain why—that I was disowned unless or until I re-married Fredson, who had raped me . . . I'll tell you in a minute how I learned the whole truth from Alphie, my supposedly insane brother.'

"Anna Maria saved me. She tells me she met my mom at the sanitorium and pledged to help me should need arise. Perhaps that really happened, perhaps it didn't, but what's important is that I have in Anna Maria what they call out here a *comadre*, a sort of second mother. Thanks to her I've trained as a nurse. I'd rather get down on my knees and scrub toilets in the men's room of Grand Central Station for a year than go through nurses' training again! But now that I'm at St. Anne's I can begin to repay your mother by helping others. I agree with you: material things beyond what you call an 'endowment' have scant appeal." Scampy paused to taste her spaghetti sauce.

"St. Anne," I said, "is patron saint of miners. That means she was an earth mother before Christians started borrowing from pagan mythology. Anyone associated with St. Anne is an earth mother. Everybody loves an earth mother. Therefore, to love you is not an infatuation. Therefore, I can marry you. Imagine that."

"Drop dead," Scampy said. "Dinner's ready."

She had transformed into a dinner table the card table I'd scrounged from a rubbish heap. For the first time in years it had a checkered tablecloth, serviettes, a complete set of cutlery and candles to go along with tin plates, tin cups and the rest of the wine. The spaghetti was too good to be spoiled with conversation. We ate greedily. When we finished, Scampy resumed her story.

"You need a full stomach for this one," she said. "Pencils out . . . Define voyeurism."

Voyeurism was a Shootout word meaning sexual gratification derived from watching the sex act, usually from a hidden vantage point. I was able to supply Scampy with the definition and added,

"Mum told me that Woodbridge observed Shiflit with your mother."

"O.K.," said Scampy, "but she couldn't tell you, because Elizabeth, herself, didn't know, that Alphie was forced to observe those sex acts, himself. As a matter of fact, Alphie, after years of psychiatric treatment at his private nursing hospital in upstate New York, only recently was able to dredge up the horror from his past. He wasn't at that time yet four years old."

Woodbridge had taken the little boy into a soundproofed room having a glass window through which observers could see into a bedroom without being observed from the other side. Here Alphie was tied to a chair, gagged, and forced to watch the conception of his sister. In the opinion of a psychiatrist, Woodbridge had wanted to "toughen up" his only son for the purpose of making him his heir and future Chairman of Corporation.

From what I had seen of or heard about Alphie, the story of his mental disturbance rang true. Once again I recalled he had fired a pistolet point-blank at his father's face in a photograph. He had given me Scampy's photograph but threatened to kill me if I tried to make love with her. He had become Shiflit's slave, trafficking in drugs for him, perhaps innocent of assisting him in persecuting me at Cripple Creek, but signing an affidavit falsely accusing me of raping Scampy. Broken on a psychological rack I couldn't begin to imagine, Alphie had been locked away, presumably because he was a greater danger to Woodbridge than Grandma Irene and Elizabeth Woodbridge had ever been.

"What Alphie knows," Scampy was concluding, "can bring down the House of Woodbridge. I know, you know, the psychiatrist knows. Anna Maria doesn't know about Alphie, but what Elizabeth told her has already put her in danger. Is there anyone else who knows all or part of the story?"

Scampy's question caught me completely by surprise. Why had I been such a clot as to go and tell everything about Woodbridge and Shiflit to Golly!

"You look pale," Scampy said.

"You shaved me," I said, groaning and burying head in hands.

"I've been living under a stone," I said, still groaning. "That's because I've seen a ghost—and the ghost is me, the Ghost of Secrets Past . . . I told Golly everything in a letter! Not long after, she changed horses in midstream, went to Woodbridge College, met Woodbridge and married him. She must have perceived something in my letter, something which triggered that incredible sequence of events."

"Blackmail? You gave her the dirt." Lacking a sarcastic tone, Scampy's voice seemed to show she empathized with my feelings of fury at myself.

"If it was blackmail," I raised my head and tossed into the discussion, "she would show Woodbridge what she had on him, take the money and run, but she married him, rendering her testimony moot. She's good people. Her father devoted his life to paying off *his* father's gambling debts. The effort killed him. Her mother is a stickler for doing right. Golly's like her parents. Once she sets her course there's no stopping her . . . I think *he* married her in a belief she was a pastoral chick from across the railroad tracks, another Union maid under his control. And I think she has never told him what she knows about him."

"Wait," Scampy said, coming and placing a forefinger over my lips. No one had ever done that to me before, and I wasn't ungrateful to have my verbosity, the result of loneliness, shut off before I talked bull feathers. Arms on hips, she looked down at me. "I think," she said, "you've just put your finger on something: Golly's upbringing and the he-gets-it-in-the-neck warning . . . Nice girls leave home. Nice girls sometimes marry tycoons, and tycoons, as I know better than most, are idiots. Does Golly hate men? I think not. I think she really loved you. But your letter triggered something, made her realize she wanted something more than happiness with you, and it had to be a combination of her father's sacrificial sense of honor and her mother's righteousness. She wanted to be a saint, a revolutionary saint. She wanted to put the Shiflits and the Woodbridges of the world into the grave. If opportunity arose, as it did when she went to college in Denver, she would wipe Woodbridge, Pa-pa, off the face of the earth and one day do the same to Fredson."

"If she is a murdersome martyr," I cut in, "why has nothing happened?"

"She has the power," Scampy said, "but, I believe as a nurse, she also has the mothering instinct. She's not a killer. What did she get? Unhappiness and some real estate . . . Mr. and Mrs. Woodbridge, according to newspapers, have had an enormous castle built up the Hudson. He doesn't go into the city as much as he used to. Fredson hangs around Corporation with nothing to do. I bet he won't resist another tour with the Guard in Colorado. Did I tell you a strike is imminent? The militia will be called in. Fredson will be spoiling for another crack at Captain Dare."

I said nothing but stood up, fetched pipe, tobacco, and matches, and returned to the table only when I was smoking and had had a few moments to reflect upon Scampy's news. I knew from what I had observed during my stay at Homesteader's in 1910 that Dare was preparing for a future strike. From Mum's letters to me in Taos I also knew that relations between Union and Corporation had been worsening ever since the Baldwin-Felts detective agency had been hired to crack down upon organizers brought in from Denver. Miners who had been scabs in 1904 were now members of Union, assuring bosses they were content with their lot, privately infuriated by working conditions at odds with their images of a Promised Land. Hundreds of miners were being killed by explosions in gassy mines, and yet mine owners blamed the disasters on the miners, themselves, and denied compensation to widows. A familiar sight now was that of a thousand miners marching behind coffins from the churches of Los Tristes to the Mesa Miners' Union Cemetery. Dare had tried everything in his power to persuade mine owners to meet with him at a conference where grievances could be discussed, chief among these being a simple one, recognition of the right to organize. The owners had dismissed his overtures out of hand. He had even written to Woodbridge at his castle on the Hudson, congratulating him on his marriage to a young woman whom he, Dare, knew personally and held in the highest regard. Woodbridge had never replied. It was appalling, my beloved country having no better use for its young than to drive them to desperation and get them killed.

"I thought you once said to me in Paris, when you were telling me and writing down for me that rather spurious tale of Shiflit's childhood," I continued, "that you had him under your thumb. You needn't tell me why you said all that. When Shiflit comes along, a sick monster, you cling to fantasy about him, that he's a pussycat, in order to avoid having to admit you allowed yourself to be deceived. We're all in the same boat, there. I almost love Woodbridge in spite of all I know about him. I'm damned proud of you . . . You mention Captain Dare. Of course, you must see him every day at the ranch. It seems he has taken you into his confidence. Has he sent you and Dawn Antelope on some sort of mission?"

"Am I that obvious?" Scampy's smile was wistful.

"Well," I said, "when a registered nurse comes barreling across the desert to see me for a few hours, earns honors as cleaning lady of the year, cooks a dinner that French chefs would die for, brings me new clothing and wine from New York, and has news of a war involving all of us, she must want, I regret to say, something other than my beardless body."

"O.K.," said Scampy, "here's the deal."

A few minutes later I realized that I was, indeed, involved in a war and was needed back in Los Tristes. Mum and Dare had been too respectful of my life as an artist to seek my assistance, but Scampy had accepted the role of intruder. As soon as the strike began in the fall, Homesteader's would be vulnerable to attack even though safeguards had been put in place since the Laredo Desperado had blown up the old house with Daddy in it. Dare was often away from home, either at Union H.Q. or at meetings in Denver or in Indianapolis. The place was guarded by Andy and two boys. Since Shiflit and others had tried previously to harm Mum, not just Dare, there was reason to believe they would try again. "I can look after myself, Tree," Scampy said, "but your mother will feel more secure if you're there. Bring your rifle."

"My rifle? The militia will confiscate strikers' weapons and give them to the mine guards to slaughter us . . . It has all happened before. Remember Cripple Creek? If I hadn't pulled you into my arms, that cavalryman would have decapitated you . . . By the way, what *are* you doing tomorrow?"

"Gun-running," Scampy replied with poker face.

"Gun-running!"

"Try not to wake up the whole town . . . And do keep *this* secret."

"Ouch. Cross my heart."

"You just put your finger on it again," Scampy said. "The militia will eventually come and confiscate weapons. In the meantime your job is to protect Anna Maria. Captain Dare is going to do everything in his power to prevent violence. He will not call strikers to arms unless there's a threat of extermination . . . As you know, hundreds of miners have lost their lives in explosions. At one time there weren't enough coffins available to bury the dead. Captain Dare had to order extra coffins from Santa Fe. Then he remembered an incident in the Philippines when rebels put weapons in coffins, smuggled these into one of our camps, and used the Trojan Horse method to capture the camp. Southern Colorado is flooded with spies. He can't just purchase guns for delivery to Union . . . This is where I come in. I work at the hospital. I have no obvious connection to Union. I'm going to Santa Fe with a purchase order for 300 coffins—with 300 Winchester rifles nailed up inside them— and I will see to it that these are shipped to an undertaker in Raton and warehoused until there is a need for them. Since Raton is just over the pass from Los Tristes, coffins with guns can be quickly delivered from there to Union."

An hour later, well past midnight, we were still talking. I happened to recall she had used an odd phrase. " 'Threat of extermination': what did you or Captain Dare mean by that? He has used similar language in the past. It's as if he's haunted by an apocalyptic vision."

"Exactly," Scampy said and went on after a pause. "Conrad. *Heart of Darkness*. I read it after Captain Dare spoke of it one night at the dinner table . . . A splendidly civilized gentleman from Europe goes to the Belgian Congo and reverts to savagery. Remember? He keeps a diary of some sort. In it he expresses his innermost desire where the natives are concerned: 'Exterminate the brutes!' Well, to Captain Dare, the phrase is a prophecy for the twentieth century and beyond. There will be an ever-increasing demand for the extermination of peoples everywhere. The 'extermination psychosis', he calls it. It will spread like a cancer world-wide. Tens of millions of innocents will be exterminated. And, to him, what happens in Los Tristes won't be another labor-management dispute, another seemingly trivial part of the history of industrial relations. For him, the battle in southern Colorado is for human survival. We are the brutes. We are about to be exterminated."

"Speaking of brutes," I said, lifting Merlin into my arms, "the dog wishes to ask you a question."

Scampy studied me, eyebrows furrowed.

"What's that, Merlin?" I said, pretending to catch his words. "He says, 'Will you marry me?'"

"Merlin! Do you really think I'm a bitch?"

I put the dog down and clutched my stomach to show I'd been shot. "Sorry. Thought he was a magician. One more chance? Please?"

"I'm going to bed," Scampy said. She rose and went into the bedroom. But left the door partly open.

"I really do think we ought to get married," I said to her through the open space.

"Drop dead," she said.

"I take it," I said, "that's an affirmative . . . Goodnight . . . I'm off to the caravan named Endless Rue."

I waited for a reply. After a little while it came. "I love your painting," she said, "especially the little boy who is sitting down to supper before a glowing fireplace . . . The boy is you. He's happy because he has a family . . . Goodnight . . . At six I want a cup of coffee, splash of milk, two teaspoons of sugar. I like an egg over easy, no salt, and a croissant with butter and marmalade. I like to be spoiled . . . I love you."

She wasn't just fast on the draw. She was the fastest gun in the West. "I love you, too," I blurted out. I decided to have another look at my painting in the studio. I had painted the picture out of imagination, not consciously realizing that I was still a little boy who had once been happy in a home and yearned to be happy again.

PART IV

Chapter Fifteen

Ever since growing up enough to identify our realm of Sad People—not just the city or region of *los tristes* but the human world of sorrow and folly, of limited knowledge and power—I had conceived of our Door, *la puerta*, both as a boundary and a bondage and as an entrance to a free and higher plane independent of the social order. It was the plane from atom to cosmos of the unknown and untamed, accessed by love and conscience and the creative spirit of the imagination and intuition and sometimes made manifest in the lives of saints and mystics or in some ordinary experience of timelessness. For men to unite, it seemed to me, we needed to share an absolute valuation of human ties, not merely man-made laws and authorities, and we needed to be responsible, reverently and ultimately, to the unconquerable awe and mystery of life.

The way of art had opened my own door to all that was greater than myself. It was as if I could live vicariously in the soul of the people, and it was self-validating in its relevance to the dignity and worth of the individual.

My loved ones were now threatened by a blind social order. The artist, too, was threatened.

Upon returning to Los Tristes in summer of 1913, I began to frequent Cousin Jack's in order to catch wind of the whereabouts of Jefferson Jones. We, Dare, Mr. Jefferson and I had long suspected the Desperado of blowing up the homes of labor organizers, presumably at the behest of or with the consent of Shiflit and ultimately of Woodbridge. Since I, together with Andy and two Union boys, Biff and Chuck, was guarding Homesteader's from another attack, we had to be alert should the Desperado, who had disappeared, show up in town after the strike began on September 23. Meanwhile, mine guards and pit bosses were being sworn in as deputy sheriffs. Gunmen of the West Virginia-based detective agency, Baldwin-Felts, patrolled the streets. Finally, because General Case and Lieutenant Shiflit had been spotted in uniform together at the Imperial Hotel, we surmised that the National Guard would be converging on the strike zone as soon as the latest governor in Denver had evidence—probably faked—of violent rebellion.

The proprietor of Cousin Jack's, an easy-going fellow named Bill, told me he hadn't laid eyes on "Jeff Jones, that gentleman" for years but "heard tell" he was making motion pictures in New York.

On the night of July 29, I was having an Irish whiskey at the bar in Cousin Jack's when a group of miners wearing red handkerchiefs burst through the swinging doors with a he-goat in tow. It was hot in the smoke-filled room, so hot no one was dancing and the fiddler, a Napolitan miner, was having a drink with me at the bar. Everyone was in a mood for entertainment out of the ordinary. Maybe the goat could perform tricks like dogs and bears, and the miners would hold out their caps or persuade Bill to give them drinks on the house.

After dragging the goat to the middle of the dance floor, one of these miners slit its throat with a bowie knife. He and the other miners raised the roof with a yell of triumph.

Now, Bill didn't take kindly to having a dead goat on his floor. He suggested to the miners by means of gestures, for their utterances were in Italian, that they leave the establishment and take the carcass with them.

The goat-killer threatened Bill with the bowie knife and screamed in a voice bordering on hysteria, *"Pozz' fini in dint ospedale!"* Then he, followed by the other Italians, pushed through the crowded room, shouting huzzas as they exited through the swinging doors and leaving the goat to be removed by busboys.

"Well!" I exhaled, turning to the Neapolitan. "For the love of Pete, what was that all about?"

My friend from Naples, the fiddler, explained that his countrymen had been reenacting the assassination of somebody named King Umberto I on a 29th of July by an anarchist named Bresci.

"Oh," I said. "You would think from the intensity of the ritual they were reaching a sexual climax . . . What did the imitation regicide, Bresci, say to Bill?"

"He say he wish Bill end his days in a hospital for the insane. . . *Nuzzer visco?*" The fiddler pointed to my empty glass.

"*Prego.*" Another whiskey was just the job. If anyone needed to end his days in a hospital for the insane—an Italian curse of the first magnitude—it was the king-killer.

At the dinner table at Homesteader's next evening I raised the matter. There were loved ones, Dare at head of table, Mum opposite him, Scampy (now Miss Elizabeth Eliot, R.N.) at my side, Mr. Jefferson and Dawn Antelope opposite us. Having described the ritual sacrifice in gory detail and been greeted with a mixture of applause, ugly faces, and dramatic noises associated with throwing up, I said to my stepfather, "Kyle, with rednecks like our boys from Naples to manage, your task as district manager of Union seems almost impossible. When you go on strike, the last thing you need is violence. You'll lose the sympathy of the nation. You'll be held responsible for riot and rebellion."

Dare raised his eyes to meet my gaze and half smiled. "Our boys from Naples," he said quietly, "assumed they would have the approval of the tribe and felt insulted when Bill had no respect for the monarchy and mistook the king for a goat. Their ritual had to do with the magic of rebirth, like the inevitable replacement of winter by spring. The king is dead. Long live the king . . . I'll get you my Frazer, and you can read him at your leisure, perhaps while you and Chuck and Merlin have the graveyard shift and you're trying to stay awake from the tedium of guard duty . . . I do have a problem keeping strikers under control, but, if we have the renewal of hope on our side, we may stay united."

After dinner Dare fetched from his library dog-eared volumes of Frazer's *The Golden Bough*. I wasn't about to yield to the temptation of reading it while I was on duty. Although I wasn't a trained soldier, I had learned in the mines, at the Académie, and in my studios the discipline of concentration. In addition—and to my surprise—I had a compulsion to do what was appropriate and right even if my ideas of order were in conflict with conventional wisdom.

So I read Fraser in off-duty hours, seeking to discover in his researches into antiquity what Dare had been driving at.

On several continents in ancient cultures, it appeared, priest-kings were murdered by their successors either on the expiry of a set term or whenever some public calamity, such as drought, dearth, or defeat in war, indicated a failure in the king of his natural powers. Since a principle of regeneration abided in rebellion, it might, Dare seemed to be implying, inspire strikers to pull together against the "kings" of finance and industry. By sacrificing for the common good, as in a ritual, strikers might cease to fight among themselves and, instead, show the "kings" that their powers were limited and decrees unqualified according to human values. The trick, indeed, was to create and sustain a harmonious relationship among all parties concerned. On the other hand—here, Frazer's book seemed particularly relevant to modern times—once the rebels resorted to violence, they instituted a kingdom of their own and abrogated their right to the primordial succession of brothers.

All this analysis was but speculation on my part. That labor organizers had to be a tough lot, however, there was no denying. Michael Livoda, a Croat, had arrived in Walsenburg to recruit for Union some Slavic miners. The sheriff, who controlled for himself the saloons and brothels and, for Corporation, the ballot boxes of his county, had Livoda arrested, hustled to the railroad tracks, and ordered to start walking, trailed by thugs in the saddle. If he dared to return, the sheriff warned Livoda, he would be killed. A few months later, Livoda returned and was again arrested. This time he was kicked and cursed, his nose smashed in; had he not covered his eyes, he would have been blinded. Finally released, he took refuge in a coal shed. It was two days before a Union friend could get a doctor to him and a week before he could stand up or seat himself without assistance. He went back to organizing. Then there was an Italian organizer, Gerald Lippiatt by name. He had arrived from Denver to confer with other organizers. At Dare's urging he left his revolver at Union H.Q., having been warned to give a wide berth to Baldwin-Felts gunmen out in the streets looking to provoke organizers into a fight. Lippiatt went for a walk along Commercial Street. About 8:30 p.m. two Baldwin-Felts gunmen deliberately butted him with their elbows. Driven by a code of honor, Lippiatt returned to H.Q., got his gun, went back to Commercial Street, challenged the detectives and shot one in the leg before he crumpled, himself, his body riddled with bullets. The stories of these organizers were well-known to miners, as were the stories of Captain Dare and Mr. Jefferson, both of whom had miraculously escaped when their houses were blown up, though one had lost to the flames a certain Dr. Penhallow and the other had lost wife and children. And, of course, Mother Jones had been harassed and imprisoned so often that she was likened to Jesus Christ and to the patriots of the American revolution of 1776.

As much as I admired organizers in general, my devotion was to the ones I had personally known for ten years, those who had cared for and mentored me after I'd been kidnapped and left to die. They were truly loved ones. While I was destined to have but one family, to love its members for the natural ties, if for no other reason, I was not a victim of divided loyalties. Two of my progenitors, Rufus Obadiah Dautremond and Alpheus Woodbridge, were scoundrels of the first order. I couldn't repudiate them or sever connections, but I could be a renegade and obey only the dictates of my heart. I had three fathers, the biological one who had remembered me in his Will in spite of his tyranny, the soldier of fortune who had saved me and married my mother, and the gentle former slave who had created his own fraternity of Worthy Brothers. And I had two mothers, Mum and Doña Luz. There were also two beautiful young women I cared about, if but one of them, Scampy, cared for me enough to be my wife. Golly renounced personal happiness. Scampy, after all, was friend, companion, lover (once in Paris), betrothed (without words or rings or lawyers or clergy, but with commitment). We lived in separate *casitas* and had our separate passions, I in art, she in nursing, but we were cocooned in paradox, at-one with one another whether together or apart.

The murder of Lippiatt had awakened 12,000 miners and their families, perhaps as many as 20,000 persons in the coalmining communities of southern Colorado, to the brutal possibilities of another strike. As horrible as the strike of 1903-1904 had been throughout Colorado and the West, with bull pens, deportations, and kangaroo beatings still bitterly recalled, the Pinkertons, as compared with the Baldwins, had been relatively benign. Working conditions of 1903, as compared to those of 1913, had been relatively safe. The old-timers from England and Wales had been wise to the dangers of damp and of roof-collapse; when they became pit bosses and superintendents, they had collaborated with the working stiffs in avoidance of accidents. Now old-timers were replaced by inexperienced scabs. Pit bosses and superintendents, allied with mine owners, not only ignored dangerous conditions but also fomented hatred, forcing miners to compete for jobs and favors. More and more miners were being killed every year by explosions in gassy mines that hadn't been properly ventilated.

"Ten years ago," Dare remarked to me one day, "a worker's life wasn't worth a mule's, but he was still worth a nickel. Now he's not worth a nickel."

Union leaders had met with him in Denver and decided to call the strike. With half a million members nationwide, Union had funds for a protracted strike. Many demands, such as the 8-hour working day and the end of cheating by checkweighmen, had already been passed into law, but these laws were not enforced. The most important demand was for the right to organize and bargain.

After the meeting Dare set to work to establish more than a dozen tent colonies along a 50-mile front where the high plains met the coal-producing foothills of the Rockies. The main colony would be at Quivira, a whistle stop (depot, post office, saloon) five miles north of Los Tristes and two miles north of the Medina Ranch. Quivira was planned as a small city for 1,300 strikers and their families, about 200 tents in rows, a headquarters tent and a Red Cross tent, one extra-large tent reserved for a school and for community dances. Tent floors would be timbered. Heavy Excelsior stoves would be installed. Each tent would have a supply of fuel and water. Beneath the floors of tents designated for families pits would be dug as shelter in the event of an attack. At a central location a platform would be erected so that mass meetings could be held. Sanitary trenches were to be excavated. Communication lines were to connect Quivira H.Q. with Union H.Q. in Los Tristes. A baseball diamond would be marked out. A leader for each of twenty-one ethnic groups would be appointed, each leader to be obeyed in everything by the people of his group. These leaders, in turn, would be responsible either to Captain Dare or to Mr. Jefferson.

Once Dare had the colonies established and in readiness for the exodus of strikers from the company-towns, he began to brood over the success of the operation. The "extermination psychosis," as he called it in our conversations, loomed as something more than a literary prophecy. It had been evident for 400 years in America in massacres and relocations of the native population. In the Philippines it had been evident in the slaughter of "Goo-Goos." Now it was showing up in what was cavalierly called "industrial relations." In the coal-producing regions of West Virginia, Baldwin-Felts gunmen had beaten pregnant women to death; there in Paint Creek an armored train had sped by a colony and sprayed the tents of sleeping miners with machine-gun fire.

On a warm September afternoon before I was scheduled for graveyard, Dare took me in his Ford truck to inspect the "industrial colony" of Quivira. As much as I marveled at his accomplishments there, when I brought our conversation around to military preparedness, he became truculent.

"Of course we're exposed," he replied to my comparison of Quivira to Paint Creek. "I can see perfectly well that our tents are backed up against the main line of the Colorado and Southern Railroad. We can be attacked by machine-gunners on a train. Of course their gunmen can come pouring out of the hills, but our people will be coming out of those same hills, expecting new homes. You saw what happened at Doña Luz's last time the poor wretches were evicted from their homes and straggled down from the canyons. We had nothing ready for them. This time we're ready. The exodus takes priority over security."

After a deep breath he changed tone. "If the militia are called in and Shiflit has command, we're sitting ducks. Not enough guns, not enough ammo, the only breastworks that arroyo over there outside the tents. If extermination proves to be the order of the day, I have, as you know, a stash of Winchesters in Raton, but, until a call to arms becomes absolutely necessary, our best defense is to show the world that we're defenseless . . . If we die here, we'll leave an indelible imprint on the civilized world."

I noted that Dare had, as usual, a .45 caliber revolver strapped to his waist.

I must, like Dare, have had a stomach for lost causes. Otherwise I might have stayed in Taos and painted. I'd taken my chances in the miner's trade, and I hadn't hesitated to help Golly in covering up the killing of Shorty. I wasn't cut out to be a soldier. I had a Remington rifle, and I'd never fired it. Still, I was pulling guard duty, usually from dusk to dawn, and, if the Laredo Desperado had charged my sentry post, I would have shot him.

After months of protecting loved ones, I was coming to the conclusion that I had little to worry about. If anything did happen on my watch, Merlin's barking would sound the alarm and Chuck's

Remington would hit the target. Daytimes, Andy and Biff were probably so sure nothing would happen, they were secretly slapping their thighs in merriment, knowing they were paid for nothing and more than their worth.

The Desperado, it turned out, had in fact become a motion picture star. Why would he want to shoot or blow up labor organizers when he could make ten times as much money imitating Buffalo Bill without having to inconvenience himself with speech, bullets, Calamity Jane or horse manure? As for Shiflit, in spite of his being Dare's nemesis from what Scampy had told me, I had to figure him for a brain-fart. Like a child unable to focus attention on any task for more than a few minutes, he was capricious as folly, one moment playing soldier, next moment playing K.O. Kid, next moment obliging Elizabeth Woodbridge, always dreaming of becoming Chair of Corporation, especially if he got to commit incest on his way to the top, as clever as the Devil when it came to quoting, out of context, scripture for his purpose but totally unprepared to control his destiny or accept and suffer the consequences of his monstrous perversity.

In these circumstances I had to make an extraordinary effort to maintain a semblance of vigilance. While I was corralled at the ranch, Mum, Dawn Antelope at the wheel of the Overland, would go out shopping upon the slightest whim, and Scampy insisted on walking to town to catch the trolley car bound for St. Anne's Hospital. On days off she was in Quivira stocking the Red Cross tent with supplies. She was planning to open a canteen there on the first day of the strike, serving free milk to children, free hot coffee to their parents. Although I tried to impress upon her the fact that Elizabeth Eliot, R.N., could be recognized by Shiflit, kidnapped, drugged and forced to re-marry him in New York, she just shrugged.

No, I wasn't cut out to be a soldier, but that didn't mean I wouldn't fight to keep open the door of the sad people.

$\approx\approx\approx$

September 23, 1913

For several days prior to the strike on September 23 rain and snow, driven by freezing winds, had been turning into mud the winding, unpaved roads leading from company-towns to tent camps. Before dawn of the 23rd, armed guards at the company-towns began evicting from their homes the strikers and their families. Littering the muddy streets were tables, chairs, brass or iron bedsteads, mattresses, clothing, pictures, dolls, Bibles from Old World countries, gaily painted gramophones. While waiting in the rain for any kind of conveyance, many women, some of them nursing babies, squatted in the mud. Once wagons were piled high with possessions and the women and children were seated atop the piles, the exodus began, soon consisting of wagons and pushcarts strung out in lines a mile long. When wheels were stuck in mud, families got out and pushed, joined by unknown strikers who spoke in foreign tongues. When wagons were rolling again, Slavs, Greeks, Montenegrins, Russians, Finns, Austrians, French, Italians, Portuguese, Lebanese, Mexicans, Japanese and others sang the Union's *Battle Cry of Union*:

> *Union forever! Hurrah, boys, hurrah!*
> *Down with the Baldwins and up with the law,*
> *For we're coming, Colorado,*
> *We're coming all the way,*
> *Singing the battle cry of union!*

At the mouth of a canyon leading down to Quivira, Captain Dare was frequently observed in the act of helping to lift a wagon sunk in mud to the hubs. Toward nightfall in Quivira, after the rain had stopped, a thousand strikers and their families stood in the torchlit meeting area and cheered their mud-splattered leader who was up on the platform shouting through a megaphone his welcome to their new home, the tents at which American flags were fluttering wildly. After the meeting he pitched in to help the men who were building swings and see-saws for children, putting up clotheslines,

338

or covering cracks in floor boards with scraps of worn-out linoleum.

All day Elizabeth Eliot, R.N., had been serving milk and coffee at her canteen and also treating sick and injured patients at her Red Cross tent. Although she wore a raincoat and a souwester, she had been soaked through and through and felt too exhausted to come home in one of the Union cars. Shivering with cold she spent the night in her tent and came home as I was having breakfast. After changing into warm, dry clothes, she had coffee with me in front of a blazing fire and said:

"There was one very brave twelve-year-old boy who had been beaten by a mine guard before the exodus began. His family had gone over to an office to return some of the company's keys. The guard said to the boy, 'Here's a goodbye present for you, you double-crossin' son of a bitch redneck!' With that he slugged and kicked the boy. When I saw the boy's face, I felt sick to my stomach. His eyes were swollen shut. He was missing several teeth. His skin was a black and blue jelly mixed with congealed blood. When I had finished cleaning and bandaging his wounds, he whispered to me, 'No one must hear of this, Mother. If anyone should ask, tell them the wagon tipped over on me.'"

September 24, 1913

The wind subsided and a hot sun came out. Wash sagged on clotheslines strung between tents. Up by the railroad tracks a hundred women and children had gathered. As a trainload of scabs passed by them, headed up the canyon toward company-towns vacated twenty-four hours earlier, the crowd shouted obscenities and hurled rocks. Captain Dare and Mr. Jefferson ran alongside the tracks and yelled, "No violence! No violence!," until the train clattered to a vanishing point.

That night many scabs, upon discovering that they were replacing strikers, tried to get away from those remote and heavily guarded company-towns. Until they paid off their board, lodging, and railroad fares, they were told, they had to work. Their shoes were taken away from them. The scab who had the money or the whiskey to bribe a guard might escape. Upon his arrival in a tent camp Mr. Jefferson and other leaders would feed him and escort him to Union attorneys in Los Tristes to make affidavits.

∼∼∼

September 30, 1913

During the early nights of the strike the mine owners bankrolled by Corporation ordered guards to sweep the Quivira camp with searchlights. There were eight of them, large 32-inch lights whose 5,000 candlepower beams had a range of several miles. Anyone or anything caught in the beams, an automobile, for instance, was subject to attack by machine-gunners positioned in the hills. Every night, all night, sleepless strikers and their families could see these lights penetrating the flimsy fabric of their tents.

On the night of September 30 a miner with a rifle was clearly picked out by searchlight beams. Strangely, no machine guns chattered from the direction of the hills. *"¡Hola, hermanos!"* the miner called out to a group of strikers who were playing cards. The miner had a white handkerchief tied to his uplifted rifle and in his free hand a bottle. The strikers recognized him, a Texas mine guard named San Luis, formerly a miner who liked to pass a bottle of whiskey around. One of the strikers who was pulling guard duty, not playing cards, called out, "Beat it, San Luis. I'd be pretty sorry to see you get killed."

San Luis laughed. "You big mistake, *amigo*," he said. "You know me. I am a square man, no trouble man. I freezing my ass off. Let's drink, old time's sake. Anything wrong for me over here? What do I trouble to you fellows over here?"

After such a cordial invitation the strikers let San Luis come and squat in their midst and pass the bottle.

Just as the party was becoming convivial, San Luis stood up and ran toward the railroad tracks as fast as he could. At the same time rifle shots were fired from the embankment there. Luke Vahernik, a Slav and one of the card players, collapsed with a bullet in his brain. Out of darkness galloped dozens of horsemen firing carbines at tents. As soon as they disappeared back into the dark the snouts of machine guns were observed protruding from an armored car about 150 yards away. The machine guns opened up, raking tents, shattering household goods, most bullets striking dirt, occasional bullets, tracers, arcing into blackness. As suddenly as the attack started, it ceased.

People staggered from tents. A woman shrieked. Others were heard to wail and shout. A little boy lay dead on the ground. A little girl, though alive, had been shot in the face.

The Baldwin-Felts detective agency had had an ordinary automobile shipped down from Denver to Corporation factories in Pueblo. Steel plates three eighths of an inch thick were bolted to the sides of the car. Two machine guns were mounted on a floor of solid wood. This contraption, soon to be called "The Death Special" in newspapers throughout the country, had on the night of September 30 been hidden behind a slight elevation where searchlight beams did not reach.

October 27-28, 1913

After the night of the Death Special, Captain Dare and Mr. Jefferson could no longer completely control the strikers. An organizer in Denver had supplied them with seventy-one rifles, .30-.30 caliber, and 5,000 rounds of ammunition. When a blizzard blotted out the Los Tristes region on the night of October 27, 300 armed strikers from various camps slipped silently into the hills in-between searchlight sweeps and attacked company-towns. Before noon of the 28th telephone and telegraph wires had been cut, railroad tracks had been blown up, tipples and cages had been set on fire, and ten mine guards and deputies had been killed.

Lieutenant Shiflit was appointed commander of company

guards. He immediately urged the governor to send Guard troops to southern Colorado. By tricking the government into an intervention, he spared Corporation the expenses of waging war against the people of the United States.

〜〜〜

November 1, 1913

On October 31, the governor having issued orders for Guard troops, a long train carrying General Case and the militia screeched to a halt at the Quivira depot a mile east of the tent colony. Lieutenant Shiflit was waiting with automobiles and had Case driven to meet Captain Dare, other Union officers, and leaders of the various nationalities.

At the headquarters tent General Case promised Captain Dare that the Guard was to be impartial. It would disarm mine guards as well as strikers. It would send mine guards out of the state. It would keep watch against the importation of scabs.

After the general had left to have a Guard tent camp established near Water Tank Hill a few hundred yards from Quivira colony, Dare telephoned Union H.Q. in Los Tristes. "Notify the other colonies to have as many people here as possible tomorrow," he said. "The militia will be marching out in full parade. We want to give these Tin Willies a proper welcome."

On the first of November, as soon as Case's cavalry was seen in formation, 1,500 men, women, and children marched down the road to meet the soldiers. Handkerchiefs and flags were waved. Dressed in white, children sang *The Union Forever* and *Marching Through Georgia* to the accompaniment of an improvised Yankee-Doodle-Dandy band. There were a few drums, a few jew's harps, some tin horns and Milenko's flute.

Later in the day, outside the tents, strikers piled up a heap of thirty old guns. Alarmed that they were cheating on promises he had made, Dare demanded, "Where are the rest?" A child in the crowd stepped forward and dropped a popgun on the pile.

Before too many days had passed Dare learned that serviceable guns out of the thirty had been given to mine guards who had supposedly been disarmed and sent out of the state.

There were two companies of militia, K and B. Company K, commanded by a Denver attorney, treated the miners with respect. These militiamen came to dances in the big tent, ate dinner with strikers and played games there. Company B was composed of mine guards and professional gunmen who had volunteered to wear the uniform of American troopers. The commander of Company B was Shiflit.

December, 1913

Mother Jones was eighty-three-years-old. In December she spoke to a reporter about her desire to be called upon by the Union to go to Los Tristes where General Case had made the Imperial Hotel his personal headquarters.

"The call can't come too soon," she said to the reporter. "Case will throw me in jail. I would bet on that. He'll do it because he doesn't know any better, because he doesn't know that persecution always helps instead of hinders any battle. And let him do it. Let him have his men, disgracing their uniforms, shoot me. I'm prepared for that, too. I wish they would. It would mean a wave of feeling over this country that would crush Case and everybody like him. It would mean certain victory . . . But I don't suppose they'll shoot me. I guess even Case knows better than that. They'll throw me in jail, and before they get me out they'll wish they'd never done it . . . I've sat on a bumper inhaling mule farts, and it smelled better than those sons of bitches."

She had been in Colorado in 1911 to organize coal miners. In October of that year she went to Mexico to receive assurances from President Madero that the new revolutionary government would permit the organization of workers. In 1912-13 the Paint Creek strike in West Virginia had focused national attention on Mother

Jones to a greater degree than ever before. Her trial and conviction by a military court, followed by her imprisonment in February, 1913, created such a furor that the U.S. Senate ordered a committee to investigate conditions in that state. And, more than ever before, her speeches were being reported, speeches in which she appealed to the entire country with themes of sacrifice and humiliation, saying,

This earth was made for you, was it not? And it was here a long time before Corporation came upon it. The earth was here long before they came, and it will be here when their rotten carcasses burn up in hell . . . Did Jack ever tell you, "Say, Mary, you go down and scrub the floor for the superintendent's wife or the boss's wife and then I will get a good room in the mine?" I have known women to do that, poor fools. I have known them to go down and scrub floors like a dog, while their own floors were dirty . . . You will be free. Poverty and misery will be unknown. We will turn the jails into playgrounds for the children. We will build homes, and not log kennels and shacks as you have them now. There will be no civilization as long as such conditions as that abound, and now you men and women will have to stand the fight.

January 12, 1914

At eight in the morning of the fourth of January the militia arrested Mother Jones at the Los Tristes depot. It was exactly what she wanted to happen, as was the immediate aftermath: she was "deported" to Denver on the next northbound train and warned against returning to the strike zone. As soon as she arrived in Denver she bought $500 worth of shoes at wholesale prices. She intended to return to Los Tristes and distribute the shoes to strikers and their families. On the eleventh of January she evaded detectives who had been keeping her under surveillance at her Denver hotel and went to Union Station an hour before a train was scheduled to leave for Los Tristes. Customarily, as she knew from experience, the cars were made up out in the yards a long distance from the platforms where passengers would be permitted to board them at the appropriate time. She could rely upon most train crews to do her bidding. Out in the yards, then, she slipped a Pullman porter a few dollars, asked him to tell the conductor to let her get off before the train reached the Santa Fe crossing in Los Tristes, climbed into her berth and was sound asleep when the train pulled up to the platform.

Early on the morning of January 12 she alighted from the train, walked into Los Tristes, checked in to a little hotel across the street from the Imperial, ate a hearty breakfast and retired to her room. Three hours passed before Case learned of her presence.

He called the governor. "Impossible!" he ranted.

"Impossible," the governor agreed. "Deport her."

A few minutes later the general and a squad of militia stood in front of the door to her room. He offered her a choice: return to Denver or be placed under house arrest at St. Anne's Hospital.

"Nothing doing, General," she replied, opening the door. "I am free, white, and a bit over twenty-one. This is a free country, and I've got a right to go where I damned well please."

Taken to a waiting automobile and driven to the hospital, she was incarcerated in a small room with a cot, a chair, and a table. Two soldiers guarded her door; other soldiers guarded the hallway and elevator entrances, and from her window she could see a soldier walking up and down outside the hospital, bayonet flashing in sun.

She had been imprisoned without charges and not allowed visitors or communications of any kind. All she had to do, the way she saw it, was get pen and paper from nurses who brought her meals, then get one of the nurses to smuggle letters out to all the leading newspapers in the United States.

She enlisted Scampy in the plot.

'Miss Eliot," she said in a low voice above a whisper one morning as Scampy, having served breakfast, was airing out the room and fluffing pillows, "you've been very kind and brave, trusting me with the secret of your upbringing in the home of Mr. Alpheus

Woodbridge, widely regarded as my mortal enemy. Your secret is safe with me. Now I must ask you to consider very carefully to undertake for me a mission fraught with danger to your person. Fetch me those letters under the mattress . . . If Washington took instructions from such as Case, we would be under King George's descendants yet. If Lincoln took orders from Case, Grant would never have been victorious. Do you follow what I am saying?"

Scampy tucked the letters into her undergarments and said, also in low voice, "When I was a girl, Mother, I was in Cripple Creek and might have been beheaded by one of General Case's Cossacks. I owe you so much for your humanitarian acts."

Mother Jones bristled. "I'm not a humanitarian," she hissed, glaring over the rim of spectacles. "I'm a hell-raiser."

As Scampy was leaving the room, Mother Jones beckoned for her to approach. "Miss Eliot," she said, holding Scampy's hand in both of her hands, "I've met Mr. Woodbridge. I am not his mortal enemy. I believe the human is very deeply planted in his breast. The pathetic scenes we witness in great conflicts must eventually touch the better side of our nature. We only pass through this life once. Let us do all the good we can for humanity, making a better place for those who come after us. I am convinced that Mr. Woodbridge would rather lose all his wealth than have recorded in the calendar of the future the brutal scenes of starvation and despair that you and I see every day. He has deceived himself into believing in a principle, that workers are independent contractors and that he is the one upholding their freedom . . . In the better days to come, child, we will all meet each other as human beings without distinctions of wealth and class."

Scampy admired Mother Jones for her faith in Woodbridge and the future but suspected the old lady of sappiness.

A week after Scampy mailed the letters there was a hue and cry in newspapers from Denver to New York ridiculing Case and deploring his persecution of Mother Jones. One cartoon showed a poor old woman stretched out in a hospital bed, crying, "Oh, doctor, help me, I'm dying," while an unshaven soldier was sticking a bayonet in the doctor's stomach, saying, "No admission to you no matter how sick th' old woman is!"

~~~

January 23, 1914

From Los Tristes to Denver and cities between them the call had gone out to the women of Colorado to gather for a demonstration and parade in behalf of Mother Jones. After great difficulty a parade permission was obtained from General Case. With everything set for January 23, women and children, as many as a thousand of them, made their way to the city and at the appointed time began to move across the bridge and up Commercial Street. According to onlookers, of whom Doña Luz was one, most participants were shabbily-dressed; fortunately the weather was mild. The parade reached Main Street and turned east toward the hospital. No soldiers were in sight. Paraders sang *The Battle Cry of Union* and carried banners proclaiming support for Mother Jones.

Suddenly, three blocks east on Main, a line of cavalry appeared, General Case sitting horse in front of his men and facing the oncoming parade. The cavalrymen had sabers out of their scabbards. Infantry filled the street behind the cavalry.

The women advanced.

"Not another step," Case boomed. "Turn back!"

The line of women wavered for a moment but continued to advance. Case spurred his horse forward but wheeled and rode toward his men. A sixteen-year-old school girl caught his eye. "Get back there!" Case cried and brushed against her with his horse. The girl was too frightened to move. "I said get back there!" Case yelled again, kicking her with his foot. He hadn't noticed that women at the head of the parade were already threading their way through the line of mounted troopers. An officer rode up. Before he could speak, the general's horse became frightened and backed into a parked buggy.

General Case was thrown from his horse.

The women screamed with laughter.

Red-faced, Case rose to his feet and roared to his men: "Ride down the women! Ride down the women!"

Laughter turned to screams of terror as cavalry mounts plunged forward. Sabers flashed. Mrs. Maggie Hammons was slashed across the forehead. Mrs. George Gibson's ear was almost severed. Mrs. Thomas Braley threw up her hands in front of her face, and they were gashed. A cavalryman, leaning from his horse, struck Mrs. James Lanigan with the flat of his saber, knocking her to the ground. Another cavalryman leaned from his saddle and smashed ten-year-old Robert Arguello in the face with his fist. Mrs. Verna, who had been marching in the van of the parade with an American flag, was pursued by a cavalryman who tore the flag from her grasp and all but trampled her with his horse.

Mounted again, General Case continued to yell, his voice drowned out by the shrill cries of panic-stricken women and children.

"*Great Czar Fell!*" the *Denver Express* said in a double banner. "*And in Fury Told Troops to Trample Women.*"

"*A craven general tumbled from his nag in a street of Los Tristes Thursday,*" the lead story read, "*like Humpty-Dumpty from the wall. In fifteen minutes there was turmoil, soldiers with swords were striking at fleeing women and children; all in the name of the sovereign state of Colorado. For General Case, having lost his poise on his horse, also lost his temper and cried, 'Ride down the women.' Then there was bloodshed. The French Revolution, its history written upon crimson pages, carries no more cowardly episode than the attack of the gutter gamin soldiery on the crowd of unarmed and unprotected women.*"

~~~

April 17, 1914

Colorado was going bankrupt. Its governors, elected by means of Corporation backing, had shouldered the costly burden of waging war against the American people, and now it was financially necessary to withdraw from the strike zone 800 of the 1,000 troops. The last of the militia was ordered home on April 17. Under the pretext of looking for hidden guns, they had looted the tent camps of anything that might be described as "valuable" in Larimer Street pawn shops; a drunken spree followed. Furious, General Case returned to Denver. In effect, his martial law went with him.

That same afternoon of the seventeenth, sixty gunmen marched along Commercial Street to the armory where Lieutenant Shiflit swore them into a newly-formed volunteer force. Although they wore the uniform of the Guard, they reminded old-timers of the outlaws who had once roamed the West in gangs.

When a corporal from the militia set out on horseback from the Quivira depot, his horse tripped over a length of taut, double-stranded barbed wire half-hidden by snow. Thrown, the corporal lay injured, and Lieutenant Shiflit, who was in the depot, demanded that the person responsible for setting the wire be found and brought before him. Not long afterwards a boy named Orf was dragged into the depot and accused of having deliberately planned the accident. Orf denied the accusation, but when Shiflit pressured him into naming the guilty party, Orf quickly responded, "Mr. Jefferson."

Shiflit struck the boy with the back of his hand. "I'm running this neck of the woods," he shouted, "not a runaway slave from Marse Jefferson's plantation and not an ex-Army captain who had Filipino boys executed for pilfering rations!"

Some while later Mr. Jefferson was brought before Shiflit and accused of deliberately placing the wire. Shiflit struck him in the face with his fist and screamed at the top of his voice, "I am Jesus Christ, you son of a bitch! I am Jesus Christ! My men on horses are Jesus Christs, you goddamn son of a bitch!"

Mr. Jefferson made no effort to resist. "You beat it over to the colony and cut every goddamn wire," Shiflit screamed at a trooper who had a pair of wire cutters. "And the first man that interferes with you, shoot his head off!"

∾∾∾

April 18, 1914

I was accustomed to springtime in Colorado and New Mexico. Warm, dry, cloudless days would suddenly be interrupted by blizzards, the snowdrifts piled as high as six feet in a matter of hours. Then a splendidly bright sun would come out with equal suddenness, a dazzling snowmelt would begin, and early daffodils would blow their yellow horns. But winter had been hard on the people of the tent colonies. Supplies of coal had become so scarce that they were only used for cooking in the stoves and not for heating. Produce obtained through the Union commissary was now in short supply. Almost gone were the fish and game caught by strikers. Seeing wives and children ravaged by hunger, the men were growing desperate. Although some were planting vegetables—and flowers—around the tents, most wanted an end to the strike.

Had it not been for Doña Luz the situation at Quivira might have become unbearable.

Life at the Medina ranch was no longer what it had been when I had lived there and earned my keep in the St. Mabyn's. As long as Doña Luz had her children and boarders to help with chores and expenses, the ranch had prospered. First, Carmencita married Orlando. The two of them had moved to the St. Mabyn's company-town; they now had three children. Then Dare, having rebuilt Homesteader's, had moved back there, Mr. Jefferson allotted a *casita*, I in the meantime having decamped to France. The other boarders, all save Milenko, had drifted away to points unknown, a vanishing breed of bindle stiffs; Milenko, too, had moved to St. Mabyn's, to bachelor barracks. When Golly left home for Woodbridge College in Denver, only Nono and Aladino remained. They were usually so busy in the mines they had little time or energy to run a farm. Doña Luz had accomplished what she could until the strike came along. Then Nono and Aladino took their rifles and joined the strikers just up the range at Quivira. Doña Luz harvested crops by herself. With the help of neighbors, she cooked and canned thousands of jars of fruits and vegetables and had all the livestock and chickens slaughtered, smoked, iced-down, nothing for sale, everything reserved for the strikers. Shortly after the New Year, again with the help of neighbors, she loaded cars with the stores of food. In Quivira, she distributed these free to the people. She boarded up the house and outlying buildings and went again to Quivira, this time to look after Nono, Aladino, Carmencita, Orlando and three grandchildren in a family tent and to teach children in the big tent the rudiments of reading and arithmetic.

After the death of Don Fernando, Mr. Jefferson had become a sort of surrogate husband to her. To the best of anyone's knowledge their feelings for one another were just part of the air they breathed. There had never been a hint of intimacy, no special words or glances, no knowing looks, no distinctions blurred between landowner and handyman. There were nevertheless understandings between them which seemed to extend beyond the acceptances of friendship or the fraternal bonds of Union. They formed a tableau, proud and silent as if photographed in a wedding pose, intrepid as compassion itself.

There had been a time, Golly had told me, when one of Luz's distant cousins from the twelfth-century Picuris settlement had been captured and lynched by Texas Rangers. From the moment the girl, Luz, heard the news in her home in Santa Fe, the very idea of time had become incomprehensively different, not a dream but a wakeful horror without relief save for the imperative of communicating love by word and act. When the labor organizer known familiarly as "Congo" and officially as Mr. Jefferson lost family, house, and home in the dynamite blast, Doña Luz did not hesitate to enlist Don Fernando's help in bringing him into their family. "He feels out of place," she had said.

"It will be difficult," Don Fernando had said, shaking his head following a torturous day of work in the mines. "They say, though he refuses to quit organizing, he breaks down and weeps at all hours. He goes to Cousin Jack's and drinks himself into a stupor while sitting at the bar and staring at the absolutely motionless figure of Jefferson Jones. *Señor* Jefferson is too consumed with sorrow to make the slightest move, himself, except in the manner of a sleepwalker."

"We must go tonight," Doña Luz said, "to show him that we understand."

They dressed in black. Don Fernando wore black shirt, black pants, black belt, black socks and black shoes and settled a black *sombrero* on his head. Doña Luz wore widow's weeds, including a black lace veil. They took their best buggy to town and waited on Main Street for the half-crazed organizer to emerge from Cousin Jack's. Just as midnight was tolled from church bells the powerful figure of a dark man was seen stumbling through the swinging doors and standing, swaying on the boardwalk as if trying to gather his wits. Doña Luz went and stood close to him. When his eyes focused on her presence, she lifted her veil and said, "I'm sorry about your family. There's something magical about an uncle. Come along."

The big dark man burst into tears. Doña Luz put her arms around him. After a while she guided him to the buggy. He fell fast asleep in her arms as Don Fernando drove them all home under a star-filled sky. The next morning the children came and woke up a man they called "Tío Congo." He was amazed to find himself on a comfortable bed in a small, clean room, an odor of bacon and eggs wafted up from a nearby staircase.

In the Quivira tent colony Doña Luz knew that her place was to be near to Mr. Jefferson.

She brought Mr. Jefferson to the Red Cross tent. The nurse, Miss Eliot, cleaned and sterilized his bloodied, swollen face. Apart from a split lip and a slashed eyebrow, a wound she couldn't stitch up without a doctor's permission, as she explained to Mrs. Medina, he was fit to go.

Meanwhile, as I was coming off the graveyard, and a light snow, which had been falling during the night, was surrendering to blue skies, Mum came and told me Dare was eating breakfast and wanted to have a word with me in private. I shook the snow from my Stetson and joined him at the table in the ranchhouse.

District leader of Union, he no longer presented himself in a rancher's costume such as the deerskin shirt he'd been wearing at Peniel but looked, almost, like a slim, tall Teddy Roosevelt, minus the mustache and glasses: three-piece suit, dark with pin stripes, starched shirt and collar with black silk bow tie. He'd put on weight during his first years of marriage to Mum, but the responsibilities of his job—his territory roughly equivalent to half of France—were beginning to show in his countenance, which was pale, circles beneath eyes, graying hair at temples.

"Siddown, son," he said. "Flapjacks and molasses and coffee black as sin. Your mother sure knows how to spoil us. I keep saying, 'Anna Maria, let me hire a Mexican lady to do the cooking,' but she insists she loves doing it." He paused, face clouded over. "Shiflit has gone bugs," he resumed in lowered voice. "He's 'Jesus Christ'! He proves it by punching out Mr. Jefferson, who did the right thing, didn't offer, lives to tell the tale . . . Shiflit's up to something. You've got Case back in Denver, and, two bits, Corporation idiots want to settle this strike before President Wilson wakes up to what is going on in Colorado . . . Shiflit is preparing to wipe us out. Eat your breakfast. I'll fill you in."

The day before the Colorado Supreme Court was to decide that Mother Jones was entitled to a writ of habeas corpus, General Case had released her from confinement in the hospital and had her deported to Denver. This activity, Dare believed, confirmed his long-held suspicion that Case's "martial law" was a sham. Shiflit and the leftover Guard had, therefore, no authority. They didn't have the right to search the colonies for weapons or, in fact, order strikers to do anything. Still, the process whereby the bogus "Guard" could be replaced by Federal troops was delayed. The Mines and Mining Committee of the House of Representatives in Washington had only just begun to investigate the coal strike. That the intransigence of Woodbridge was recognized as the very crux of the problem, President Wilson seemed to comprehend, but Wilson was distracted by an ambition to invade Mexico. As a consequence, he, Dare, had to decide whether to issue a call to arms.

"Years ago, I foresaw the possibility of a call to arms," he said, still in lowered voice, "but it's the last thing I ever wanted to put into effect. Look at your goat-killers from Naples. We have plenty of bloodthirsty miners, and their patience is rolled out thin. If I arm the strikers for self-protection, we could have the bloodiest outbreak of labor violence in our history, but, if I don't arm them, Shiflit will, I swear, exterminate them. You're a historian. You know that Mother Jones has stirred up sympathy for the downtrodden. But she won't be writing the history books. We could have a massacre here, and hardly anybody will notice—unless we fight. So I've decided to prepare us to fight back at a moment's notice. We're going to truck in our 'vegetables' from Raton to Union H.Q. where we can then fetch them in under an hour."

Vegetables? I almost bit on them before a code kicked in and I realized he was referring to the 300 Winchesters in Raton. I nodded and let Dare explain his plan.

April 18, 1914

There are coincidences which turn out to be the outcome of a conspiracy. Since the conspirators, we will assume, have taken precautions to conceal their identities, their victim will have difficulty in tracing events to a cause and will probably chalk them up to chance, fate, karma, or some hidden influence, baleful, bizarre, or just plain silly. He or she has to have a few faint clues or a stroke of luck in order to be relieved of the persistent torment of a cold theory.

In what I am presently about to relate, namely, a conspiracy to murder Dare, coincidences abounded. If I reveal them in the sunshine of hindsight, the fog of mystery begins to be burned off.

First, Dare and I suspected but had no proof that Jefferson Jones had dynamited both Mr. Jefferson's home and Homesteader's and that he was acting on Shiflit's orders.

Second, our suspicions would later prove to be true, but what we didn't know was as follows. We didn't know that Shiflit, using Corporation funds, had paid Jones and a camera crew to come to Los Tristes in the middle of April under the pretense of filming "Wild West" scenes. We didn't know that Jones and crew, at mid-morning of April 17, would be in Kit Carson Plaza, Jones expecting Dare's arrival there. We didn't know that Andy, our security guard and my friend, was a Baldwin-Felts suck who had been instructed to lead Dare into Kit Carson Plaza.

Why April 17, why mid-morning, why Kit Carson Plaza? Earlier that month Dare had asked Andy to set aside that date and time. He would be relieved of guard duty and would accompany Dare and me to the Union car pool where we would pick up trucks. Our mission would be to collect "vegetables" in Raton for delivery to the colonists. To get to the car pool, Andy knew, they would have to pass through Kit Carson Plaza.

Third and finally, there was something that no one knew. Ever since Shiflit had been left in command of militia, Dare had been wearing a bullet-proof vest.

Dare's plan, as explained to me over breakfast, was for three of us, Andy included, to walk to town and collect trucks from the car pool and bring them back to the ranch. Early next morning, before dawn, we would drive to Raton. If we got stuck in mud and were delayed, and if anybody wanted to know what we were doing, we were collecting fresh produce from Raton and returning with it for distribution in the Quivira colony. It was important to understand that our mission was dangerous.

Dare leaned in. "You and I, but not Andy, know those 'vegetables' are contraband. If we are caught with it, I wouldn't put summary execution past Shiflit. Or, if I am caught and the two of you can get through, you are to carry on . . . If you want to back out, you're free to do so."

I be dog, *that* stung! Actually, after months of guard duty, I was ready for action and said so. At the same time I was visited by what seemed a bright idea. "Sir," I said, "I have an idea for ending the war."

His expression was quizzical. "Shoot," he said.

"It's like this, sir," I said and proceeded to tell him about Mum's old letter, the one containing Elizabeth Woodbridge's confession about Woodbridge's voyeuristic complicity in having her impregnated by Shiflit. This document, if added to my own sworn testimony about Grandma Irene, about Woodbridge's encouragement of Shiflit's incestuous marriage, about Woodbridge's shackups with Pia, about Mum's imprisonment in the Sun Palace, about the burning of Ganny's apartment and sundry other cock-ups, the most hideous being Woodbridge's attempt to "toughen" Alphie, a little boy, by forcing him to observe Scampy's conception, would bring Woodbridge to the table for fear of exposure. If he refused or reneged on the deal, I would go straight to the New York newspapers with the scandalous materials.

When I had finished my explanation, Dare looked at me and shook his head. "Tree," he said in a sort of schoolmaster's tone, "that's the dumbest idea I've ever heard. In the first place, though I agree that your dirty old grandfather is terrified of scandal, he's a business man. You don't threaten business men with blackmail unless you're reckless as Shiflit. Next, your case is not as strong as you believe it is. Grandma Irene lives in a hospital for the insane and thinks she's in love with a phantom named St. John Beauchamp. Elizabeth Woodbridge's 'confession,' as you call it, is hearsay. As for Pia, it's common knowledge that rich men in New York, Philadelphia, and a few other cities keep mistresses. You can bet your bottom dollar Woodbridge is proud that he bedded my former wife. He could be the toast of the town! And, unless Alphie and his psychiatrist are put under oath, you can't expose Woodbridge's monstrosity there. And so on . . . Believe me, he has ways of silencing us as long as he continues to flatter Shiflit into thinking he's heir to Corporation . . . Jesus, Tree, threaten that tycoon, and you won't be the only one Shiflit will nail in the coffin. Your mother will not be spared, Miss Eliot will be . . ."

"I'm calling my grandfather long-distance!" I flung out, rising in a tantrum from the table.

"The lines are down," Dare said coldly. "Even if you could get through to New York or to his castle on the Hudson, what are you going to say to the employee who answers the call? 'Hi. This is Rountree Penhallow, Jr., son of Mr. Woodbridge's bastard. I must speak to him at once.'"

"I'll not be mocked," I said. Dare wasn't listening.

He was already knotting a red handkerchief around his neck, pulling on a sheepskin coat and settling his Stetson over the long yellow-gold hair Mum wouldn't let him have cut off. I finished my coffee and followed him out the new blue door. At the gate Andy fell in with us. We headed for town, boots crunching in sun-brightened snow.

Far from holding it against Dare for scolding me, I felt more than ever grateful for our relationship. He had reason to believe that the world, not just a few thousand miners, was headed toward the brink of annihilation. Still, he could also look steadily ahead and envision a coming world of consciousness, one in which peoples would emerge, as through a door, and converge in a sanctuary of at-one-ment.

At the Imperial Hotel, Andy said, "I know a short cut to the plaza through Felicidad Lane. This way." We followed him. Presently Kit Carson Plaza opened to our view.

Carbon-arc lamps encircle the small plaza and bathe it in an eerie white light like that emitted by the searchlights above Quivira. Gunmen are leaning against buildings, puffing on cigarettes. There is a man standing on a makeshift platform. Cap to shoes he is dressed all in white as if for a tennis match or a cruise on a private yacht. He is busily cranking a motion-picture camera which is pointed in the direction of an illuminated cowboy. Over and over the cowboy snatches a six-shooter from hip-holster and twirls it in his fingers with effortless dexterity. His ice-blue eyes are lit up like silver bullets as they focus on Dare, who is also illuminated as, without hesitation, he comes and stands not ten feet away from the cowboy and well within range of the camera. Once more the cowboy snatches six-shooter from holster. However, instead of twirling it in his fingers, he squeezes off six deafening rounds of ammunition. Dare, who should be pitching forward a corpse, blood puddling in snow, slowly slips his .45 caliber revolver out of holster and shakes it in the cowboy's face.

"Howdy, Jeff," he says.

I've seen pantomimists in the streets of Paris, Barcelona, and London. Usually they are naked except for codpieces, their bodies plastered blue-white as they pose, motionless as gods. The Laredo Desperado, clothed as a cowboy, is a pantomimist. True, he blinks his eyes, as flummoxed as the rest of us at the invincible Captain Dare, but, composure restored, he flops and lies spreadeagled in snow in the attitude of a crucifixion.

∽∽∽

April 19, 1914

Acting as if nothing much had happened, Dare waved to the camera man and walked from the plaza to the car pool, Andy and I shuffling along behind him, both of us wondering the same thing: how could anybody so full of bullets still be alive?

"It was blanks," Andy muttered to me, shaking head. He looked nervous.

"Sure," I said. "Blanks." A ringing in my ears told me that the Desperado had fired real bullets. Nor had my eyes deceived me about the Desperado's aim at point blank range. But I didn't want to jump to conclusions until I had a chance to speak with Dare in private. I changed the subject while we were walking. "It's a good thing we're trucking in vegetables to the colony. Tomorrow's Easter for the Orthodox. The Greeks will be celebrating, wearing traditional costumes and playing baseball. Our delivery of fresh produce will be good for morale."

"Oh?" Andy's mind seemed to be elsewhere. "Reckon."

We picked up three trucks and parked them at Homesteader's. That night Dare and I had our talk.

" 'Be thou a spirit of health, or goblin damned'?"

He chuckled. "I come in questionable shape. You're right about that, but I'm not a ghost. There are indentations of bullets in my steel vest—shown upon request. To tell you the truth, I wasn't sure the thingamabob would work. If he'd aimed at my head, I'd be a goner . . . See my hands? They started trembling only about an hour ago. Delayed reaction. Battlefield shakes. Sometimes you do things automatically, not thinking about danger until it is long gone . . . Now, I'd be obliged if you say nothing about my vest. If you protect yourself, people tend to believe you're cheating, whereas, if you march into a hail of bullets without any protection, they admire you to pieces. Trouble is, you're dead."

Before dawn the next morning, Sunday the nineteenth, Dare, Andy, and I formed our column of trucks and headed, engines whining and sputtering, into the up-grades of the rock-ribbed Raton Pass. About halfway to the summit we were forced to halt for a roadblock. At first I thought maybe some boulders had tumbled onto the turnpike. Then, out of the shadows appeared a dozen or so uniformed deputy sheriffs. They pointed rifles at Dare.

I climbed down from my driver's seat in order to hear what was being said. Dare remained in his truck. "What's the trouble, boys?"

"Sorry, Cap'n," said a deputy, motioning with rifle. His tone was deferential, his meaning firm. "Turn off, step down, and put your arms over your head. You are under arrest for the murder of Jefferson Jones."

Chapter Sixteen

A grownup at last, I had begun to ponder the nature of evil. How was I to identify and confront it in myself and in others? I hoped to become a good, free, fulfilled, self-transcending human being, to the rear of my betters but not too damn bad. If the door to the future of Man were opening as Dare believed it was, I wanted to be ready for a new world of consciousness, ready to emerge out of the self-centered self and converge, uncoerced, with peoples of the planet. I had faith in that future, being already endowed with faith in the existence of dimensions beyond ordinary knowing, the wild and unknown, and in an order of values superseding the man-made. As a creative person, not as a philosopher or theologian, I believed the mystery of Creation was past finding out. Precisely for that reason there had to be the concept of sacredness in life and an imperative to preserve it.

The destructiveness of evil persons seemed consistent. A Shiflit behaved as if he were above reproach, in his own eyes always innocent while others were always guilty. If someone reproached him, he felt impelled to harm or destroy him or her. If entire categories of human beings seemed to reproach him simply by being different, he wanted to exterminate them. Since he was blind to evidence of his own evil, he was always seeking scapegoats. To do his scapegoating for him, he liked to employ other persons, such as the Laredo Desperado, or other agencies, such as the military or the Law.

Many people tried to hide their destructiveness from themselves as well as from others. They mistook violence for strength; in fact it was weakness. One of the hardest things to learn, because it seemed to be a position of weakness, was to try to overcome violence with nonviolence. This was Dare's teaching. In the end, the nonviolent would triumph, their cause being just. On the long road to victory, however, the violent would seem to win the day, their victims sacrificed to a future they would never live to enjoy. Dare wanted to arm his strikers and lead them in battle, but, if he met violence with violence, he would delay the day of retribution. For some time I'd been learning that rebellion in the name of brotherhood was noble. When rebellion became revolution, however, it ended as another tyranny, often one more murderous and brutal than the oppression it replaced.

Dare had foreseen this dilemma long before the strike was called. Given that Corporation might prefer to wipe out rebels rather than recognize Union, he decided to have arms available for defense. It was not his intention to provide strikers with these rifles unless or until a moment came when the alternative to defense was annihilation. In the meantime he and Mr. Jefferson would encourage the strikers to turn guns over to the militia voluntarily and at the same time discourage strikers from resorting to violence. It was a tall order. Once the strike began, there had already been a few isolated incidents in which strikers went into the hills to kill mine guards and burn down coal company buildings. Now that Shiflit had under his command a large number of gunmen augmenting his militia, Dare's call to arms seemed imminent. Still, Dare didn't want strikers armed before the situation looked hopeless. Armed, they would begin what would appear to the American people and government as a bloody insurrection.

As previously noted, the plan he divulged to Mr. Jefferson and me only was this: the rifles would be collected, trucked over the pass, and stored at Union H.Q. If a call to arms became necessary, rifles could be delivered quickly from there to Quivira.

The arrest of Dare on Sunday, April 19, as he, Andy, and I

were on our way to Raton in three trucks had left me responsible for that delivery. The arrest came as a shock to me like the bite of a dog. Dare, I was sure, hadn't anticipated the Desperado's death. Of course, he hadn't anticipated, either, being ambushed and shot by the Desperado the day before. It was a wonder to me that Dare hadn't killed the Desperado on the spot! Dare had been saved because he was wearing a bullet-proof vest. He could have retaliated but didn't. Was that a sign of strength or weakness? I understood the thrust of his spirit: create a new awareness of the interconnection of everyone.

After the arrest, as I was driving up the pass, Andy in his truck behind me, I could no longer rely upon Dare's leadership. I had to focus on the matter of a betrayal. Hadn't the Desperado been tipped off that Dare would be entering the plaza at a certain time? Who knew in advance that Dare would enter the plaza by a route unusual for him? I didn't have to pause more than an instant to suspect that Shiflit had hired the Desperado to murder Dare or that Shiflit, following failure of the ambush, had murdered the Desperado in order to lay the blame on Dare. I did have to ponder Andy's loyalty.

On the steep approach to the summit of the pass I shifted into low gear and had time to think the matter through. Having to distrust a fellow miner who'd been helping me to guard the ranch was an unpleasant duty. Andy, a simple soul, had thought nothing of cheating when he was a mule driver. It had been his job to supply miners at their drift with ample empty cars on time and collect cars full of coal on time. A miner's wage packet depended upon production. If for any reason the mule driver failed to deliver and collect cars on time, production declined, with it wages. Therefore it was common practice for miners to bribe the mule driver into making swift rounds. Dare and I, when we buddied up in the mine, had never hesitated to offer Andy bribes, and he had never hesitated to accept them. Later, when Dare hired Andy as a guard at an exorbitant rate, one hundred dollars a month, he did so to prevent the boy from taking a job with Baldwins. But Andy had a wife and child to support. He might be tempted to earn extra money as a spy or tool of Baldwins. In particular, Andy had known before April 19th that Dare would be passing through Kit Carson Plaza on his way to the motor pool, and on that day he had steered us to the plaza via a short cut. Yes, I was thinking, Andy had been an accomplice, though perhaps an ignorant one, in an attempted assassination. Wasn't there on the morning of the 19th a strange, sheepish expression on his face? The good news was, he believed we were headed to Raton to collect vegetables for delivery to the colonists at Quivira. The bad news was, once he learned we were collecting rifles, not vegetables, our enterprise was faced with a considerable amount of danger. It's like this, I was saying to myself as I reached the summit, crossed the state line, and began the descent to Raton. If Andy drives his truck packed with rifles to Union H.Q., he would be double-crossing Baldwins. Therefore he probably will warn Baldwins over the telephone to have us stopped. Hadn't Dare cautioned me about "summary execution" for smugglers? Sure, he liked to mock my imagination of disaster, but if Andy tipped Shiflit off about my running guns for Union, I might expect from Shiflit the same fate as befell the boys in Samar.

I would have to send Andy to Coventry, isolate him, employing Witness Hall, the undertaker in Raton who had been storing the Winchesters inside coffins and was expecting our arrival. He had long been a friend of the Dares, father and son, and was said to be an ardent Union sympathizer. Witness Hall was in fact a legendary "mountain man" or "sourdough." He'd been mentioned in my *Book of Knowledge* as having rubbed elbows with Kit Carson and Wyatt Earp. He had constructed a toll road through Raton Pass as an improvement to the Old Santa Fe Trail. When coalmining operations prospered in northern New Mexico Territory, he began, logically enough, his undertaking business, building a funeral parlor and a warehouse across the street from the Santa Fe Railroad depot.

When we parked the trucks at the warehouse, I told Andy to stay where he was while I went into the office. It was the first time, as far as I could remember, I had ever given *orders* except to Merlin the dog. It surprised me how readily Andy obeyed me, pulling his hat down to cover his eyes and easing in to a mid-morning nap. I was under orders myself. I had to get the rifles into Los Tristes and out of the hands of hot-headed strikers unless Mr. Jefferson, now in command, issued the call to arms.

When I came in, Witness Hall was in his office polishing silver handles on a coffin. There wasn't much to see, a desk with some papers on it, a telephone, over the desk a faded picture of a naked floozy and, hanging on a string, what was unmistakably a dried human scalp, presumably Indian.

"Whar's Cap'n Dare?" he asked, straightening up and glaring at me through bifocals. He was short and bald and fat, his trousers hitched over belly with red suspenders, his old sourdough's voice sounding hollow as if it were being blown through a Peruvian pan-pipe.

I answered his question and introduced myself.

"You the gov now?" he said in dubious tone, grin revealing missing teeth. "Cap'n arrested for murder? I'll be a freckle-faced snicklefritz."

"Sir," I said, "how am I going to load two trucks with 300 rifles?"

"Well," he said, "you ain't. You might could pack a hunnert each truck, total two hunnert, the rest leave with me. . . Now, let's cut the cackle and get to the horses. One, never much keer'd for Alpheus Woodbridge and them fellas who starve the pore so's they can buy toothbrushes for poodles. Two, I got thirty-five Greeks here itchin' to jine the fight soon's they sober up from their Easter celebration. Problema solved. You give leftover guns to the Greeks. They tote them over the mountains on foot, meetcha couple days."

My face felt warm. "Sir," I stammered out, "I can't do that! My orders are, all the rifles go to Union headquarters until there's a call to arms. I pre-chate the Greeks wanting to help, but I'll have to come back tomorrow for the last load."

Witness Hall squinted at me hard, sucked gums, ran tongue over tobacco-stained teeth. "High-minded, ain'tcha, Mr. Penhallow," he finally said. "You let me handle the Greeks any which way I please, or I get orders d'reck from the cap'n . . . You ready to load?"

I wasn't so dumb I didn't understand what the old Indian killer was getting at. The Greeks, once armed with two or three rifles apiece, wouldn't be going either to Los Tristes or Quivira but into the mountains as a guerrilla force to attack Corporation property – exactly what Dare wanted to avoid. I decided as a practical matter to take the 200 rifles and leave the remaining hundred to hungover Greeks. I needed Witness Hall's help with my other problem, Andy. I explained it to him.

"The wrath of God rests on him," Witness Hall said after a long silence. "Hell waits his coming with its eternal darkness and despair . . . Tell you wot, Mr. Penhallow. Leave this Mr. Andy to me. If he ain't a livin' corpse by the time the 5:30 to Al-be-kirk come 'round the bend, he'll wish he was a real one. I've got a Greek named Louis can drive your other truck."

I went outside, woke up Andy, and broke the news: delivery of vegetables from Cimarron had been delayed. As Mr. Hall would explain, we had to run for our lives. Now, the only thing I had heard about Cimarron, New Mexico, was that Buffalo Bill and Calamity Jane had filled the ceiling of the local hotel with bullet holes. Anyhow, Andy probably believed Cimarron was in California, a place so covered with snap beans and kale it was totally green.

As soon as we entered the office, Witness Hall lit into Andy. "The Baldwins are on your trail, son," he said in a solicitous tone. "You better take a seat, get a grip."

Andy sat and declared, "If Baldwins bother me, I'll call the police."

"Son," Witness Hall snapped back, "the Baldwins *are* the police. They's ouchonder right now, aimin' to air-dance you and Mr. Penhallow."

"What fer?"

"Remember, Mr. Andy, yestiddy? That dude with the camera? Well, they warned him. Told him *vamoose*. Didn't much keer for his knowing too much. He didn't pay no nevermind, pore fella. Look wot happened to him."

"What happened?" Andy said, eyes like white pool balls.

"Well," Witness Hall went on, "the Laredo Desperado was firin' blanks, right? Why? Thing was, he was tryin' to get everbody's attention, warn about Baldwins, they gonna wipe you-all out. You didn't pay no nevermind, now, didcha, and hit's too late. That camera man, you see, he thought a bunch of Baldwins was his pals on account he was secretly suckin' for them. What he didn't know, them Baldwins kill their sucks as soon's they ain't got no more use for them. Fact."

Witness Hall paused a long time, staring Andy straight in the eye, then went on, lowering his wheezy voice as if Baldwins were right outside the door listening. "Mr. Camera Man, he went back to the Imperial Hotel. Know wot he find in his bed? A dead rat, that's wot. It done been hanged by the neck with a red shoelace, sorta like the red kerchief you wearin'. There was a note stuffed up the rat's little ass, sayin' 'You're next' . . . Mr. Camera Man, boy, he get pictures of the air dance so quick his face is white as his white suit. He stole him a horse and come over the Santy Fee Trail, excuse me, the Witness Hall Turnpike, just like you done. Only, you cain't escape them Baldwins, no sirree bob. They got him, and they got him legal, him bein' a horse thief now . . . They got him ouchonder in Hangman's Holler . . . I better shut my mouth. You don't really want to know wot happen next. I hate to see you young fellas strung up."

"Guh?" I couldn't make out what Andy was saying. It sounded like *guh*. I could see his eyes, though. If they were pool balls before, they were now ready to pop out and roll into pockets.

Witness Hall leaned in and said in a spooky kind of whisper, "They th'owed a thick rope 'round his middle. They pulled him up the hill to Hangman's Holler. They flicked him with riding-whips while he writhed and twisted. They tore his fancy clothes from him down to the waist. They moved the thick rope from his waist to his neck. They th'owed the thick rope over the sturdy branch of a tree. They ax'ed him, any las' words for the little wifey and kid. He had a little wifey and kid, you see? Anyway, he said he was plumb sorry he done taken a coupla dollars from Baldwins, he jus' wanted a teensy-weensy bit extry for the wife and kid, he would give the money back with interest. Shoot! It was too late! They hanged him! Now, Mr. Andy."

When Witness Hall paused again, I fastened eyes on the Indian scalp. I was beginning to believe the Baldwins were going to get me as well as Andy.

"Mr. Andy," Witness Hall continued, "you better believe hit. Let's step over to the funeral parlor. I'll show you the body. Sorta cold now. Real peaceful . . . I been polishin' up silver handles for Mr. Camera Man's casket."

Andy looked scared pasty. I jumped in and told him my plan for escape. Baldwins were swarming over the depot and might bust into the office any old time, I was saying. If we let Mr. Hall nail us into coffins, though, we would be hidden until the 5:30 train to Albuquerque pulled in, at which time Mr. Hall and his band of Greek unionists would stow the coffins, us inside, into the baggage car. "One thing more," I said. "Mr. Hall will draw up legal papers for you and me to sign. We have to swear we died of our own free will. We don't want Mr. Hall to be charged with kidnapping. If the Baldwins come snooping around, the conductor will show them the documents. Also, once we're safe in Albuquerque, he'll pry us loose and set us free. We can raise hell until the coast is clear for us to return to Los Tristes!"

Witness Hall telephoned Louis, the Greek, to fetch us some venison sandwiches and bottles of Manitou Springs medicine water to tide us over for the rest of the day until 5:30. Meanwhile, Andy and I wandered about the warehouse selecting our coffins. I picked one smelling of fresh cedar and featuring velvet cushions in the bottoms and fresh-air vents covered with cotton wool to keep out wasps and worms. Half an hour later, after Louis came, we tucked in the picnic and Andy stretched and yawned, saying he might's well get some sleep in his coffin, just not to nail him in yet in case he needed to pee before Albuquerque. I had to lie down in my coffin, too. I was no sooner in it than I fell asleep.

I woke up to the *clink-wink-wink-eek-eek-whap* of a nail's being driven into the lid of my coffin. I could feel myself being carried a pieceways until I could hear, coming closer and closer, the steam hissing out of a train's power nostrils. Never having been buried alive before, I didn't know what I was going to do if Witness Hall, Louis, and enough Greeks to fill the Trojan Horse sent me F.O.B. to Albuquerque along with Andy. It all turned out all right, though. Louis pried the lid off. I climbed out of my coffin in time to see Andy's being lifted into a baggage car. Before long, the train whistled loud enough to waken the dead, chugged out of the station. I watched the tail lamps of the caboose dwindle down to little red dots like smoldering eyes belonging to an evil genius, me.

Only, as I was on my way back to the warehouse, expecting to find men loading the trucks with rifles, I discovered one truck obviously had already been loaded while I slept. The trouble was, Louis was cranking it up to a sputtering start. And he drove off.

Witness Hall was waiting for me in his office. "I done tol' Louis wot you said, them rifles got to go to Union H.Q., not to Quivira, but you can never tell with him, he lives by the three 'f' words—fish, fight, and the other one. Don't worry about it, son. You still got one hunnert rifles to deliver according to your orders."

Like Orlando and many a poet and painter, I had always liked the word *dusk*, the palpable darkness following golden twilight. In Raton, though, with shadows closing in as I sat in an undertaker's office with my head in my hands and contemplated my failure to prevent an outbreak of bloody revolution, dusk was just another word for mornings that would never come again. With Louis's delivering rifles directly to strikers in Quivira and thirty-five Greeks well-armed for guerrilla warfare in the mountains, the Union's struggle for freedom and justice would be put down as an aberration and Dare would be hanged for treason as well as murder. Although I had Witness Hall's permission to use his telephone, one look at the scalp and I hesitated. His *dusky* past hovered over my future and that of my country like a jeremiad about sin.

Like a condemned criminal deciding to speak a few last words, I took out my wallet, found on a piece of paper the numbers I would be calling, and got through to an operator who rang Mr. Jefferson, H.Q., Quivira.

"Uh-huh?"

His voice exuded melancholy.

"Sir. Tree."

"I wonder what wrong with you."

"I'm still in Raton. They arrested Captain Dare."

"Heard that. Laredo Desperado dead. Imagine."

I told him I'd be delivering the "vegetables" to Union H.Q. about eleven o'clock. After unloading them, I should arrive at the colony before dawn.

"Uh-huh," he said slowly. "Congratulations. The sheep done learned him to be a wolf." After a pause he recovered his King James Version. *"Except those abide in the ship, ye cannot be saved!* The ship is Union! They has machine guns in place. Don't drive near the colony. Park in the Black Hills. Soon's you here, he'p Miss Eliot at the Red Cross nex' door. Anything happen to me, her and you mobilize the womens and chi'ren in the Black Hills. They's a couple of flags here in office. Take them flags with you, unnerstan'? Boss Man?"

"Sir?"

"They's fixin' to wipe us out."

"Know what, sir?" I said, wanting to get my words right. "You don't know how many people love you."

"Pre-chate it."

"Coronado," I said in order to distract him, "pestered the Pueblo Indians so much they decided to get rid of him. They told him about a city of gold in the desert where you are now. He went. All he ever found was sky and grass, an ocean of grass. The city didn't exist. The Indians had called it Quivira. If you live in a place that doesn't exist, nothing can happen to you."

"It exists now," Mr. Jefferson said. "After they wipes us out, that's when it don't exist . . . You take care of yourself, Worthy Brother. You take care of yourself and Miss Eliot, you hear, Worthy Brother Penhallow."

He clicked off. He had just admitted me to the best fraternal society since the Last Supper.

Mum, whom I called next, already knew more about Dare than I did. She and a crowd of unionists had been down to the county courthouse where he was being held in jail in the basement. The windows to his cell had been broken. She asked a Union organizer whether the crowd had broken the windows. He told her that the windows had been purposely broken by the police back in the winter. First, they would wet prisoners down with hoses. Then they would lock them in that cell so they would come nigh to freezing to death. Mum stormed into the courthouse to lodge a protest. She was told Captain Dare couldn't receive visitors or packages until he made bail. She said she would pay bail. They told her nothing doing, it was Sunday. She went outside where the crowd was trying to sing *The Battle Cry*.

"Dreary," Mum said. "How are you?"

"Fine," I said. I told her Jefferson Jones had almost certainly been murdered by Shiflit. I told her I was going to the colony to mobilize the women and children for a march into town. Would she arrange accommodations for them?

"Good!" she said. "It's time to stop guarding me at the ranch. I can take care of myself. You do what you have to do. Goddamnit, you're finally an outlaw!"

A third time lucky, the operator put me through to Miss Eliot, Red Cross, Quivira. When I heard Scampy's calm voice, I exhaled happy air.

"Hi."

"You O.K.? Mr. Jefferson sounds like the end of the world is in the trend."

"I'm O.K."

"Sorry if I woke you up."

"I can't sleep," Scampy said. "I haven't slept or eaten anything for two days and nights. You heel, you haven't been here to dance with me. I have a patient from Armenia. She looks like a Byzantine madonna, dark circles around big round eyes. I delivered her baby boy an hour ago. She's here in the tent, says her man is fighting in the mountains. You?"

"I'm in Rat. The Spanish word for *mouse* is *ratón*. The best-laid plans of mice and men. Dance?" I asked on a rising inflection. "Your ex, the creepy-crud you call 'Fredson' may be planning to wipe the colony out, and you've been *dancing?*"

"Drop dead," she said. "Today is Orthodox Easter. The Greeks roasted a lamb on a fire and drank barrels of beer and wore national costumes, the *vrakes*, and there was a dance. They're good people. In costume the men look a bit like Edgar Allan Poe in a ballerina's skirt and tights, but I wouldn't pick a fight with them."

"You got that right, honey," I said.

"Today," she went on, "they played baseball, and then there was the dance in the big tent—fiddlers, accordion players, a little rag-time, whirling, flinging and reels. Bow to yer partners! All hands around! Ladies in the center, gents around! Grape-vine twist! Swing yer partners! You jilted me, you jerk."

"Mum says I'm an outlaw," I said. "Outlaws don't dance."

"I had a good time without you," she said. "I was *la plus belle redneck du monde*. Had a good-looking partner, too."

I said nothing.

"Nono," she said. "Your old sweetheart's brother. He and Doña Luz and their whole family were there, minus the pariah . . . I braced myself with hands on his shoulder. We met in the center, bowed, and danced back again, right hand, left hand, swinging around and shuffling feet to the squeaking of fiddlers, everybody clapping hands in rhythm, especially some pretty little Mexican girls dressed in red polka dots for fiesta . . ."

I had to clear my throat. "Honey," I said, "you're making it hard for me to be serious. I believe in your equal rights. I don't tell you what to do. If you think I'm giving you orders, please talk to Mr.

Jefferson . . . I'll be there about three or five. I want you to pack your stuff and go to the Black Hills now, tonight. Mr. Jefferson wants both of us to lead the colonists on a march to town."

I was expecting Scampy to get angry, but she just sounded exhausted. "No more skinny girls with curls and ribbons. No more sunburned housewives with breasts like porcelain cantaloupes. No more *Guantanamera* and *De Colores* . . . It's true. Nono says the militia have machine guns on Water Tank Hill. While I was watching the ball game, five militiamen came to the diamond, one mounted, all armed. The soldier on horseback pointed to the roasting lamb and said to the Greeks, 'You have your big Sunday today, and tomorrow we'll get the roast!' He seemed to be hinting at something. I asked Mr. Jefferson what it might be, and he says Union camps have been set on fire before. Oh. Mr. Jefferson's face is still swollen from the great K.O. Kid's cowardly assault. The lip is still bleeding some, though I've bandaged the slashed eyebrow . . . I'll start moving my things to the arroyo and tell everyone to head for the Black Hills . . . I love you."

The line went dead. I got through to an operator. She said she couldn't get Quivira anymore. I wondered if the militia had cut the line. My Remington was on Witness Hall's desk. If anyone tried to stop me on the road to Los Tristes, I, for the first time in my life, was resolved to shoot.

I drove to Union H.Q. without incident, unloaded the truck, set out in it for the Black Hills, arriving there just as the eastern rim of the prairie was beginning to glow. Aurora, goddess of the dawn, was on her way; *le crépuscule du matin*, "the twilight of the morning," was wakening little birds in the forest around me.

> *And smale fowles maken melodye*
> *That sleepen al the night with open yë*

Chaucer had heard little birds more than 500 years ago. Less than a hundred years ago Arnold had praised the tranquility I was feeling now, a westering moon declining behind the Sangre de Cristo, chimney smoke from hundreds of tents a mile and a half away scumbling dark foothills. The mood didn't last. Arnold's tranquility in *Dover Beach* had been appearance, not reality. His sea, like my ocean of grass, brought in an eternal note of sadness followed by the clash of ignorant armies.

Some strikers ghosted out of the forest, evidently disappointed to discover that I was not delivering rifles as Louis had done. I saw his truck parked about a hundred yards away.

No searchlights swept the colony. I began to see in the distance a partially clad woman stringing up laundry, children running about as if on Arnold's beach, their laughter surging in waves. A few men were smoking pipes, apparently chatting as if they were on street corners in Paris, Salonika, Helsinki, Yokohama. When the sky brightened, what had been crystals on Water Tank Hill emerged as machine guns and a pair of field glasses, this pressed against the head of a uniformed insect.

I, too, surveyed the scene. There were two tent camps, the strikers on one side of the Colorado & Southern tracks, the militia on the other. As if indifferent to hostility between the camps, freight trains had for months been keeping to regular schedules, often stopping for an hour or two and blocking views across the tracks. Well back from the tracks was Water Tank Hill on one side and an *arroyo* on the other side. It, the *arroyo*, I was thinking, would be deep enough to afford protection from machine gun fire. Once the colonists left their tents and gathered in the *arroyo*, they could follow its winding path to the safety of the Black Hills. To be sure, many tents had deep dugouts under the floorboards, and Dare wanted families to hide in them in the event of an attack. Had he considered what might happen to people in these dugouts if, as Mr. Jefferson seemed to expect, the tents were set on fire? I had done well to advise Scampy to urge colonists to begin an evacuation. I shouldered my rifle and set off at a run along the *arroyo* in the direction of the colony, hoping to find Scampy and hundreds of colonists already crouched there with blankets and what-nots. Instead, I found several dozen strikers who, armed with the new Winchesters, were watching for any movements on Water Tank Hill. One of them was Louis. Instead of upbraiding him for disobeying orders—he who was risking his life as a volunteer in solidarity with fellow miners—I shook his hand, letting him off the hook, and asked him what he was expecting.

"Charge," he said, pointing toward the militia's camp. I took him to mean, if an attack began, he and others would delay the charge of the militia until tents had been evacuated. I asked him if he were acting under orders from Mr. Jefferson. For reply, he shrugged—and pointed toward tents by the railroad tracks, the headquarters tent and the Red Cross tent. I shuddered inwardly. If the machine guns opened fire, the first tents to be shredded into lace-like tatters would be those of Mr. Jefferson and Scampy. Scanning further, I spied Doña Luz outside her tent at the northwest corner of the colony. She was shielding her eyes against the glare of the rising sun. I waved to her. She, recognizing me, waved back. When the strike is over, I was thinking, I would visit her at the Medina ranch and show her some of the pictures I had painted in Taos, using the materials she had given me as well as Don Fernando's magical box. Thanks to him and her, I'd come a long way from the bourgeoisie and become an artist of the people.

A few minutes later I was standing outside the Red Cross tent from inside of which came the muffled caterwaul of a baby. I went in and found the Armenian madonna, a mere girl, giving suck to a swaddled creature with eyelids tightly closed and an expression of inconsolable fury on its face in-between sips of breastmilk. When the madonna looked up, there was a clear stream of joy running through her countenance.

"Miss Eliot?"

The madonna tossed her head sideways, meaning Scampy was in Mr. Jefferson's tent. I turned and rushed there. Scampy, wearing a blood-spattered nurse's uniform with Nightingale pin, stood up from behind Mr. Jefferson's desk and came and kissed me. "I missed you," she said as we parted to gaze upon each other. To me, she was a maiden in a myth, but from the lines written on her brow I could tell that the field of mortals was getting on her nerves. "We have to hurry," she said before explaining the situation.

Mr. Jefferson had asked her to stay on duty until morning. He had received a telephone call from Shiflit, who claimed Mr. Jefferson was holding an Italian miner against his will in the colony, a miner named Carindo Tuttoilmando. After searching his books for names of miners on the payroll, Mr. Jefferson informed Shiflit that no one named Carindo Tuttoilmando was or had been in camp, whereupon Shiflit declared the camp had to be searched. Mr. Jefferson swore he would never permit another search because the militia would steal things and insult the women. Besides, since the military authority was no longer in commission, a sheriff and a warrant would be necessary before a search could be conducted. Shiflit threatened force, giving Mr. Jefferson an ultimatum, change his mind by sunrise or pay the consequences. "The telephone rang not fifteen minutes ago," Scampy said, gaze still fixed upon me. "It was Fredson. He told Mr. Jefferson to meet him at the railroad tracks for 'negotiation.' I know because Mr. Jefferson came to my tent, informed me what had happened, asked me to hold the fort and gave me instructions what to do in case of . . ."

"The Death Special," I said, interrupting. "The same old trick. Only, this time Mr. Jefferson knows he's walking into a trap . . . What instructions?"

"I'm to grab the megaphone and warn everybody to run for their lives."

We lowered gaze. "Tell the Armenian madonna to run for the *arroyo*," I said as I rolled back the top of Mr. Jefferson's desk and picked up two big flags, each neatly folded in triangles. Scampy grabbed the megaphone as she scurried out of the tent, followed by me, the flags tucked under my left arm, the strap of my rifle gripped by my right hand. A minute later, as the madonna, hugging baby, was running past me, Scampy and I headed for the railroad tracks.

Dozens of colonists were standing quietly on their side of the tracks. Facing them from the other side of the tracks were at least a hundred armed men, a few militia mixed with gunmen without uniform. Between these groups and standing, facing each other on the tracks were Mr. Jefferson and Shiflit, the latter looking as if he were still in Bagapundan, campaign hat, belt, boots, the butt of a Krag touching ground, the former, face swollen and bandaged, wearing a three-piece suit and old fedora, red handkerchief at neck and no sign of a weapon. On both sides a great hush had fallen, but I couldn't hear what Mr. Jefferson and Shiflit were saying.

Then it happened.

Quick move of Shiflit's hands as he swings the Krag over his head and brings it swiftly down upon Mr. Jefferson's head, breaking the stock into pieces. Mr. Jefferson's arm, too late in coming up to avoid the blow, reaches for the sky, then he staggers away from the tracks, pitches forward, lies still. Four militiamen dash forward, aim rifles at Mr. Jefferson's back, fire into him a fusillade of shots.

A militiaman brought Shiflit a megaphone. Lifting it, he roared, "YOU LOUSY SUMBITCHING REDNECKS! ANYBODY WHO TRIES TO BURY THIS NIGGER WILL BE EXECUTED! HEAR ME? NOBODY COMES NEAR HIS BODY! THE BIRDS AND THE RATS WILL TAKE CARE OF HIM! PSALM 109: 'AND THEY HAVE REWARDED ME EVIL FOR GOOD, AND HATRED FOR MY LOVE. LET HIS DAYS BE FEW. LET THERE BE NONE TO EXTEND MERCY TO HIM!' THE WORD OF THE LORD."

Suddenly Shiflit, the militia, and the gunmen turned and ran from the tracks, war-whooping until they were safely spread out behind breastworks on Water Tank Hill.

KA-BLAM!

Dynamite bomb exploded behind militia tents.

Cha-cha-cha-cha-cha-cha . . .

Steady bursts of machine gun fire, bullets kicking up dirt, like inverted teardrops, at our feet.

Sun, golden sky.

∾∾∾

Once I believed there could be no scream like the scream of blinded mules being hoisted into mines and out of the world of sun-scented grass, but there is no scream like that of women and children in a panic as machine guns rake their homes and bullets zing.

In the tent colony strangers had become neighbors. Now neighbors became strangers again. Women and children came rushing out of tents, running in all directions.

Scampy lifted the megaphone and shouted, "NOW LISTEN! NOW LISTEN CAREFULLY! THE MILITIA ARE GOING TO DESTROY US! REPEAT: THE MILITIA ARE GOING TO DESTROY US! I BEG OF YOU, RUN FOR YOUR LIVES! RUN FOR YOUR LIVES! THIS IS THE FIRST AND LAST WARNING I CAN GIVE YOU!"

More women and children rushed out of tents. Some headed back to collect an umbrella or a pisspot. Others could be seen moving iron beds and dislodging floorboards in a scramble to find shelter in dugouts. Bullets richocheted off stoves where pots were left burning. As bullets raked dirt at our heels, Scampy and I ran from tent to tent, peering into them in order to make sure no one was huddling inside too paralyzed with fear to move. I overheard her matter-of-factly saying to some old people, "Better hit it for the *arroyo*, from there you'll be guided to the Black Hills." We ducked, we ran in zig-zag patterns. I watched as a young woman stooped to put her shoe back on and, stitched with bullets, fell into a lifeless heap at my feet.

There was no time to think of time. Perhaps half an hour passed, perhaps an hour, always the machine guns chattering before Scampy and I flung ourselves down in the *arroyo* where strangers were becoming neighbors again. I still had the flags clamped between my arm and ribcage. I placed the Remington at my side. After a time that was no time we were joined by Louis and another Greek. The two were aiming and firing new Winchesters at Water Tank Hill.

"Where are the other rifles you brought?" I asked Louis.

He waved an arm vaguely toward the mountains. "Americans," he said. He seemed to be saying that immigrants now thought of themselves as citizens.

After another time that was no time the other Greek poked head and shoulders above the *arroyo*, took a bullet in the neck, and slid back into a patch of snow at our feet. Blood poured from his wound. Scampy stuck her thumb in it. "How do you feel?" she asked the Greek with a nervous smile.

"Why are my feet in the air?" he asked. His feet were not in the air. He died.

Louis pointed at my flags. When I understood that he wanted a flag for a shroud, I gave it to him. He draped it over his compatriot and said, "American now."

"Look," Scampy said.

Machine gun fire and rifle fire became desultory, then stopped. Peeping over the top of the *arroyo*, I saw Shiflit about two hundred yards away. He was waving a revolver in the air and leading the charge of massed troops across the railroad tracks and into the tent colony, the sound of war whoops coming to me as they must have come in the Philippines to *insurrectos* about to die for their country. Some troops swarmed into tents, emerged with bicycles, violins, sewing machines. Other troops poured oil on brooms, set the brooms on fire, spread fire from tent to tent. Flames shot sky-high. An awful wailing could be heard. I looked at Scampy. Some women, we realized, had returned to their tents, now ablaze. Shots were fired. Bodies lay crumpled on the ground. A white St. Bernard dog picked up a piece of smoldering timber and ran away with it in his mouth. Smoke billowed from the last of the tents. Troops heaved bodies into piles and blew them up with dynamite.

Hundreds of jackrabbits sprang out of holes and hopped about.

Then it happened.

The whistle of a Colorado & Southern freight train shrieks. The train rumbles past us, slows, screeches, halts on tracks, dividing the camps. The troops cannot be seen. Water Tank Hill cannot be seen. The body of Mr. Jefferson can be seen. Jackrabbits can be seen. They jump like popcorn in a hot skillet.

The locomotive and dozens of steel-plated cars loaded with coal did not move. Smoke from the wiped-out tent colony dwindled to wispy, greasy coils. Scampy and I—Louis having deserted us to join the revolutionists in the mountains—rounded up the hundreds of survivors in the arroyo and sent them on their way to the Black Hills. We could hear the militia getting drunk in their camp. If Shiflit lost control of his troops, especially the gunmen without uniforms, there was a chance they would move the machine guns to positions where the women and children in the Black Hills could be exterminated.

A gaunt striker with a gray handlebar mustache came running toward us in the *arroyo*, behind him another striker who had a Winchester gripped in his hand. I recognized the first striker as Milenko, though I hadn't spoken with him for years. The other striker I didn't recognize. Milenko was yelling, "Mr. Tree! Mr. Tree!" breathlessly. When he came close to me, he nodded to his friend, also a Croatian. "Come quick," said this man, "Madame Luz. Thirteen body. No good."

We followed the two men to the northwest corner of what had been the colony, stepping gingerly among ashen heaps of furniture and grotesquely twisted iron beds until we came to a group of strikers who had finished laying out bodies which had not been bloodied or charred. Someone pointed to a black hole nearby. The bodies had been plucked from it, bodies of men, women, and children who had been asphyxiated in their last oubliette.

I recognized the family, Doña Luz in her flowered print dress and black silk shawl, Carmencita, Orlando next to her, their three children beside them. Nono and Aladino were there, a total of eight Medinas gone, leaving alive only Golondrina, the pariah in her castle on the Hudson.

"Mr. Tree?"

I swung around just in time to identify Milenko as the one who slugged me in the stomach and left me sprawling. He grabbed my Remington and emptied my pockets of ammo, then stood and said over me, "*Mi idemo tražiti ima li još pravice na svietu!*" So saying, he trotted into the shadow of freight cars. His compatriot translated, "He say we are going to find out whether there is still justice in the world." He, too, fled for the mountains.

I struggled to my feet. My head felt light and relieved of time.

Then it happened.

In a time that is no time I go from the Black Hole of Quivira to the body of Mr. Jefferson, having ghosted through an open door into a bright light beyond the sad people. Mr. Jefferson's skull has been crushed. Bullets have entered the back of his head and exploded, removing his face. I unfold the flag and drape it over Mr. Jefferson. I am shrouded in golden light . . .

Time was returning to me.

Train whistle shrieked.

Freight cars clanked. Not ten feet away from me steel wheels screeched. The Colorado & Southern, gliding over rails, announced its departure, *la-lump la-lump la-lump* beginning to come in ever shorter intervals, creaking cars beginning to speed past me like a curtain being drawn aside, bringing in realization of my exposure and imminent execution.

I felt myself leafing out in my soul.

I collected heavy rocks, placed them on the flag to keep it from blowing away. Suddenly Scampy was beside me, again having alighted in the field of mortals. She gripped my hand. Our fingers were intertwined.

Then there he was, Shiflit, not twenty paces away on the stage that was the other side of the tracks. Rigid his posture, right arm stretched out and clutched in the right hand a .45 caliber revolver aimed directly at us.

I wanted life and the life I wanted was beside me, holding my hand.

It was a strange thing, what was happening, so unlike the time I faced Shiflit's firing squad. I felt no fear, no victim's shame, no sorrow too much for me.

But Shiflit didn't shoot.

He lowered the revolver.

Smirked.

There didn't seem to be any point in sticking around.

"Shall we?" I motioned to Scampy, doing the Lord This and Lady That bit. We were shrouded in a golden light, one of those useful mists with which ancient goddesses protect heroes. We strolled away from Shiflit. Pretty soon we found ourselves out in open, scorched grasses.

"Perhaps, darling," I ventured, "Ahab has his humanities, after all."

"Ahab's, yes," Scampy said. "Fredson's need some work. You do know, don't you, why he didn't pull the trigger? He still believes he is Pa-pa's heir and future Chairman of Corporation. It just wouldn't do to, as you say, bump us off, you Pa-pa's disreputable grandson, I his daughter and daughter of Elizabeth Eliot Woodbridge. Besides, where humanities are concerned, Pa-pa has just enough left of them to be frightened by the scandal of a massacre of innocents and revolted by Fredson's murder of us. He's married to a woman with sanguine heart. She'll have his permission to leap to her revenge."

Almost 500 people, mostly women and children but a few wounded men and a few of the old and the blind, were sitting in hushed groups in the forest of the Black Hills. Those unable to walk could ride in the trucks. The rest, Scampy and I would lead to town. By now Mum would have aroused the citizens of Los Tristes to welcome the refugees.

They, the ordinary people of Los Tristes, weren't sad people all of the time or even much of the time, and they, unlike so many in a world of sadness, were what they appeared to be, good. I lifted my eyes unto the golden light enveloping the great oubliette out of which all souls would some day be emerging.

Epilogue

QUIVIRA MASSACRE and MASSACRE OF THE INNO-CENTS: these and similar headlines were splashed across newspapers in the country. "Muckrakers," a catchy term at-tributed to President Roosevelt and used to describe writers with a flair for exposing corruption in high places and sometimes for advancing a political agenda, descended upon Los Tristes. The fo-cus of the stories was almost entirely upon the deaths of women and children in the Black Hole and upon Woodbridge's alleged re-sponsibility for the tragedy. The cruelty of the militia and the "well-financed gunmen" received notice, too, but little was given to the murder of Mr. Jefferson or to the bloody rampages of strikers in the mountains.

It was widely reported that the entire Medina family had been asphyxiated. Few people knew that a daughter survived. Almost no one was aware of her marriage to the terrible—and untouchable—tycoon. I was one of the very few, Doña Luz having confided in me, and my heart was cut for Golly. Not only had she been treated as a pariah by her family, but also under strict orders from her husband she had relinquished connection to miners, unionists, and persons of Mexican descent. Doña Luz had no idea, as Mum and I did, that Woodbridge had once stuck a lighted cigarette into a wife's cheek. Doña Luz did know, though, about a fabricated story circulated in New York: the shy and beautiful Mrs. Celestine Woodbridge was said to be descended from an admiral of the Spanish Armada.

Defeated in 1588, he, according to the story, had swum ashore in Cornwall, had immediately abjured Roman Catholicism, sworn allegiance to Queen Elizabeth and married into the landed gentry. In my opinion, Golly, like her mother, was proud of her heritage. They were, as I knew, Americans before there was an America. Perhaps, just perhaps, she was enough of an actress to adopt a pseudonym for the sake of pursuing revenge.

On April 28, 1914, President Wilson ordered federal troops into Colorado. They arrived on May Day during a heavy rain. The National Guard had to go home. Union called an end to the strike. Once again and for decades thereafter, gassy mines exploded, miners by the thousands died in accidents or from disease. Not until 1935 did Congress finally act to legalize unions and collective bargaining.

On the Sunday following the Massacre undertaking parlors in Los Tristes were filled with mourners. Hats in hand, hundreds of miners filed past the biers of compatriots, solemnly touched cold brows, and crossed themselves. For the next two days separate Orthodox and Roman masses and burial ceremonies were held. Alone because Scampy was on duty at the hospital and Mum was in Denver securing the services of an attorney courageous enough to resist the judicial system, I attended the Roman.

The bodies of the Medinas and other victims lay in caskets in a chapel, branched candles burning, a silver censer swinging. Mr. Jefferson's body was so horribly mutilated that his casket was closed. The weather cleared to misty sunlight, lovely as a dream of Provence, and the Sangres glowed pink-orange. As a mile-long funeral procession followed hearses down Main to Commercial and over to the Mesa Miners' Union Cemetery, the people of Los Tristes turned out en masse. Leading the parade was Mother Jones, head bowed; a thousand miners marched in pairs, wearing black arm bands, red handkerchiefs, and caps, some flying flags and banners. At the cemetery, after caskets were lowered, Mother Jones stood on a platform to give a speech.

"Has anyone ever told you, my children," she said, "about the lives you are living here, so that you may understand how it is you pass your days on earth? Let us consider this together, for I am one of you, and I know what it is to suffer . . ."

Just as Mother Jones began to paint her picture of the life of a miner from boyhood to early old age, a uniformed chauffeur came up to me and pointed to a black Rolls-Royce parked far away from the cemetery. "Mrs. Woodbridge," he whispered in my ear.

"The labor movement," Mother Jones was saying, "was a command from God Almighty. He commanded the prophets thousands of years ago to go down and redeem the Israelites that were in bondage, and he organized the men into a union and went to work. And they said, 'The masters have made us gather straw. What are we going to do?' The prophet said, 'A voice from heaven has come to get you together.' They got together, and the prophet led them out of the land of bondage and plunder into the land of freedom!"

Following the chauffeur, I braided my way through the crowd and presently stood by the Rolls in the shadow of cottonwoods. The chauffeur opened the back door and motioned for me to go in and take a seat. As I was doing so, I glanced at the woman by whose side I would be sitting, dressed as her mother would have dressed in weeds with black lace veil. Doña Luz had so dressed when she rescued Mr. Jefferson from despair and when she buried Don Fernando. Golly had lost him and now her mother, two brothers, a sister, a brother-in-law, a niece and two nephews. She looked as stiff and frozen as the Juneau Ice Cap. I wondered if I would be cold-tongued for abandoning her in Los Tristes in order to live a bachelor in France.

"I need corroborating evidence," she began abruptly, no greeting, no glance in my direction.

"Hello? Can I help you, Golly?"

"Evidence of my husband's first wife's intercourse with a *bello bruto* named Shiflit."

"Oh," I said. "You want to talk about the beast who massacred your family. Or is there something else?" I was stalling. Thoughts

387

and sensations needed sorting out, lawyerly talk of "intercourse" mixed with sexual innuendo, "beautiful brute" being a sophisticated version of the attraction of Beauty to Beast, plus a request for "evidence" I'd forgotten she knew I possessed. Presumably she wanted Mum's letter, the one she had written to me from St. Aignan about Elizabeth Woodbridge's confession, the letter I had been keeping at the First National Bank of Los Tristes. I planned to bait Woodbridge with it in hopes of setting Dare free from jail. Yes, of course, I almost muttered to myself out loud, I wrote Golly from Paris all about that letter. She would consider it, since she had once contemplated taking up a study of law, as "corroborating evidence" for what I had written about Woodbridge and Shiflit. "The letter to which you refer," I said, "I need it, myself. And I'll tell you why, though I'm under no obligation to do so."

"Blackmail?" Golly said.

"Call me anything you like," I flung back at her with an aggressive tone I didn't want to use, "but hear me out before we cross swords over our lousy ancestors' sweepstakes, my real slave trader against your make-believe Spanish Armada admiral . . . Captain Dare is under arrest for a murder he didn't commit and a revolt he tried to prevent. He will be tried by a judge and jury owned by your husband. He will be hanged—unless, that is, my old grandpa, your husband, Madame Stepmother, uses his influence to have a conviction annulled. I intend not to blackmail him for gain but to strike a gentleman's business agreement with him: he sets Dare free in return for the letter, or all his peccadilloes and sanctimonious Machiavellianisms will surely be revealed in public."

"I didn't realize you could be such a shit," Golly said in a tone of voice more coy than censorious. " 'Sanctimonious Machiavellianisms' reminds me of your juvenile games."

"*Touché,*" I conceded. "I've gotten into a bad habit of slandering people who are destructive. Shiflit, for example, I call a 'brain-fart' so I won't be terrified of him. I'm not proud of some words that pop into my head. Maybe I am a shit. I want to be better than that."

Golly glanced at me for the first time, studied me, her voice relaxing as she spoke. "I called you a name. We're even and can talk without rudeness . . . Give me the letter. I'll see that everything is taken care of . . . My husband is extremely vexed by Lieutenant Shiflit's latest behavior. I shot and buried Shorty without your assistance. Remember? I give you credit for drawing a red herring across the track, know what I mean? Let's just say that Captain Dare, whom my husband actually holds in the highest esteem, will be acquitted by the state Supreme Court, come hell or high water . . . Send the letter. My address is, Mrs. Alpheus Woodbridge, Glen Eden, Nyack, New York."

"I'll be sending you the letter," I said, "with love and shit."

We said nothing for awhile.

"*Bueno*," she finally said. "Lieutenant Shiflit has been acquitted by a military court in Denver."

"You are full of surprises, Golly!"

"He was charged with murder and arson. The prosecution confined its case almost exclusively to the foul curses he had allegedly overheard being shouted at scabs and militia by the women of Quivira. The alleged curses are so offensive to the tender sensibilities of soldiers that any soldier who hears them is justifiedly enraged enough to kill. Dear, dear, courtroom had to be cleared before sweet Lieutenant Shiflit could be induced to repeat the vile words! Similarly, the murder of Tío Congo was justified on the basis that, in conference with the lieutenant, he used dirty words, probably 'Have a nice day.' What about the evidence that Tío Congo, known to the court as 'Jefferson', was killed when Shiflit broke a Krag rifle over his head? The prosecution argued that the rifle was old and defective, that its stock could easily have been broken, and that Shiflit had only tapped Jefferson over the head like a schoolmaster with a cane. Not guilty, darling, not guilty . . . By the way, I'm having the ranch fixed up and *la cueva de los olvidados* converted into a luxurious brothel."

I had no idea what Golly was driving at. "Our cave a brothel? You must be joking."

When Golly lifted her veil, her smile was tight. "Mamá hated

389

being an empty-nester. That's why, after I was engaged to my future husband, I had to insult her, preventing her from trying to change my mind, know what I mean? She had the house boarded up before she went to the colony. I'm having it cleaned and painted so that my gentleman caller, so to say, will not think he's being lured into an unsatisfactory environment."

"Brothel?"

"Oh," Golly purred, "just a figure of speech . . . Look."

Golly undid the top button of her frilly black blouse and extracted a gold chain with a rusty key dangling from it. "The Yale lock," she said before tucking the key back. "You're a slow-pokey, Mr. Penhallow . . . Did you know that my husband was once upon a time as innocent as you are? He was abandoned from the day he was born and raised an orphan. I don't suppose it has ever occurred to you, Alf was once as naked and penniless as Adam."

It was true. Apart from his matriculation at Yale and subsequent adventures in Alaska, my grandfather had seemed to have no history. "If he was Adam, that explains his interest in apples. He told me he keeps a paper sack full of them on the sill outside the bedroom window."

"Yes," said Golly, a dreamy expression on her face. I ventured, "You love him, *don't* you?"

"My dear Mr. Penhallow, do you believe I would marry a man I could love? I'll admit I wanted nothing to do with the drudgery and toil of a miner's wife, the frequent childbearing, the widow responsible for the care of her children but without means of support. I'll admit that my husband has been a heartless and rather humorless financier. If you insist, I had every intention of killing the man I married, not, heaven forbid, for his money but to avenge the death of my father and other miners. But his Foundation distributes tens of millions of dollars to charities. He never knew his real parents. He never had the benefit of a mother's caresses. He was born during an Irish famine and somehow dumped in an orphanage named St. John Beauchamp's in Manchester, England. Its operators were straight out of a novel by Dickens, very cruel, addicted to laudanum, know what I mean? And then some rich Yankees with Yale pieties, the Woodbridges, happened to visit the orphanage and found the five-year-old *muchacho* with curly hair and an impish smile perfectly adorable." Pausing, Golly peered through the windshield at the distant cemetery, frowned and lowered the veil. "Get out!" she screamed suddenly and bitterly. "That letter you wrote me from Paris was a pander! You made me dedicate my life to killing the enemies of the people! If you hadn't told me about my future husband, I would have waited for you! Don't get me wrong. Don Fernando would be very proud of you, and I have my own private collection of your French nudes and New Mexican landscapes. Don't speak to me until you're famous!"

"In that case," I said, "we may never speak again! I doubt very much I shall ever be famous!"

≈≈≈

Did I say that people tell me stories?

From 1914 to 1964, fifty years, I never saw Golly again.

I did hear about her through reports in newspapers, over the radio, or on TV. She was pigeonholed as the reclusive young widow in a "castle" called "Glen Eden" in Nyack, the Director of the Woodbridge Foundation since the death of Alpheus Woodbridge in 1928 from choking on an apple. As for my "fame," I really owed it to her: in 1964 she arranged for a retrospective of my paintings to be exhibited at the museum she had had built at a cost of millions of dollars, The Woodbridge Museum of Modern Art in New York. Other than that exhibition, I'd been little noticed in the art world. Obsecurity had left me free to paint, to travel, to raise a family. Scampy and I, married after I returned in 1919 from the war in France, had moved from Los Tristes to Walt Whitman country near the tip of Long Island. We had three children and seven grandchildren.

From time to time I turned over in my mind certain thoughts about Golly, especially her "confession" about getting revenge on the man she married. Scampy, after all, when the Medina family was killed during the Quivira Massacre, had predicted that Golly's "sanguine heart" would lead her to take revenge on both Woodbridge and Shiflit. And that was an odd thing. Not long after Golly and I had our meeting in her Rolls near the cemetery, Shiflit disappeared, never to be heard from again. He had last been seen, according to Denver police, in the company of a "prostitute" at the Brown Palace. Some Colorado National Guard troopers suggested that he had gone to Mexico to fight alongside Doroteo Arango, "Pancho" Villa. Hamilton Eliot, Scampy's grandfather, hadn't seen Shiflit in New York after the massacre in Colorado.

Intuition, plus Golly's reference to the Cave as a "brothel," did lead me to suspect that she was responsible for Shiflit's disappearance. Or was I confusing him with Shorty? I, since hearing Scampy's opinion, imagined Golly as a wrath, someone whose fixed idea of destiny involved retributive justice. Upon receiving my letter from Paris, had she hardened her heart to become, in Scampy's phrase, a "revolutionary saint" determined to overthrow tycoonery from the inside? Hadn't she said so herself? Hadn't she written to me in Paris that Woodbridge could be deceived by a "chick"? If the "chick" were she, wasn't she a Cassandra and a Clytemnestra, the one prescient, the other poised to assassinate a king?

Mum having put up a bond for $35,000, Dare was released from jail to await trial. The Union relieved him of his duties. He resumed life as a rancher. Meanwhile in Los Tristes a grand jury made its report: "The evidence produced before us clearly shows that the crimes in Colorado were committed by armed mobs acting in pursuance of well-defined, carefully matured plans, having for their object the destruction of property and human life." Accompanying the report were indictments of 124 Union members, the most notorious of them being Kyle Deville Dare. He was accused of murder, arson, and conspiracy in restraint of trade.

The trial was conducted in the summer of 1915. As expected, the judge, the prosecuting attorney, the bailiff and all the members of the jury had either worked for Corporation in the past or were currently on Corporation payrolls. As expected, Dare was convicted and sentenced to life imprisonment at hard labor without parole. All but one of the jurors had recommended that he be hanged. Led away in shackles, he had little hope that his appeal for a new trial would be heard. He had no idea I was counting on Golly to persuade Woodbridge to intervene in the process and have the conviction annulled, vindication effected. Eventually the state Supreme Court threw the case out on various counts of legal malfeasance. Dare and almost all of the 124 indicted miners were exonerated. For the first time in years, it seemed, the judicial system was in good working order.

I shall return to the matter of the trial presently. First, though, I have a shorthand summary.

Antituberculosis drugs were announced in 1952.

Dare and Mum lived, as the saying goes, long and happy lives on the ranch. Although his "extermination psychosis" was evident in two world wars and especially by the introduction of nuclear weapons, he was not alarmed by vicissitudes of the future. If anything, he believed more fervently than ever that Man's consciousness was in the process of evolving to the point where certain ancient philosophies were on the cutting edge of a world culture. Science, too, was showing that humankind was one, that everything in the universe was interconnected, that a planetary imperative could not be ignored and that, among other signs of increased awareness, we were confined to one Earth and the rights of women, workers, minorities and children had to be recognized.

When Ganny became too old and infirm to take care of herself, Mum brought her to live, together with a full-time nurse, at the ranch. Ruby, too, came to live there, also with a private nurse. Dawn Antelope, who was given a generous pension, retired to the Taos Pueblo. Grandma Irene Penhallow could not be persuaded to leave Harrow House. Mum, however, with the help of Florrie

Natters, enriched the endowment of Harrow House through a trust fund. Specifically, patients, should they feel strong enough to defy their families, were to have pre-paid granite tombstones with their names and dates inscribed on them.

Pia continued to draw alimony support from Dare until her death in an automobile accident in 1925 in New York.

It had come out in court that Andy had indeed been paid by the Baldwins to steer Dare toward Kit Carson Plaza. When Andy approached me outside the courtroom, he forgave me for my trick in Raton. Inside his coffin, he told me, he'd enjoyed a splendid vacation away from a nagging wife and a baby who cried all night.

I return to the trial of Captain Dare.

According to the prosecution the motion picture shot in Kit Carson Plaza had "captured" Dare's "cold-blooded" murder of Jefferson Jones. Even though the film was silent, it was "clear" that, one, Jones never fired a shot, Dare remaining upright, and, two, Dare menaced Jones with a gun and fired it, Jones having been seen to fall in snow and remain motionless, "beyond a reasonable doubt dead as a doornail." With "no sign of remorse" Dare had "strolled away" from "the scene of the crime" in the company of "shady-looking characters."

On cross, Dare's lawyer produced witnesses who swore to events contradicting the silent film as credible evidence. One, following the dumbshow in the plaza, Jones and the camera crew had gone to Cousin Jack's for drinks. Two, when Jones went to the Imperial Hotel to meet with Lieutenant Shiflit, he had accused Jones of multiple failures to carry out orders, notably the assassination of Dare, and then, using a service revolver, had shot Jones through the heart. Three, indentations in a bullet-proof vest belonging to Dare proved that Jones had actually initiated a confrontation.

The judge had all such exculpatory evidence thrown out.

The prosecution circulated to jurors a batch of old newspaper clippings. One of these "proved," it was said, that Captain Dare was "the infamous Butcher of Bapagundan" who had ordered the execution of Filipino boys. Another clipping "proved" that Dare had murdered Dr. Rountree Penhallow of Colorado Springs "in a fit of jealous rage." Because Dr. Penhallow was "protecting Dare's estranged wife from harm," Dare planted dynamite under his own house, lured the good doctor there, and "blew him nearer to God."

When Dare's lawyer objected to the introduction of irrelevant, unsubstantiated allegations from the defendant's past, the judge overruled him. The defense was allowed to call witnesses who testified to Dare's sterling character. Far from planning the destruction of property and human life, Dare had gone to extraordinary lengths to preserve peace, encourage friendly relations between strikers and militia, cooperating with militia in the search for weapons, even discouraging women and children from using foul language as scabs passed by the colony.

The prosecution demolished these witnesses. All were members of Union. One was a Socialist, another was a bigamist, still another had spent time in the penitentiary for hurling a plate of porridge at a Baldwin-Felts detective.

After denying Dare's petition for a new trial, the judge leaned over the bench and grumbled, "Have you any statement as to why sentence should not now be pronounced against you?"

Dare rose to his feet.

This is what he said:

> The court has asked me what, if anything, I have to say why sentence should not now be pronounced against me.
>
> During argument on that very question, through which I listened, not in a personal way, but so far as possible as a citizen of our common country, I had supposed that many and unanswerable reasons supporting my view had been given to the court. Therefore, in the court's interest at this moment I must recognize a mere formality. It is plain that nothing I can say will change your fixed determination so far as you have the power to have me hanged or start me down the dark path of imprisonment for life.
>
> It is proper that a man so situated, especially when, as in my

case, he is the victim without fault of an utterly unscrupulous persecution, should be permitted to enter his protest against injustice.

Fortunately, what I have to say is warranted by bigger considerations than any personal to me. So far reaching are they that I feel I have a right to ask you to hear my views with the same courtesy I have used during my trial through your rulings. About to be condemned by you I will, therefore, make answer to your question in the following way.

First of all, in the name of the courts of my country, which I respect, I protest against your right or power to pass any judgment against me. It is undenied in this case that you were appointed to the bench recently for the trial of myself and my associates, fresh from the employment of the very Corporation which has pressed and engineered these prosecutions. Yourself a coal company attorney, engaged to assist as a practicing lawyer in the trial of cases arising like mine out of the industrial disturbances of 1913 and 1914, you had no right to sit as a trial judge in the case of any striking miner. You were so deeply prejudiced against me that my case was a travesty of justice from the start.

Second only to the resolution with which you hold your seat upon the bench, was the method adopted by you for selecting from the regular jury box provided by law, and you ordered an open venire. This method was exactly adapted to procure what none were surprised to discover: a hand-picked jury of coal company partisans. The jury so chosen was naturally subject to the self-same Corporation influences which, with hue and cry, now seek to drive me to the gallows or the penitentiary. It matters not that I was utterly guiltless of the charges against me. It matters not that the prosecution never proved that I fired a shot or did other than seek to avoid the violence which menaced the cause dearest to my heart. It matters not that it became necessary for the prosecution to invoke legal doctrines of conspiracy which, if applied impartially, would convict the leading coal operators in the country, under the direction of Corporation, for the deaths of men, women, and children at Quivira on April 20, 1914.

Such practices, however astonishing to our people in general, do not surprise one who has observed our industrial history. From long experience I recognize the power of wealth, the magnitude of our industrial problems, and their effect on our existing social system. I can understand, for I have seen how men who seek a living realization for the workers of the world of the old ideals of justice and equality; who endeavor to open the eyes of their fellows to the true economic conditions that surround them as they seek their daily bread, are persecuted, defamed, and even in exceptional cases hounded to the gallows by those who control the wealth and privileges of our generous country.

I have seen some masters of finance within and without this state using the full powers of government to divide the workers, to crush the hopes and aspirations in their breasts, and to extinguish the kindling light of intelligence in their souls in full realization of the fact that understanding brings the fixed desire for the higher and nobler things in life, including a dream of equality of opportunity some day for the children of the rich and poor alike. And it is not overstatement to say that I am here today because, with others, I have patiently, without bitterness, yet persistently, for years sought these things—a wider chance in life for those who toil, a higher type of democratic citizenship and a social system of industry which gives promise to mankind and denies autocratic power over the lives and liberties of the great mass of workers to the masters of millions who have usurped government authority itself.

Those who, like myself, have continued to worship at the ancient altars of human liberty and justice in this country have been marked for annihilation.

In receiving sentence of death by hanging or of life imprisonment at hard labor from this court I can do so with

397

the knowledge that I have broken no law and committed no crime, unless it be that I am a coal miner, honored by my fellow workers with their years of confident faith that my devotion will stand even this acid test for the maintenance of their principles.

Dare paused, sucked in a deep breath. The judge bit his lips and glared at him. Dare went on:

In a word, the reason this court should not pass judgment as I see it is that, by doing so, it will openly violate every principle of justice for the promotion of which our courts exist. Solemnly facing the gallows or iron bars and prison walls, I assert my love for justice and my faith in its ultimate triumph—not a justice of theory but of reality, extending to men, women, and children whose proper equality of opportunity it embraces, and with utmost earnestness I want it understood that my one satisfaction in my lot—separated though I be from those who are dearer to me than life—lies in the belief that this, my undeserved experience, may help awaken others to the living wrongs in our world, calling today as definitely as in the past for remedy.

It is a privilege and a duty even by sacrifice to advance our priceless cause. I am, therefore, ready to receive the sentence this court should declare itself without either authority, right, or justification to impose.

Given that my grandfather was a tycoon and that Scampy had grown up in his mansion, we should have known more about tycoons in general than did most people. As a matter of fact we knew little more about them than what we read in the popular Press or in novels or saw in movies. Like most people we stereotyped tycoons. When, therefore, we pondered the mystery of Woodbridge's character, we tended to regard him as a type and to overlook the evidence of his ordinary and conventional habits and of a metaphorical stenosis of his heart. He was in fact remarkably dull, not stupid but dull. We still wanted to cast him in a glamorous light and to attribute to him the lofty ideals and noblesse oblige of a born aristocrat.

A typical tycoon had the Midas touch. He struck gold or manipulated the stock market or invented a gadget. Like as not, he founded a corporation. When it grew into an octopus with tentacles creeping into various corners of the world, it assumed a life of its own and became too big to be restrained, not even by its founder. A typical tycoon married an actress and built a castle, first looting Europe of cloisters and art, transporting stones to vacant lots as large as golf courses, then assembling the stones into a building with 100 unoccupied rooms and towers like silos on Iowa hog farms. A typical tycoon hired an English butler, an English nanny, a French chef and an assortment of maids, gardeners, and mechanics. A typical tycoon gave cocktail parties for politicians, playboys, showgirls, and robbers. A typical tycoon suffered from an unrequited love, taught Sunday School, and became a philanthropist, avoiding taxes while making sure that the money taken from the poor was never given back.

What Scampy called "the homely touch" endeared tycoons to the masses. Usually a tycoon's homely touch was revealed in an interview, a ghost-written memoir, a biography or a muckraking movie. The public's appetite for scandal was surpassed by its love for homely touches such as a tycoon's lonely childhood, an irrevocable loss of a mother or a toy, the overcoming of adversities and of addictions of all kinds. If it was learned after his death that he had always kept a bottle of American ketchup on his twelfth-century refectory table, someone was sure to insert a notice about him in the *Times*, "Come back, all is forgiven."

Woodbridge's homely touch was the apple.

One afternoon in the summer of 1964, I, having received a summons from Golly to pick her up in Nyack for the drive to New York for the grand opening of "Penhallow: A Retrospective of His

399

Paintings" at The Woodbridge Museum of Modern Art, pulled up to her "castle" on the Hudson in my battered 1936 Ford. Evidently, Golly wanted me to herself, because she insisted that Scampy meet us at the museum for the martinis and hors d'oeuvres that enable connoisseurs of art to battle the boredom of actually having to look at a painting. I had warned Golly in advance what to expect: a 74-year-old curmudgeon with shoulder-length gray hair, a scruffy gray beard, an antiwar t-shirt, paint-splattered Levi's torn at the kneecaps and an Ivy League tweed jacket purchased at Goodwill for 59¢. My motto, I told her to test her for snobbery, was "Screw the Bourgeoisie." If she could swallow that, I promised to behave myself. Actually, though I didn't let on, I was so excited about seeing my paintings again, most of which I'd forgotten about, that I could have been recruited to be a classic of respectability, a confidential bank clerk with a brolly.

The most amazing thing about Glen Eden was that it wasn't a "castle" at all but a small French chateau, façade intersected with tall windows framed in gray shutters. Though she had renounced happiness, Golly had lived in beauty.

Golondrina, as always lovely as her name, was waiting for me at the front stoop, no maids or butlers in sight, and, I must say, she was dressed in elegant simplicity, the perfect summer dress, the perfect pearl necklace on ballerina neck, the perfect bonnet over the long light-gray hair. She was gaunt-looking, though, and I feared she might be putting on for me another kind of show. At sight of me she suppressed a smile. "The artist," she said.

I opened the passenger-side door for her, glad it didn't disintegrate in my hand. "Sorry about the pumpkin, love," I said. "All my fairy godmothers travel on brooms."

Seated, we studied each other for a long, silent minute. Her perfume, like Mum's, was Provençal. It made the odors of oil and grease bow down. "Before we say anything else," I said, "I want to thank you for being in my life—and for the exhibition."

"It's overdue," she said, "and it's not what you think."

"Meaning?"

"Buttering up your conscience. I've done things I shouldn't have done, and I've paid the price. All I ask of you is understanding. No special moral consideration."

I switched on the ignition. "You know me," I said. "I'm the man with invisible fireflies for you."

"They were visible," Golly said quietly. "I'm glad to see you, I'm happy for you, as I told you many years ago, my father would have been very proud of you . . . Now. I have an inoperable brain tumor. I have a deathbed confession to make . . . You drive. I'll talk. Remember the key I showed you at the cemetery? Remember the letter you gave me, your mother's letter about her encounter with Elizabeth Woodbridge? Remember the letter you wrote me from Paris, Dante's *Inferno* inscribed with my husband's and Shiflit's sins, their blindness to them, your compassion for sinners?"

"Of course," I replied. "I assumed you used the letters to have Captain Dare set free by the state Supreme Court."

"Well," Golly said, "we'll get to that in a minute . . . I suppose you've assumed I killed Shiflit. I gave you plenty of hints that I intended to seduce him and lock him in the Cave. No one else but you would have guessed how he disappeared."

"Go on," I said after a pause to thread through traffic. "*Did* you kill him?"

"I intended to," she said. "I lost my nerve. I accepted my fate: he would kill me. Then he had an accident. He fell and broke his neck. *Then* I locked him in the Cave."

I thought and said, "You had no Law to go to. Just like with Shorty. That day you were sad. You've been sad ever since. As you say, you paid the price."

"Yes."

"And, like a sinner in *Inferno*, you blamed my letter from Paris for being a "pander' because it inspired you to prostitute yourself to powers-that-be in order to destroy them."

"Yes," Golly said. "I hired a bulldozer to fill up the Cave. I sold the ranch. Next time you visit Los Tristes you won't find the ranch, house, or Cave. It's a shopping center now with a hamburger

401

franchise atop Shiflit's bones."

I drove slowly. Parts of her story were clear, parts left to implication.

It was like this . . .

Woodbridge is furious with Shiflit after the news of the Quivira Massacre is spread across the country, furious with himself for consenting to blackmail, Chairmanship of Corporation in exchange for silence about Shiflit's intercourse with Elizabeth and marriage with their daughter, the voyeurism, the procurement of Pia and all the rest of it. "I'm going to Los Tristes for the funeral," Golly says, "and afterwards I have my own business to settle with Fredson Shiflit." She and Woodbridge exchange knowing glances. Has he not always divined in her character a fellow killer? In Los Tristes she has the ranchhouse cleaned up and freshly painted and personally tidies up the Cave to serve as a love-nest. After the funeral she dismisses the chauffeur, drives the Rolls to Denver, and tracks down Shiflit. Dressing herself to look like a prostitute, she spends the night with him at the Brown Palace. There she coaxes him into believing a plan suggested to her by Elizabeth's ordeal: Woodbridge wants a son; therefore she is to stay with Shiflit until a child is conceived, but they most conduct themselves with the utmost secrecy, slipping out of town to go to her old homestead near Los Tristes. If he wishes to confirm this plan with Woodbridge, he has but to reach for the telephone. He doesn't think the call will be necessary. Once they are alone at the ranchhouse she knows she must be patient, getting Shiflit, whose very touch is repulsive to her, to trust her. She gets him accustomed to her in the Cave. In the middle of one night she smothers him with kisses, declares love for him, and physically exhausts him. He falls asleep. She sneaks up the eighteen-foot ladder. Free under a star-frantic sky she slams the heavy steel trapdoor shut over the entrance to the Cave and locks the lock. Out loud, arms lifted in exaltation, she cries, "Never wrassle with a girl who has a Yale lock! Mierde!" However, she bursts into tears and has to seat herself, sobbing, on the trapdoor. Beneath her, suddenly, Shiflit bangs on the door, screaming, "Let me out! Let me out! I love you! Darling! We'll go to Rio!" She covers her ears, she mustn't give up and crawl, she knows he will kill her, and yet, helplessly, moving as if in a trance, she inserts the key, turns it, and is about to throw away the lock when, after a curse, Shiflit is silent. Have rotten rungs of the ladder collapsed under his weight? Has he fallen? "Freddie, are you all right?" No answer. Heaving the trapdoor aside, she climbs down the ladder, at bottom of which she steps on his body. She lights a candle, goes to him, feels for his pulse. Nothing. The scourge of God is dead. For a moment she considers driving the Rolls to Los Tristes to inform the police about the accident, but they, she knows, are gunmen, killers of her family. Like Captain Dare, she will be arrested. Presently she is driving to Denver to catch a train, praying she doesn't carry the spawn of the Devil.

"Tell me, Golly," I said as we crossed over Washington Bridge, "did you use the letters to persuade Grampy Alf to have Dare's conviction thrown out by the Supreme Court?"

Golly was shaking her head. "I'm sorry. I broke my promise. I heard that Captain Dare was exonerated, and I was relieved, but I was saving the letters for another kill. My husband, I originally thought, was like other tycoons, believing he could get away with anything he wanted but, deep down, so terrified of scandal he, if exposed, would be forced into retirement or to take his own life. Everyone thought so. You thought so. You wanted him to be humiliated in the Press. At first, when I hated him, I was going to give the letters to the papers. Then I thought of a better idea: show the letters to Mr. Hamilton Eliot, First Vice-President of Corporation and my husband's trusted brother in Skull & Bones . . ."

"I knew him," I offered. "Mr. Eliot was my wife's grandfather. He attended our wedding. He gave us a house and studio on Long Island. When I met him, he was no longer Vice-President but the Chairman of Corporation. An honorable businessman."

"I'm coming to that," Golly snapped back. "This all happened when you were in France."

"First Lieutenant, Twenty-Eighth Division, wounded at Chateau Thierry," I said. "So what happened? We're on Riverside Drive. Twenty minutes to go, kiddo."

She shows the letters to Hamilton Eliot. A small man who smokes a small pipe, he is, as she knows, Mr. Probity. The letters horrify him. He keeps saying to Golly, "I never knew, I never knew." He purchases a pistol, puts it inside a briefcase, and, one evening, turns up at the front door of Glen Eden. He shows her the pistol in the briefcase. She is thrilled. Don Fernando had sacrificed his life by working in the mines in order to pay off his father's debt of honor. It seems altogether fitting that her husband redeem his honor by committing suicide. Mr. Eliot knocks on Woodbridge's study door, enters it, has a long talk with Brother Alpheus, leaves the pistol with him and returns to sit with Golly in the living room and wait for the telltale crack of the pistol. Mr. Eliot uses a small handkerchief to mop perspiration from his brow and bald head. He and Golly exchange anxious glances for about fifteen minutes. Finally, they hear not only the shot but also what sounds like the jingling crash of tambourines. They nod solemnly to one another and tiptoe into the study expecting to find another noble Cato fallen on his sword, a metaphorical one, to be sure, and the victim just a Midas of New York, Yale graduate, accidental imperialist.

Mr. Alpheus Woodbridge, instead of being a good boy, lying on the Persian carpet in the obligatory puddle of blood, is still seated in his swivel chair, feet still up on his mahogany desk, pistol in his right hand, an apple in his left. He is studying the apple as if to decide which bite will cause the least disturbance to his dentures. He is also aware that "Ham" and "Celestine" must be seeing a ghost.

"A damned good shot, if I do say so," he exclaims and waves at a corner of the study at a shattered chandelier. It had been dangling from the high ceiling by a thin wire now severed by the pistol shot. "I want to thank all of you, Celestine, Ham, and that scapegrace, Rountree, who thinks he has me snookered with libelous poppycock. Well, I trusted my managers to tell me the truth, and they betrayed

my trust by telling me only what they thought I wanted to hear. And you three, two present, haven't hesitated to speak what you believe to be the truth. I could shoot you now. However, a great man is magnanimous. Ham, you shall be Chair when I retire. Celestine, you shall direct the Foundation."

Golly lit an Old Gold as we rumbled down Broadway. "Until that moment I had dreamed of seeing my husband dead."

"Don't tell me," I asked with a suppressed laugh, "you fell for his 'superman' jargon?"

"Don't be ridiculous! And it wasn't the magnanimity, though that was real, believe it or not. I didn't tell you that he had his son, Alphie Junior, released from a private nursing institution and given a position of trust in Corporation—where his career has been exemplary . . . I cursed myself with a dream and ended by helping him to fulfill his dream of giving his fortune away. That night I changed."

I thought and said, "It was the apple."

Golly, I could see out of the corner of my eye, had her turn to be taken by surprise. Smoke coiled out of her open mouth. "How did you know, Tree?"

"Oh," I said, "the homely touch."

After we drove up to the museum entrance, a valet sped off with my Thrifty Sixty. I tipped him a dollar for being neither supercilious nor obsequious. Unaccustomed to valet service, this one being my first, I added a "never before" at 74 to my lifetime collection of signposts to one's arrival as a grownup.

Over a hundred of my paintings had been assembled, some pieces dating as far back as St. Aignan, Académie Julian, and Taos days. I was glad that Scampy joined us for the tour because any museum as large as an indoor Colosseum for cattle auctions always makes me feel a bit antheap-y. Besides, I needed support for the ordeal of perusing pictures by a fellow with a strange name, "Rountree," although I knew I'd encountered him somewhere in the world of sad people.

The three of us ambled from gallery to gallery, followed by photographers and fans whose eyes tugged at Golly like piglets at a sow's teat. I must admit, I enjoyed the paintings. I was good, though not as good as Leonardo.

Not too damn bad.

Afterword

THE DOOR OF THE SAD PEOPLE is a novel patterned after real events culminating in the Ludlow Massacre of 1914. Out of more than one hundred books consulted for their historical content, four have been indispensable: Barron B. Beshoar, *Out of the Depths: The Story of John R. Lawson, a Labor Leader*; Zeese Papanikolas, *Buried Unsung: Louis Tikas and the Ludlow Massacre*; George S. McGovern and Leonard F. Guttridge, *The Great Coalfield War*; and Mary T. O'Neal, *Those Damn Foreigners*. Thomas Andrews's *Killing for Coal: America's Deadliest Labor War* (2009) appeared too late to be considered during composition of the novel.

Words and speeches of Mother Jones are quoted (with minor emendations) as they appear in various documents. The speech attributed to the fictional Dare in 1915, as he is about to be sentenced to life imprisonment, was actually given in similar circumstances by the real-life labor leader, John R. Lawson. Anecdotes about St. Aignan, France are based on unpublished family documents.

Valuable information, for which I am especially grateful, has been gleaned from the following sources: Linda Atkinson, *Mother Jones*; David Haward Bain, *Sitting in Darkness*; Fawn M. Brodie, *No Man Knows My History*; John Brophy, *A Miner's Life*; Mark Caldwell, *The Last Crusade*; Helen Clapesattle, *Dr. Webb of Colorado Springs*; Colorado Coal Mining—Trinidad Project—Oral History Program—California State University, Fullerton, 1971; David Alan Corbin, *Life, Work, and Rebellion in the Coal*

Fields; Dale Fetherling, *Mother Jones, the Miners' Angel*; Walter H. Fink, *The Ludlow Massacre*; Herbert G. Gutman, *Work, Culture, and Society in Industrializing America*; Gardiner Harris, "Dust, Deception & Death," in *The Courier-Journal*, Louisville, Kentucky, April 19 and 21, 1998; John Higham, *Strangers in the Land*; Joseph Husband, *A Year in a Coal-Mine*; Louis Hyde, ed., *Rat & the Devil*; Mother Jones, *Autobiography*; Stanley Karnow, *In Our Image*; Emma F. Langdon, *The Cripple Creek Strike*; David Lavender, *One Man's West*; Priscilla Long, *Where the Sun Never Shines*; Stuart Creighton Miller, *"Benevolent Assimilation"*; Alan Nevins, *John D. Rockefeller*; Katherine Ott, *Fevered Lives*; M. Scott Peck, *People of the Lie*; Andrew F. Rolle, *The Immigrant Upraised*; Sheila M. Rothman, *Living in the Shadow of Death*; Joseph L. Schott, *The Ordeal of Samar*; Dorothy Schwieder, *Black Diamonds*; Edward M. Steele, ed., *The Speeches and Writings of Mother Jones*; Tom Tippett, *Horse Shoe Bottoms*; and David Thoreau Wieck, *Woman from Spillertown*.

Biography

Alexander Blackburn was born in Durham, N.C., where his father was at Duke University a teacher of writers, including such future luminaries as William Styron, Mac Hyman, Reynolds Price, Anne Tyler and William deBuys. Blackburn carried a passion for writing across his academic training at Andover, Yale, UNC Chapel Hill, and Cambridge University (Ph.D. in English). After graduation from Yale he volunteered in the U.S. Army during the Korean War. After stints teaching creative writing at the University of Pennsylvania and world classics at the University of Maryland's European Division, he pioneered in the teaching of those subjects at the new University of Colorado at Colorado Springs, where he founded and edited *Writers' Forum*, a literary journal dedicated to discovering and publishing writers from the West. Blackburn has edited two anthologies of stories by Western writers, and recently he discovered, selected and edited *Gifts From the Heart*, memories and chronicles by the daughter of a Latino cowboy. *Gifts* was a finalist for the 2011 Colorado Book Award. Groundbreaking critifcal studies by Blackburn have also been published: *The Myth of the Picaro* (North Carolina), *A Sunrise Brighter Still: The Visionary Novels of Frank Waters* (Ohio University Press) and *Creative Spirit: Toward a Better World* (Creative Arts). His memoir, *Meeting the Professor: Growing Up in the William Blackburn Family* (John F. Blair), identifies true educators as great-hearted artists. The main thrust of Blackburn's literary endeavors has been as a novelist. *Kitty Pen-*

tecost, Suddenly a Mortal Splendor, The Voice of the Children in the Apple Tree, and *The Door of the Sad People* are available or forthcoming in original or revised form. For his work as educator, novelist, critic and editor, Blackburn has received the prestigious Frank Waters Award for Excellence in Literature. He lives in Colorado Springs with his wife, Dr. Inés Dölz-Blackburn, Chilean-born author and professor of Spanish Language and Literature.

About The Type:

The Door of the Sad People is set in **Bookmania**. Bookmania is the name given to the typeface designed by Mark Simonson, and based on Bookman, a classic 150-year-old font originally named Old Style Antique. It was designed by Alexander Phemister in 1858 and first produced by the Miller and Richard Type Foundry of Aberdeen, Scotland. Type fonts, like ladies' hemlines or men's ties, fall in and out of fashion over time. Bookman is no exception. Widely used during the 1960s and '70s, it has fallen out of favor in the decades since. Until now. Simonson's version, with its multiple sets of numbers, stylistic alternates, ligatures, small caps, swash small and italic, plus an extensive range of accented letters, five different weights, and a walloping 3,177 glyphs per font make Bookmania a designer's dream! "Its combination of historical research, intelligent design and comprehensive features makes this the one Bookman to rule them all."

— with thanks to Rob Keller, MOTA Italic
Berlin, Germany

Have you seen
our other
Rhyolite Press
Publications .. ?

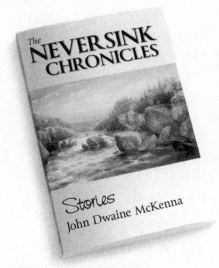

THINK YOUR HOME IS YOUR CASTLE?
. . . NOT IF THE GOVERNMENT WANTS IT!
READ

THE NEVERSINK CHRONICLES

Seventeen linked stories showing what happens to us, the
ordinary folks, when the government takes our property away.
It's all about the water . . . our most precious resource and increasingly scarce commodity.
We don't stand a chance . . .

CIPA EVVY Award Winner, 2012
1st prize, Best Fiction

$15 at bookstores everywhere, or direct from the publisher:
www.rhyolitepress.com

ISBN 978-0-9839952-0-3

Praise for *The Neversink Chronicles*

"A gifted and natural born story teller with command of dialog and dialect. Congratulations!"
—Clark Secrest, Author, *Hells Bells,* San Diego, CA

"A gifted storyteller. An amazing first book. Keep writing, you have a great future ahead of you."
—Allison Auch, Copy Editor, Durango, CO

"Hated parting with the manuscript, as I knew things were changing quickly in *Neversink.* That's when you know you have a great book in your hands."
—*Leigh Daily*, Paralegal, Boulder, CO

"This is a book to read over and over. The people are real, the life is true and the author has to have been everywhere and met everyone to have captured all of these personalities so well. I'm waiting for more from him."
—Mary Lelia, Austin,Texas

"'Just Another Day', gave me chills remembering my own Vietnam experience".
—Skip Mooney, Financial Consultant, Manitou Springs, CO

". . . and the winner, First Prize for fiction, 2012 goes to . . .
The Neversink Chronicles"

18th Annual CIPA Awards Ceremony
Denver, CO May 17, 2012

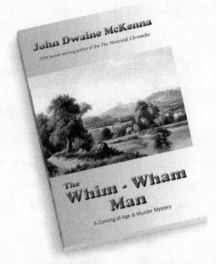

The Whim - Wham Man

A STORY THAT HAS IT ALL...
A CRIME YOU CAN'T FORGIVE
A PLOT YOU COULDN'T IMAGINE
AND A CHARACTER...
YOU'LL NEVER FORGET!

There's no sanitary way to write about murder.
"The Whim-Wham Man," a gut-punching novel of a teen-aged
boy whose idyllic life in rural Colorado comes crashing down
when reality and adulthood rush in after the brutalization and
savage killing of two young girls... **It's a helluva yarn.**

CIPA EVVY Award Winner, 2013
2nd prize, Best Fiction

$15 at bookstores everywhere, or direct from the publisher:
www.rhyolitepress.com

ISBN 978-0-9839952-2-7

Praise for *The Whim-Wham Man*

"It's a helluva yarn."
—Dick Kreck, Author of *Murder at the Brown Palace* and *Smaldone*

"Great Job! It got my blood boiling! Then it got my mind thinking."
—Linda Comando, Publisher and Editor of *The Tri-Valley Townsman*

"It was like eating popcorn . . . I couldn't quit. Congratulations. I am looking forward to more Jake McKern novels."
Bill Calls, Scottsdale, AZ

"This short book with the odd title is the hard-to-put-down story of a 15-year-old youth who grows up in a hurry when a grisly tragedy strikes his family."
—Mary Jean Porter, *The Pueblo Chieftain*

"Well-written, so compelling I couldn't stop reading until the last page."
—S.M. Albany, NY

"*The Whim-Wham Man* is the most thought-provoking novel I've read in a long time. Thanks for writing it."
—Kathy Hare, *The New Falcon Herald*

". . . and the silver award winner for fiction 2013 is . . .
The Whim-Wham Man."

19th Annual CIPA EVVY Awards, Denver Co
May 10, 2013

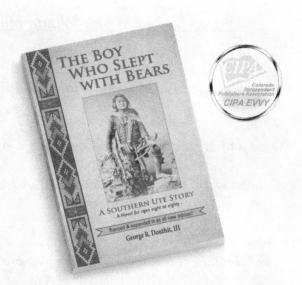

THE BOY WHO SLEPT WITH BEARS

Pulled from the pages of history, a fiction novel that tells the heart wrenching and heartwarming story of Tomas Dequine, or Sak-wa-ma-tu-ta-ci, 'Blue Hummingbird' in his native tongue, a thirteen-year-old Southern Ute boy whose family and way of life are being crushed by the onrush of white European settlers in 1880s Colorado . . . a time when the Utes were being driven off of their ancestral lands to be resettled on reservations. Told in a warm, grandfatherly voice, Douthit's novel is a past winner of a coveted golden CIPA-EVVY award for fiction. It has been read and loved by ages eight to eighty, and contains a reader's guide and bibliography.

One of our hottest novels!

CIPA EVVY Award Winner, 2005
1st prize, Best Fiction

$15 at bookstores everywhere, or direct from the publisher:
www.rhyolitepress.com

ISBN 978-0-9839952-8-9

<u>Praise for *The Boy Who Slept with Bears*</u>

I loved this book. The author, George Douthit, does a beautiful job of taking a young Ute boy and "brother bear" paralleling their lives and trials. This book made me feel like I was right their in the tepee with Tomas and his mother. This book also made me think about the Ute Indians and the many hardships they had after they were forced to move to the reservations. I love how the writer begins to blend history, culture, and symbolism all into one story. Being a Colorado native I really loved the use of historical fact mixed with fiction. I rarely read a book that I want to not end and this was one of these books. I grew to understand Tomas and his relationship with the earth and brother bear. This book is a great book for young and old alike.
Valorie R. Hornsby, Interior Designer

George Douthit's book *The Boy Who Slept with Bears*, is the moving story of a Southern Ute boy coming of age at a time when the Ute traditional territories were being overrun by non indians during the gold rush and the Utes removal to reservations. The author captures the boy's desire to avenge his father's murder at the hands of white soldiers. He steps from boyhood into a man's world while struggling to hold onto his traditional beliefs. Though fictional, Douthit weaves true historical details of the Southern Utes and a legendary grizzly bear named "Old Mose" into a masterful story that leaves the reader enthralled and captivated.
Vickie Leigh Krudwig, Author, *Searching for Chipeta*

A terrific read for both young and old! Outstanding! *The Boy Who Slept with Bears* is the best book about native Americans I've ever read. Please send two more copies for my nephews.
Leonard Foxworth,

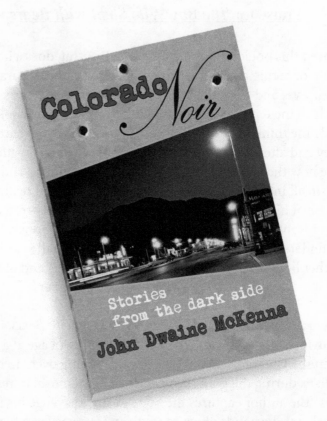

Colorado Noir is a walk on the dark and wild side of America's
most controversial city. Ten stories and one novella.

$16.95 at bookstores everywhere, or direct from the publisher:
www.rhyolitepress.com

ISBN 978-0-9896763-0-4

"This guy is the next Tom Clancy"
Bill Hill, USAF (Ret)

Colorado Noir by John Dwaine McKenna

2014 Silver Medal Winner for Fiction/Mystery/Noir

Coming soon!
from the award winning
pen of Alexander Blackburn . . .

THE VOICE OF THE CHILDREN
IN THE APPLE TREE

Printed in the USA
CPSIA information can be obtained
at www.ICGtesting.com
LVHW052250301223
767812LV00008B/331